Also available from
GENA SHOWALTER
and Harlequin TEEN

Intertwined

GENA SHOWALTER

HARLEQUIN®
TEEN

HARLEQUIN®
TEEN

ISBN-13: 978-0-373-21022-0

UNRAVELED

Recycling programs
for this product may
not exist in your area.

This edition published by arrangement with Harlequin Books S.A.

For questions and comments about the quality of this book please contact us at Customer_eCare@Harlequin.ca.

www.HarlequinTEEN.com

Printed in U.S.A.

Again, this one is for the real Haden, Seth, Chloe, Riley, Victoria, Nathan, Meagan, Parks, Lauren, Stephanie, Brittany and Brianna. Notice that none of your characters have sprouted horns and tails. I can't promise it won't happen in the next book, but I can tell you that Auntie GeeGee can be bribed....

This one is also for fellow authors Jill Monroe, Kresley Cole and P.C. Cast. I know, I know. You see their names in all my dedications. But I promise you, they deserve every bit of praise. A writer's life is often solitary and those three talented beauties remind me that there's a world outside my computer—and that there's a party nearby with my name on it.

This one is also for my amazing editor and darling friend, Margo Lipschultz. This woman continually goes above and beyond the call of duty for me. Her insights are brilliant and I'm a better writer because of her!

This one is also for The Awesome, aka Natashya Wilson, another amazing editor and advocate in my corner. This lady rocks!

Also, to Harlequin for always being willing to take a chance on my (weird) ideas. To my family for the continued support. And to YOU, my readers. From the bottom of my heart, thank you.

Despite everything I said above, though, this book—like *Intertwined*—is mostly dedicated to me. What? Writing it was hard.

PROLOGUE

ADEN STONE THRASHED ON his bed, his sheets falling to the floor. *Too hot.* Sweat poured from him, causing his boxers, the only thing he wore, to stick to his thighs. *Too much.* His mind...oh, his poor, ravaged mind. So many flickering images tangled with consuming darkness, horrid chaos and brutal pain.

Couldn't take...much more... He was human, yet scorching vampire blood now flowed through his veins. Powerful vampire blood that allowed him to see the world through the eyes of its donor, if only for a little while. That wouldn't have been so terrible—he'd experienced it before—except he had ingested blood from *two* different sources the night before. Accidentally, of course, but that didn't matter to his scrambled brain.

One source—his girlfriend, the Princess Victoria. The other, Dmitri, her dead fiancé. Or betrothed. *Whatever.*

Now their blood fought a vicious tug-of-war for his

attention. A toxic back-and-forth. No big deal, right? Over the years, he'd fought zombies, time-traveled and talked to ghosts; he should be able to laugh about a little ADD. Wrong! He felt as if he'd drunk a bottle of acid with a chaser of broken glass. One burned him while the other sliced him to pieces.

And now he was—

Switching focus again.

"Oh, Father," he suddenly heard Victoria whisper.

He winced. She'd whispered, yeah, but, *too loud*. His ears were as sensitive as the rest of him.

Somehow, he found the strength to push through the pain and center his gaze. Big mistake. *Too bright*. The heavy gloom of Dmitri's surroundings had given way to the sparkling colors of Victoria's. Aden peered through her eyes now, unable to even blink on his own.

"You were the strongest man ever to live," she continued in a solemn tone, and Aden felt as if *he* were the one speaking, his throat rubbed raw. "How could you have been defeated so quickly?" *How could I not have known what was happening?* she thought.

She, her bodyguard, Riley, and their friend Mary Ann had driven Aden home last night. Victoria had wanted to stay with him, but he'd sent her away. He hadn't known how he would react to the two different types of blood inside him, and she'd needed to be with her people in their time of mourning. For a while, he'd tried to sleep, tossing and turning, his body recovering from the beat down it had given—and received. Then, about an hour ago, the tug-of-war had begun. Thank God Victoria had beat feet. What a freaking nightmare it would have been to see himself through her eyes, in his current pathetic condition, and know what she was thinking.

When Victoria thought of him, he wanted her stuck on the word *invincible*. Barring that, he'd make do with *hot*. Anything else, no thanks. Because *he* thought *she* was perfect, in every way.

Perfect and sweet and beautiful. And his. Her image filled his mind. She had long, dark hair that tumbled down her pale shoulders, blue eyes that glittered like crystals and lips that were cherry red. Kissable. Lickable.

He'd met her only a few weeks ago, though he felt as if he'd known her forever. Which, in a warped kind of way, he had. Well, at least for the last six months, thanks to a heads-up from one of the souls living in his head. Yeah, as if vampires and telepathic blood weren't enough of an oddity, Aden shared his head with three other human souls. More than *that,* each soul possessed a supernatural ability.

Julian could raise the dead.

Caleb could possess other bodies.

And Elijah could predict the future.

Through Elijah, Aden had known he would encounter Victoria before she'd ever arrived in Crossroads,

Oklahoma. A place he'd once considered hell on earth, but now considered The Awesome, even though it was a total breeding ground for so-called mythical creatures. Witches, goblins, fairies—all enemies to Victoria—and of course, vampires. Oh, and werewolves, the vampire protectors.

And, okay. That was a lot of freaking creatures. But if one myth had been true, it kinda made sense that *all* myths would be.

"What am I going to do with—" Victoria began again, drawing his attention to the present.

He really wanted to hear her complete that sentence. Before she could utter another word, however, his focus switched. Again. Darkness suddenly enveloped him, consuming him, chasing away his connection to Victoria. Aden's thrashing on his bed renewed, pain exploding through him just before he linked with the other vampire. Dmitri. *Dead* Dmitri.

Aden wanted to open his eyes, to see something, anything, but his lids were seemingly glued together. Through panting breaths, he smelled dirt and…smoke? Yes. Smoke. Thick and cloying, itching his throat. He coughed, and coughed, or was Dmitri coughing? Was Dmitri still alive? Or was the body only reacting because Aden's thoughts sparked through their shared mind?

He tried to move Dmitri's lips, to force words to emerge, to gain someone's attention, but his lungs seized, rejecting the ashy air, and suddenly he couldn't breathe at all.

"Burn him," someone said coolly. "Let's make sure the traitor stays dead."

"My pleasure," another replied, a gleeful edge to the tone.

In the darkness, Aden couldn't see the speakers. Didn't know if they were human or vampire. Didn't know where he was or—the first man's words finally sank in, consuming his thoughts. Burn...him...

No. No, no, no. Not while Aden was here. What if he felt every lick of flame?

No! he tried to scream. Again, no sound emerged.

Dmitri's body was lifted. Aden felt as if he were suspended from a wire, head flopping back, limbs forgotten. Nearby, he heard the crackle of those dreaded flames. Heat wafted to him, swirling around him, enveloping him.

No! He tried to thrash, to fight, but the body remained motionless. *No!*

A moment later, contact. And oh, yes. He felt it. The first streams of fire flicked against his feet before catching...spreading. Agony. Agony unlike anything he'd ever known. Skin, melting. Muscles and bones, liquefying. Blood, disintegrating. Oh, God.

Still he tried to fight, to pull away and run, and still the lifeless body refused to obey. *No! Help!* Impossibly, the agony intensified…smoldering over him, eating him up bite by tasty bite. What would happen if he remained linked to Dmitri until the very end? What would happen if he—

Pinpricks of light winked through the darkness, bloomed and locked together, until he was once again seeing the world through Victoria's eyes. Yet another switch. *Thank God.* He was panting, so drenched with sweat he was practically swimming, but despite the change, residual pain—far greater than the acid still swishing through his veins—slithered from his feet to his brain, and he wanted to shout.

He was—shaking, he realized. No, Victoria was shaking.

A soft, warm hand pressed against his—her—shoulder. She looked up, vision blurry from her tears. Moonlight glowed in the sky, he saw, and stars twinkled. A few night birds even flew overhead, calling to each other in…fear? Probably. They had to sense the danger below them.

Victoria lowered her gaze, and Aden studied the vampires surrounding her. Each was tall, pale, striking. *Alive.* Most were not the monsters storybooks painted them to be. They were simply detached, humans a food source they couldn't afford to care about.

Vampires lived for centuries, after all, while humans withered and died. Exactly as Aden was soon to die.

Elijah had already predicted his death. The prediction sucked, yeah, but it was the method that sucked more: a sharp knife through his very necessary heart.

He'd always prayed the method would miraculously change. Until now. A knife through the heart beat burning to death inside a body that didn't belong to him any day of the week. And when the hell was he going to catch a break, huh? No torture, no fighting creatures, no waiting around for the end, just flunking tests and kissing his girlfriend.

Aden forced himself to concentrate before he worked himself into a rage he couldn't hope to assuage. The vampire mansion rose behind the crowd, shadowed and eerie, like a haunted house melded with a Roman cathedral. Victoria had told him the house had been here, in Oklahoma, for hundreds of years, and her people had "borrowed" it from its owner when they first arrived. He'd taken that to mean the former owner had supplied the vampires with a nice lunch buffet—of his organs.

"He was powerful, you're right about that," a girl who looked to be Victoria's age said. She had hair the color of newly fallen snow, eyes like a meadow and the face of an angel. She wore a black robe that bared one pale shoulder, traditional vampire garb, but somehow she seemed…out of place. Maybe because she'd just popped a Juicy Fruit bubble.

"A great king," another girl added, placing her hand

on Victoria's other side. Another blonde. This one had crystalline eyes like Victoria and the face of a *fallen* angel. Unlike the other girls, she wore a black leather half-top and black leather pants. Weapons were strapped to her waist, and barbed wire circled her wrists. And no, the wire wasn't a tattoo.

"Yes," Victoria replied softly. *Darling sisters.*

Sisters? He'd known Victoria had them, yeah, but he'd never met them. They'd been locked in their rooms during the Vampire Ball meant to celebrate Vlad the Impaler's official awakening from his century-long slumber. Aden wondered if Victoria's mother was here, too. Apparently, she'd been imprisoned in Romania for spilling vampire secrets to humans. Vlad's orders. A real nice guy, that Vlad.

Aden was human, and he knew way more than he should. Some vampires—like Victoria—could teleport, traveling from one location to another with only a thought. And if word had already reached Romania that the vampire king was dead, mommy vamp could have arrived in Crossroads seconds later.

"He was a terrible father, though. Wasn't he?" the first girl continued while chewing gum.

The three shared a rueful half-smile.

"He was indeed," Victoria said. "Unbending, exacting. Brutal to his enemies—and sometimes to us. And yet, it's so hard to say goodbye."

She peered down at Vlad's charred remains. He was the first human ever to change from human to vampire. Well, the first anyone knew about. His body was intact, though burned beyond recognition. A crown perched haphazardly atop his hairless head.

Several rings decorated his fingers, and a black velvet cloth draped his chest and legs.

His dead body still lay where Dmitri had dropped it. Was there some kind of protocol about moving a royal corpse? Or were his people still too shocked to touch him?

They'd lost him the very night they were to be reunited with him. Dmitri had burned the guy to death just before the ceremony and claimed the vampire throne as his own. Then Aden had killed *him,* which meant Aden was now supposed to lead the bloodsuckers. Aden, of all people, of all *humans,* which was honest to God *craziness.* He'd make a terrible king. Not that he wanted even to try.

He wanted Victoria. No more, no less.

"Despite our feelings, he'll have a place of honor, even in death," Victoria said. Her gaze swept past her sisters to the vampires still looming around them. "His funeral must be—"

"In a few months," the second sister interrupted.

Victoria blinked once, twice, as if trying to jumpstart her thoughts. "Why?"

"He's our king. He's *always* been our king. More than that, he's the strongest among us. What if he's still alive under all that soot? We need to wait, watch him. Make sure."

"No." Aden felt the glide of Victoria's hair on her shoulders as she shook her head violently. "That will merely offer everyone false hope."

"A few months is too long a wait, yeah," the green-eyed gum chewer said. Her name was Stephanie, if he was reading Victoria's thoughts correctly. "But I do agree waiting a little while before burning him is smart. We'll let everyone get used to the idea of a human king. So why don't we compromise, huh? Let's wait, oh, I don't know, a month. We can keep him in the crypt below us."

"First, the crypt is for our deceased humans. Second, even a month is too long," Victoria gritted out. "If we must wait—" she paused until they nodded "—then let's wait…half a month." She'd wanted to say a day, maybe two, but had known the suggestion would be met with resistance. And this way, *Aden* would have time to acclimate to the idea of being king.

The other sister ran her tongue over her very sharp, very white teeth. "Very well. Agreed. We'll wait fourteen days. And we *will* keep him in the crypt. He'll be sealed inside, preventing any lingering rebels from hurting him further."

Victoria sighed. "Yes. All right. You agreed to my stipulation, so I'll agree to yours."

"Wow. No one had to throw a punch to win the argument. The changing of the guard is working in our favor already." Stephanie popped another bubble. "So, anyway, back to Daddy Dearest. He's lucky, you know. He died here, so he gets to stay here. Had he kicked it in Romania, the rest of the family would have spit on his crypt."

There was a beat of stunned silence before gasps of outrage flooded the congregation.

"What?" Stephanie splayed her arms, all innocence. "You know you're thinking the same thing."

Thank God Victoria wouldn't be heading off to her homeland for the funeral. Aden wouldn't have been able to travel with her since he lived at the D and M Ranch, a halfway house for "wayward" teens, aka unwanted delinquents, where his every action was monitored.

Everyone assumed he had schizophrenia because he talked to the souls trapped inside him, which had earned him a lifetime of institutions and medications. The ranch was the system's final effort to save him, and if he blew that chance, he'd be carted away. Boom, done, goodbye. Hello, lifetime of confinement in a padded room.

He'd lose Victoria forever.

"Shut your mouth, Stephanie, before I do it for you. Vlad taught us to survive, and kept the humans unaware of us—for the most part. He made us a legend, a myth. He also taught our enemies to fear us. For that alone, he has my respect." The blue-eyed sister—Lauren; her name was Lauren—tilted her head to the side, suddenly pensive. "Now. What are we going to do about the mortal while our fourteen-day reprieve is ticking away?"

"Victoria's...Aden?" Stephanie's brow wrinkled. "That's his name, right?"

"Haden Stone, known by his people as Aden, yes," Victoria replied. "But I—"

"We'll follow his rule," a male voice said, cutting her off. "Because, and stop me if you've heard this one, he's our ruler." This came from Riley, a werewolf shape-shifter and Victoria's most trusted guard, as he approached the half-circle the girls formed. He glared at Lauren. "If you don't understand that, let me know and I'll break out the hand puppets. He killed Dmitri, he calls the shots. End of story."

Lauren scowled at him, her fangs sharper than before. "Watch how you speak to me, puppy. I'm a princess. You're just the hired help."

More gasps reverberated.

Aden kept losing sight of the crowd, but they suddenly filled his line of vision as Victoria studied them, ready to leap into action if someone attacked her sister. Clearly they didn't like that the wolf had been insulted. But then, neither did she. Wolves deserved respect—far more than what had been demanded even for Vlad. Wolves could—

Aden cursed as Victoria blanked her mind, forcing herself to concentrate on what was happening around her. Wolves were more important than vampires? he wondered. More important than vampire *royalty?* Why?

Riley laughed with genuine humor. "Your jealousy is showing, Lore. I'd be careful if I were you."

Lauren ignored him this time, swinging her crystal eyes back to Victoria and snapping, "Bring Aden here tomorrow night. Everyone will meet him. Officially."

And kill him before the fourteen days "ticked away?"

"Yes." Victoria nodded, but not by word or deed did she reveal her sudden trepidation. "All right. Tomorrow, you shall meet your new king. In the meantime, we shall *mourn.*"

The conversation ended, everyone properly chastised.

Victoria sighed and peered over at the body of her father. Which meant *Aden* peered over at her father. He considered the charred remains, speculating about what the king had looked like before. Tall and strong, surely. Had he possessed blue eyes like Victoria? Or green like Stephanie?

Vlad's fingers curled into a fist.

Aden stilled, sure he'd just hallucinated. And he must

have, he rationalized, because Victoria had not seemed to notice the earth-shattering event and he'd watched through her eyes.

Vlad's fingers uncurled.

Once again, Aden stilled, waiting, gauging, heart thumping against his ribs. He hadn't imagined that. He *couldn't* have imagined that because even as the thought formed, those fingers twitched as if trying to make another fist. Movement, true movement, and movement equaled life. Right?

Why hadn't Victoria noticed? Why hadn't anyone? Maybe they were too lost to their grief. Or maybe Vlad's once-immortal body was simply expelling the last hints of his existence. Either way, Victoria needed to be told what he'd seen.

Victoria, Aden projected, desperate to gain her attention.

Nothing. No response.

Victoria!

She petted Vlad's arm before rising, intending to instruct the biggest of the vampires to carry him inside for burial preparation. Obviously, she didn't hear him.

And then it was too late. His world shifted, realigned, darkness closing in around him. No, not darkness. Light. So much light. Blue-white flames covered Dmitri's entire body, and therefore *Aden's* body. Scorching him, blistering what was left of him.

This time, Aden did scream.
He did thrash.
He also died.

ONE

MARY ANN GRAY STUDIED HERSELF in the full-length mirror in her bedroom. Makeup—light and unsmeared. Dark hair—not a tangle. Perhaps even, dare she think it? Silky. Clothes—an unwrinkled lacy T-shirt and clean skinny jeans. Shoes—hiking boots. She'd replaced the plain white laces with thick pink ones, giving them a feminine flair.

Okay, then. She was officially ready.

Breathing deeply, shaking a little, she gathered her books, stuffed them into her backpack, swung that pack over her shoulder and headed downstairs toward the kitchen. Where her dad was waiting. With breakfast she would be required to eat.

Her stomach churned in protest. She'd have to fake-eat because she doubted she would be able to keep a single bite down. She was simply too knotted with nerves.

From the living room, she heard pans clattering, water pounding into the sink and a man sighing in…defeat?

She stopped just before snaking the final corner and leaned her shoulder against the wall, losing herself to her thoughts. A few weeks ago, she and her dad had entered new territory. Ugly, deceitful territory. *We'll always be honest with each other,* he used to tell her. All. The. Time. Of course, at the same time, he'd been feeding her lies about her birth mother. The woman who had raised her had not given birth to her, but had in fact been her aunt.

In truth, her real mother had possessed the ability to time-travel into younger versions of herself, yet he'd refused to believe her, had considered her unstable. She couldn't prove otherwise, either, because she was dead and her spirit had moved on. Lost to Mary Ann forever.

God, the loss still hurt.

Mary Ann had gotten to spend one day with her. One amazing, wonderful day because Eve, her mother, had been one of the souls trapped inside her friend Aden's head. Then, boom. Eve was gone.

Tears burned Mary Ann's eyes as she remembered their parting, but she blinked them back. She couldn't allow herself to cry. Her mascara would run, and then she'd look like a domestic abuse victim when Riley arrived to pick her up.

Riley.

My boyfriend. Yes, she'd think about him instead,

looking forward to the future rather than wallowing in the past. Her lips even curled into a small smile as her heart raced uncontrollably. She hadn't seen him since they'd attended the Vampire Ball together, when his king had been murdered and Aden had been named the new vampire sovereign. Not that Aden wanted the title—or the responsibilities that would surely come with it.

Sure, that had only happened on Saturday. But two days apart felt like *forever* when Riley was involved. She was used to seeing him every day at school, as well as every evening when he snuck into her room.

And, to be honest, she'd never liked anyone the way she liked him. Maybe because there was no one quite like Riley. He was intense and smart, sweet (to her) and protective. And *sexy*. All those muscles...honed from years of running as a werewolf shape-shifter and fighting as a vampire guardian. Both of which forged the many facets of his personality.

While acting as guardian, he was unemotional and distant (to everyone but her). He had to be, to do such a violent job. But as a werewolf, he was soft, warm and cuddly. *I can't wait to cuddle him again,* she thought, her grin spreading.

"Are you going to stand out there all day?" her dad called.

She snapped to attention, grin fading. How had he known she was there?

Just get the morning's emotional bloodbath over with. Raising her chin, she marched the rest of the way into the kitchen and settled at the table, dropping her backpack at her feet. Her dad set a plate of pancakes in front of her, the scent of blueberries and syrup suddenly coating the air. Her favorite. Her stomach had settled considerably as she'd thought about Riley, but even so, she didn't think she could eat. Or rather, didn't want to risk the possible consequences. Like vomiting in front of her brand-new boyfriend.

Her dad eased into the chair across from her. His blond hair was spiked around his head, as if he'd raked his fingers through it a few thousand times, and his usually bright blue eyes were dull, with dark circles underneath them. Lines of tension branched from his mouth, making him look as if he hadn't slept in weeks. Maybe he hadn't.

Despite everything, she hated seeing him like that. He loved her, she knew that. But that was what had made his betrayal sting so badly. And by "sting" she meant toss-her-into-a-meat-grinder-and-use-the-pieces-as-fish-bait.

"Dad," she said at the exact moment he said, "Mary Ann."

They peered at each other for a moment, and then grinned. It was the first easy moment they'd shared in weeks, and it was…nice.

"You go first," she told him. He was a doctor, a clinical psychologist, and he was tricky as hell. With only a few words, he could get her to spill her feelings without her realizing she'd even opened her stupid mouth. But she'd chance a spilling today because she had no idea how to kick things off.

He heaped a few pancakes onto his plate. "I just wanted to tell you that I'm sorry. For every lie. For everything. And that I did it to protect you."

A good start. She followed his lead and filled her plate, then proceeded to push the food around, pretending to eat. "To protect me from…?"

"The stigma of thinking your own mother was unbalanced. The thought that you had somehow…that you had…"

"Killed her?" The words croaked from Mary Ann's suddenly tight throat.

"Yes," he whispered. "You didn't, you know. It wasn't your fault."

Her real mother, Anne—known to Aden as Eve—had died giving birth to her. That happened sometimes, right? No reason for her father to blame her. But then, he didn't know the whole truth. He didn't know that Mary Ann muted paranormal abilities.

She had only just learned of it herself, and all *she* knew was that her mere presence prevented people—and creatures—from using their "gifts."

If not for Aden, she never would have discovered even that. He was the biggest paranormal magnet of all time. (And if he wasn't, he should be. 'Cause anyone who was stronger—shudder.) Her mother had weakened each day of her pregnancy, little Mary Ann literally sucking the life right out of her. And then, at the moment of her birth, Anne/Eve had simply slipped away.

Right into Aden, Mary Ann thought with a sigh. Aden, who had been born on the same day, in the same hospital. Aden, who had also drawn three other human souls—ghosts—right into his head.

Only, Anne/Eve hadn't remembered Mary Ann right away, her memories wiped when she'd entered Aden. Once they'd figured everything out, her mom had been granted the thing she'd wanted most in life, that which she'd been denied by her death. A single day with Mary Ann. And once her mom had gotten her wish, she'd vanished. Never to be seen or heard from again. *Stomach… churning…again…*

Her dad didn't know any of that, either, and Mary Ann wasn't going to tell him. He wouldn't believe her. He would think she was as "unbalanced" as her real mom had been.

"Mary Ann?" her dad prompted. "Please. Tell me how you're feeling. Tell me what you thought when I—"

The doorbell rang, saving him from finishing and her from having to form a reply. Heart dancing wildly, she popped to her feet. Riley. He was here. "I'll get it," she said in a rush.

"Mary Ann."

But she was already racing from the kitchen to the front door. The moment that thick cherry wood swung open, Riley visible through the netted screen, her stomach calmed completely.

He smiled his bad boy smile, half wicked, half *really* wicked. "Hey."

"Hey." Yep. *Sexy.* He had dark hair and light green eyes. He was tall, with the body of a dedicated, can't-be-sacked football player having an affair with weights. His shoulders were broad, his stomach roped. Tragically, she couldn't see those mouth-watering ropes under his black T-shirt. His jeans bagged a little on his strong legs, and he wore boots caked with dirt.

Wait. Had she just given him a total body scan? Yep. Cheeks heating, she brought her gaze back to his face. Clearly, he was trying not to laugh.

"Do you approve?" he asked.

The heat intensified. "Yes. But I wasn't done," she added. He wasn't beautiful in a male model kind of way, but he was ruggedly appealing, with a slightly crooked nose—probably from being broken so many times—and a strong jaw. And she had once kissed him, right on those gorgeous lips.

When will we kiss again?

She was ready. More than ready. That was the most fun her tongue had ever had.

He opened his mouth to say something, then snapped it closed. Footsteps echoed behind her, and she turned. Her dad approached, her backpack dangling from his arm. She closed the distance between them, claimed the pack and stood on her tiptoes, kissing his cheek before she could talk herself out it.

"I'll see you later, Dad. Thanks for breakfast."

The tension in his face eased just a bit. "See you later, honey. I hope you have a wonderful day."

"You, too."

His gaze shifted to the boy still standing in the doorway. "Riley," he acknowledged stiffly.

They'd met once, but only briefly. Her dad didn't know it, but Riley was older than he was. By, like, a hundred years. As a shape-shifter, Riley aged slowly. Very, *very* slowly.

"Dr. Gray," Riley returned, respectful as always.

"Mary Ann," her dad said, attention returning to her. "You might want to take a jacket."

It was the first of November and every day was a little colder than the last. But she said, "I'll be fine." Riley would keep her warm. "I promise." Pleasantries done, Mary Ann returned to the door, pushed the screen open with her shoulder, and grabbed Riley's warm, callused hand. She shivered. She loved touching him. As a human *and* a wolf.

As they walked, he confiscated her pack with his free hand.

"Thanks."

"Not a problem."

Morning was in full swing, though the sun was muted behind clouds and the sky a dark gray. Blackbirds were squawking continuously—they stayed in Crossroads all year round—and the air was cool and crisp. Still hand-in-hand, they bypassed the few houses surrounding hers.

Each house was shaped like a train station of yore, with posts, decks, colored wood and sloped two-story roofs. Once they'd passed the very last one, they approached a brick wall about half a mile ahead, a heavily populated forest directly behind it. The trees there were thick, their leaves now yellow and red.

Her dad assumed she and Riley took the long route to school, staying on well-traveled, paved roads. *Not* cutting through the forest. Her dad was wrong. Sometimes a girl needed to be alone with her boyfriend, with no prying eyes. Or ears. The walk to Crossroads High was one of those times.

"I can't believe how much time has passed since I last saw you," she said.

"I know. I'm sorry. Feels like eternity to me, too. I

wanted to see you, believe me, but more vampires have been popping into the house in preparation for Vlad's funeral."

"I'm sorry," she said softly, squeezing his hand. "About his death. I know you respected him."

"Thank you. We have to wait fourteen days before we can hold the funeral—no, thirteen now, I guess. After that, Aden will be officially crowned king."

"Why wait fourteen days for the funeral?" She did *not* want to imagine what the corpse would look like after lying around for two weeks.

Riley shrugged. "He was king. The people want to make sure he's dead."

"Wait. He could be *alive?*"

"No."

"But you just said—"

"The people want to make sure he's dead, I know, but they're in shock, hopeful. Nothing like this has ever happened to them before."

She could understand that. She'd been a mess after both her moms had died. "Aden will be happy to have a reprieve, at least. He's not looking forward to being king, I don't think."

"Oh, he's already king, no doubt about that. Not even Vlad could recover from such a severe burning."

Again she found herself saying, "But you just said—"

"I know, I know. The thing is, alive or dead, Vlad isn't ruling us and *someone* needs to rule us or there'll be chaos, deserters and takeover attempts."

With a human in charge, there'd probably be chaos, deserters and takeover attempts anyway.

"And everyone is…eager to meet Aden," Riley went on, "to discover his plans for the clan."

Eager. Yeah. Right. *Sorry, Aden,* she thought, suspecting he would balk when he heard. *Looks like you're gonna have to take one for the team.*

"Now that the life and death issues are out of the way, you've gotta tell me. Are you okay?" Riley cast her a concerned glance. "After everything you witnessed…I've been worried."

"I'm fine, I promise." And she was. Yes, at the ball she'd seen humans reduced to nothing more than living plates of food by the bloodsuckers. Yes, she'd seen Aden fight and ultimately kill one of those bloodsuckers by burning him as he'd burned Vlad, and then stabbing him where he was most vulnerable: his eyes. And yes, those bloody images might haunt her for the rest of her life.

But she *was* alive, thanks to Aden and Riley, and everything else kinda stopped mattering when compared to that.

"So, are *you* okay?" she asked. He was a warrior and

she had probably insulted him by even asking, but she needed to hear him say it.

"I am now," he replied, and they shared a smile. A smile that melted her like ice cream in the sun.

Okay, so. *Remind him of the rest of the "life and death issues" so you can concentrate on something else.* Like cleaning Riley's tonsils. "It's probably a good thing nothing's going to happen with the vampires for two weeks. We have a meeting with the witches to attend. Or rather, Aden does." Ugh. She hated even thinking about those witches. How powerful they were. How uncaring. How she would literally die if Aden didn't make it to that meeting.

Several days ago, those witches had cast a spell over them. A freaking death spell. If, in the next five days, Aden failed to attend some sort of meeting with them, Mary Ann, Riley and Aden's girlfriend Victoria would die.

That simple. And that complicated.

No one knew where the meeting was being held or even where the witches were staying. Which made it impossible to meet with them.

Maybe that had been their intention all along.

Stomach churning again…

And yet, the prospect hardly seemed real. They had cursed her with death if Aden failed to attend their meeting, yet Mary Ann felt fine. Healthy, whole, as if she had decades ahead of her rather than days.

Would her heart simply stop working? Or was she fooling herself? Would nothing actually happen, the spell just a joke? A means of terrifying her?

She'd spent all last night researching witches and spells and ways to break those spells. The information differed, depending on the source. The source she most believed, however, was Riley, and he said spells, once uttered, sparked to unbreakable life.

The muscles in Riley's hand twitched, returning her drifting mind to the present. "Believe me, I haven't forgotten the meeting." His voice was toneless now.

Trying not to scare her? Too late. Even though the prospect didn't seem real, she was still scared out of her mind. He believed in the witches' power completely. Which meant he honestly believed everyone in their group would soon die.

"Any idea where that meeting will be held?" she asked, even though she knew the answer.

"Not yet, but I'm working on it."

So frustrating! Not that she was frustrated with him, of course, but with the entire situation.

"It'll be okay," Riley said, as if sensing her growing upset. He probably did. He could read auras, and therefore emotions. "We'll figure everything out. I promise. I would never let anything bad happen to you."

She trusted him. She did. More than anyone else in her life. He never lied to her. He gave her the facts, straight up, unvarnished, no matter how harsh they were.

Finally they reached the wall, though they weren't even close to the gate, and stopped. Without a word, Riley leapt to the top of the seven-foot structure, his graceful movements making the jump look seamless. Grinning, he leaned down and offered her a hand.

Even that, she had to use all of her strength to reach—and she probably looked like a spastic rabbit, hopping up and down as she stretched to connect with him. Yet the moment she clasped his fingers, he pulled her the rest of the way effortlessly.

"Thank you. For everything," she said as she balanced on the ledge. "And not to change the subject, but do you think Tucker will be okay?"

Tucker. Her former boyfriend. They'd rescued him from the Vampire Ball, where he'd been the night's snack of choice.

Riley jumped to the ground on the other side. Again, the motion was seamless, the impact of landing barely registering. "He'll survive. Unfortunately," she thought she heard him add with a twinge of jealousy. "He's part demon, remember?" He held up his arms, waiting for her. "Demons heal faster than humans."

She'd done this so many times she didn't hesitate; she, too, jumped. He caught her and settled her to her feet, letting her slide down his beautiful body, their gazes locked together. Her palms lifted and flattened on his chest. His heart was pounding. As was hers.

"Demon. As if I could forget." That demon blood was the only reason Tucker had dated her. She'd calmed him, he'd confessed after their breakup. A breakup he had fought. Not because he loved her, but because he'd craved more of the calming, as if she were a sedative. Maybe she was.

Sometimes she wondered if that was why Riley was with her. Because she calmed him, too. He was a supernatural creature, after all, and her presence alone had to soothe the brutal, ferocious beast inside him.

If so, she would still want to be with him. She was already addicted to him, *enjoyed* his wildness. But she would still wish he wanted her for her, not for what she could do. Still. She could always content herself with the knowledge that she now soothed rather than drained, as she'd done to her own mother.

"You look sad," Riley said, head tilting to the side as he studied her. "Why?"

Thoughts of her mother always brought melancholy, but that wasn't the reason for the emotion he was sensing. "I'm..." What could she say? She didn't want to lie to him, but she didn't want to admit her fears, either. That the girl she was might not supersede the ability she possessed. She'd seem needy and her self-esteem low. *Are you? Is it?*

Without warning, Riley swung her to the left. She yelped as her entire world spun. Her back was suddenly pressed against a tree trunk, though she wasn't jarred in the least. Strong hands had padded the collision, so much so she wouldn't have known anything was behind her if not for her inability to move away. Not that she wanted to move away.

Riley pinned her completely in the next instant, caging her in, his hands at her temples.

"Are we under attack?" she managed to say. Had something—or someone—threatened them? Had—

"You're beautiful, you know that?" he said, voice husky.

No threat, then. She melted. "Th-thank you." Though she wasn't sure she agreed. She could maybe be called "cute" on her best days. She just, well, she had a baby face. A little rounded, dimpled. Olive skin like her mother—the only attribute she did like—and light brown eyes. "So are you. Beautiful, I mean."

"I am not." Said with disgust, though his eyes were as bright as emeralds. "I'm manly."

A laugh escaped her. "Manly. Definitely. I don't know what I was thinking, calling you beautiful." Exquisite was a better word for those rough features. "Forgive me?"

"Always." He leaned down, his nose at her throat, and sniffed. "Have I ever told you how good you smell? Like sugar cookies and vanilla."

"That's my lotion." Was that breathless voice really hers?

"Well, your lotion is going to get you nibbled on."

That had been the plan. "Yeah?"

"Oh, yeah."

His head rose, but only slightly, and their noses touched at the tip. He was breathing heavily, and so was she, so every time she inhaled, *she* scented *him*. She might smell like cookies, but he smelled like the forest around them. Wild and earthy and *necessary*.

She cupped his nape, her other hand returning to rest just over his heart. The beat was faster now, so fast she couldn't keep count. His heat enveloped her like a winter coat, keeping her toasty warm, just as she'd known he would.

"Riley?"

"Yes?" That single word was a low, rumbling growl.

"Why are you attracted to me?" Oh, God. Had she really gone there? And yep, she'd sounded needy.

"Fishing for compliments, darling? Well, I can play. I'm with you because you're brave. Because you're sweet. Because you care about your friends. Because every time I look at you, my heart beats out of control, as you can probably feel, and all I can think about is being with you longer."

"Oh. That's nice." A silly reply, but she didn't know what else to say. He'd just rocked her entire world. And now she wanted to rock his. "Kiss me." Inch by inch, she closed the distance between their mouths.

"My pleasure." And then their lips met.

Automatically she opened for him, letting his tongue thrust inside, and it was like being struck by lightning. Electrifying. *So good.* He tasted as good as he smelled, just as wild, just as earthy. Just as necessary.

His fingers slipped under the hem of her T-shirt and settled on her hips, branding the sensitive skin there. He urged her away from the tree and closer to his body, and she eagerly followed that urging. *So good,* she thought again.

This was their second kiss, and it was far better than the first. Which she wouldn't have thought possible. That kiss had consumed her. This one lit her up and burned her all the way to her soul.

They stood like that, lost in each other, for several minutes, still tasting, hands wandering—though not daring too much—and utterly enjoying.

"I love kissing you," he rasped.

"Me, too. I mean, I love kissing *you.* Not myself."

His chuckle brushed her cheek with warm breath, and goose bumps broke out from there to her neck. "While we're at school, I won't be able to think about anything else. Just this. Just you."

With a moan, she tugged him down for more. The tangle of their tongues excited her as nothing else ever had. The feel of him against her, so strong and sure, thrilled her. Other girls might look at him and crave him, but it was Mary Ann he turned to with desire in his eyes.

Yeah, but because he really wants you or because you calm his wolf?

Stupid fear.

She stiffened, and Riley pulled away from her. He was panting, little beads of sweat on his brow.

"What's wrong?" he demanded.

"Nothing."

"I don't believe you, but you'll tell me the truth later, after the flames have died and I can think properly. Won't you?"

He couldn't think properly? She almost grinned. "Yes." Maybe.

"And anyway, we needed to stop."

The same words he'd uttered last time.

She was having trouble catching her breath or she would have sighed. "Yeah. I know." Disappointing, but indisputable. "If we don't, we'll be late for school."

"Or we won't make it to school. At all."

Plus, she didn't want her first time to be out in the open. Not that she would tell him that.

They reluctantly parted and kicked into gear, heading toward Crossroads High. She couldn't help herself. She reached up and traced her fingertips over her lips. They were swollen. Probably red. Definitely moist. Would everyone know what she and Riley had been doing with only a glance?

Twenty minutes later, not nearly long enough, they reached the edge of the woods and stepped onto school property, the massive building coming into view, forming a half-moon of three stories. In several places, the roof pointed toward the sky. Salmon-colored brick was decorated with multiple black and gold banners that read *Go Jaguars.*

The lawn was manicured, the grass slowly fading from green to yellow to off-white. Cars sped through the parking lot and kids rushed up the concrete steps, bypassing the flagpole without a glance.

In front of the closest set of doors stood Victoria. Alone. She was pacing, hands wringing together in agitation. She wore a black T-shirt and matching miniskirt, dark hair flowing down her back. A beam of sunlight bathed her as if drawn to her, causing the blue of her eyes to practically glow.

The younger the vampire, the more time they could spend in the sun, Mary Ann knew. The older they got, the more the sun burned and stung their skin. Surprisingly sensitive skin, since it was so thick and hard, like marble, that even a blade couldn't cut through it.

Victoria was still at an age—eighty-one or something like that—where the sun didn't bother her. Like wolves, vampires aged slowly.

For the first time, that thought upset her. Victoria and Riley would age at the same rate while Mary Ann would wither, becoming a hag. Oh, God. How mortifying! And now she wanted to slap the vampire girl around a bit, just on principle.

"Have you seen Aden?" Victoria asked the moment they reached her. Normally she was pale, but today she was chalk white.

"No," Mary Ann and Riley said in unison. She recalled the last time she'd seen him. They'd snuck him into his room at the ranch and he'd flopped onto his bed. He'd been pale, shaking, sweating, breath shallow as he fought for every inhalation.

She'd thought he would rest, and rest would heal him. What if—

"Well, he wasn't at the ranch this morning," Victoria rushed on. "But he was supposed to be there so we could walk to school together."

"Maybe he's inside," Riley said.

The vampire's concern didn't lessen. If anything, her hand-wringing became more insistent. "He isn't. I checked. And the tardy bell will soon ring. You know he can't be late. He'll get into trouble, be kicked out, and you also know he'll do anything to avoid being kicked out."

"Maybe he's sick," Mary Ann said, not believing her own words. If that were the case, he would have been at the ranch, still in bed. And Victoria was right. Aden was never late to school. Not because he feared being sent away, but because he never missed an opportunity to spend time with his princess. He worshipped the girl.

"I'll hunt him down." Riley glanced at Mary Ann before she could tell him she would be coming with him. "You'll stay here with Victoria."

"No, I—"

"I can move faster without you."

Embarrassing but true. "All right. Fine. Just be careful."

"Riley," Victoria began. "I—"

"You'll stay, too," he reiterated.

With the many creatures that now prowled the streets of their small town, he wouldn't leave Mary Ann without a guard. His protectiveness was as fine a quality as the six-pack on his stomach.

Victoria nodded stiffly. "You're my soldier, you know. You're supposed to obey my orders."

"I know, but it's my king out there. Sorry to tell you

this, babe, but he now comes first." With a final glance at Mary Ann, Riley spun on his heel and strode away, soon disappearing into the trees.

✝WO

ADEN AWOKE WITH A JOLT, a shout of pain caught in his throat, wild gaze cataloging his surroundings. Bedroom. Desk. Dresser. Plain white walls. Planked floor.

His bedroom in the bunkhouse at the ranch, then.

Alive. He was alive, not burned to a crisp. Thank God. But…

Was he intact? He patted himself down while looking himself over. Skin? Check. Smooth and warm, tanned rather than deep-fried. Two arms? Check. Two legs? Check. Most important—was he now a girl? No. Thank God, thank God, thank God. He expelled a sigh of relief, sagged against the mattress and took stock of everything else.

Sweat soaked him. His hair was plastered to his head, and his boxers looked like they'd…like he'd… His cheeks flushed with heat. If Shannon, his roommate, saw him like this, he'd be teased about having a wet dream. Albeit good-naturedly. That's just what friends did. Still. No, thanks. He—

Saw the bottom of Shannon's bunk, and his eyes widened. There were deep grooves in the wooden slats, as if he'd clawed and kicked at his friend's bed. Repeatedly. He glanced at his fingernails, and sure enough. They were ragged and bloody, with wood shards embedded underneath them.

Great. What else had he done while crashing on vampire blood?

Worry about that later.

"Elijah?" he asked. Time for roll call.

Present, the psychic said, knowing the drill.

One down. "Julian?" The corpse whisperer, as they called him. A single step into a cemetery, and hello, walking dead.

Here.

Sweet. Two down, one to go. "Caleb?" The body possesser.

Yo.

Rock on. The gang was all here.

Once, Aden had wanted them gone. He loved them, but come on. A little privacy would be nice. But then he'd lost Eve. Her name might have been Anne in her real life, but she'd always be Eve to Aden.

He missed her, his motherly time-traveler. Missed her

terribly. Now he wasn't sure he could deal with losing the others. They were a part of him. His best friends. His constant companions. He *needed* them.

As always, that line of thought made him feel guilty. They deserved their freedom. *Wanted* their freedom. Maybe. Since Eve had left, they hadn't asked him to figure out who they'd been before taking prime real estate in his head, as if they were afraid he would succeed and they, too, would have to leave and experience the unknown.

Where Eve had gone, none of them knew. They only knew that she'd disappeared and hadn't returned.

So what's going on? Julian asked.

What he means, Caleb said, *is that our dreams were hot. And not the good kind of hot. We burned, dude. Burned.*

And most of us normally don't share your dreams, Julian added.

Well, Elijah did, but that was because Elijah was psychic and his visions were Aden's. Tonight, last night, *whenever,* hadn't been a vision, though. It had been real, a mind-merge, but now, pieces of his memory were missing. He remembered seeing Victoria, feeling those flames, then meeting her…sisters? Yes, her sisters. But nothing else stood out. The rest of what happened was blurred at the edges, as if his mind couldn't process what it had seen. If that were true, though, why did he remember being burned alive? Why did they all remember *that?* Shouldn't that be what they forgot? Something too painful to recall?

So? Julian prompted. *An explanation would be nice.*

"Vampire blood," he reminded them. He couldn't just think his replies because they couldn't hear his inner voice amid the chaos. "We saw through two other sets of eyes."

Oh, yeah. And speaking of vamps, Caleb said. *Where's ours?*

Victoria, he meant. *She's mine,* Aden wanted to snap, but didn't. Caleb the Pervert couldn't help himself. He lived for girls and "nookie" he might never get. "She's supposed to meet us here and walk to school with us." What time was it?

Before he could check the clock on his desk, his bedroom door swung open, and Seth and Ryder strode inside.

"—Shannon won't mind," Seth was saying. Seth Tsang. An Asian last name, though you couldn't tell his race from looking at him. He'd streaked his black hair with red, and had blue eyes and pale skin.

Ryder Jones, who was behind him, arched a brow. He, too, had dark hair, but his eyes were brown. "You sure? You know how possessive that dude is with his stuff."

Aden grabbed the sheets and jerked them over his sweat-soaked lower body. "Hey, guys. Knock much?"

They ignored him.

"So what're you looking for?" he grumbled.

Again they ignored him. In fact, they didn't even glance in his direction.

"Just check the desk," Seth told Ryder, and the boy shuffled forward to obey.

Aden frowned. Once, these two had hated him. Once, but no longer. They'd reached a truce after their Treat-Everyone-Like-Crap idol, Ozzie, had been kicked off the ranch—and, as of this weekend, sucked dry by vampires. Not that they knew that part. They were as clueless about the "other" world as he had once been.

So why the silent treatment now?

"Where is it?" Seth muttered, crouching in the closet and rummaging through the clothes on the floor, wrist turning and revealing the snake tattooed there.

"Where's what?" Aden repeated, sitting up.

Yet again, they ignored him.

Shirts and jeans were tossed over Seth's shoulder, followed by shoes. At the desk, papers crunched under Ryder's hands. Several minutes passed. Aden kept up a steady chatter—"this joke isn't funny, try something original, will you just talk to me already?"—to no avail. He finally stood, sheet falling away, forgotten, and stalked to the desk.

With every intention of beating some sense into Ryder, he reached out. Except his hand wisped through the boy's body.

No way. No damn way.

Aden's heart pounded against his ribs as he tried again, shaking this time. Again, his flesh wisped through Ryder's and he could only stand there, wide-eyed and reeling. How was that possible? How *the hell* was that possible? He'd burned to death, yes, but in someone else's body. He'd thought... He'd assumed... Was *he* dead, too? Truly, no-coming-back dead?

No. No way. But... Blood freezing in his veins, he stalked to Seth.

"Found it," Seth said, standing. He held a book triumphantly in the air. A book about vampires. Any other time, Aden would have floundered over Shannon's chosen reading material. "Shannon's weird, dude. He's always reading this crap. Saves us a trip to the library, but, frickin' *please*. I've never written a report about wackos with fangs before and I don't want to start now."

"Mr. Thomas is the weird one, my man. We're supposed to write about how evil the bloodsuckers are, like they're real or something. I can't take that crank seriously, you know. I'll probably fail, but ask me if I care."

His shaking intensifying, Aden tried to wrap his fingers around Seth's wrist. Nothing. No solid contact. Bile burned a path up his throat. His arm thudded heavily to his side, and he stumbled backward, black winking over his eyes, dizziness rushing through his head.

The answer to his question? Dead. He was really dead. That was the only answer that made sense.

The boys raced from the room, mumbling about stupid new tutors and dumb homework assignments. Aden just stood there. Doomed to live the rest of eternity as a ghost?

God, was this how the souls felt? Trapped, out of control, lost?

"Guys," he whispered, not knowing how to begin. If he was a ghost, he couldn't help them figure out who they'd been in their other life. And if he couldn't help them figure out who they'd been, they could never be free of him. If that's what they still wanted. "I think—I— This is—"

"Hello, Aden."

The male voice came from behind him, and he spun. There, in the doorway, was the D and M's brand-new tutor. Not for him or Shannon since they attended Crossroads High, but for all the others. Mr. Thomas had shown up the day of the Vampire Ball, and Dan had hired him on sight. Which was completely unlike Aden's guardian. No background check, no intensive interview, just, "You're perfect!"

Even weirder, the boys acted like they'd known him

forever, already comfortable complaining about him. Aden hadn't met the man officially, but Victoria had secretly pointed him out. Mr. Thomas, as it turned out, was not a let's-all-learn-and-grow kind of tutor. He was a fairy and Victoria's enemy, here to find out who was helping her.

The man didn't look like Aden's idea of a fairy—small, female and winged. Instead, he was tall, lean, his skin golden and even a bit glittery (okay, *that* was fairylike). And never had Aden seen a more perfect face. There wasn't a single flaw. Perfectly spaced blue eyes, a perfectly sloped nose, perfect lips neither too full nor too thin.

And it was embarrassing as hell that Aden had noticed. Anyone found out, and they'd take away his man card or something.

"You can see me?" He gulped. "Hear me?"

"Yes."

"Am I...dead?" Saying the word was more difficult than thinking it. And how could the fairy see and hear what Seth and Ryder hadn't been able to?

A chuckle rumbled from the fairy, almost like a thrum of a harp. "Hardly. You're...somewhere else."

He wished he could take comfort from that. "Some-where else?" When everything looked the same? "Okay. Where am I? How'd I get here?" He plowed his fingers through his hair. "What's going on?"

Aden, Elijah said, and there was a warning in his tone. *I have a bad feeling about this.*

Dread instantly filled him. Elijah's bad feelings were, well, *bad.*

"So many questions." The man *tsk*ed. He waved to the chair at the desk. "Sit, please, and I will endeavor to answer you. After you answer me, of course."

What should have been a simple request struck Aden as a threat. And with Elijah's wariness, he suspected a fight would soon break out. He did a weapons check. He had nothing on him, but there were knives hidden in his boots. Boots he wasn't wearing and might not be able to touch. Boots that were…tucked neatly beside the bed, he saw.

"Sit, Aden." Two words, both layered with authority.

This time Aden sat. Without going for those blades. He didn't want to play his (potential) ace unless absolutely necessary.

Blood will run before this meeting ends, Elijah said.

Ours? Caleb asked with annoyance and a hint of fear. *'Cause I like ours and don't want to give up a single drop.*

"My name is Mr. Thomas," the man said before Elijah could respond, walking forward and stopping only a few feet away from Aden's chair. He anchored his hands behind his back and braced his legs apart. A war stance.

Aden knew it well. He'd stood that way many times—just before launching himself at the person threatening him. *Concentrate.* The plain, ordinary name didn't fit the man's smooth features in any way, and had to be an alias. If it wasn't, Aden would plant a big, fat wet one right on his lips.

"You want answers," he said, wondering, *About what?* "Then you'll have to tell me what I want to know. First. How are we here but not here? How am I alive but invisible?"

There were several beats of heavy silence. At first he thought Thomas meant to strike him for using his own tactics against him. With every second that passed, fury grew in those blue eyes. Fury and indignation.

Finally, though, the fairy said, "Your people would call this place another dimension, though it is the true realm of the Fae." Despite his expression, his words were calmly stated.

Fae had to mean fairy. And another...dimension? Was that even possible? As soon as the question hit him, he wanted to roll his eyes at his own stupidity. After everything he'd seen and done recently, *anything* was possible. "So, just to clarify, I'm not dead?"

"This constant need for reassurance is tiresome, so listen carefully, because I will not repeat myself again. You are very much alive. *But* you are in another dimension, therefore humans cannot see or hear you."

If Thomas was to be believed, Aden wasn't a ghost. He could return to Victoria, to his friends. "And you brought me here?" A croak.

"Yes."

"Why?"

Another tension-laden pause stretched between them. Clearly, getting answers was going to be like pulling teeth.

"Because," Thomas finally said on a sigh, "I had met all the students—but you."

There at the end, the fury had returned to the man's eyes, this time blended with disgust.

Oh, yes. Blood will run, Elijah said on a trembling breath.

"From a knife?" *Please, please don't say from a knife.*

Don't know, was the reply. *Can only see the river of red.*

"What do you mean, from a knife?" Thomas demanded.

He must not know of Aden's reputation as the boy who always talked to "himself." "Sorry. I wasn't speaking to you."

"Then to whom were you speaking?"

A question he'd been asked a thousand times by a thousand different people.

Maybe we *should. Run, I mean,* Caleb said, all his bravado gone. *Before we bleed.*

I'm with Caleb. It's not like we know how to fight a fairy.

Caleb suddenly snickered, amusement momentarily obliterating distress. *Fight a fairy. Do you hear yourself, Jules?*

"Quiet, please," Aden snapped, and Thomas hissed in a breath.

"Do not speak to me like that, little boy."

Rather than explain, Aden rubbed his temple to ward off the coming ache. "There was no reason for you to meet me. You won't be tutoring me." He couldn't run, as Caleb had suggested. Where would he go? Plus, he wasn't anxious. Yet. He still had those blades. Maybe.

"No." Thomas started forward, one step, two, then paused, thoughtful. "But I will be killing you."

Okay. *Now* he was anxious. Aden leapt to his feet. If Thomas issued another threat or made another move toward him, he'd dive-bomb the boots. And if he couldn't clasp the blades inside them, he'd run like hell, despite his lack of direction.

"Do not even think of bolting, Haden Stone."

"No one calls me that." Not since he'd inadvertently butchered his own name as a kid and called himself Aden, and everyone else had followed suit. "I killed the last guy who did. True story."

Far from intimidated, Thomas barked, "Sit. I answered your questions. You will now answer mine."

Uh, that would be a big, fat no. He wasn't waiting

around for the second death threat, he decided. The fairy's anger level had just jacked up a notch. "Sure thing." Aden faked left, Thomas following him, and then spun right, ducking around the tutor and swiping at the boots. His hand ghosted through the leather.

He cursed under his breath as he sprinted for the door, not allowing himself to wallow in disappointment or fear. Only, some kind of invisible wall blocked him. He slammed into it hard and fast, the shock of impact reverberating through him and tossing him backward. Thomas was in front of him a second later, pushing him the rest of the way down and stomping one of his boots on Aden's neck.

Instinctively, Aden wrapped his hands around the man's ankle and shoved. The foot remained planted.

Bright blue eyes peered down at him, and if they'd been guns, Aden would have been blown to bits. "Several weeks ago, an electric shock split through my world, creating a doorway into yours. A doorway we cannot close. The source of that shock has been traced to this ranch. And now to you. I feel the energy wafting from you even now, tugging at me, drawing me. Even increasing my power." The last was said in a drugged whisper. A *needy* whisper.

Increasing his power? Then why would he want to kill Aden?

Aden tried to form a reply, but the only sound that left

him was a gasp for air. He continued to struggle, clawing at the man's leg, shoving. *Breathe, need to breathe...*

He couldn't die here. In this...dimension? He just couldn't. No one would know what had happened to him. Not really. They'd just assume Crazy Aden had relapsed and split.

Suffocation doesn't cause bloodshed, Elijah said. *Stay calm. This isn't the way you're going to pass on. You know that.*

Kick his ass! Caleb shouted.

Kick it good, Julian agreed.

They needed Eve, their voice of reason. But some of what Elijah had said did penetrate his fog of panic. Suffocation wasn't the predicted end for him. Thomas was simply trying to scare him.

"We had hoped to keep you alive, to use you to finally close that doorway," Thomas continued. "And yet, what do I find when I walk into your room to introduce myself? The stink of vampire. Our greatest enemy, the race that once tried to slaughter us."

"I'm sure...they had...good reason."

A muscle ticked in the fairy's jaw. "Tell me, Haden Stone. Are you aiding them? Planning to lead them into this dimension to attack us?"

And just how was Aden supposed to lead the vampires here when he had no idea how he'd gotten here in the first place? "Can't...speak...anymore."

The pressure eased on his neck. "There's no reason

for you to answer my questions. I know the truth. You *are* aiding them, and that is why you must die."

Aden kept his hands on Thomas's ankle, taking a moment to catch his breath and making a production out of gasping as he stealthily searched the room for some sort of weapon he could actually use.

All he discovered was his own determination. Over the years, he'd fought too many corpses to count, their poison working through his body, weakening him, sickening him. Yet still he'd won. Every time. He would *not* let a fairy defeat him.

Use your hands, Elijah prompted. *Unbalance him.*

Aden curled his fingers under Thomas's boot and jerked with every ounce of strength he possessed, upsetting the big guy's center of gravity and finally sending him tumbling down. Aden was standing a moment later, assuming the same this-is-war pose the fairy had adopted earlier.

"That was not wise, boy."

Though he'd never seen Thomas move from the floor, the voice came from behind him. *Directly* behind him. Warm breath trekked over the back of his neck, making him cringe. Slowly Aden turned, knowing a sudden movement would cause the fairy to strike. They faced off. Aden was tall for his age, just over six feet, yet Thomas towered over him.

"I do not like to see humans suffer, and would have ended you painlessly. But…" An eerie smile lifted the man's lips. "I told you not to fight me. You disobeyed. Now I will show no mercy."

Blood, Elijah gasped.

This was it, then. The big one.

"Bring it," Aden said.

Suddenly the room's only window shattered and a giant black blur flew inside. That blur—Riley in wolf form, Aden realized—landed, green eyes glowing, lips pulled back and sharp white teeth bared. A furious growl echoed from the walls.

Get back, Aden.

A command from Riley, whispered straight into his mind, blending with the others, yet still Aden heard it. "You can see me?" he asked, even knowing the wolf was too distracted to reply. If so, could Riley see Thomas? Could Thomas see Riley?

"Mistake, wolf," Thomas said, turning to face Riley. There was enough menace in his expression to kill.

Apparently the answer to both of Aden's questions was the same. *Hells yes.*

Without any more warning, the two leapt at each other, meeting in the middle of the room in a tangle of claws, biting teeth, odd bright lights and shimmering blades that appeared out of nowhere.

No question about *this.* As Elijah had said, blood would flow.

This match would be to the death.

✝HREE

Yep. True to Elijah's prediction, true to Aden's suspicions, blood ran.

Riley chomped at Thomas's neck, and his sharp claws swiped at the man's chest. The scent of burning cotton and flesh filled the air, smoke rising from Thomas's shirt. Screams followed as a shaking Thomas grabbed thick hunks of the wolf's fur and tossed him hard and fast. The animal flew into Aden, who in turn flew into the wall.

Plaster cracked and paint chips sprayed. Air was knocked from Aden's suddenly deflated lungs.

Riley was up an instant later, again leaping for the fairy; the two twisted together as they fell. When the wolf's nails next slashed, the scent of burning flesh intensified and blood sprayed. A few drops hit Aden in the face, and they were oddly chilled, like ice shards. When the fairy's blades moved at lightning speed, *Riley's* blood sprayed. Hot, like prickles of flame.

Help him, Julian cried.

This is why I'm a lover, not a fighter, Caleb, whose bravery had returned now that a wolf was taking the beating for them, said.

Breathing should have been impossible, but Aden managed to drag in a few mouthfuls of air as he lumbered to his feet. Dizziness hammered at him, and he swayed. "Elijah?"

Of course, the psychic knew what he was silently asking. *How* could he help? He had no weapons, and couldn't leave the room to get to any.

I don't know, Elijah said, agonized.

"Will Riley win, then?" He spoke quietly, not wanting to distract the wolf and *cause* his defeat.

I don't know, the psychic repeated in that same agonized tone. *I see the blood, washing through this home, bathing everything and everyone.*

So much? And from this fight? Or something worse?

Over and over Thomas tossed Riley aside, and over and over Riley returned, a catapult of wrath and teeth. For some reason, he'd stopped using his claws. Furniture was smashed to pieces and more walls were ruined, *including* the invisible one, allowing the combatants out of the room and into the hallway. The fight then moved to another bedroom, the door smashed into puzzle pieces that would never fit back together. Aden followed. Somewhere along the way, Thomas lost his grip on his knives and dropped them. Aden tried to pick them up and insert himself into the action—multiple times—but the blades he couldn't touch eventually vanished and the fairy and the wolf moved so quickly, they would appear in another location before he even realized he'd missed.

And why were they able to destroy the walls, doors and furniture, but nothing else?

The boys who lived at the D and M Ranch—Seth, Ryder, RJ, Terry and Brian—were in the entrance hall, each with a book in hand. Some were reading, some were pretending to read. None noticed the vicious fight unfolding around them.

Not even when their chairs were seemingly over-turned and shattered. They just sat there. On air. Riley and Thomas ghosted through them, imperceptible, un-felt, unheard. Blood splattered over the boys, too, but again, they didn't notice. Perhaps couldn't even see it.

So freaking odd, all of it. Thomas had open wounds that were bleeding profusely, and yet he seemed stronger than ever. Riley, on the other hand, seemed weaker, his jumps slowing down, his snarls becoming slurred, and yet his wounds had already closed, healed.

What was weakening him?

Aden noticed that Thomas only punched to unhinge

Riley's jaw from whatever body part the wolf had decide to munch on. Then Thomas would tilt his head back and practically offer his neck to the wolf, rather than allow the animal to bite down on his hands. Why?

And rather than immediately batting Riley away, Thomas would flatten his palms on the beast for several seconds, allowing the wolf to do whatever he wished. That was stupid. That was—necessary?

Were Thomas's hands somehow able to weaken Riley? That would explain Thomas's determination to keep his hands free. That would also explain his lack of concern over his own injuries. What did a few cuts matter when your opponent would soon be too feeble to fight you off?

"What can I...do?" This time Aden's whispered question trailed off. He knew. The answer had already slapped him, cold, hard. Stinging.

You know, Elijah said, and if he'd sounded agonized before, he sounded pulverized now. Clearly, he had realized the answer, too.

What? Julian asked. *What are we going to do?*

Aden gulped. "Caleb. You're up."

I'm u...p—oh, hell, no!

He hadn't needed to explain. By requesting Caleb's aid, they all knew what he now planned. They were going to possess Thomas's body.

No. No, there has to be another way. If he'd had a body

of his own, Julian would have been shaking his head and backing away.

"Sorry, guys." This had to be done. For Riley. Hell, for himself.

The pain, Julian moaned. *We've endured enough. This will wipe us out.*

This is the only way, Elijah said. *The fairy has to perish.*

"We've been through worse." Like burning alive. Nothing could be worse than that, he was sure. "And if I'm going to kiss Victoria again, I've got to save her bodyguard."

Hate to be the harbinger of bad news, but Aden's right, Caleb said, suddenly leaping on board the Plan Save The Day bandwagon. He'd do anything for another kiss. *We'll survive this. Even if Thomas doesn't. That's all that matters.*

Aden focused on the two opponents. Riley lay on the floor, several feet away from Thomas, but inching forward as best he could, still determined to win. Having just been tossed like a rag doll, Thomas brushed big chunks of plaster from his chest and stood. His shirt was in shreds, his skin flayed, yet that skin was finally weaving back together, as if he'd somehow absorbed the wolf's ability to heal.

Thomas smiled smugly as he approached the wolf and crouched down. "Tell your princess not to send a boy to do a man's work. Oh, wait. As you won't be leaving this room, you won't be telling her anything."

Riley's eyes were glittering green fire and hate-filled.

The fairy sighed. "I admire your courage, wolf. Therefore, you will not die dishonorably. Know that I am not a mere Fae servant, but a prince. Indestructible. The moment you entered my realm, you were destined to die. But there is no shame in your death. You should see this as the favor it is."

A favor? Hardly.

Echoing Aden's sentiments, Riley growled.

Frowning, Thomas reached out. "Again, I admire your courage. A shame you serve the vampires. Would you, perchance, be interested in switching allegiances?"

Another growl. A clear no.

"Well, then, I am sorry for this, but it must be done. I'll be swift, wolf."

What are you waiting for? Whether the question came from himself or the souls, Aden didn't know. Riley was his friend, for the most part, and he couldn't allow a friend to be hurt. No matter the pain involved.

Just before fairy palm met wolf fur, Aden—who had obviously been forgotten—sprinted forward. He didn't stop when he reached the fairy. He stopped only when he was *inside* the fairy.

One touch of skin against skin, and thanks to Caleb,

he could meld his body with someone else's. Morphing from solid mass to insubstantial mist was painful, as Julian had said, not to mention maddening, terrible and shocking. But he did it. He bonded to Thomas, a shout of agony ripping from his throat.

The voice he heard, however, was not his own. This one was deeper, huskier. Thomas's.

Panting, sheened by a cold sweat, Aden fell to his knees. There were sharp lances working through him, and he wanted to pound at his chest, tear at his skin, anything to stop them. Each of his bones was like a blade against his muscles, cutting. Worse, this pain was only the beginning.

Thomas screamed inside his head. *What are you doing? How did you do that? Release me!*

Usually Aden could block the person's thoughts. Could take them over so completely, they never knew what had happened. But creatures of myth and legend, he was coming to learn, were quite different from humans. They knew. And they hated.

"Riley," he said in that deep voice. "This is Aden. I'm inside the fairy. I have control of his body."

Green eyes pierced him, searching for signs of truth.

Aden could feel the power surging through him. So much power. *Riley's* power, too, as if the fairy had not only weakened the wolf, but had drawn his energy inside his own body. Animalistic, wild pulses warmed the chill in his blood. They sang in his mind, more beautiful than a chorus of angels, drugging him.

This could be addicting. Once more, he couldn't tell who spoke, him or the souls. Maybe all of them at once. Part of him wanted to remain inside the fairy's body forever, losing himself in that warmth and power, forgetting what had to be done.

Act quickly, Elijah demanded suddenly. *Or you will never leave him.*

He would leave. In just a little while. What would a few more minutes hurt? That music…so peaceful…

The sooner you leave, the sooner we'll be able to see Victoria, Caleb added.

Victoria. Yes. Being with her was even better than this, he thought, at last focusing on the task at hand. "Riley. Tell me what you need me to do so that you can defeat Thomas."

The wolf studied him, then nodded as if he were satisfied Aden had truly possessed the body.

"Tell me, and I'll do it. Whatever it is."

A moment passed. The wolf frowned, snarled. Waited. Whatever reaction he wanted from Aden, he didn't get. In the end, he hobbled to his feet and tripped his way to the nearest closet, disappearing inside.

"Riley," Aden called. He knew the wolf wouldn't abandon him here, but he had no idea what was going on.

Was Aden supposed to follow him?

There was a bright light, several grunts, then the rustle of clothing. Just as Aden was stepping forward, Riley emerged in a pair of jeans. No T-shirt, no shoes, just those ill-fitting jeans that couldn't be snapped.

How had he touched the cloth? Wouldn't his hand have ghosted through the material like Aden's had?

Riley's normally suntanned skin was now pale, the blue veins underneath visible. His cheeks were hollowed out and his eyes slightly sunken and bruised. There were a few cuts on his chest, as if his ability to heal in a snap had abandoned him.

"Fairies can't hear werewolf thoughts." Even his voice was fragile. "That must mean you can't either while you're in there, because I was telling you what to do but you gave no reaction."

So. He'd expected a reaction. Because bad news had been delivered? "Tell me again."

Do not aid him, Thomas roared inside his head. *He is the enemy. His masters will destroy your world and all the humans who populate it. Do you hear me? Kill him!*

Aden tuned him out as best he could.

"I need to plunge a blade through his heart," Riley announced.

No! The protest came from Thomas and Aden simultaneously.

Fabulous. From Caleb.

Dear God. From Julian.

Blood. From Elijah.

"Is there another way?" Aden managed to ask past the lump in his throat. "A way to leave him here, prevent him from causing any more harm?"

"No. There's no other way. He's a fairy. Like all his kind, he has the ability to borrow strength from immortals, temporarily possessing *their* abilities. More than that, he's a prince. If he lives, he'll raise his army and come after us."

"I don't like the thought of killing him." Even though Elijah, too, had said it was the only way. "He protects humans." Victoria had told him. Still. Had he not known, he would have realized the truth the moment he'd stepped inside the fairy's body. The knowledge was there, swimming through his mind with the same potency as the warmth. Humans were like children. Irresponsible, feral children, but loved by the Fae nonetheless.

"He'll kill you if given another chance," Riley said.

"I know." That knowledge was there, too. "But I don't care." He could take care of himself. He hoped.

"He'll kill Victoria," Riley added coolly.

Low blow. The wolf knew Aden would do *anything* to protect her. His hands clenched, and his eyes closed. His heart pounded in a staccato rhythm as he condemned another creature to death. "All right. God. Let's do it."

"Are you sure?"

Sure he wanted to take a knife through the heart? No. "Yes." He wondered if he would die with the fairy the same way he'd died with Dmitri. If so, would he come back to life?

Yes, you will die, but yes, you will come back, Elijah said, calming him. *Still. You'll wish you'd stayed dead. You'll feel the stabbing as if it was your own.*

Okay. Bye-bye calm. Here was the pain he'd feared before possessing the prince. He'd known Thomas would have to be injured and subdued in some violent way. Stabbing, though…

For Victoria.

"All right, then," Riley said, resolved.

Aden opened his eyes and nodded. "I'm ready."

Riley returned the nod, and unsheathed a blade from his back pocket. A blade that belonged to Aden.

Do not do this! Thomas commanded.

"You didn't arrive with that," Aden said to distract himself from the sharp, deadly weapon soon to be embedded in his chest.

"While I was in the closet, I slipped back into the human dimension and gathered what I needed." Riley shrugged those wide shoulders. "Then I slipped back."

"That easily?"

"That easily." All of Riley's nonchalance and confidence faded as he lumbered forward, paused and frowned. "You won't be harmed when I do this?"

"No. I've been assured I'll live." *For the most part.*

"My king—"

"Don't call me that," he snapped, and Thomas gasped in shock.

King?

Again, Aden ignored him.

"If there were any other way..." Riley continued.

"I know." He was surprised by how sad he suddenly was that hatred and intolerance had brought them to this point.

For several minutes, neither of them moved or spoke.

"Maybe you should lie down for this," Riley said, shaky now.

"All right." Aden studied his surroundings. The fight had ended inside RJ's bedroom. The bunk bed had been toppled, but one of the mattresses was on the ground. Aden forced the prince's body to stride over to it and lie down. By the time he stilled, he was shaking worse than Riley.

What was a stabbing compared to being burned alive? He could do this.

You'll regret this, the prince snarled.

"If you would just promise not to harm Victoria."

Riley had already closed the distance between them and now blinked at him, clearly offended. "I would *never* harm her."

"Not you. The prince."

That, I can never promise. Your Victoria—oh, yes, I know her very well—she is a spawn of Vlad, and her sister Lauren was to be my brother's bride. A peace offering, a uniting of the races. Only, Lauren killed him before the ceremony and admitted she had never meant to wed him. Spat with enough acid to burn. *Should I live, Victoria will die. A sibling for a sibling. My vengeance will not be denied.* At least the fairy hadn't lied. "Even at the cost of your own life?" Aden demanded, and this time Riley ignored him, knowing he conversed with the prince.

Hear me well. I've already killed three members of her family. The rest will follow.

"Three?" he gritted out. "That's not a sibling for a sibling, is it? Who did you kill?"

Cousins. Not nearly enough of a sting. I want them all. The entire royal family.

"Then you are a murderer and you have brought this on yourself."

I am a murderer? What are you?

Hesitant, Riley raised the knife. "Ready?"

"I—"

She is vampire, Thomas said, cutting him off. *You are*

a human. All you'll ever be to her is a blood-slave, addicted to her bite. And still you kill for her?

Flickers of fury ignited in his chest. He was more than Victoria's blood-slave. He wouldn't believe otherwise. "Yes. For her, I'll do *anything*."

For my brother, I will do anything. You might kill me, but you'll never break me. And Haden? Somehow I'll make you pay for this, even from the grave.

"Ready?" Riley repeated then. Determination radiated from him, but that determination was waning. "I want to get this done before I change my mind."

Deep breath in, hold, hold, slowly release. Aden was tense, which would cause more pain, but that wasn't going to change the final outcome.

"Ready?" Riley repeated a third time. Sweat dripped from his hand.

"Ready." He could do this. He would not chicken out. "Do it. Do it now!"

"I'm sorry." The blade fell, a blur. Plunged deep. Cutting through bone, muscle and into the vital organ. Burning, stinging…destroying. Aden screamed, loud and long, and his voice soon broke from the strain.

The heart, though, continued to beat. At first. Each pump slid the knife deeper, cut worse, burned more. Blood flowed from the wound, soaking his chest, the mattress. Droplets even bubbled up into his throat, choking him, before rising into his mouth and spilling out, warming his cheeks.

Rivers, Elijah said, as if in a trance. *Flow.*

Caleb, Julian and Thomas were howling. They weren't feeling Aden's agony, he knew from experience, and he was glad to spare them that. But they *were* feeling the residual effects of his mental anguish.

Calm down, he told himself. For them.

But the pain never eased. Not when it felt as if every drop of life had poured from him. Not when his limbs chilled, so heavy he could no longer lift them. Aden could have abandoned the body at any time, but he wanted to spare Thomas every bit of pain he could. Besides, he had to know. For his peace of mind, he had to know when it was over. He had to know what he would one day have to bear himself.

A few moments later, Aden died for the second time that day.

FOUR

A few minutes earlier
Crossroads High

MARY ANN PLOPPED HER TRAY on the lunch table and settled across from the too-beautiful Victoria, who had just sat down herself. Shannon, Aden's friend from the D and M, was beside her, a gorgeous black boy with green eyes that reminded her of Riley's. Once, she'd even thought he was the wolf dogging her every step.

Beside Mary Ann was Penny Parks, her stunning best friend and next-door neighbor whose platinum hair, blue eyes that were prettier than sapphires and pale, freckled skin had fueled the wet dreams of many Crossroads High students.

A (regular) girl could get a complex, surrounded by all that perfection.

Victoria focused her own baby blues on Shannon. "Question. Did you see Aden this morning?"

Shannon had just taken a big bite of his pizza. He chewed as he shook his head, then swallowed. "He was gone before I woke up."

"But you saw him last night?" Mary Ann asked.

Another nod.

So where was he? What was he doing?

She sighed.

"So. What's your deal?" Penny suddenly asked Victoria, changing the subject. "You don't even pretend to eat. Or drink, for that matter. Are you anorexic? Is that how you stay so skinny?"

"Penny," Mary Ann said, slack-jawed. Loosely translated: *Rude!*

"What?" her friend asked, all innocence. "I'm curious. Ask any teacher here. Curiosity is for the learning-inclined."

Victoria glanced between them. "American food is… unappetizing." Another translation: *Because it wasn't blood.* "I prefer to eat at home."

"I dig." Penny nodded, clearly buying the misdirection. "Where're you from, anyway?"

"Romania."

"Spooky. Your accent isn't thick, though. Lots of traveling? One parent from someplace else?"

Victoria nodded, noncommittal.

Blithely Penny continued. "So why'd you move to

Oklahoma, of all places? Isn't that, like, hickville to someone like you?"

"Enough with the inquisition," Mary Ann said on a sigh. Victoria had only attended the school for a few weeks, but the vampire had held herself aloof from everyone except Aden, Mary Ann and Riley all that time because she hadn't known how long she would be here or what her father, Vlad, would order her to do. And really, she considered humans a food source, not a playground of friendliness. Though Mary Ann liked to think the vampire was softening because of Aden.

Aden. *Where are you?* Had Riley found him already?

Riley. *Hurry up!* Every minute he was away, her worry for him increased. And for Aden, of course. With that dumb death curse hanging over their heads…oh, God. She hadn't needed the reminder on top of everything else. *Couldn't…breathe…*

She'd been on edge all day. She'd been distracted, too, and had no idea what her first three classes had even covered.

Victoria's gaze met hers, and they shared a moment of silent communication.

Entertain me, Mary Ann mouthed.

I can't. You entertain me, Victoria mouthed back.

This sucks.

I know. And not the good kind.

A joke. The first she'd ever heard Victoria tell, though she doubted Victoria realized the humor of her statement. Mary Ann's lips twitched into a grin. Entertainment achieved. Intended or not.

"When will this day end?" an exasperated Victoria asked everyone at the table.

"Not soon enough," Penny muttered.

Why was she muttering now? She'd seemed so carefree only a minute ago.

"I—I—like it here," Shannon said, stuttering slightly. He'd admitted to being teased about that stutter his entire life, but it was getting less pronounced every day. "You know how r-rare it is to meet someone who accepts you for who you are?"

Now she did. Now that she knew she merely calmed people with otherworldly powers, and they weren't actually charmed by her. But whatever. Riley liked her for herself. Oh, the things he'd said to her this morning. *Pretty. Brave. Caring.* She'd be getting high off those compliments for weeks.

She moved her gaze through the room. Kids shuffled all around them, either running to get in a line—tacos and pizza slices were on today's menu—or trying to find their friends in the vast bench-filled cavern that was the cafeteria. Plain white walls circled them, livened up (or marred, depending on your perspective) by the occasional poster proclaiming school spirit. The noise level was high today and suddenly scraped at Mary Ann's nerves.

"Hey, Penny. Wanna come to my house later?" a jock asked as he strutted past their table. The boys around him chuckled. "We can study anatomy."

Penny's cheeks reddened.

"Jackass," Mary Ann shouted, her hands fisting. Some of the conversations around her tapered to quiet, and many sets of eyes pinned her in place. Cussing was unlike her, but the word had just sprung from her, unstoppable.

Penny was pregnant. With Mary Ann's ex-boyfriend's baby. That had been hard to get over, since the two had cheated on her. And really, she was still dealing with lingering feelings of hurt and distrust, but she loved Penny and was working on forgiveness. Still. That didn't make her friend a slut, nor did it mean these boys had a right to tease her.

The jocks stopped, facing Mary Ann as one. A frowning Shane Weston stepped to the front, big and strong and clearly angry. "You better shut your mouth, Gray. Tucker isn't here to protect you anymore."

Mary Ann opened her mouth to reply, but no words emerged. *Coward! Say something. Anything.* She remained still, silent. She'd never been any good at confrontation, and now, when she needed the courage Riley had praised, she found none. Shame filled her.

"That's what I thought," Shane said with a laugh.

"G-get the h-hell out of here," Shannon suddenly growled.

"What? Are we making you angry, and we won't like you when you're angry? Whatever, Stutter." Laughing again, Shane and his gang wandered off.

"Shall I kill him for you?" Victoria asked without any inflection in her tone.

"Yes," Penny snapped as Mary Ann rushed out, "No." Penny had no idea that Victoria really would do it. Her fangs were hidden right now, but she could drain Shane Weston dry in seconds.

Victoria shrugged. "If you change your mind…"

"We need to change Mary Ann's mind. I'm all for jockicide." Penny pushed to her feet as if she hadn't a care, but hurt lingered in her eyes. "Anyway, I've got a paper due next hour, and I haven't even started it."

"N-need help?" Shannon asked, standing before she could answer.

He meant to protect her, Mary Ann realized, in case anyone else insulted her. That brought tears to her eyes, because dang it, she missed her own protector.

Penny blinked in surprise, but strode around the table and linked their arms. "Sure. You any good with Sylvia Plath?"

"No."

"Excellent. You can help me make everything up."

They laughed as they walked off, Penny throwing a smile and finger-wave over her shoulder at Mary Ann.

Alone at last.

Mary Ann propped her elbows on the table and leaned toward Victoria. "We've got to work on your…humanness." Was that even a word?

The vampire furrowed her brow. "What do you mean?"

"You can't just go around offering to kill people. That'll get you into all kinds of trouble."

She raised her chin, and Mary Ann caught a glimpse of her stubborn core. "I welcome trouble."

"Fine. But Aden doesn't," Mary Ann reminded her.

Gradually, Victoria's chin fell. "You're right." She pushed out another sigh. "Sometimes I wonder if I'm the right girl for him. If perhaps…" she twirled her fingertip over the tabletop, tracing some sort of design "you wouldn't be better suited for him."

"Are you kidding?" One, Victoria might have phrased the words like a suggestion, but there had been fury in her tone. And two, Mary Ann adored Aden, but she didn't crave him the way she craved Riley. "That boy worships you."

Some of the tension left Victoria's shoulders. "Yes, but sometimes, when we're all together, you'll laugh and he'll watch you, and there will be such…*longing* on his face. When that happens, I want to rip out your trachea. Sorry, but it's true."

Okay. She'd been close to dying *before* the curse, and had had no idea. Perfect. "I can tell you for sure that he doesn't like me as a girlfriend. Aden and I...we will only ever be friends. Our different—" She looked around, making sure no one was listening. Everyone seemed to be going about their day, eating and talking, unconcerned about her and her conversation. "Our different abilities make us want to run from each other most of the time. It's a miracle we're even friends. Besides, can you imagine wanting to kiss the guy who housed your mom?"

Victoria shook her head, but still didn't appear completely convinced.

"Maybe that longing shows up because he wants to make *you* laugh like that. Let's face it, I've known you for weeks and I've seen you smile once. Maybe. You might have been grimacing."

Now Victoria blinked over at her. "Are you saying I'm...depressing?"

"Will you want to rip out my trachea if I am?"

Crystalline eyes narrowed. "Maybe, but I won't allow myself the luxury."

"Thank you. Then, yes. I am. Just...lighten up, maybe. Tell a joke every now and then. Aden's had a lot of seriousness in his life, you know? A lot of bad. Now he needs good."

What? You're a doctor now? Well, she *had* always wanted to help people.

"I...I— Well, I hate that the boys think it's okay to leave us behind." Clearly, the subject of humor was closed. "They treat us like we're damsels in distress." Like Mary Ann, Victoria propped her elbows on the table. She rested her chin in her upraised hand.

Mary Ann didn't know if the girl would take her advice or not. Time would tell. "I agree," she replied, allowing the change of topic without comment. "And it's irritating." *But you* are *a damsel in distress, and that's the real reason you find it irritating.* Proof: she hadn't punched Shane in the nose like he'd deserved.

Disgusted with herself, Mary Ann pushed her tray aside, even the scent of the pepperoni pizza suddenly hurting her stomach. She should be starving by now, she mused. First she'd skipped breakfast, and now lunch. But she'd been unable to think about taking a bite without wanting to barf.

"I mean, I understand that I can do a lot of good here," Victoria continued, unaware of her inner turmoil. "I can protect you, of course. And I've convinced all of Aden's teachers that he's here today so that he won't get into trouble and be kicked out of the ranch."

Victoria could make anyone do or believe anything

she wished with only her voice. Mary Ann secretly called the ability "Voice Voodoo" and nearly peed her pants in fear every time she thought about it. Stripping in public just because a vampire told her to? Yeah, it could happen. That, and a lot worse. Thank God they were on the same side.

The litany of her skills persisted. "I'm also a trained fighter. More than that, I can't be hurt. I'm an indestructible vampire, for God's sake."

Mary Ann didn't bother to point out that her father—an indestructible vampire—had just been killed. Or that her former fiancé—an indestructible vampire—had soon followed Vlad the Impaler to the grave.

"First, you don't need to protect me. I'm not helpless," Mary Ann said, her irritation clear. *Didn't you just admit to yourself that you are, in fact, a damsel in distress? And isn't a damsel in distress, what? Helpless.* "There's no need for you to play babysitter."

Victoria uttered a dejected sigh. "I didn't mean to offend you. I'm new to interacting with humans. You have always been my food source, nothing more. Or rather, my delicate, easily destroyed food source." Her lips twitched there at the end.

A grin? Now?

Victoria was attempting to joke with her, just as Mary Ann had instructed, but Mary Ann's shoulders slumped in nervousness rather than amusement. Here was yet another reminder of the death and destruction that could be waiting around the corner. A vampire could drain a human in seconds. A werewolf could rip human skin into shreds. But...

Maybe there was a way to fight them.

The stray thought had her tilting her head, considering her options. She didn't want to fight Victoria or Riley, of course, but she did need to learn how to defend herself. Then maybe they'd see her as more a help than a hindrance.

"What if—" she began at the exact same time as Victoria said, "Riley told us—"

Mary Ann laughed. "You first."

"I was saying that Riley told us to stay here, but that doesn't mean we have to obey him. I mean, he and Aden might need us. And if we save them, they'll have to thank us for coming to their rescue."

Slowly Mary Ann smiled. "True. Where would we go, though? How would we find them?"

"I would—" Victoria stiffened, frowned, then blinked. "Did you hear that?"

Listening, Mary Ann glanced around the cafeteria. Same kids, same inane chatter. "Hear what?"

"That scream." The vampire massaged her throat with one of her hands. "So much pain...I've never heard anything like it." She jumped up, her chair skidding backward. "And I think...I think it belonged to Aden."

Mary Ann was on her feet in the next instant, as well, heart hammering, blood chilling. Something hot and hard banded around her wrist, and then a strong breeze was ruffling her hair. Her feet lost their solid foundation, and suddenly she was floating, flying. She yelped in shock.

The kids, the tables, even the walls around her vanished. In a snap, thick tree trunks and orange-gold leaves took their place. Sunlight gleamed from the gray sky, murky, yet still too bright for her startled eyes.

An unruffled Victoria stood beside her.

"What just happened?" Mary Ann rasped. And why did she feel like she was going to fall over and vomit? Black spots replaced the light as her stomach churned mercilessly.

"I teleported us to the forest. I can only travel short distances, so we'll need to do this several more times before we can reach the ranch."

Wait. They'd just *teleported?* Out of school? "Did anyone...see us?" God. Now she couldn't breathe, the air freezing in her nose before reaching her lungs.

"I'm not sure. We'll find out tomorrow."

Great, she thought, swaying with her sudden lightheadedness. "A little...warning next time. Okay?" She hunched over, sweat pouring from her, even though that winter storm was raging inside her veins.

"Mary Ann?"

"Yes?"

"Here's your warning."

Once again a hot brand circled her wrist. Once again the ground disappeared from beneath her. Once again she was floating, flying, wind ripping through her, splitting her into thousands of pieces, then fitting her back together again in an instant.

This time when she focused, she realized they were in a neighborhood. Small, kind of rundown houses surrounded her. Those pesky blackbirds were squawking and flying in every direction, as if something had startled them. Next to her was a street—with a car driving past. The driver rubbernecked, trying to look at them as long as possible. Had he seen them appear out of nowhere?

He'll think he made a mistake. Don't worry about that now. "Don't…just…rest…" *Words—form properly, damn it!*

Another cuss word. Excellent. At this rate, she'd soon sound like every other kid at school.

No time to mourn that development, however. The black spots were expanding in front of her eyes, thickening, some of the circles now touching. The snowstorm inside her raged out of control, becoming a blizzard, and she shivered. Ice. Her new most-hated thing.

"Just a little farther," Victoria said. There was no sympathy in her tone, only worry. "Okay? Yes?"

For Aden. For Riley. Mary Ann could do this. She straightened. Nodded.

Victoria wasted no time. Hot brand, ground gone. Mighty wind. Unwanted chill. Mary Ann in pieces— pieces that could be lost forever. What if she didn't fit back together the right way? What if she— God, she really was a liability. She really was the weak link of their circle. She couldn't even handle being teleported.

That will change. I'll learn to fight, no matter what's required of me, she told herself as she solidified in…she looked around, only fragments of her surroundings registering past the ever-growing black. A train track, too-tall grass that was yellow, brittle. A snake slithered and hissed over the rusted iron. Shouldn't it be hibernating?

"Mary Ann?"

She knew what Victoria was asking. Was she ready to go again? "Just…do it," she said. "Finish this."

Brand. Wind. Chill. Ground. Stop.

Brand. Wind. Chill. Ground. Stop.

"We're here."

Finally. Mary Ann's knees gave out and she collapsed, sucking in as many breaths as she could. Which wasn't many. Dizzy, so dizzy. Air too thick, still too cold. Only one thought made any sense at the moment: teleporting sucked.

"The ranch is just ahead. When you're able, stand and walk. Yes? I am going inside now."

Victoria didn't wait for her reply—not that she was in any shape to deliver one—but bolted away, a blur of motion. *Fight. Fight this!* If she didn't, and Riley was inside, he would come after her, wanting to help her. He would see her like this. He would view her as weaker than he already did.

A minute passed. Maybe an hour. But finally, Mary Ann clawed her way from the darkness, her head clearing enough that she was able to stand, the air thinning enough that she was able to breathe. Her knees knocked together, but she didn't let that stop her from tripping forward. She had yet to warm, so every step was like pushing her legs through sludge.

Finally, she reached the ranch's bunkhouse, where Aden stayed, a log cabin-type structure next to a bright red barn. She found his window, saw that the glass was pushed up, out of the way. Inside she climbed, just kind of throwing her body through. She plopped unceremoniously to the floor.

"Mary Ann!"

Riley's deep voice penetrated the lingering fog in her mind.

Relief and dread, that's what she experienced. If he said anything about her presence or current condition, she'd…what? Nothing, probably. *Coward.*

Not for much longer.

"I was just coming for you, baby. Are you okay?" His strong arms wound around her and gently tugged her to her feet.

"I'm fine. You can let go." *Don't let go.* "Where's Aden? *How's* Aden?" Her lashes lifted, and her gaze met Riley's. As always, her heart constricted. He was just so beautiful. So much a warrior. But right now, despite that, he looked like death walking. He was shirtless and covered in dried blood. "What's wrong with you?"

"Come. See for yourself."

FIVE

MARY ANN EXPECTED TRAGEDY. Death, even. She was braced for the emotional impact, whatever chose to flood her—grief, remorse, sorrow. A combination of all three. What she saw surprised her, and it was *happiness* and *relief* that flooded her.

Aden's room was neat. Clean. The papers on the desk were tidy, and the air was wonderfully sweet, smelling of roses and honeysuckle. Aden lay on the bed, buried under the covers. He was a little paler than normal, with dark circles under his closed eyes, his black hair—with its blond roots—in tangles and matted to his scalp. His body was shaking, but otherwise appeared healthy and whole. She flattened a hand over her thumping heart and grinned.

And yet, Victoria sat beside him, patting his hand, tears streaming down her face. Why the tears? He was alive.

"I don't understand what's going on," Mary Ann said, burrowing deeper into Riley's side.

"He reeks of Fae." Victoria shimmied under the covers and curled herself around Aden. "My poor baby," she cooed. "You're so cold. Like ice. Let me warm you."

Aden, asleep or not, must have recognized his girl-friend, because he turned toward her, slid his arms around her waist and held on tight. Gradually, his shivering ceased.

"What's wrong with smelling like the Fae?" Mary Ann asked. All she smelled was the roses and honey-suckle. And it was good. She inhaled deeply, savoring, wanting a bottle of the scent to take home and bathe in.

In fact, when she closed her eyes, she could imagine herself twirling in a meadow, thickets of roses stretching toward her, a rainbow of soft, fragrant petals. Warm air. Birds singing. Hazy blue sky, fluffy white clouds. The images calmed her, and her stomach settled completely for the first time that day.

"The stink lingers, and our people will never follow him like this. They will rebel. They will demand a new leader. But to gain one, they will have to kill him." Tears fell from Victoria's eyes again. "And he's supposed to appear before them. Tonight!"

The last was a screech.

"That's not the worst of it," Riley said gravely. "I haven't told you how he came to be in this condition."

Mary Ann's eyelids cracked open, the field and colors fading away. So. Weird. For a second, she would have sworn she'd truly been in that meadow.

Riley said something in a language Mary Ann didn't know, and Victoria paled. "Mr. Thomas to the humans," he finished in English.

"Who?" Mary Ann asked. "And what did you say? Before?"

"I spoke the name of the Fae prince who dragged Aden into Fairy Tale," Riley said. "The human tongue cannot pronounce fairy names, and so they use shortened versions while here. Anyway, he once swore a blood oath to destroy every member of Victoria's family for their part in his brother's death."

"Aden is now part of the royal family," Victoria gasped out.

"As you can see, he's fine, for the most part, but... there was a fight," Riley continued. "I was losing. Aden possessed his body, allowing me to kill the—to win."

Wait. Fairy...tale? "Fairy Tale is..."

"A dimension that coexists next to ours, as well as looking into ours. Meaning, while they're there, they can see us, yet we can't see them. Which is why they have all developed God complexes, and consider themselves masters and protectors of this world."

Another dimension? Seriously?

Why are you surprised? Mary Ann was coming to learn that *every* creature she'd once thought belonged solely to, well, fairy tales, actually existed. They coexisted secretly. Or not so secretly now.

Victoria looked up at Riley, expression as grave as his tone had been. "Where is the prince now?"

"Still in Fairy Tale. Aden can raise the dead, and I didn't want a fairy prince zombie on the loose, so I whisked Aden here as fast as I could. There's a lot of cleanup needed, though, and I have to do it before another fairy discovers the remains—" His gaze skittered to Mary Ann. "I mean, uh, never mind. I just need to take off for a few minutes."

She knew he feared her reaction to the violence of his nature, to the things he'd done—and would one day do. She also knew war would erupt if "the remains" were found. More than it already had.

So, there was no contest. Whatever he needed to do to survive, she wanted him to do. She released him. "Go on, then. We'll take care of Aden while you're gone."

He'd gone rigid, waiting for her response, and now relaxed. "Thank you."

After a swift, hard kiss, a whispered, "Be careful," Riley was striding into the closet, soon gone from view. There was a murmur of falling clothing, then…nothing. Frowning, Mary Ann walked over and peeked inside.

He was gone. Vanished. Reeling, she made her way to the only chair in the room and plopped down. Her feet sighed in pleasure, even as her mind continued to whirl.

Was Riley now in Fairy Tale? Was there a doorway in the closet? If so…talk about weird!

"He'll be okay, right?" she asked Victoria.

The vampire was focused completely on Aden, brushing her fingertips over his face and kissing the line of his jaw. The opal ring she always wore glinted in the light, as if rainbow shards were trapped inside. "Yes. He'll have to rip open a doorway, which is why he moved out of sight, and then he'll—"

The bedroom door suddenly swung open. A boy stepped inside, one Mary Ann had never met. He stopped when he spotted Victoria in bed with Aden and Mary Ann sitting at the desk. His eyes narrowed, his mind clearly assessing the situation. He possessed the same dangerous edge as Riley, as if he'd done things—difficult, dangerous things.

"First, how come Aden gets all the hot chicks?" he said, his voice rough. "And second, who are you and what the hell are you doing here?"

Uh-oh. Caught. Aden was supposed to be at school. If Dan, his warden, found out he was ditching, he could be kicked off the ranch. Second, no girls were allowed here. If Dan found out about her, Aden *would* be kicked off the ranch.

So, either way, he was screwed.

Victoria sat up, her gaze never leaving the newcomer. "You will leave this empty room and shut the door behind you. You saw no one." Power wafted from her voice, so much power Mary Ann had to rub her arms to remind herself that she was not on the receiving end of that command. "You will not return today."

"Empty. Leave. Will not return." The boy nodded, his eyes glazed. He turned and shut the door behind him.

With barely a pause, Victoria refocused on Aden, as did Mary Ann. He appeared more relaxed, his color higher, the bruises fading.

"He's healing," she said, her relief palpable.

"Yes," the vampire replied without looking at her. Despite the progress, the worry must not have left her.

She needed a distraction. "I'm a power neutralizer," Mary Ann said. "So how can you use your Voice Voo—uh, command while I'm here?"

"You do not stop Riley from shifting, do you?"

"No."

"Because the ability is natural, part of who he is. The same is true with me. Most of my powers are natural, what I was born to do. Like teleporting. You didn't stop me from doing that, either."

Too bad about the teleporting. And *most* of her powers?

As in *many*. How many weird things could she do? And also, what wasn't natural? Not that Mary Ann would ask. She and Victoria were friendly, for the most part, but the boys were the glue that held them together. Not affection. Not yet. Perhaps that would come in time.

"What a terrible week this has turned out to be," Victoria muttered. "My father killed, a witch death curse unleashed and Aden injured by the Fae."

The witches. Ugh. How could she have forgotten, even for a second? "Have you ever been summoned to a witches meeting before?"

"No. Usually, the witches and the vampires avoid each other. They are...well, their blood is our greatest addiction." Her eyes closed, and she licked her lips, as if she were imagining drinking from one. "The taste is...I can't even describe it. There's nothing like it, and one sip can enslave us."

Great. Neither of them knew what to expect, then.

"We've always maintained distance from each other, and have an unspoken pact. We do not use them for sustenance, and they do not bespell us. Until lately."

"So you're uncomfortable around witches."

"I suppose."

"And you're also at war with the Fae."

"Yes."

"And you hate goblins."

"Anyone with sense does."

Were vampires allied with *anyone?* Well, besides were-wolves, their trusted protectors.

Maybe you joined the wrong team.

The stray thought hit her, and she blinked. Wrong! She'd joined the right team. She'd joined Riley's team. How dare her mind consider anything else.

Are you seriously angry with your own brain?

She hated that cynical inner voice. Besides, what other team would she have joined? The witches? Yeah, that would have been nice. Wasn't like they could curse her every time she angered them.

Oh. Wait. They *could.*

But, God, if she could just talk to a witch. Ask a few questions, figure this thing out. How, though? It wasn't like the witches were wearing signs around their necks announcing what they were, or popping up at school or this ranch and asking if there was anything they could do for her.

But Victoria and Riley could spot them at a glance. What if they went into town—where most of the creatures were congregating, trying to figure out how they'd been summoned to Crossroads and not yet realizing Aden was the source—and kidnapped a witch?

Her eyes widened. Of course. Kidnap a witch, ask questions, get answers and boom. Success. Death curse reversed.

She could have danced.

Of course, she'd never kidnapped anyone and had no idea how to go about it. But she'd figure something out.

Who are *you?*

The old Mary Ann never would have considered such a risky plan. This was a new world, however, and she had to adapt. Or die. She wasn't ready to die.

"Let's backtrack to the witches…" After she outlined her plan to Victoria, the vampire glanced over at her for the first time since she'd entered the room and nodded thoughtfully.

"Excellent."

She beamed.

"I had not thought you so mercenary, Mary Ann."

Slowly her "beam" dimmed. "What do you mean?"

"Only that I approve of your plan. Kidnap and torture for information. And after the meeting, we can even bargain for our captive's release. If the witches vow never to curse us again, she lives."

And if they refused to offer such a vow? Mary Ann's stomach hollowed. No way would she commit murder. And torture? No! In her mind, she kind of expected the witch to offer answers in exchange for freedom. Easy, done. Just like that. Clearly, Victoria thought differently. And that she could resort to brutality so easily and without a hint of remorse…

First, you didn't mind Riley acting all He-mannish. Second,

Victoria's a vampire, remember? Raised by one of the most vicious men in history. So for eighty years, and by her own admission, Victoria had viewed humans as food, nothing more, nothing less. Life had no true value to her. Besides, witches weren't human, Mary Ann didn't think, but they *were* a source of irritation to the vampire. Irritations were probably to be snuffed out immediately. Painfully.

That's what Vlad the Impaler had most likely done, and that's what Victoria assumed she needed to do. Someone would have to teach her otherwise.

So. New task to add to Mary Ann's ever-growing list. Teach Victoria to respect other species. Hopefully, Riley wouldn't need the lesson, as well. If he did, however, she would give it to him. There would be no killing unless absolutely necessary.

Unless absolutely necessary? *Who are you?* she wondered again. And just how was she supposed to teach a vampire and werewolf anything when they were far older than she was and had a lifetime of experiences she couldn't even imagine?

"When is he going to wake up?" Victoria suddenly asked.

Mary Ann pulled herself from her thoughts. "When his body is ready, I suppose. Rest is healing."

"I wish…I wish I could turn him into a vampire. Then his skin would be indestructible."

She really needed to eliminate that word from her vocabulary. Vampire skin could be burned by *je la nune;* at least, that's what she thought Aden had called it. He'd also said *je la nune* was fire dipped in acid then wrapped in poison and sprinkled with radiation. Or something like that. That's what was hidden inside of Victoria's ring.

What a painful way to die. Mary Ann wasn't sure Aden would prefer that to the few cuts and bruises he had now.

"He's going to die, you know?" Victoria said softly. She rested her head on Aden's chest, as if she were listening to his heartbeat. Silky black hair spread around her shoulders and draped over the arm she had wrapped over Aden's stomach. Together, they looked like a magazine ad for a fancy perfume. "Has he told you yet?"

"What's to tell? All humans die."

"No. He'll die. Soon."

At first, Mary Ann could only blink over at her, certain she'd misheard. Then, as the words penetrated— *He'll die. Soon.*—they became real. All the moisture in her mouth dried, her limbs shook and her heart did that hammering thing. "How does he know he's going to die?"

"One of the souls inside his head is psychic. A death predictor."

"Wh-when is this supposed to happen? *How* is it supposed to happen?"

"A knife through the heart. The other, the timing… that, he doesn't know. Only that it will be soon, like I told you."

Soon. What was soon, though? A day? A week? A year? And a knife through the freaking heart? Dear God. An even worse way to die than from the *je la nune*. He really did need tough vampire skin.

Why hadn't he told her?

"Why can't you turn him?"

"Attempts were made to turn humans in the past. None were successful."

"Can't we—?"

"Stop it from happening, now that we know about it?" Victoria laughed without any trace of humor. "No. Apparently, that will only make things worse for him. He told me that stopping a death, once it's been predicted, does not change the outcome, only the way that outcome is achieved. And when changed, that outcome becomes far more excruciating."

Aden. Dead. Soon. No! Tears burned her eyes, stinging down her cheeks. "How does he live with that knowledge?" *Don't talk like that. Something can be done. Surely.*

"I don't know. But I don't think I could. He is human, yet he is stronger than I will ever be." She traced something over his heart, but Mary Ann was too far away to tell what that something was. If she were guessing, though, she would say it was the same thing Victoria had traced on the tabletop in the cafeteria.

"And you're sure you can't make him a vampire?" There *had* to be a way to save him.

"I am sure. Our blood is…different than yours and in large doses, which would be required to turn someone, it drives humans to insanity and death. Sometimes the vampire trying to do the turning dies, as well, though no one knows why."

No way Aden would risk Victoria's life. That she knew. "How did you become vampire, then?" The question emerged broken, hoarse.

"I was born this way. My father was the first to change, you see. He was a blood-drinker, even as a human, and slowly found himself changing. His skin thickening, his hunger for everything else fading away. His body no longer aging. He had his most trusted men and their females drink blood, like him, and they, too, changed. He then had his beloved pets, the wolves, drink. They changed, as well, though they became vicious. It is their offspring, like Riley, that you see now, able to shift into human form."

"Why can't Aden drink *that* blood? What your father and his people drank?"

"He drank from people, Mary Ann, and those people are long gone. Dust in the grave."

"But if *Aden* drank from people...maybe..."

"That, too, has been tried. That, too, has failed."

So that was it? They were supposed to give up and watch Aden die? *Soon?* No. Absolutely not. She refused. There had to be a way to save him, she thought again. *Please let there be a way to save him.*

Suddenly Riley strode from the closet, wiping his hands together and claiming their attention. He was fully dressed now. His clothes were wrinkled, torn and bloodstained, and there were streaks of dirt on his face and arms.

"It's done," he said, and there was no emotion in his voice. "No one will know a prince was killed in Aden's home." His gaze raked Mary Ann, ensuring she was okay, before moving to Aden and Victoria. "How is he?"

"Better."

As if he'd heard the question, Aden moaned.

Both Mary Ann and Riley stilled before rushing to the bed and crouching beside him. Mary Ann latched onto his hand and squeezed.

Victoria rose over him, on her knees, and patted his cheeks. "Can you hear us, Aden?"

Slowly he blinked open his eyes. There was a collective intake of breath as they waited...waited... He focused, though his multicolored irises, a mix of brown, blue and green, were glassy.

"Victoria?" he asked groggily.

"I'm here. How are you? Is there anything I can get you?"

He frowned, his head tilting to the side. He blinked again, and his frown deepened. Then he shocked everyone by snarling, "No!" grabbing Victoria by the shoulders and throwing her behind him as he popped to his knees. "Don't you dare touch her!"

Startled, Mary Ann followed the line of his gaze. She saw...no one. "Aden?"

"How are you still alive?" he demanded. "Riley killed you. I felt you die!"

"Aden?" Victoria approached him again and curled her fingers around his forearms, urging him down. "Who are you talking to?"

"The prince." He remained where he was, balled his fists and raised them, ready to strike. "The prince who had better be leaving."

"He's *here?*" Riley demanded.

"Yes."

"But that's impossible. I mean *really* impossible. I just buried him."

SIX

BURIED HIM.

The words penetrated the fog drifting through Aden's head, and he rubbed his face with a shaky hand. Not happening. This was so not happening.

Buried him.

He once again maneuvered Victoria behind him, but Thomas continually reached through him, trying to touch her. No, not just touch her. Kill her. There was hate in the fairy's eyes. Only good news was Thomas's hand ghosted through Aden *and* Victoria, every try.

Riley had already grabbed Mary Ann and pushed her against the wall, his body covering hers like a shield. His predator's gaze circled the bedroom, searching, his body waiting to act.

Buried him.

Plausible, because Aden had taken a death-blow for him. He shuddered, remembering. The pain... He'd never experienced anything like it. In fact, there wasn't a word to describe it. *Excruciating* was like a gentle massage in comparison.

And that's how *Aden* was going to die.

Which meant he would have to experience that again. Chest ripping open, organ tearing, blood spilling. The cold consuming him, turning his bones to brittle ice. No. No, no, no. He refused. No one should have to endure that kind of death. And twice? Not just no, but hell, no. He'd think of something, *do* something, anything, to prevent it.

Yeah, he'd tried to save people in the past, hoping to circumvent the deaths Elijah had shown him. And yeah, they'd then died in other, more painful ways. But to Aden, there was nothing more painful than a knife through the heart. He'd take anything else. In a heartbeat. Stupid pun intended.

"Why can't I touch her?" Thomas snarled.

"Back off. Or—" What kind of threat would scare a fairy? "Or you'll regret it." Not the best, but all his foggy brain could come up with.

Finally, panting and skin glistening with sweat, the prince stilled. "What did you do to me?"

Good question. "Just leave her alone." Slowly, Aden moved from the bed…his legs had better cooperate… yes! He remained standing, arms splayed to block any new attempt. "In fact, just leave."

He stiffened as a thought occurred to him. *Make you*

pay for this, even from the grave, Thomas had said before the knife plunged. Pay. Grave. *Grave.* Oh…crap. Had Aden earned himself a vengeful fairy-slash-ghost-slash-sidekick?

"Aden. What's going on?" Victoria demanded, as the prince shouted, "I can't! I tried." She moved in front of Aden before he could stop her, ready to fight his demons for him. "Tell me what to do, and it's done."

"Victoria," he said. He couldn't stand the thought of her hurt. And despite everything, this could be a trick. What did Aden know about fairies and their afterlife? Thomas could be waiting for the right time to strike. For real.

"There's no one here, Aden. Just us. The prince is dead. Riley buried the body, like he told you. Yet you see him still?"

"Yes. But you can't see him? Can't hear him?"

A chorus of "No" rang out.

So. No one but Aden could see or hear Thomas, and Thomas couldn't touch anyone. Maybe this wasn't a trick, then. Besides, Thomas wanted Victoria and all of her family dead—enough to die himself—and wouldn't have waited for the right time to strike. He would have simply struck. Aden should have considered that before.

The prince really was a ghost.

At least you didn't suck him into your head, Julian offered helpfully.

Dude, Caleb said. *Like that's a silver lining.*

The souls had been quiet ever since he'd taken that knife to the chest. Hearing them now, as if nothing had happened, was both a relief and a curse. They were alive and well, but he didn't need the distraction right now.

Thomas was here to haunt him.

Sickness churned in his stomach, threatening to revolt. He'd encountered ghosts before. Hell, the souls inside him were ghosts without bodies. And yeah, he now knew Thomas couldn't hurt Victoria, but that didn't lessen his concern. This ghost wasn't simply a deceased human. No telling what Thomas would be able to do.

"Leave," he said to Victoria. He latched onto her arm and spun her around, then flattened his hand on her lower back and urged her forward, toward Riley.

"Wh-what?" She was so shocked by his words and actions, he knew, she offered no resistance.

"You have to leave." Not once did he remove his gaze from Thomas. Just in case.

"I don't understand."

"You, too, Riley. Take Victoria and go." He wanted to explain, but didn't want Thomas to hear that Mary Ann blocked supernatural abilities, just in case other fairies were able to see and hear him. He didn't want the fairies to know that she even blocked Aden's. That, when she was around, he didn't hear voices. That he didn't see ghosts or wake the dead. Except when Riley was with her. Somehow, Riley muted her ability to, well, mute. One day he'd figure out how. Until then… "For God's sake, go!"

Riley frowned but nodded. "Yes, my king. I'll keep both girls safe."

"I thought I told you not to call me that." Aden was no one's king. "And Mary Ann needs to stay."

"No." Green eyes narrowed on him. "Mary Ann goes with me, and that's final."

An argument? Now? For once, he would have preferred the reverence. "Actually, Mary Ann stays. That's an order."

Her dark head peeked from behind Riley's shoulder. She made a slashing motion over her throat, silently telling him not to go there. Thomas watched, gauging. Deciding what next to do?

There was a pause, heavy and tension-filled. Finally, Riley growled, "Yes. *My king*. All shall be as you *order.*"

Aden pressed his lips together to stop his retort. He was getting what he wanted; he could let the sarcasm slide.

"Aden?" Victoria said, and he could hear the question—*why are you doing this?*—in her musical voice. Worse, he could hear the hurt.

He suddenly hated himself. She'd endured enough hurt lately, and he didn't like adding to the mix.

Don't be so harsh with her, Aden, Caleb scolded him. *You know I only want to show her a good time.*

A good time. Yeah. That's all Aden wanted to show her, too. Always. She'd spent her life obeying one rule after another, sheltered, not really allowed to laugh, yet here he was, pushing her away without explanation.

Moment they were safe, he'd tell her why. And then he'd tease her until she laughed. He'd only heard her laugh once, and still dreamed of hearing that tinkling sound again.

Please don't tell me you're listening to Caleb now, Julian snapped. *We've got work to do.*

Yeah. Sexy work.

You are such a pervert.

Boys. Elijah sighed. *Is arguing necessary? Now?*

Looked like Elijah had taken over the role of mother hen now that Eve was gone.

"Aden," Victoria repeated, drawing him back to the present.

He ground his teeth, irritated with himself. His concentration sucked, even in times of great danger. "Call me later," was all he said, still unwilling to explain while Thomas could hear.

"I'll do more than that. I'll return for you this evening." Victoria grabbed Riley's hand before the wolf could protest. "My family wishes to meet you, and *their* wishes are not something you can ignore."

With that, the two were gone.

A second later, Thomas vanished, as well. A second after that, the souls inside of Aden gasped, as they always did when Mary Ann muted them, fading from his mind, falling into the black hole they'd once told him about.

They despised that black hole, but they didn't complain. They loved Aden. They wanted him happy, and they knew these private moments were necessary.

As necessary as letting them go, he thought, guilty again.

Aden sank to the ground, his back sliding against the wall. Yeah, he was going to have to set them free, no matter how much he might want to keep them. First, though, he had to figure out exactly who they had been as humans. Then he had to help them finish whatever was keeping them bound to the earth. To him.

That's how he'd lost Eve. Once he'd given her what her human self had wanted most—a day with her daughter—she had disappeared in a snap.

So much to do, he thought. *Overwhelming.* First up, it seemed, was meeting Victoria's family. The sisters he'd already seen in that vision. Laurel and...no, that wasn't right. He wracked his brain. Their names remained just out of reach.

"Is the fairy..." Mary Ann began.

"Yeah. He's gone." But most likely, Thomas would return the moment Mary Ann left the ranch. What would Aden do then? He couldn't keep her here all day and all night.

"Good. Now don't take this the wrong way, okay?" She walked to the bed and threw herself on the mattress, bouncing up and down. "But you really need a shower."

He glanced down at himself, heat blooming in his cheeks. Streaks of blood decorated his chest, and sweat had dried his boxers to his skin. "The bathroom is down the hall. Will you stay here? I'll hurry."

"I'll stay," she said with an impish grin. "Now, less talking and more showering."

As weak as he was, he had to use the wall to unfold from the floor and stand. And while digging through the closet for clothes, he fought wave after wave of dizziness. Finally, though, he was in the bathroom, having managed to stalk down the hall without running into any of the other boys, hot water streaming down his body, cleaning him inside and out.

His first private shower, he mused. He wondered how far Mary Ann's ability stretched—and he wished he could enjoy the solitude more. Yeah, *really* enjoy it. Instead, he had to hurry as promised.

When he finished, he dressed in a T-shirt and jeans and headed back to his bedroom. Just before he reached the door, the scent of peanut butter sandwiches drew him into the kitchen. There was a tray piled high with them, but no boys in sight. They should be here, studying.

You killed their teacher, remember?

Sad and guilty once again, Aden confiscated two of the sandwiches, eating each in two bites, and searched the rest of the bunkhouse. All the chores were done, so the boys *had* been here. The wood floors were polished, the oak table and scuffed chairs dusted. The walls were scrubbed clean and smelled of soap.

A few months ago, those walls had been filled with horseshoes and pictures of the ranch as it used to be a hundred or so years ago when it had first been built. But then two of the boys had gotten in a fight, and one of them had used a metal horseshoe to bash up the other. Or so Aden had heard. Dan, the owner of the ranch and the guy in charge of their care, had taken everything down.

There was no sign of the boys anywhere. Were they okay? Where had—

Laughter suddenly rang out.

At the far window in the entryway, he brushed the curtains aside and looked out. An overcast sky fashioned a gray canopy over the D and M as the boys played football in the field between the main house and the bunkhouse.

Aden experienced a momentary pang of jealousy.

Once, that's all he'd craved. Friends, games. Acceptance. Now he finally had it, for the most part, but he also had a little too much on his plate to enjoy it.

"You're gonna get into trouble," he told them, even though they couldn't hear him. Dan wasn't here—his truck was gone—but Meg, his wife, rarely left the main house, and she would report what had gone on.

But no tutor, no studies, Aden supposed, and his guilt increased. Dan was going to have to find a new tutor, having no idea why Mr. Thomas had "left" as suddenly as he'd appeared.

Aden liked Dan. Respected him. A lot. The man was honorable and truly wanted to give the boys here a better life. Yet time and time again, Aden made *his* life more difficult. *Don't think about that now.*

Back in his bedroom, Aden found that Mary Ann was still on the bed, though she was propped against the headboard and reading one of Shannon's books. The door clicked shut behind him—no lock, though, since Dan had removed them—and she looked up.

"Much better," she said with a nod.

"Thanks for staying."

"My pleasure." She set the book aside and straightened. "How are you feeling?"

"As good as I smell."

She laughed exactly like he wanted Victoria to laugh. "That good, huh?"

"Sorry you had to stick around."

"I didn't mind. I wanted to talk to you about something, anyway."

He sat at the desk, marveling that the room was perfect, nothing out of place. After Riley and Thomas had ravaged the entire building in that other dimension—which still freaked him out—he'd expected *some* sign of what had happened. Yet there was nothing. Not even a speck of blood.

"Are you listening to me?" Mary Ann asked with another laugh. "I thought the souls were quiet when I was with you."

He grinned sheepishly. "Sorry. I'm so used to being inside my head, I often get lost in there."

"Well, I was saying that you know how to fight."

"Yeah." He should. He'd been fighting his entire life. Other mental patients, doctors, other foster kids. Zombies that Julian, the corpse whisperer, raised from eternal slumber.

"Well," Mary Ann said, squaring her shoulders. "I want you to teach me."

He arched a brow, not sure he understood. "You want me to teach you how to kick as—uh, how to fight?"

"How to defend myself and how to attack, yes."

There was a big difference in what people needed to do to defend themselves and what they needed to do to attack someone else. A big, *dangerous* difference. "Riley won't like it."

She shrugged, swirling a finger along the cotton comforter. "He'll have to get over it. I *need* to do this. I don't want to be a liability anymore."

That, Aden understood. Perfectly. "I'll teach you."

She clapped as if he'd just told her she'd won the lottery. "Thank you."

"My pleasure," he said, mirroring her earlier words. "So when do you want to start?"

She whipped her cell phone from her back pocket and checked the time. "We have a few hours until I have to be home from school. And I can't believe I'm saying this, rather than rushing back to class, but…why not now?"

Those sandwiches had given him strength, though he wasn't one hundred percent racer ready. Still. He nodded. This girl had been the first person to accept him for who and what he was; he owed her. "We'll have to go out back. The boys are in the front, and it'll be better if they don't see us."

"Sounds good to me."

Outside, the clouds were thicker than they'd been even a few moments ago when he'd peeked through the window, the air chilled and laced with dew. A storm was on its way.

He positioned Mary Ann on the grass, then moved in front of her. "First up, defense. And to do that, you have to learn how people will strike at you. Which means I'll have to strike at you."

Determined, she nodded. "Okay. I'm ready."

The next few hours passed quickly, and by the end, they were sweaty, grass-stained and exhausted, but mostly wet and muddy. A fine drizzle had started fifteen minutes ago. Mary Ann was pretty bruised up. Fine, Aden was, too. He'd been jabbed, punched, poked and tripped. And yeah, he'd done the same to Mary Ann. Experience was the only way to learn. Because, if she was afraid of pain, she would cower rather than act. So he'd had to show her she could withstand anything.

Surprisingly, she had. Better than he'd hoped.

"So tell me what you've learned so far," he said, standing in front of her again.

"Screaming is good. And punching people in the throat is far more effective than punching them in the face or stomach. Plus, throat punching is something anyone can do, even fragile little girls, since it doesn't take much force to do a lot of damage there." This last was said in a mockingly deep voice, mimicking him. She tightened her borrowed jacket around her middle. The only time they'd stopped practicing was when he'd gone to fetch her that jacket from his closet. "I should use my fists as if they're hammers, or even hit with my open palm."

"Good. What else?"

"Anything can be used as a weapon. Rocks. Keys. A purse."

He nodded. "What else?"

"I shouldn't use my toes when I kick. There's not enough power there. I should use the flat part of my foot. Oh, and kneeing my attacker in the groin is acceptable. Even encouraged. So is eye-poking. I shouldn't be afraid to cause this person pain, since their main goal is to hurt me." She spoke as if she were reciting gospel. "If my back is to them, I should try and elbow the guy—or girl—in the face. That causes a lot of pain and stuns them, allowing me to try and get away."

"Good. Now let's put some of that information to the test. I'm going for your neck this time," he warned her. "My plan is to choke you. Do you remember what to do?"

She nodded. "As quickly as possible, I'm to move both my arms between yours and hit your elbows with mine."

"And?"

"And knee you in the groin."

"Yeah, but let's just pretend on that last one. And by the way, an attacker won't usually give you a heads-up."

Her lips quirked at the corners. "Much as I wish otherwise."

Next time, he wouldn't warn her what he was going

to do. He'd just act, and she'd have to figure out what to do without forethought. "Ready?"

"Read—"

Leaves rattled a few yards away, and they both turned.

"Aden? Mary Ann?" Shannon had just stepped from the forest, a backpack dangling at his side.

"Hey," they called in unison.

"I—I wondered where you'd gone after lunch," Shannon said to Mary Ann.

Guilt danced in her eyes. "I should have told you I was leaving. I'm sorry. But if you're home, that means school's out, and I have to leave again now." She closed the distance to Aden and kissed his cheek. "Will you be okay?" she whispered. "Because the fairy's going to come back. The moment I'm gone, he's going to come back."

"I know. And yes, I'll be fine," he lied. He had no idea how to deal with Thomas, or how far Thomas could roam. Still. He gave Mary Ann a gentle push toward the forest. "Go home before you get into trouble with your dad."

"I'm going to call him and tell him I'm heading to the library. Which is true. I want to dig around and see if I can find any books on spells, that sort of thing. I'll keep you updated."

"Thanks."

"Welcome. And thank *you* for the lessons. Not that my gratitude will save you from my ferocious wrath during our next lesson."

"Those are fighting words, girl," he said with a laugh. "But maybe you should go home and change before you hit the library." He gazed pointedly at her muddy jeans.

"Will do!" Laughing herself, Mary Ann took off, stopping only to kiss Shannon on the cheek. When she reached the line of trees, a pair of green eyes and bared white teeth flashed through a thick bush.

Animal…hiding. The realization jolted him, and Aden sprinted forward. But then Mary Ann uttered another laugh, the sound just as free and happy.

Riley, he realized, stopping. A pissed Riley, at that. That scowl had been for Aden's benefit, he was sure. Had the wolf watched the defense lesson? Or had he witnessed the kiss Mary Ann had bestowed upon his cheek?

He'd find out. Later. First, he knew, Riley would walk Mary Ann home.

Thank God, Julian said. *We're back.*

What happened while we were gone? Caleb asked. *Why are we outside?*

Were you…fighting? Elijah demanded.

"Guys," he muttered. "I'll have to explain later."

Shannon reached him, clearly concerned. "W-where

were you t–today? I told Dan you'd already l–left for school this morning, so you're clear on that front."

"Thank you." Aden was still amazed that he and Shannon were friends. They hadn't started off that way, but they were pretty tight now. And it was nice. Even so, he couldn't tell Shannon the truth. Boy knew nothing about the real world and the creatures populating it, and that was for the best. "Come on. Let's go in, and I'll tell you everything." Yet nothing.

They headed into the bunkhouse, where the others were already washed up and in dry clothes, watching TV in the living room as if they'd just finished up their schoolwork like good little boys.

Aden waved at them, and kept moving. He and Shannon needed to talk, but what he would say, he still didn't know. After that, he needed some time alone to talk to the souls. Where he would go, though, he didn't know.

"Well, well," another familiar voice said when he entered his room. "Look who's back. Me."

Freaking fantastic, Caleb grumbled.

Not good, Elijah said with a sigh.

Aden didn't have to look around to know that the ghost prince had indeed returned. His hands curled into fists as he wondered if he'd ever lead a normal life.

"Aden?" Shannon said beside him. "You okay? The

guys asked if y-you wanted to watch Sports Center with them."

At the same time, Thomas said, "Tell me what you did to me. Tell me why I'm here, why my people can't see or hear me. Why no one but you can. Tell me!"

The voices blended together, making the words intelligible. He knew then that he wouldn't be having a conversation with Shannon anytime soon. Nor would he find that private moment with the souls.

Not knowing what else to do, Aden covered his ears and threw himself on his mattress to wait out the storm.

SEVEN

TUCKER HARBOR HUDDLED in the corner of a dim, damp crypt, surrounded by darkness and flat-out creepiness. A spider might have just crawled over his hand, and was that a mouse squeaking? He would have given anything to *see*.

He hadn't wanted to come here. He'd been lying on a hospital gurney, hooked to all kinds of monitors, drugs pumping straight into his veins, chasing away the pain. Yet *the voice* had called to him, drifting through his head, and he'd found himself unhooking the tethers, rising, walking, finally running, desperate to be wherever *the voice* wanted him to be.

Unfortunately, getting here hadn't been that difficult. No one had tried to stop him, and his "gift" hadn't been on the fritz. Tucker had cast illusions—something he'd been able to do his entire life. Whatever he envisioned in his mind, he could create around him. Or rather, make people think was around him.

If he pictured a gutter, a gutter would seem to encase him. If he pictured a circus, a circus would seem to appear, with him in the center ring. On his way out of the hospital, he'd pictured himself as the wall beside him. Outside, he'd pictured himself in a T-shirt and jeans, rather than this paper-thin gown.

So now, here he was. In pain, again, still weak from the vampire bites he'd endured only a few days ago—or maybe hours ago, he didn't know anymore. Time was just…time. Ticking away, but not part of his awareness anymore. Maybe because he didn't care.

Which he didn't understand. He'd been tied to a table as if he were dessert, and vampires—real-life freaking bloodsuckers—had been allowed to simply lean over and bite him. Anywhere they had desired. He'd wanted to die. But then, as the blood had drained from him, his body growing cold, his conscious mind dimming, he'd wanted to live. So badly.

Then Aden Stone and Mary Ann had come to his rescue. He'd been so grateful. He'd thought, *I'm going to turn my life around. I'm not going to cause trouble anymore. When I want to do bad things, like grinding my fist into as many faces as I can, watching the blood pour and hearing the screams echo, like stealing and fighting and hurting my mom with mean words just to hear her cry, I'm going to ignore the urges.*

Yet now, without the threat of death hovering over him, without the utter helplessness, without the drugs, he wanted to do all of those things again. And he couldn't ignore the urges. On the way here, he'd punched a middle-aged man he'd never met, felt the guy's teeth cutting into his knuckles, and had laughed. Laughed. Because he'd liked inflicting pain.

I'm a monster.

The only time those kinds of urges left him was when he was with Mary Ann. They'd dated for several months, and for those several months he'd been blissfully happy. Of course, being Tucker, he'd managed to ruin everything.

She'd taken off one night, so he'd visited her neighbor and best friend, Penny Parks. He and Penny had tossed back a few beers, had stupid unprotected sex, and now Penny was pregnant with his kid. Or so she said.

Part of him believed her. The human part of him that hated when he acted like a maniac. The other part of him, the part where all those urges churned, didn't want to believe her.

He needed Mary Ann again. Not as a girlfriend. Just as a friend. He wasn't sure he'd ever really wanted her romantically. He just liked how she made him feel. She would fix him, make him better again. And maybe then he could be a better dad to his kid than his own father had ever been to him.

Somewhere in the dark, he heard the whisper of cloth against flesh, the sound somehow far more obscene than the squeak of that mouse. Then, "You came," a hard, emotionless voice said from the darkness. "Good boy."

The voice. Only this time, it wasn't inside his head.

As his heart pounded out of control, Tucker straightened. He still couldn't see anything. There wasn't a single beam of light in this crypt, and dust layered the air. Dust and death. "Y-yes. I try to be." He would try to be anything this man wanted. "Who are you?"

"I am your king."

Four simple words, but they changed Tucker's life. Irrevocably. Yes. He belonged to the owner of that voice. It was strong, powerful, almost as if magic floated from each syllable, wrapping around him, tightening...tightening...controlling. More than being what this man wanted, Tucker would do whatever was asked of him, whenever it was asked. Happily.

"Vlad," he said, knowing the name deep in his soul. He inclined his head in reverent greeting, even though he couldn't be seen. Or could Vlad's gaze pierce the darkness?

"Yes. I am Vlad. And there is someone else you know, Tucker. Someone I am deeply interested in. Aden Stone."

A statement, not a question, yet Tucker replied anyway. "Yes." He couldn't help himself. Must please Vlad. Must always please Vlad. "I know him."

"You will watch him."

"Yes." No hesitation.

"You will tell me everything you learn."

"Yes." Anything. Everything.

"That is good. I am counting on you, Tucker. Do not let me down. Because, you see, he took my crown, and when the time is right, I will take it back."

THE NEXT FEW HOURS of Aden's life passed in a blur. Shannon realized something was wrong with him and tried to distract him, telling him about his day and how Mr. Klien, their chemistry teacher, had had him stand at the front of the class doing finger-strengthening exercises the entire period for dropping one of his test vials.

At the same time, Thomas continued to barrage him with rapid-fire questions. "Why can't my kind see or hear me anymore? Why did I disappear into a black hole after the vampire and werewolf left?"

At the same time, Elijah demanded they discuss the coming vampire assembly. Plans needed to be made. What if there was a rebellion and someone tried to dethrone him?

At the same time, Caleb outlined what Aden should wear to impress Victoria enough to make out with him. Black leather was a top contender. Whipped cream, too.

At the same time, Julian wrote an I'm-sorry poem for him to give to Victoria. *Oh, sweet darling, my heart bleeds. But you love blood. And I am mud. Forgive me.*

That's when Caleb became mocking, and Elijah incensed. Blah, blah, blah.

Through it all, Aden even thought he heard wolves howling in the background. *Arf, arf, arf,* he thought mockingly.

His head throbbed. He couldn't keep up with the chatter, the words and sounds doing more than blending together. They were creating an ever-increasing buzz that hammered against his skull.

Finally, he gave up. He rolled over, closed his eyes and tried to block out all of them. Peace. He just needed a little peace.

Soon, lack of rest and dying-by-proxy twice caught up with him, and he drifted in and out of agitated slumber. No, slumber wasn't the right word. He wasn't asleep, but he couldn't move. Even when Shannon shook him, he couldn't move or respond. It was like someone had tied his arms and legs to the bed. Like his eyelids had been taped open, and he couldn't blink, even when his eyes dried and burned.

What was wrong with him?

He was vaguely aware of Shannon leaving the room

and returning with Dan, who looked him over with concern. Dan tried to talk to him as he undressed Aden and tucked him under covers, but still Aden couldn't answer. One, his jaw was as useless as the rest of him, and two, he simply couldn't wade through the sea of voices, his awareness still being tugged in too many different directions.

Besides, Dan would think he was crazy—like everyone had always called him—if he answered something incorrectly.

Finally, Dan left and he sighed with relief. Short-lived relief. On and on the souls chattered. On and on Thomas spewed demands. Then Dan returned with Dr. Hennessy, Aden's newest therapist, adding something more to the mix.

Dr. Hennessy looked him over, as well, frowning but not concerned. The doctor was a short, balding man, with wire-framed glasses and cold brown eyes, and he never showed any type of emotion. He was clinical, impersonal and always radiated shrewd awareness.

Questions were hurled at him. Aden could only decipher two words: *catatonic* and *regressed*.

Were they talking about *him?*

Of course they were. Pills were shoved into Aden's mouth, and he tried to spit them out. Dr. Hennessy pinched his nose closed and held his jaw still, his purpose clear. If Aden wanted to breathe, he'd have to swallow.

"Take your medicine like a good boy, Aden," the doctor said crisply. "You've had these before. I'm not giving you anything new." A sigh. "Still determined to resist? Well, if you don't take them, I'll simply give you an injection. Wouldn't you prefer to avoid a needle?"

Only when his lungs screamed in protest and his throat began to convulse did he swallow. A second later, he could breathe.

He sucked in mouthful after mouthful of air, but his I'm-going-to-live happiness disintegrated when he realized what he'd swallowed. Those pills always fogged Aden's brain and put the souls into a stupor, two things he loathed. Two things *they* loathed. More than that, he needed to be clear-headed tonight. He needed... The blood-brain barrier was broken almost instantly, and dizziness washed through him.

The fog he'd feared appeared behind his eyes, thickening, spreading, fuzzing his thoughts.

"Sorry," he managed to croak out, jaw once again working. "So sorry."

Julian was the first to quiet. Then Caleb, then Elijah, who fought the hardest to remain heard. *You'll need me, Aden. Tonight is...tonight is...*

Even Thomas, standing beside Dr. Hennessy, glaring down at Aden, began to waver, shimmer, there but not there, an outline without substance.

"He'll need to visit me tomorrow morning," Dr.

Hennessy was saying to Dan as he straightened, wiping his hands together in a job well done. "First thing."

Dan crossed his arms over his massive chest. He was a former pro-footballer, tall, wide, pure intimidation with pale hair and dark eyes. "He has school. If he's well enough, and I think that he will be. He always pulls himself together quickly."

"He can miss one day."

"No, actually, he can't. His studies are just as important as his therapy."

Thank you, Aden wanted to say, but didn't allow the words to move past his lips. No reason to encourage attention or unwittingly admit he understood what was being said. Dan cared about the boys here. Truly cared. Even about Aden, as his insistence proved.

"I'll bring him to you immediately afterward," Dan continued. "How about that?"

"I highly recommend you reconsider. This boy doesn't need to be in school, around normal children. I could take over his—"

"Excuse me, Dr. Hennessy," Dan said tightly. "I may not have a fancy degree, but I know this boy better than you do. He's a good kid with a lot of heart, and he's doing well here. He's excelling in school with those so-called normal kids, and he's even made new friends and gained confidence. He's doing better than ever and I will not disrupt that progress."

"Yes, but he still talks to himself. And today, well, he lost himself inside his mind. I would hardly call that 'better than ever,' Mr. Reeves. Would you?"

Dan stuffed his hands in his pockets, going all "well, shucks," on the doctor, a sign Aden recognized as growing annoyance. "We all occasionally regress, as you said, but he's pulling himself together."

"That's the pills."

"That's the boy's strength of will."

Slowly Aden relaxed, rubbed a hand over his face. His vision was slightly blurred, his movements sluggish, but at least his mind was quiet. Still. Poor souls.

The two men continued their conversation a while longer, until finally it was decided that Aden would attend class, then immediately be driven to Dr. Hennessy's office for a session.

Great. Those sessions were nothing but a pain in the ass. The *good* doctor always wanted to touch him. Nothing overt, and nothing too creepy, just a hand-holding, skin-to-skin thing. That, on top of the fact that he had to be in therapy at all, aggravated the piss right out of him.

At last the men left, and Aden gingerly sat up. His stomach burned as if a fire had been set there, and that burn rose into his throat, his brain. More fog, more dizziness. He closed his eyes. In the distance, a wolf howled.

So he hadn't imagined the howling. Riley must be nearby.

"S-sorry, man," he heard Shannon say.

His lids cracked open, and he saw that Shannon was beside the bed and crouched in front of him, his features tight with concern.

"D-didn't want to get Dan, but didn't k-know what else to do. You were really o-out of it. Never seen you l-like that."

"Don't worry about it." He blinked, doing his best to focus. "What time is it?"

"About ten-thirty."

That late? Wow. Riley really would be here any minute. How was Aden going to sneak out now? Dan would check up on him throughout the night, Aden knew that he would. Apparently, that's what people who cared about you did. Checked on you. It was new and wonderful and yet, hell on the social life.

Something clanked against the window, and both Aden and Shannon turned. The glass rose, then Riley was there, smoothly climbing through. He was dressed in a black suit, was cleanly shaven and had his hair arranged in perfect spikes. In his arms, he clutched what looked to be a garment bag.

"Shannon," he acknowledged with a stiff nod.

Shannon, who was used to Aden's nightly visitors, nodded in return. "Riley."

"I've gotta borrow our boy for a little while."

Shannon frowned. "He's b-been sick and needs his r-rest."

Riley frowned, too, gaze darting to Aden. "Sick? Again? How?"

"Again?" Shannon's focus swung back to Aden. "When were you s-sick before? What was wrong?"

Oh, yeah. Aden hadn't explained—or lied, as he'd planned—so Shannon had no idea how iffy things had been for him.

"Shannon," a musical female voice said from just beyond the window. Victoria had arrived. "You are tired. You must sleep now."

"Sleep," the boy muttered, yawning. "Yeah, I'm pretty tired." He scaled to the top of the bunk bed and lay down. He was softly snoring a few seconds later.

So much power in one little voice, Aden thought. A voice she used liberally, but always to help him, so he didn't want to complain. Even though a part of him sometimes feared she'd one day use that voice *against* him. How would he combat the compulsion to do what she wanted if, like, he made her mad and she told him to do something tragic?

Don't think like that. She cares about you.

He blamed the drugs for his illicit thoughts.

Still outside, she moved backward one step, two, though remained in a beam of light spilling from the room. Her dark hair was piled on top of her head, he noticed, and several ringlets framed her pale face. Her eyes had been outlined in black and black glitter sprinkled on her lids. His favorite? Her lips were painted bloodred.

From what he could see, she wore a silky black robe with thin straps on both shoulders and a neckline that dipped low in the center. New favorite, he thought. He even liked the metal bands winding around her biceps like thin, bejeweled snakes.

She was breathtaking.

Mine. The thought was his own, no one else's. Because she was. His.

"Aden," Riley said, claiming his attention. "You were sick?"

Aden nodded, and had to blink against the sudden renewal of dizziness. Stupid pills. He explained what had happened, what had been done to him. How he'd been drugged.

Riley shook his head. "I don't know how you deal with all those voices anyway. But don't beat yourself up about it. One slip-up in how long? A year or more? That's reason to celebrate. You know, at a vampire mansion. Like, now."

At least the wolf wasn't snarling at him.

"Help him dress, and I'll ensure Dan stays away from this room for the rest of the night," Victoria said from her outer post, and then was gone.

Riley unzipped the bag he held. "I seriously hope you're not going to make me do all the work."

"Please. I'd have to be dead to let you put your hands on me." Aden stood—and almost tumbled back on his bed, his knees were so weak, but he managed to remain upright, and held out his hands. Several articles of clothing were thrust at him.

He dressed quickly, and realized he was now wearing a suit almost identical to Riley's. Black, silk, expensive. He brushed his hair and teeth, then splayed his arms wide, silently requesting inspection.

"Better, but not done yet." Riley held out his open palm.

Aden saw what rested in the center and actually backed away. "No. No way."

"You must."

The ring—*Vlad's* ring—glistened with a luminous shimmer in the light. Bad idea, all the way around.

"Your coronation ceremony will take place in thirteen days and—"

"Thirteen days," he interjected. That seemed relevant somehow. Familiar. "So why wear it now?"

"As a symbol of your power."

Power? Please. He had no power. Not any that mattered.

"We must go," Victoria said suddenly, at the window again. "Everyone is waiting."

Riley arched a brow at him and shook the ring. "You're king, ceremony or not, and the vampire king wears this ring. Always. Your people won't take you seriously without it, and you're going to have a hard time being taken seriously anyway since you're human."

"Thanks for the newsflash." *I don't want to be king,* he thought, but he reluctantly pinched the band between two fingers and slid the thing in place. A large opal stared up at him, casting multihued beams in every direction. His foggy mind could have studied those beams forever, lost.

He'd wear the ring tonight because, in their minds, he *was* king. According to their laws—of which he knew only this one—he who killed the king became king. But Aden planned to appoint someone else, someone deserving, someone competent and equipped. And soon. *Without* letting himself be killed.

"Go." With a push from Riley, he was stumbling toward the open window.

Chilly air enveloped him as he climbed out and strode toward a dark blue sedan the pair had hidden a few yards from the ranch. Stolen, no doubt. They didn't own a car, so Victoria "borrowed" one when she needed to be driven somewhere. Or rather, have Aden driven somewhere. All the while, crickets sang and wolves continued to howl.

"Goblins out tonight," Riley explained as he settled

into the driver's seat. "Though they're thinning out, and should be contained soon."

Goblins. Little monsters who liked to eat human flesh. Aden hadn't met one yet, but had heard the stories about sharp teeth ripping through human bodies like a knife through butter. Little wonder he wanted to put off that introduction as long as possible.

Aden and Victoria had claimed the backseat. She had tried to sit in front, in the passenger seat next to Riley, but Aden had grabbed her hand and tugged her back with him. She could have fought him, but allowed the restriction, silent.

Once they were on the road, she withdrew a cologne bottle from the center console and sprayed him from top to bottom. Soon he was choking on the scented mist that clogged the air.

"Enough," he said, waving his hand in front of his face.

"This is necessary. Believe me, you don't want to smell like the Fae when you face my people."

"So I still smell like him?"

"Yes," she and Riley said in unison.

Great. Not at his best mentally *and* he reeked. What a night. "So where's Mary Ann?"

"Home," Riley said, and there was all kinds of fury in his tone. The kind of fury Aden had been expecting since the wolf's arrival. Which meant Aden had just opened a big can o' crap. "There's no reason for her to be involved in this. Plus, she checked out some books at the library and is currently reading them, hoping to learn everything she can about the witches. And speaking of Mary Ann—" his voice rose with every word "—why the hell were you shoving her around today?"

Yep. Crap. "I'm sure you asked her, and I'm sure she explained that I was teaching her to defend herself."

"No, I didn't ask her. I figured the defense thing out on my own, thanks, but I wanted to chat with *you* about it first. Did you have to be so rough? She's only a human."

"*I'm* only a human. And yeah. I had to be rough. That's the only way to learn."

"No, it isn't. In fact, I'm taking over her lessons."

Oh, really? "Sorry, but she didn't ask you. She asked me. So *I'll* be the one continuing with her lessons." He could have relented. Wasn't like he cared one way or the other. But allow Riley to boss him around? Multiply "hell, no" by "dream on" and divide by "suck it," and the answer was "the wolf could bite the big one."

That earned him a thick and heavy silence.

Aden sighed and dropped his head against the seat rest. He needed Riley on his side tonight. More than that, he had a thousand questions he needed answered. How was this meeting going to go down? What was expected of him? Was there anything he should or shouldn't say?

Anything he should or shouldn't do? But as he sat there, peering up at the car's roof, mind drifting, churning, he could only make himself care about Victoria.

She'd sat through his exchange with Riley, stiff and too quiet, as if she didn't dare breathe because she might miss something. Was she jealous of the time he spent with Mary Ann, as he was often jealous of the time she spent with Riley? Or was she still hurt about earlier? Or both?

Either way, he didn't like it.

He'd dreamed about her for six months before he'd actually met her, and in that time, she'd become the most important part of his life. A part he needed, craved. Like Mary Ann, she accepted him for who and what he was, and had from the beginning. Even though her own people considered him unworthy—not to mention his own. She understood what it felt like to be considered different. She was a princess, set apart. And hadn't he vowed just today to only ever make this princess laugh?

"Just so you know," Riley gritted out. "If you hurt her again…"

"You'll call me a bad name?" Aden retorted. "Or maybe tell your friends not to like me?" He knew he shouldn't provoke the wolf. Riley's claws could rip through bone in a blink. But again, *bite the big one, wolf.*

Riley growled from low in his throat. Expected. What wasn't expected? Victoria laughed, an honest to God laugh.

"I'm sorry," she said when Riley tossed her a dark look. "But that was funny. You know it was."

"Whatever," Riley replied, but there was now suppressed amusement in his tone.

Aden's chest puffed up. He'd done that. He'd caused that reaction without even trying. But then Victoria's laughter subsided, and she once again refused to look at him.

More. He had to have more. "Victoria," he began. "About what happened—"

"I know," she said on a trembling exhalation. "I already figured out your reasons for ditching me at the ranch."

Oh, God. Was she going to cry? "I didn't ditch you, I swear."

"Well, I know that, too."

He shook his head, confused. There'd been no trembling that time. "Wait. You just said I did, in fact, ditch you. So...you're not mad at me?"

"I was at first, but then I wasn't. Don't you see?" Grinning, she clapped, clearly proud of herself. "I've been teasing you since we picked you up. I was using exaggeration. Like a human. Did I do good? Did I fool you?"

His lips twitched in relief and pleasure. They had a *lot* to work on in the humor department, but he said, "You did real good." And she had. She was trying to drop that ever-somber air. For him. "You look beautiful, by the way."

"Thank you. So do you. Practically edible."

His lips twitched again. Edible—the highest form of praise from a vampire.

Her hand slid over his and their fingers twined. As always, her skin was hot, smooth. Perfect. "Thank you, by the way. For what you did with the fairy," she said, suddenly serious.

"You're welcome."

"I wish I could reward you, but instead, I'm taking you into a potential war zone. Are you scared?"

"No." But he should be, and he knew it. "The drugs have made me a little detached."

"Perhaps that's a blessing. Fear can be smelled, and most vampires really like the taste of it."

He snorted. "Baby, even if I was afraid, I doubt anything can be smelled except my perfume."

Another laugh bubbled from her, bells tinkling together, and he grinned. Twice in one day. He couldn't have been prouder.

"As I told you, my sisters are in town," she said, then explained something about a fourteen-day waiting period. He didn't tell her that he'd met her sisters already in the vision. Not that he recalled much more. But with that thought, another formed. There was something he needed to tell her. Something urgent. For the life of him, however, he couldn't remember what it was. "Lauren is…"

"Hardcore," Riley finished for her.

Victoria rolled her eyes. "She is not. He says that only because they used to date, but Lauren broke up with him. *Anyway.* Lauren is strong, opinionated and determined not to like you. She's a warrior and one of the fiercest among us. She'll come around, though. Stephanie, my other sister, is very humanlike. She used to sneak out of our home, to my father's fury, and socialize with the food, as he would say. She might just be your biggest supporter."

"Good to know I have one. Has your mother arrived yet?" Aden knew her mother had been locked away by her father, a punishment for revealing vampire secrets to humans. Upon Vlad's death, though, Aden had decreed the woman free. His first act as king.

The title had him shaking his head. Weird, and not at all suitable for him. He could barely manage his own life.

"No," Victoria replied. "She can't teleport like me, and so she would be traveling by human methods if she had agreed to come to Crossroads. But she didn't, preferring to stay in Romania."

In protest of Aden's rule? he wondered.

"Nothing like this has ever happened before, you know. My father has *always* ruled us. He was the first of us, after all, and he believed humans were good enough to be food or blood-slaves, but nothing more." Victoria tapped a finger against his chin. "I'm sorry, but that is the mindset you will be up against this night."

The car slowed as a tall iron gate came into view, the bars opening to welcome them. Two wolves sat at the sides, watching. Guards? Further up, a five-story, sprawling mansion consumed acre after acre. The black brick and black-shrouded windows pandered to every eerie stereotype there was, but perhaps that had been done on purpose. A way to keep humans at bay.

The roof dipped and rose into several points, knifing into the sky, where the moon seemed to have shifted away, looking elsewhere, as if afraid to peek inside the home. That was probably for the best.

Last time Aden had been here, a vampire had tried to murder him. That same vampire *had* murdered an acquaintance of his. He wondered what awaited him inside *this* time.

EIGH✝

I WANT YOU to stay home tonight.

But I want to go with you. Be with you. I want to help Aden.

I'd rather you were safe.

And that's how Riley had left it. He'd called, dropped the "stay home" bomb and hung up before she could protest again. Now, at close to eleven, Mary Ann paced through her bedroom. Each of her walls was painted a different color—pink, blue, green, red—and those colors blurred together. Half of her wood floor was covered by a multicolored rug that somehow managed to clash with the walls. A decorating scheme her mother—her real mother—had loved and her aunt, the woman who had raised her, had carried on.

What was happening at that vampire mansion? Was everyone okay? Had the vampires accepted Aden without protest?

Clearly, Riley viewed her as weak. A hindrance. She'd

suspected, but this…this was proof. And she didn't like it. Wouldn't stand for it. But what could she do?

She couldn't kidnap a witch on her own. That was just craziness. One, she didn't know the extent of their powers or how they wielded that power. Even though she'd spent the last few hours studying every book she'd checked out at the library, as well as scouring the Internet yet again, looking for obscure details. Anything. There was tons of information out there, most of it conflicting.

Witches drew their power from the elements. Witches drew their power from inside themselves. Witches were good, benevolent. Witches were bad, evil, servants of the devil. Witches liked to perform ritual sacrifices. Witches were merely delusional.

You're getting sidetracked. You were thinking about why you can't kidnap a witch. Oh, and two, she doubted she could subdue someone physically just yet. And three, where would she keep the witch? In her closet? Her dad wouldn't find anything odd about that. Yeah. Right.

Still. Waiting for Riley, Victoria and Aden to do something grated.

She wasn't the best at spotting witches, but she *could* do it. Riley had taught her how. So. Maybe she could go into town and count how many witches were out there, discover what they were doing and where, exactly, they were congregating. Or even find out if none were out there. Tomorrow, she could report her findings, *helping* her group instead of dragging them down.

Go ahead and pat yourself on the back. Because yeah, it was an excellent plan. She wouldn't get out of the car, of course. She wasn't that stupid. She would simply drive around, people-watch—or rather, *creature*-watch—and take notes. And, even better, she would take Penny with her as backup.

Yep. An excellent plan.

Mary Ann left her tank and jammie shorts on, and pulled on a long-sleeved shirt, jeans and a jacket. She anchored her hair in a ponytail, slipped on her tennies, grabbed her purse and stuffed her cell, keys and voice recorder—a gift from her dad to help her keep track of her thoughts—inside, then wrapped the long strap around her shoulder and hip.

Excited, nervous, she switched off her lamp, then arranged her bed to look like she was lying in it. At the room's only window, she opened the glass and peered down…down. Her bedroom was upstairs, and there were no nearby trees to scale. Smart daddy, digging up her supposed only way down. But he hadn't been able to alter the shape of the roof. If she dropped a wee bit, she would hit the first story. From there, she could drop and roll to the soft grass below.

Simple. Easy. *Please be simple and easy.* She'd never snuck out before. Never really broken any rules before.

Now, she was breaking every single one of them. But this was a new world, she reminded herself, which meant new rules were needed. And the first new rule she was implementing was that the survival of her team was more important than curfew.

Dad would not agree, her conscience shouted.

Well, Dad didn't have all the facts.

Palms sweating, Mary Ann hoisted herself out. She maintained a somewhat steady grip on the ledge, allowing her legs to dangle. Deep breath in, deep breath out. The air was no longer layered with mist, but was chilled nonetheless.

She let go. Her feet hit—*thud*—and her knees buckled. She slid along the shingles before catching herself on the gutter, sprawled out, scratched and bruised. Well, *more* scratched and bruised. Her workout with Aden had left her unbelievably sore. And in places she hadn't even known she possessed!

She panted, grateful for the shadows as she waited for her dad's light to turn on and his head to peek out his window. One minute passed, two. Her arms shook. There was nothing, no movement.

In the distance, several wolves howled.

She gulped. Riley? Had he spotted her?

Probably not, she quickly decided. He would have called her cell, texted her, something. So who did that leave? His brothers? She knew they were out there, patrolling the area and fighting goblins, but she'd never met them. And if they had spotted her, they would have contacted Riley. Right? Right. So again, she would have been called or texted. That she hadn't been had to mean no one was watching her.

Okay. You can do this. Slowly, she inched her way over the final edge. The shaking in her arms intensified as she once again dangled. Had the first-story roof always been this high up? Couldn't have been. She would have noticed. *Just do it.*

Mary Ann let go and fell.

When she hit, her legs were jarred, her kneecaps slamming straight before bending. She flipped backward, rolling far more inelegantly than she'd intended, air knocking from her lungs and dirt and grass filling her mouth.

Thank God she still hadn't eaten. She would have vomited for sure. But it was odd, her lack of appetite. More and more, she was actually…repulsed by food. The thought of it, the smell of it. Ick. Even odder, she wasn't weak from lack of nourishment.

Two days had passed. Shouldn't she be shaky?

Think about that later. She popped to her feet and stumbled next door to Penny's house, stopping at the large oak next to Penny's widow. *Lucky.*

Stars winked over Mary Ann's eyes as she gathered a few small pebbles and tossed them. *Clink. Clank.* A moment passed. Nothing. How frustrating. Would people wake up if she shouted "fire"? 'Cause this was ridiculous.

Three more stones were needed before the glass rose and Penny stuck out her blond head. She rubbed the sleep from her eyes and yawned as she searched the night for whatever had disturbed her. Her hair, usually straight and gleaming prettily, was in tangles around her face.

Her jaw dropped when she spotted Mary Ann. "What are you doing?" she whispered fiercely.

"I need your help. Get dressed. And bring your keys." They'd take her Mustang GT. Mary Ann was still saving to buy a car for herself.

Penny didn't ask any questions. She simply smiled, blue eyes gleaming, and nodded. "Give me five," she said, and closed the window.

Mary Ann used the time to catch her breath. Her lungs were so grateful, they finally stopped burning. Then another howl rent the air, this one closer, and Mary Ann's lungs were forgotten. She spun, nervously studying the gravel road, the homes, the trees. Leaves and branches rattled together as if something—or someone—was out there, just waiting for snacktime.

Hurry up, Pen.

A few minutes later, the front door of the house squeaked open, then closed with a snap. Mary Ann whipped back around. And there was Penny, clad in one of her favorite baby doll dresses—pink with white lace—flip-flops on her feet, hair straight and gleaming again, strolling forward without a care. As if they were headed to school. As if it wasn't beyond cold and close to midnight.

"What are you doing?" Mary Ann demanded quietly, racing over to her friend. A cloud of expensive perfume enveloped her. "Your parents—"

"Won't care, believe me. The shock of my new 'condition' wore off and they gave me a pardon. I'm no longer grounded for life. Besides, I rarely sleep anymore, so they hear me padding around the house at all hours. Sometimes I get bored and take off." She shrugged. "No big. So where we going?"

"Let's get warm, then talk."

When they were situated inside the car, buckles in place, the engine revved and Lady Gaga blasted from the speakers. Penny turned down the volume and pulled out of the driveway.

Mary Ann said, "I'm sorry I woke you up. If I'd known you were having problems sleeping, I would have—"

Penny laughed. "No worries, girl. I've been trying to begin your miseducation for years. The fact that you asked me to sneak out is priceless. So I'll ask again. Where we going?"

"Tri City."

"Really? Why? It'll be dead this time of night."

Maybe. Maybe not. "I just want to drive around and see if anyone's out."

"Try again. I don't believe you. There's something else...expecting someone in particular to be there? Someone like, oh, I don't know, the oh, so gorgeous Riley?" The last was said in a sing-song voice. "'Cause he's the only person I can think of who could make Mary Contrary finally come out to play."

"Mary Contrary," Penny's childhood nickname for her. And she had been. Very contrary. A bundle of energy her parents hadn't been able to tame. Until her mom—aunt—died, and then Mary Ann had changed. Happy smile—gone. Laughter—gone. Wild spirit—crushed. In their place, a need to please her dad had grown. She'd become somber, a little withdrawn. She'd even developed a fifteen-year plan for her life. College, doctorate, internship, open up her own practice. Like her dad. Now...goodbye, fifteen-year plan. She had no idea what she'd do tomorrow, much less next year. And she was happy about that. Finally free.

"Well?" Penny prompted.

Mary Ann ignored the question. She didn't want to discuss Riley with Penny, and not because Penny had slept with Mary Ann's last boyfriend. To her surprise, that was even less of an issue than it had been at lunch. She just, well, her feelings for Riley were so new, so...

intense. She could barely process them herself and didn't want anyone else trying to do so.

"Is the baby keeping you up?" she asked.

"Probably," Penny replied, allowing the subject change without comment.

"Any word from Tucker?"

Her friend's baby blues clouded over. "Not a peep."

Tucker was a moron.

After the Vampire Ball, she, Aden, Riley and Victoria had taken him to a nearby—yet not *too* nearby—hospital for a much-needed transfusion. Earlier she'd called his room to check on him and was told he'd taken off. Now, he was out there somewhere, armed with knowledge that could be dangerous to her friends.

Had he told anyone that vampires were real? Riley had made him vow not to—Victoria would have Voice Voodooed him, but vampire compulsion apparently didn't work on demons—and Tucker had seemed adamant in his agreement. But as Mary Ann well knew, Tucker was a very good liar. What was he doing? Where had he gone?

"How'd Grant take the news?" Grant was Penny's on-again off-again boyfriend. Currently off. Probably forever off now that Penny was pregnant with someone else's kid.

"He won't speak to me. Unlike you, he's not forgiving."

"I'm sorry."

"No big," she said again, but she couldn't mask the pain in her voice.

They were quiet the rest of the drive, each lost in her own thoughts. Finally, though, they reached their destination. Red brick building after red brick building came into view, some crumbling, some brand-new, but each spaced far enough apart to accommodate larger than necessary parking lots. The streets curved, lamps shining on each side. Every stoplight was currently green.

Not that traffic was moving. In fact, just the opposite.

"Wow," Penny said. "Gotta say, this is a little unexpected. Seriously. Is that Mr. Hayward, my Trig teach?"

Probably. People were everywhere. Human and nonhuman, though an untrained eye wouldn't be able to tell the difference.

None of the stores were open, but that didn't matter to the loiterers. They had lawn chairs and beer coolers, and music blasted at full volume—all evidently encouraging a multitude of sins involving the removal of clothing. The lawn chairs—major, grinding PDA. The coolers—stripper platforms for some of the girls. The music—dancing that could double as sex.

Shocking. Mary Ann shook her head, rubbed her eyes, certain she was imagining things. This wasn't what she'd expected, either. Everything was so…collegiate. Well, her idea of collegiate, anyway. One big party, an orgy waiting to happen. Shouldn't creatures of myth and legend be a little more…dignified?

"What's gotten into everyone and who are all those people?" Penny asked, awed.

She ignored the first question, and answered the second. "I have no idea." And technically, she didn't. She'd never been properly introduced to the creatures who'd chosen to mingle with the humans.

"Should I pull over?"

"Yeah, but park where we have a view of everyone but they don't have a view of us."

Penny pulled alongside Dairy Mart, killing the lights and immersing the car in shadows. She stopped, and Mary Ann scanned the crowd intently. At first glance, everyone appeared human, but she'd already begun to make out the small differences.

There were a few vampires, their skin pale, their lips bloodred. They moved with ethereal grace, as if each step was a ballet. There were fairies, careful to remain a safe distance from the vampires, their skin glittering slightly in the moonlight. Plus, they were mouthwateringly gorgeous, each one of them. The shifters, like Riley, had a purposeful stride, their expressions hunterish, as if the entire world was their dinner buffet.

The otherworld, or whatever it was called, had fully

descended on Crossroads, it seemed. And the humans were loving it, even though they had no idea what was truly going on. But...

Witches, witches, where were the witches?

"With witches, you must be careful," Victoria had once told her. "They can smile while cursing you."

They could also cloak themselves in magic so that anyone who looked at them would see only an Average Jane, easily forgettable.

"You have to train your eyes to see below the surface," Riley had explained.

Mary Ann found that she couldn't see below the surface, past the magical mask. Five minutes later, she realized she didn't need to. She saw a figure she recognized and gasped.

"What?" Penny demanded.

"Nothing, nothing." A lie without guilt. "This is just weird, that's all." Truth.

"I know. Totally weird."

One of the witches who had issued the death curse stood under a streetlamp, golden light flooding her. Long blond hair curled over a shoulder, vivid against the darkness of her coat. A breeze had kicked up, blowing the hood of that coat back to reveal her lovely, familiar face. She hadn't worn a mask before, and she wasn't wearing one now, her dark eyes watching the surrounding chaos with disdain.

"Have you ever seen that girl?" she asked Penny, pointing.

"Pretty, but no. Have you?"

"Maybe," she hedged. Full disclosure wasn't an option. First, Mary Ann needed to gain Riley and Victoria's permission. Otherwise, they might want to kill her friend to keep her from talking. Although, really. The secret was pretty much out. How could it not be? Mr. Klien, her stodgy chemistry teacher, was flirting with a scantily clad woman whose body was covered in odd tattoos.

"Can I be honest with you?" Penny asked suddenly.

"Please." *Just don't expect the same from me.*

"This is creeping me out. But should we, I don't know, join them? Act like cute little detectives and find out what's going on?"

"No!"

"Okay, okay. Bad suggestion." Penny rubbed her slightly rounded belly. "They just look like they're having so much fun, and I feel like I've been without fun *forever.*" Her tone was wistful. "So what's the plan? Just sit here and watch them?"

"Yep. When the police arrive to arrest everyone in the vicinity for indecent exposure," she said, thinking fast, "we'll have a better chance of getting away if we're in the car."

"Uh, Mary Ann? I hate to disappoint you, but the

police are already here. See the potbellied man twirling his shirt in the air? That's Officer Swanson."

"We're still staying here." Bottom line, she wasn't going to put her friend in danger. The creatures seemed to be behaving themselves, not hurting anyone, but that could change in a blink. And what if someone sensed the baby Penny carried had a demon father? What then? Would they want to spill Penny's blood? Would they want to destroy the baby?

She shuddered. One thing she knew: different "mythological" species were at war. Like vampires and fairies. And she had no idea which species liked demons and which didn't.

"Fine. We'll solve the mystery from here," Penny said, unable to hide her disappointment. "Detective Hot Pants reporting for duty."

"Good. Welcome to the team." Kind of.

Except, only a few minutes later, Penny grumbled, "This sucks. I'm officially bored. They're still having fun, and we're still sitting here watching."

"Sorry. Five minutes, and then we'll head home. I promise." So far, she'd learned nothing new.

Crap! Did the witch come here every night? Was there a party every night? If so, she'd have to nab the woman in front of a thousand potential witnesses.

So what was the best way to abduct someone from this crowded a place? she wondered. The answers slid into place as easily as if she'd been a criminal her entire life. First order of business would be noise control. A scream would draw all kinds of notice.

Second order of business would be carrying the resistant or unconscious body through the masses. Again, without drawing all kinds of notice. Third order would be storing their cargo after the kidnapping.

As her mind pondered the options and subsequent consequences, a stream of something warm rushed through Mary Ann. Her skin tingled, and her stomach growled. In seconds, that "something" soothed her, intensifying the tingle yet chasing the growl away, and she savored the sensations, wanting more, needing more, warm, so warm. Frowning, she pulled herself from her thoughts. What the—

The witch was striding toward Penny's car, she realized, her steps intent.

"Go," she shouted, slapping the dashboard. "Go now!"

"What? Why?"

"Move!"

Penny threw the car in Reverse and stepped on the gas. Tires screeched. Gravel sprayed. The car snaked a corner, and Mary Ann thudded against her window. They straightened out, speeding down the road, the crowded square soon becoming a distant speck in the rearview mirror.

Only problem? Two wolves were now running alongside them—and neither was Riley. One had white fur, like snow, and the other brown and red. Friends? Enemies? There was no time to reason it out. The farther down the road they went, the farther away the wolves edged from the car. Finally, Mary Ann couldn't see them at all.

"Okay. What was that about?" Penny demanded, out of breath though they'd done nothing physical.

"I—I don't know," she lied. Damn it! Had she blown everything? Probably. Now the witches knew she'd been there, watching. What was the chance the witch would return tomorrow?

She sighed, trying not to despair. Guess she'd find out. After she told Riley, Aden and Victoria what she'd done and they lectured her for her stupidity, of course.

Penny was right. This sucked.

NINE

WITH HER HEAD HELD HIGH, Victoria led Aden down a long—*long*—line of richly dressed vampires. He saw black velvet robes draping the females, jewels of every color sewn into the fabric, and silk shirts and pants on the men. There was a sweet perfume coating the air, a scent that thickened as he made his way up a dais, where a throne of the deepest ebony rested. A scent that thankfully canceled out his perfume.

Weird symbols were etched over every inch of the throne, symbols that seemed to hum with power, enveloping him as he sat, then holding him in place as if manacles encircled his wrists and ankles.

Victoria placed herself at his right and Riley his left, and the line started moving forward. Introduction after introduction was made. Male, female, young, old. Too many names and faces to remember, especially in his current, foggy condition.

Some regarded him hopefully, some with disdain.

Some looked past him to the large tapestry that hung along the wall. He didn't have to turn to know what image was woven there; it was burned into his mind forever. In it, Vlad the Impaler viciously fought an angry, determined mob. They had pitchforks; he had a bloody sword. At his sides were countless pikes—each with a human head perched at the top. Was that what these vampires would expect from Aden?

Most likely. He should care, he thought. Just then, he cared about nothing.

As the introductions continued, he found himself tuning out the voices and studying his surroundings. Even without Elijah, Julian and Caleb tossing out their opinions about *everything* every few seconds, Aden was still distracted, unable to concentrate. A long red carpet stretched from the dais to the front double doors. The same swirling symbols that decorated the throne also decorated the carpet.

There were no lamps present, only elaborate candelabras that produced flickering golden flames and ribbons of black smoke. On each side of the room were, strangely enough, stone steps—or bleachers—broken only by the four round columns stretching to the domed ceiling. They led to a platform where uniformed guards stood, swords strapped to their sides.

Humans sat on the steps. He knew they were humans because their skin ranged in color, from slightly tanned to darkest of mocha. Plus, their facial features lacked the perfection of the vampires. They, too, wore robes, though theirs were bereft of both jewels and sleeves. Easier access to their pulse points that way, Aden supposed. And he didn't have to ask them if they wanted to be here. They were watching the vamps with unabashed longing in their eyes.

Blood-slaves, he thought then. Victoria had once told him that humans quickly became addicted to a vampire's bite. Aden hadn't believed her at the time. He believed her now. Since then, she'd bitten him twice and each time had been…heaven. Her teeth produced some sort of chemical or drug that numbed a human's skin, then sweetly burned their blood.

"And finally," Victoria said from beside him, returning his thoughts to the present, "I'm pleased to introduce you to my sisters."

They'd reached the end of the line already? How long had he been casing the room?

"The first," she continued, "is the Princess Stephanie."

A beautiful blonde stepped forward and inclined her head in greeting. Like the others, she wore a robe. Until she reached up and pushed the material from her shoulders, and the thing whooshed to the floor, pooling at her feet. She lifted her chin, practically daring him to object. At least she'd had clothing on underneath the robe. *Now* she wore a black T-shirt with a jewel-studded rainbow in the center—the makeup on her face matched perfectly—as well as black jeans and bright red boots that hit her knees.

When he said nothing about her wardrobe switch, she relaxed.

As she chewed her gum, her green gaze roved over him. "Cute," she announced. "And oh, baby doll, you *do* give off a powerful vibe, don't you? Makes me want to touch you."

With your teeth, I'd bet. "Uh, thank you," he said. Everyone else had said only "My king" or nothing at all. Well, the ones he remembered. "Please don't be offended, but I'm asking that you...not."

She grinned, as noncommittal as possible. "So you're the one who defeated Dmitri, huh?"

"Looks like." While fists had pounded and blades had slashed, he hadn't known this was what awaited him if he succeeded. If he had... No, he thought then. No matter what, he would have done what he'd done. His instincts had taken over, and he'd wanted only to eliminate the person who had hoped to eliminate Riley and Mary Ann. And okay, fine, he'd also wanted to destroy the guy who planned to marry Victoria.

Stephanie arched a brow. "So how do you expect to rule us, human boy?"

Human boy. He shrugged; he'd been called worse. "I honestly don't know."

She offered him another grin. "Honesty. I like that. It's different."

Vlad had lied to his daughters? About what?

"So, listen," she said. "I'd really love to…toast your victory. What do you say we—"

Victoria stiffened, even grabbed his arms in a protective gesture. Riley, who stood at his other side, merely chuckled.

"We do not drink from our king," Victoria said stiffly.

What? She'd planned to toast his victory by using his neck as a juice box?

Stephanie tossed up her arms. "Ever?"

"Correct," Riley said.

Scarlet lips turned down, the lower one sticking slightly out. Her shoulders sagged. "Fine, then, but I have other questions for our future king. Like—"

"Now isn't the time for that, and you know it," Riley interjected gently. "Later, princess."

A moment passed in silence. Then another, "Fine. But I *will* ask my questions soon. They're *important*."

Riley didn't back down. "I'm sure they are. As for now, goodbye."

In a huff, Stephanie picked up her discarded robe,

swung around and stomped out of the room. A door slammed.

Only one person remained in the line. The other sister, he thought, her delicate face somehow familiar to him.

Victoria motioned her forward. "This is the Princess Lauren."

The cool blonde with the crystal eyes inclined her head in greeting. Like Stephanie, she had ditched the traditional robe. Unlike Stephanie, she wore a skintight black leather half top and matching pants. She had real barbed wire wrapped around her wrists and weapons strapped all over her body.

"So you are Aden Stone, the human I've heard so much about. I admit there's a draw to you, as Stephanie said, but you're nothing like my father."

He inclined his head in acknowledgment. "Thank you."

"That wasn't a compliment, you idiot!"

He shrugged. She said tomato; he said suck it.

Her eyes narrowed. "Like my little sister, I have questions, human. Unlike my sister, I expect, no, I demand answers this night."

"King," Riley snapped at her. "'My king.' That's how you will address him from this moment on."

Her chin rose, though she never removed her attention

from Aden. "In thirteen days, I'll call him king. Until then…"

For a moment, Aden thought she might be considering unsheathing one of her blades and tossing it at his heart, and a cold sweat broke out over his skin. Not a stabbing. Not again.

But she remained in place and said, "Besides, I haven't decided to follow him."

Riley descended the dais to stand just in front of her, nose-to-nose. "Is that a challenge?"

Above, the guards with the swords appeared ready to pounce. On Aden, Riley or Lauren, he wasn't sure. "Enough," Aden said, not knowing what else to do. *I am not king. I don't want to be king.* But something had to be done. "We'll argue about this later. As for now, glad as I am to meet a member of Victoria's family, the introductions are over. You may go." Did that sound kingly enough?

Surprisingly, yes. With a stiff nod and murderous glare, Lauren spun on her heel and stalked from the chamber. Once again, the door slammed shut. He noticed the humans were gone, too. He'd never heard them leave, but they'd somehow silently melted away.

"What now?" he asked, standing. Dizziness swept through him, and he had to grip the throne arm to remain upright. Just how long had he been sitting down?

"There's a reception in your honor." Victoria smoothed the hair from his brow, the caress gentle, warm. "Are you all right?"

No. Yes. Maybe. "What time is it?"

"Almost three."

He'd been here for four hours, then. And in three more hours, he would have to "wake up" to get ready for school. "I have to return to the ranch soon. We've got school tomorrow, and I can't miss again." He knew she could fix things with her voice, making everyone think he was there when he wasn't, but he wanted to go. He'd had to fight to be able to attend, and he wasn't going to waste the opportunity to learn, to better himself.

Yeah, he'd probably sleep through every class, because even now, he fought a yawn, but he'd still go. Maybe the lessons would sink into his subconscious.

"Just a little while longer, then I'll take you home." Her palms flattened on his shoulders before sliding around to cup the back of his neck. She pressed herself against him. "I promise."

Did she plan to kiss him? They'd kissed before, but only gently, and not for nearly long enough. He'd wanted more then and despite his condition, he knew he'd want more now. He'd want her tongue, her taste and her teeth.

A minute ticked by, then another, but she merely held

him. He tried not to wallow in disappointment. At least he cared about something now, he mused.

"This whole place is a stereotype, you know that?" he said in an attempt to distract himself. "All this black. The robes. The creep factor."

"Father loved stereotypes. Loved playing to them."

Her father. There was something Aden should know about the man, he thought, something he needed to tell her...but again, he could think of nothing. "Why did he love playing to them?"

One of her shoulders lifted in a delicate shrug. "People who encounter us think we're merely humans pretending to be vampires. We're considered weird, but we aren't considered a threat."

He understood. Weirdos were avoided, left alone. Threats were hunted, eliminated.

"The same could be said of you right now, Aden Stone." Amusement layered her tone. "My people consider you weird rather than a threat."

"And how do you know that?"

"No one tried to kill you."

"True," he said with a smile.

"And I'm proud of you, you know," she said huskily, gaze dropping to his lips, then his neck.

Was she thirsty? Please...

Riley coughed.

They ignored him.

Praise had always been a rare commodity in Aden's life, and he soaked hers up. In the institutions, the doctors had merely questioned him and the other patients had been wrapped up in their own problems. In foster homes, neither the well-meaning nor the uncaring parents had known how to deal with him, had even feared him. At the ranch, the other kids had ridiculed him at first.

"You're not embarrassed that I'm a weak human?" he asked her. Because he knew, even if she wouldn't admit it, that that's how her people saw him. Would probably always see him.

She countered with a question of her own. "You're not embarrassed that I'm a bloodthirsty fiend?" Even as she spoke, her gaze returned to the pulse at the base of his neck, which was hammering wildly. She licked her lips.

"Is my fiend thirsty now?"

"No," she croaked, arms falling away. She stepped backward, adding distance between them.

"Liar," he said, but didn't push. She refused to drink from him because she didn't want to turn him into a blood-slave. He understood, but he hated the thought of her beautiful mouth on anyone else.

They wouldn't argue about it now, though. No time.

"Come." Determined, she held out her hand. "The party is waiting."

He twined their fingers and allowed her to usher him down the carpet, Riley trailing a few steps behind. The closer they got to the doors, the more noise Aden heard beyond them. But when they passed the thick metal arches, he realized there was no one in the hallway. There were only alabaster statues of people and animals and intricately carved chests, all open and empty. What were they for, then?

Beyond another set of doorways, however, was a ball-room brimming with vampires, their werewolf guards and humans. The vampires talked and laughed, the wolves, in animal form, prowled throughout, and the humans were again on the fringes, eagerly awaiting a summons.

The cobbled walls were black, the monotony broken by long, oval mirrors, and again, the only light source was the golden glow of candles. Above, the ceiling looked like a... He frowned. Sure enough. A cobweb. In the center of the web hung a chandelier. And that chandelier had legs that stretched up, as if a spider walked along the ceiling.

Someone spotted him, and conversations halted, the sudden silence interrupting his ogling. All heads turned to him. Aden shifted uncomfortably from one foot to the other. Several minutes—an eternity—ticked by just like that. No one moving or speaking, just watching him, judging.

Should he do something? Say something?

They'd only ever been ruled by Vlad, he reminded himself. They were as clueless about this as he was. Not that he planned to rule them. He *would* figure a way out of this. Soon.

"Is he ready to see? To know?" someone muttered. Conversations started back up, the volume quickly rising. He thought he heard words like *beast*—maybe *feast*—and *horde*. Maybe *bored*.

"Should we wait until after the coronation?" someone else asked.

"Wait to see what?" he asked Victoria from the corner of his mouth.

She shifted uncomfortably, as he had done, and whispered, "They want to tell you about…they want you to know… Oh, this is difficult. I had hoped never to have to speak with you about this, but it was decided that, as king, you must know."

"Know what?"

"That we are not…alone."

Literally? 'Cause he could have figured that out on his own. Clearly they weren't yet on the same page. "You want to explain what you mean?"

"No."

"Do it anyway."

She sighed. "There is…something with us."

O-kay. Time to try another route. "If I'm going to… run things—" God, he couldn't believe he was saying that, even just to get answers "—I need to know everything. So, let's try this again. What *something* is with you?"

Twin pink circles bloomed on her cheeks. "This is so embarrassing, and you might run screaming from me once you find out."

"I've seen you eat, and didn't run screaming."

"Yes, but this is worse."

He didn't give up. "I promise you, nothing could make me run from you," he said, squeezing her hand. "And you know I like you, just as you are."

"Well, hold on to that thought." She gazed down at her feet and kicked out as if moving an invisible rock. "First, you should note that despite the familiar trappings you see here, whatever you thought you knew about vampires from your books and movies doesn't come close to the truth."

"So noted," he said dryly.

Her eyes widened. "Can you be serious?"

"I'll be serious if you relax."

The pink tip of her tongue slipped out, sliding over her lips and leaving a sheen of moisture. Of course, she didn't relax. "If you insist on knowing…"

"I do."

"Then here it is. The truth. We are...more than bloodsucking vampires." Her chin lifted stubbornly. Like her sister had done earlier, she practically dared him to protest. "There. Now you know."

"Hardly. Explain."

Again she licked her lips, her mulish vibe giving way to a nervous energy. "Aden..."

"Victoria. Just say it. Rip the Band-Aid."

Her shoulders sagged in defeat. "Very well. We are more than bloodsuckers because we have...we have monsters living inside us."

Monsters? "Again. I don't understand."

"We are possessed—wait." She shook her head, dark hair dancing over her shoulders. "I'll explain a different way. But first, the good news."

A stalling tactic, he knew, but he didn't stop her.

"The designs you see on the walls? Well, we have them burned into our skin. All of us."

"*You* have these marks?" He'd swum with her—and they'd only worn their undergarments—yet he didn't remember seeing any marks on her. And he'd looked. Hard.

"Yes. I have them."

"Where? And why?"

"On my chest. And they are...wards."

He ignored the first part of her words because yeah, he wanted to stare at the area in question, and focused on the second. "Wards?" Aden blamed the pills for his inability to fit the pieces of this crazy puzzle together.

"As I said, we each have a monster inside us, and they are true beasts of nightmares. Humans would probably liken our condition to that of demon possession. Anyway, the wards in our skin keep those monsters contained inside us and quiet, rather than walking the earth." Now *she* squeezed *his* hand. "Believe me, you never want to encounter one of these creatures. They are savage and brutal and crave the death of those we drink from. Destruction is all they know."

He was quiet a moment, trying to absorb her words. "How did you get them? And do *you* have one inside you?"

As she started to reply, five men stepped forward to form a half-moon around him, each watching him expectantly. They clutched bejeweled goblets, thick red liquid swirling inside. Blood, no doubt. He smelled the coppery tang.

"You remember your council, I'm sure," Victoria said, sounding relieved that their conversation about the monsters was over.

Not even a little. "Of course." He met her gaze, silently telling her they'd be discussing those monsters again. Very soon. Then he turned back to the…councilmen, he supposed they were called. They were older, almost identical to each other with silver hair, strong builds and only slightly lined skin. Plus, their fangs were visible, poking from their lips.

Were they hungry? For him? If he'd had his wits about him, he might have been scared. No way could he fend off five determined vampires at once. Sure, his blades were anchored in his boots, as always, but those blades were useless against such creatures.

The only useful weapon he had was Vlad's ring. Oh, yeah. He glanced down at his right hand and saw the opal winking in the light. He was suddenly grateful to Riley for insisting he wear it.

"Now that Victoria has explained about the beasts, let us move on to more pressing subjects," one of the councilmen said. Before Aden could ask what could be more pressing than monsters, he continued, "There is much we must decide upon."

"Where will you live, for one?" another said. "Here or with your humans?"

The rest jumped right in, peppering him with questions as briskly as Thomas had earlier.

"And if you *are* with your humans, how then will we call upon you when we need you?"

"Also, you must be introduced to our allies. When shall I set the meeting?"

"Also, you must choose a queen."

"And you—"

"Give him a chance to catch up," Riley barked, silencing them.

Aden was surprised when the men immediately bowed their head in agreement. Two even apologized. Riley was a guard, not a prince or a vampire at all, yet they'd obeyed him without rebuke. Very interesting.

"So, to answer your questions. I'll live at the D and M Ranch, just as before," he said, and all eyes returned to him. He traced his thumb over the ring. "I'll meet your allies sometime next week—" this week was for the witches "—but it'll have to be after school. Just let me know when, and I'll be there." Or here. Wherever. And who were their allies? As far as he'd known, the vampires and werewolves warred with *everyone*. "As for a queen, that will be Victoria." No question. Not that he was ready to get married. Not that he'd be king for long.

Again, she squeezed his hand.

All five councilmen frowned at him. "You can't simply pick the princess Victoria. You have yet to spend time with our other females," one said.

"I don't need to spend time with them," he replied. "I won't change my mind."

"Complaints will be raised," another said, irritated.

Aden shrugged. "I don't care."

"Fathers of eligible daughters will rebel, for they desire a chance, at the very least, to forge an alliance with the royal house. You don't want to cause a rebellion so early in your reign, do you?" a third asked.

"No, but I—"

"Good, good. It's settled, then." Each of the five raised their goblets, smiling now.

He shook his head. "I don't understand. What's settled?"

"You'll meet the rest of our females so that their fathers won't rebel."

Aden pinched the bridge of his nose. "No," he insisted. "I won't."

The men muttered amongst themselves for several minutes before nodding and facing him. Their determination was palpable.

"We will compromise," the tallest among them said. "You'll meet only five female vampires, not including Victoria, each chosen by a member of the council. You will rendezvous with each girl and on the day of your coronation, you will name your favorite. That favorite shall be your queen."

Uh, what now? Rendezvous equaled date, he suspected, and he did not want to date. And *five* of them?

"He agrees to your compromise," Victoria said without revealing any hint of her emotions.

Aden opened his mouth to deny her claim, but the men wandered off, slapping each other on the back in a job well done.

"Aden," she said.

His narrowed gaze swung to her. "I don't care what you told them. I'm not dating anyone else." She was the only girl he wanted. The only one he dreamed about, hungered for...

Her expression was blank, just as it had been when she'd arrived at the ranch earlier. Only this time, he doubted she was "exaggerating" to be more humanlike. This was not a "ha-ha, let's tease" subject.

"They were right." She released his hand, severing all contact. "If you refuse to date anyone else, families will complain, and complaints will lead to unrest. Unrest to danger. You face enough of that already."

Was she trying to protect him again? Or was she really okay with the thought of him seeing other girls? Because *he* might pound any guy who looked at *her* into dust. Then spit on that dust. Then flush that dust down the toilet.

"I'd rather deal with the danger," he said through gritted teeth.

"Well, I wouldn't." Her expression remained implacable, her tone dead.

"Don't care." She was mentally pushing him away, he realized. One second comforting him, the next seemingly done with him, and he didn't like it. For his own good or not.

"This must be done, Aden."

"No. I—"

"Wonderful. A lovers' spat. Let's mingle instead," Riley said, giving him a push, "and spat later."

Aden and Victoria glared at each other for a moment. Then she nodded stiffly, and he followed suit. But this wasn't over. On any level. He was *not* dating other vampires. And she was going to apologize for acting like she didn't care. Unless she hadn't been acting. Perhaps vampires saw nothing wrong with dating more than one person.

What did he know?

She had kissed him while engaged to Dmitri, after all. But she'd hated Dmitri, and had wanted nothing to do with him. Still. If that was the case, she could be seeing someone else right now. And if *that* was the case, he didn't know what he'd do. Besides involving himself in a knock-down-drag-out.

"We'll talk about this later," he said quietly, fiercely, before turning away from her.

She gave another stiff nod.

Silent, they entered the masses. Multiple hands brushed against him. Someone thrust a goblet at him and he grabbed it before it could fall and shatter. *Do not forget what's inside and accidently drink.*

"Do I scent a…fairy?" someone suddenly growled.

He froze, Victoria and Riley moving closer to flank him.

Nostrils began flaring. Many vampires cringed. Once again, the room fell silent and all eyes landed on him. Only this time, those eyes were filled with horror and hate.

Great. The cologne must be wearing off.

The vamps backed away from him, until he and his friends were enclosed in a tight circle. Riley was rigid, ready to attack. Victoria finally exuded emotion—fear. Until the werewolf guards pushed their way through the crowd and joined Riley in the circle, facing the vamps, growling for them to stay back.

Unwavering, unquestioning support. *For me.* How odd.

One dark-haired vampire who looked to be Aden's age finally stepped forward. He ignored the wolves, his cold gaze locked on Aden. "Are you already a traitor, cavorting with our enemy?"

Aden laughed. He just couldn't help himself. If escaping repeated death-attempts could be classified as cavorting, then yes, he was.

"You dare laugh?" the boy gasped out.

"You dare question your leader?" Riley snapped.

The boy squared his shoulders and raised his chin. Though he spoke to Riley, his gaze never left Aden. "I will say what most of us are thinking. He's too weak to lead us. Anyone in this room could enslave him in a matter of minutes."

Finally. The threats he'd expected. "Anyone in this room could try." Brave words, foolish words, but he meant them. He would lose, no doubt, but he would fight 'til the end. That had always been his way.

"Our enemies will assume we're as weak as you are and attack," his accuser continued. "You should never have accepted this position."

Accepted? Ha! The position had been thrust at him, and he still didn't want it, but now wasn't the time to try to find someone new. They'd assume he'd done so because he was "weak." "From what I'm told, fairies protect humans. Perhaps those same fairies will wish to ally themselves with you, now that you're being led by one of those *weak* humans they so love."

Not that he was going to lead these vampires, he reminded himself. Again. God, he was digging himself in deeper just to leave with dignity.

Still his opponent persisted. "And goblins? Do you know how to deal with them?"

"Yes. As Vlad did. By sending the wolves into the forest at night to fight them."

"And how can you send the wolves to fight them when you yourself have never fought one? That smacks of cowardice."

"I might not have fought a goblin, but I *have* fought a vampire. Need I remind you the outcome of *that?*"

Murmurs erupted. The circle was tightened. Saliva dripped from the wolves' still-bared teeth.

Finally the boy nodded curtly and rejoined the crowd. Once again, conversations resumed, and the circle expanded. Crisis averted, Aden thought, and yet, relief eluded him. Just how long was this unspoken truce going to last?

TEN

FOR ONCE, Riley didn't pick up Mary Ann to take her to school.

Had he heard about last night already? Was he angry with her?

Or had he been hurt at the vampire mansion?

Stomach churning...

By the time Mary Ann realized he wasn't coming, Penny had already left. Which gave her two options. Walk alone, miss most of first period and be considered absent, or let her dad drive her, and deal with the tardy slip. Either way promised absolute mental torture.

She was a perpetual early bird. If she wasn't ten minutes early, she considered herself late. But trying to converse with her dad...ugh. He'd ask how things were going with Riley; he wouldn't be able to help himself. She wouldn't have an answer. Not now. So he'd feel obligated to mention sex, condoms and STDs. Again.

She would burn to ash with embarrassment, so of course she'd be late forever since she would be *dead*.

In the end, she decided to walk. Her dad didn't try to stop her, but he did thrust an apple into her hand as she flew out the door. She still wasn't hungry, so she chucked the bright red fruit the moment she exited the neighborhood. A stray dog would appreciate it, rather than vomit at the very thought of taking a bite.

If she didn't develop an appetite soon, she'd have to talk to someone.

Sighing, she picked up her pace. She stuck to the main roads, which would shave at least ten minutes from her walk time. Since Riley had pounced into her life, she'd stopped taking this path.

Where are you, Riley? Are you okay? How had Aden handled the introductions? Had anyone attacked him? Mary Ann hated that she'd been left behind. Next time she'd... What? she thought dryly. Demand they take her or she'd give them the silent treatment? Cry alone in her room?

The school parking lot was full when she arrived, but there was no one out front and the halls were empty. Which meant the tardy bell had rung a while ago. As she reached for the front door, she paused. Frowned. Something warm and powerful was wafting through her, filling her nose and mouth and sliding sweetly into her stomach.

Delicious. For a moment, she closed her eyes, savoring. There really was no reason to eat when she experienced *this.* With every inhalation, she was stronger, better, happier. Then she recalled what had followed this same sensation last night, and dread overtook her.

The witch was nearby.

Mary Ann gulped and spun, hands fisting as Aden had taught her. Her gaze darted across her surroundings. Sunlight shone brightly, those stupid blackbirds singing overhead.

The yellowing grass stretched before her, interrupted only by a large oak. Perhaps she'd been mistaken. Perhaps she was wrong and—

The witch stepped from behind the trunk, and their gazes met, locked, clashed. Mary Ann's heart thundered in her chest. This morning the witch wore a plain red T-shirt and jeans. Long blond hair curled over her shoulders, stopping at her waist. Sun-kissed skin soaked up the bright light haloing around her.

"I've been waiting for you." A musical voice, yet it dripped with anger nonetheless.

Every instinct she possessed demanded she run. Last time she'd spoken to this woman, she'd been cursed with death. Still, she held her ground. She'd wanted to question a witch. Now she could. *Without* resorting to kidnapping. "Why?"

"Oh, no. You aren't the one who will be given answers. I am. Why were you spying on me last night?"

Mary Ann squared her shoulders and raised her chin. Time for a little bravery—whatever the price. "You placed a death curse on me. Why *wouldn't* I spy on you?"

A gleam of admiration brightened the witch's eyes. "True."

"And I *will* be given answers. You commanded my friend to attend one of your meetings, yet never told him when and where that meeting will be held. Tell me, and I'll tell him." *Please, please, please.*

"I don't have the information you seek." The witch never took a step, yet the distance between them was suddenly cut in half.

Mary Ann raised her chin another notch. "You're lying."

"Am I?"

Yes, she had to be. "Do you *want* us to die?"

"Maybe."

"Why?"

"You are friends with a vampire, a werewolf, both enemies to my kind, and a boy who draws us with a power we have never encountered before. To echo your question, why *wouldn't* I want you to die?"

Her teeth ground together as her own strategy was used against her. Time for a new angle, she supposed.

She forced her expression to clear, her tone to gentle. "What's your name?"

"Marie."

Mary Ann was surprised by the simply stated answer. "Well, Marie, you should know that we're going to do everything we can to stay alive."

"As would I." Marie's head tilted to the side, her study intensifying. "Do you know what you are, Mary Ann Gray?"

Hearing her own name used, when she'd never offered it, was jolting. "Me?" She laughed; she just couldn't help herself. "I'm human." Average in every way.

"No. You're something more. I can feel you feeding on me."

Her eyes widened in horror. "*Feeding* on you? Are you kidding? I am *not* a vampire."

"I didn't say you were. But you *are* attempting to drain me, and I won't allow it." With every word, Marie's voice sharpened.

Drain her? What— Oh. Yeah. "Drain" must mean "mute" in witch-speak. "I don't mute natural abilities, so you should be able to—"

"Do you purposely misunderstand me? I said nothing about muting. You are sucking at my life-force like a vacuum, trying to take everything and leave a mere shell behind."

"No. I'm not."

"Continue to lie to me, and I'll cast a truth spell on you." Now the witch's voice slashed. "Never again will you be able to lie about anything to anyone. Ever."

Could she really do that? Mary Ann experienced a wave of fury, of frustration and helplessness. And with the emotions, more of that sweet power flowed through her, filling her up, somehow soothing her. "I'm not lying now. I'm not...sucking at you."

"Perhaps you haven't yet realized what you are, then." Marie's eyes narrowed as she backed away, heading into the forest. Odd. She was pale now, her beautiful tan visibly fading. "If you return to town, I'll assume you're there to finish this."

Finish this fight between them, she meant. "You will assume correctly." *Shut up. Just shut up before she attacks!*

Mary Ann couldn't, though. She would not be the weak link anymore.

Marie disappeared behind the branches and leaves, and Mary Ann spun, quickly jetting inside the building. To safety. What had Marie meant by "perhaps you haven't yet realized what you are"?

Riley might know. He had arranged his schedule to match hers, so, if he'd come to school, she'd get to talk to him during class.

The second period bell suddenly rang.

Doors flew open and kids raced into the halls. Lockers creaked open and slammed shut. Mary Ann had to fight her way through the crowd. Great. She'd missed first period entirely, and she had a test tomorrow. Great. Mr. Klien, if he'd come to school after partying so hard last night, would have done a review today. Without that review, she would flunk.

Schoolwork didn't come easily for her. She had to slave for every A, and slave hard, but she hadn't been studying the past few weeks, her attention too focused on, well, staying alive. Last test, she'd gotten a B. Her first. And the last pop quiz? Solid D. Another hated first.

She hadn't told her dad yet. When she did, he would flip. Make that *if* she did. She kept telling herself he was better off not knowing. He had enough to deal with. Besides, she would ace the next one and her overall grade wouldn't be affected.

Oh, who was she kidding? As her peers headed into their next class, she finally admitted the truth. She hadn't told him because she didn't want the hassle of being lectured, maybe even grounded. And hey, maybe Marie really had cast a truth spell on her. Now she couldn't even lie to herself.

"Hey, Mary Ann." Brittany Buchanan walked briskly down the hall, grinning, a paper outstretched in her hand. Her chin-length red hair was the envy of every girl at school. Well, not her twin sister. Brianna's hair was the exact same color, only longer. "Glad I ran into you. Riley asked me to take notes for you in Chem."

"Riley's here?" she asked, claiming the paper.

"Yeah." The redhead sighed dreamily. "I almost passed out when he spoke to me. That boy's voice is *deep*."

Thank God he was here. If he was here, he was okay. "Where is he?" And why hadn't *he* delivered the notes? Why hadn't he picked her up this morning?

"Don't know. But, uh, are you two, like, dating, because…" Brittany bit her bottom lip.

"Yeah." *Hands off!* "We're dating." She hoped. After last night, though, he could have changed his mind. She'd been so sure of herself, so stupid. She may have ruined everything. Now witches were even visiting the school. "Thank you for the notes. I owe you. Big time."

"No problem. And as for payback, if Riley has a brother, you could, I don't know, introduce me." Brittany started biting her lip again.

"He has two." And both were dealing with curses of their own, she recalled. Anyone they were attracted to would think they were ugly. Anyone they weren't attracted to would think they were gorgeous. "I'll see if they're free."

"Thanks!" A grinning Brittany flounced off.

Mary Ann rushed to her locker, threw her bag inside and grabbed her book and binder. The halls were now almost empty, the bell due to ring in less than a minute.

Too much time gabbing, she thought, and she had to haul butt into the three hundred building.

As she barreled around a corner, a door in front of her opened unexpectedly. She stumbled as she darted around it—or tried to. An arm reached out, hard fingers banding around her wrist and jerking her into a darkened room. The moment she was inside, the door closed, locking her in with her assailant.

Her textbook thumped to the ground. *Crap!* She could have used it as a weapon. *Do something. Quick!* Fighting panic, trembling, Mary Ann struck, slamming the heel of her hand into the guy's nose, just like Aden had taught her.

He howled.

She stilled, recognizing that howl. Her heart slammed against her ribs. "Riley?"

"I think you broke my nose," he said, but he sounded amused. That amusement didn't last long, however. He flipped on the light, chasing the shadows away, and she saw that his expression was etched in violence. His eyes were narrowed, lips pulled back, teeth bared. Didn't help that blood poured from his nose.

"I'm sorry. You just, you scared me!"

The tardy bell rang, and she wanted to curse.

"Don't be sorry," he growled. "Be proud. And I'm sorry I scared you."

He didn't sound apologetic. He sounded just as violent

as he looked. She glanced away, needing a moment to calm, and saw that they were in a supply closet. The scent of disinfectant saturated the air. Cleaning supplies lined the shelves.

Deep breath in, out. Finally, her trembling eased and her heartbeat slowed. "Why are you so upset?" she asked, keeping her eyes away from him.

"I'm not."

She ran her tongue over her teeth. Someone needed a truth spell, and it wasn't her. "So where were you this morning? I waited." And waited. Oh, God. Did he hear the whine in her voice?

"After the vampire gig, I had to escort Aden home. As there was a wee bit of opposition from his new subjects, I was afraid someone would follow him and try to take him out, so I ended up camping outside his window all night and all morning."

Her hand whipped up to her throat as her gaze once again clashed with his. "Did they? Try to take him out, I mean?"

"No."

"So he's well?"

"Well, but tired. He still sees the fairy ghost, and that ghost prevented him from sleeping."

Tired and ghost-whispering were far better than mortally wounded. "Where is he now?"

"Here."

"With Victoria," she said with a nod. A statement of fact, not a question. Those two were always together.

"No. Victoria didn't attend today."

"Why? Was *she* hurt?" And why wasn't Riley with her? Usually Riley glued himself to the vampire's side, protecting her his first priority.

Tendrils of jealousy worked through Mary Ann, followed by tendrils of guilt. Their relationship shouldn't bother her. They were princess and bodyguard. If Victoria were injured, Riley would be punished. Perhaps killed.

Or maybe things were different now, under Aden's rule.

"Physically, she's fine," Riley said. "Our councilmen want her to stay away from Aden so that he can date other people."

What? "And she's okay with that?"

Riley's lips twitched. "You'll have to ask her."

"If Aden's king, how can the councilmen tell her what to do? He wouldn't allow it." Would he?

"Aden doesn't live in our home. He's new and no one knows what to make of him. Everyone is looking to the councilmen for answers, and right now, they support him. We don't want that to change, so we're catering to their desires. Besides, to deny them would cause unrest among the people. That unrest would be dangerous for Aden."

Still. Having to watch your boyfriend date other girls? Absolute torture! The thought of Riley with someone else…her hands curled, her nails cutting past skin. "Well, you could have called me. Let me know you weren't coming for me."

He tangled a hand through his dark hair, all hint of amusement fading. The fury returned, darkening his expression. "No, I couldn't have. I would have yelled."

"You're yelling now!" And for no good reason, that she could tell.

"Yeah," he said, still with that fury, but now, it was tinged with something else. Something low and raspy. His eyelids dipped to half-mast as he traced a fingertip along the slope of her nose. "But now we get to kiss and make up." Even his voice had dipped.

Yes, please. "First, why would you have yelled?" Clearly someone had told him what she'd done, but she wanted to hear him admit it before she spilled her guts. "Second, we can't kiss." She backed away from him, not stopping until she hit the door. The closer they were, the headier his wild scent became. The closer they were, the better she could feel the heat radiating off him. The closer they were, the closer she wanted to be. "I need to get to class."

"Actually, you'll have to miss it. We're talking right now."

Uh-oh. The words echoed around her, a threat. "I

can't keep putting off my studies, Riley. Yeah, I'm fine with missing Geometry right now, but anything after that? No. As you know, Spanish is my worse subject, and I need all the help I can get."

"I'll tutor you later. *Si?*"

Yeah, right. Like they'd really pay attention to their books if they were alone in her room. *"No."* The only other Spanish she could recall at the moment was: *No hay tenedor limpio, tenemos que lavar la.* There is no clean fork. We have to wash some.

That wasn't really applicable here.

"Well, you're not going to class until we discuss a few things. Namely, you went into town last night," he said, jaw clenched.

And there it was. The admission. She gulped. "Yes."

"Alone."

"Yes. How did you find out?"

"My brothers. They followed you."

The two wolves who tailed Penny's car. Of course. She should have guessed.

"They said you encountered a witch. Tell me, Mary Ann. Why would you endanger yourself like that?"

You are not the weak link. You are not the freaking weak link. "Did your brothers also tell you that I stayed in the car? Did they tell you Penny and I drove away before Marie could reach us?"

His nostrils flared in outrage. "You know her name now."

Uh-oh.

"You've talked to her." Again, not a question.

"Yes," she admitted softly.

He slapped the wall beside her temples, caging her in. He'd done that yesterday, on the walk to school, and she'd loved it. He'd kissed her, after all. Now, he just looked like he wanted to choke her. The funny thing was, she still loved it. She had only to lift onto her tiptoes and *she* could kiss *him*.

"A witch doesn't need to be close to you to bespell you, Mary Ann." If he knew the direction her thoughts had taken, he gave no notice. "She needs only to see you. You were in danger the moment you left your house. Do you not recall what I told you about spells?"

"I do," she said with a nod.

"Tell me."

A tremor slid the length of her spine. "When a spell is uttered, that spell becomes alive, its sole existence to fulfill its purpose. There is no breaking it. Ever. Even by the witch who cast it."

As she'd spoken, his gaze had lowered and remained on her lips. Tension had wafted from him before he'd snapped his attention back to her face. "That's right," he croaked. "And what would happen if a different type of death spell were cast over you?"

"I would die twice?" she asked dryly.

"Yes, smartie. That's exactly what would happen, and neither time would be pleasant."

She'd never seen Riley so fierce, so intense, but she planned to stand up to him exactly as she'd stood up to Marie. This was too important. "Guess what?" she said, flattening her palms on his chest. His heart thundered to the same erratic beat as hers. "That's a chance I'm willing to take. I'm part of this team, and I *will* help in any way that I can. How is my being in danger any different from you being in danger?"

His eyes narrowed to dangerous slits, even as he pressed deeper into her body. "I heal."

"So do I!"

"Not from death!"

But his kind could be brought back? Hardly, she wanted to snort.

She paused. Wait. *He* had been brought back. She recalled the night he'd told her about his brothers' curse. He should have been cursed that way, too, ugly to anyone he desired, but for him, the requirement of that spell had been met. He'd died, and the werewolves' version of modern medicine had brought him back. Modern medicine could bring her back, as well, she thought defiantly.

Still. Thinking of his death filled her with fear. She couldn't lose him. She needed him.

Mary Ann slid her hands around his neck and gentled her tone. "I'm not going to argue with you about this, Riley. I went into town, yes, but I'm not sorry. Marie will be there tonight, and I know where." Marie had threatened Mary Ann, as good as told her not to return. Which meant she would want to know if Mary Ann disobeyed her. Which meant she would have to be there, watching, waiting. "We can capture her."

"No, we can't." His hands settled on her waist, locking her in place. "She'll be prepared now. We'll walk right into an ambush."

Mary Ann shook her head, refusing to give up. "She thinks she's warned me away. Intimidated me." She told him a bit about their conversation, but left out the part about feeding; she didn't understand that, and until she did, she was sharing the details with no one. And even though she'd thought to talk to him about "what she was," according to Marie, she left that part out, too. Now wasn't the time. "She'll be careless."

"So you hope," he said, his grip tightening.

True. "Even if you're right, we still have the advantage. We'll be prepared for an ambush. Either way, I guess we'll find out tonight. And Riley, do not even think about leaving me behind."

"I'll do what needs to be done, Mary Ann."

Finally she rose on her tiptoes and kissed him. He didn't respond, and she tried not to let it matter. "So will I. And guess what? I changed my mind. I'm hitting second period." With that, she turned and opened the door. He released her without protest and she strode into the hall, never once glancing back.

ELEVEN

GO *AHEAD AND FLUSH* this day down the toilet, Aden thought as he and Shannon walked home from school.

Cars whizzed past them on one side, and trees stretched on the other. They were taking the main roads today rather than the forest. Riley had insisted, and agreeing had been the only way to get rid of him.

All day, Aden had been too tired to listen to his teachers. He had no idea what material had been covered, and even if he had been paying attention, the souls had been too chatty to allow him to concentrate, having just come out of their drug-induced stupor. They'd wanted to know what had happened with the vampires, but he hadn't had a chance to reply.

On and on they'd asked—were *still* asking—until he'd wanted—*still* wanted—to bang his head against the wall. It was probably a good thing, then, that Riley and Mary Ann hadn't spoken to him at lunch. Actually, Mary Ann hadn't spoken to *anyone* at lunch. She'd sat at the table, food untouched in front of her, frowning at everyone who passed. Aden would have asked her what was wrong, but trying to carry on a conversation hadn't seemed wise.

Especially since she'd looked ready to throw something at Riley's head when the wolf announced he would be walking Aden home rather than his girlfriend. But Aden had refused his escort with a firm shake of his head. Having a friend beside him, sure, good times. But a babysitter? No, thanks.

To his surprise, Riley had accepted his refusal after only a few halfhearted protests. He'd been free to go with Mary Ann, after all. Hopefully, they'd work out their problems before midnight, when their little group was supposed to meet up and head into town to hunt—and kidnap—a witch.

Aden was still reeling about that. Kidnap? Really?

Again, there hadn't been an opportunity to discuss it. Not just because of the souls, but because of their audience. And now he had to rush to the ranch so that Dan could take him to Dr. Hennessy's office for their emergency session.

"This sucks," he said.

"W-what does?" Shannon asked, flicking him a glance.

The question battered against the rest of the noise inside his head, and Aden took a moment to decipher it. "My upcoming doctor's appointment. I don't want to go."

If that stupid doc forces any more drugs down your throat, I'm going to shoot myself, Caleb grumbled.

Good luck with that, Julian replied dryly. *I don't think I ever told you this, but it's always been a dream of mine to watch a soul without a body wield a gun.*

Well, bodiless or not, we might wish we could shoot ourselves after today's session, Elijah said grimly.

"Do you know something?" Aden demanded. Elijah's predictions never failed. What the soul thought would happen, happened. Usually, he only knew when people were going to die. Yet more and more lately, he knew other things. Scary things. Like blood flowing in rivers.

"Know w-what?" Shannon asked.

This time, he didn't have to pause to decipher the words. The different conversations were finally streamlining, becoming clearer. "Sorry," he said to Shannon, cheeks heating. "I meant, this has just been such a crappy day, with Mary Ann's silence, Riley's bad mood and the doctor's visit, like I mentioned."

"Yeah. What was wrong w-with you yesterday, man? I've never seen y-you like that."

Aden wanted to confess. He wanted to trust Shannon fully. He really did. But he couldn't predict the boy's reaction to vampires and werewolves and ghosts, which meant he couldn't say a word. If Shannon told Dan, Dan would think Aden was crazy—more than he already did—and send him back to juvie or to another institution. For "help."

"Stress," he said, and left it at that. In a way, that was the truth.

"Know what you m-mean. Sometimes life just seems to be t-too much."

"Having trouble?" Aden knew kids liked to tease Shannon about his stutter, and that embarrassed the boy unbearably.

"What if I t-told you that I—I…" Shannon rubbed the back of his neck, clearly uncomfortable. His stutter was more pronounced now, which meant his emotions were jacked. "M-my parents, they knew I was d-different and—" He pressed his lips together, now mute.

"Come on." Aden grabbed his arm and tugged him into the woods completely, seemingly leaving civilization behind. Yeah, he'd told Riley he'd stick to the main roads. No, he didn't feel guilty. When a friend needed you, you delivered. "It's okay, man. You can tell me anything. Believe me." He'd been different his entire life. Hearing voices, talking to people who supposedly weren't there. Now, summoning creatures from fairy tales and nightmares.

"Yeah, but I'm not d-different like you." Horror

blanketed Shannon's expression. "I-I'm sorry. I—I didn't m-mean that in a b-bad way. I j-just…" He pushed out a shaky sigh. "I've n-never really told anyone else a-and—No, that's n-not exactly true, b-but—"

A boy Aden didn't recognize stepped from behind a tree.

Aden and Shannon drew up short.

Another boy he didn't recognize swung from around the next trunk over. Both were relaxed, seemingly un-armed. The first had pale hair, pale skin and pale blue eyes. Multiple shades of brown and gold colored the other's hair, the same shades swirling in his eyes. Both were tall, stretching over Aden's own six feet. They were leanly muscled, and both wore T-shirts and soft-looking slacks.

Not another fight, Caleb groaned.

Aden reached for his daggers.

"Riley sent us, Majesty," the pale one said, his voice deep and husky. He held up a palm in greeting. "We're his older brothers. Be glad you aren't meeting the younger brothers. I'm Nathan."

"Maxwell," the other said with a nod.

Thank God, Julian said after a relieved sigh. *Were-wolves.*

The horror returned to Shannon's expression, though Aden suspected it was because he'd almost confessed his secret, whatever it was, with strangers nearby.

"Nice to meet you," Aden replied.

Shannon tossed Aden a strange look. "M–Majesty?"

"Nickname," he muttered. To the new boys, he said, "I prefer Aden."

They nodded as they straightened from their relaxed poses.

"Why are you here?" More babysitting?

Maxwell waved his arm, motioning them forward. "To see you home safely, of course. Just in case you deviated from your promised route."

He still wouldn't feel guilty, he told herself as he surged forward, dragging Shannon with him. Nothing he could say in rebuttal, not now. Riley, though, would get an earful later.

Wish Riley would have sent a girl to guard us, Caleb said.

There are more important things in life than girls, Elijah admonished.

Name one.

A moment passed in silence.

Caleb laughed. *See!*

The list is so long I got lost in thought, the psychic grumbled.

Yeah. Right, Julian said, his own laughter blending with Caleb's.

"Guys. Please."

Shannon tossed him another strange look, and Aden motioned to their escorts, trying to pretend he'd been talking to them.

Sorry, Caleb said, repentant. *My bad. I just, I miss Victoria, I guess.*

Aden missed her, too. Monster and all, whatever she'd meant by that. He still didn't fully know. Her demon-possession example hadn't told him much. Did she morph into an actual beast or just exhibit beastly qualities? Either way, she'd been mortified to tell him.

Didn't she realize he would care for her, no matter what? Didn't she realize that this, whatever it was, made her better able to understand him and his differences, and offered more proof that they belonged together?

There was absolutely no way he'd date those other girls. That simply wasn't going to happen, whether Victoria was fine with the idea or not.

The newcomers didn't speak again, even when they reached the edge of the forest and the ranch came into view. They simply backtracked, soon disappearing. Aden didn't get a chance to ask Shannon about his problem, though. Ryder and Seth were at the edge of the property, smoking.

When Shannon spotted them, he drew up short again. Only this time, a little color flooded his face. He was… blushing? Really? Why?

Aden closed the rest of the distance. "Why aren't

you inside?" Usually, they were doing chores this time of day.

"Mr. Thomas didn't come in again today," Seth said with a shrug. He raised the butt to his lips and inhaled, his wrist turned so that Aden had a full view of the fanged snake tattooed there. "We did our chores early and called it a day."

And then they'd snuck out to smoke. Dan would rage if he saw them inhaling "cancer sticks," as he called them.

"Want?" Ryder asked, claiming the butt and offering it to Aden.

"No, thanks."

Shannon finally approached, though he remained outside the little half-circle. "Where's D-Dan?"

Ryder immediately looked down at his shoes. He handed the cig back to Seth and tangled a hand through his hair. "He had to check on his cows or something and said he'd be right back."

Maybe he'd luck out, and Dan would arrive too late to take him to Dr. Hennessy. *Like you're really that lucky.*

Shannon motioned to the cigarette with a wave of his hand. "T-then maybe you should put that out."

Ryder's head snapped up, his eyes narrowed. "Maybe you should make me."

"T-thanks for the invite, but I'll pass. I mean, why b-bother?" Shannon's hands balled into fists, and the image caught Aden's attention—as if it were important. As if it were…life-changing. Why? "You already smell like an ashtray."

Tension crackled between them, thick and palpable. Usually, they got along just fine. Clearly, though, something had changed.

"So, uh, what's Dan going to do about Thomas?" Aden asked, hoping to distract them from their anger. He brushed off his uneasiness. There was no time to ponder it now.

Seth shrugged. "He tried calling the guy, but someone else answered, a Ms. Brendal. She said she was his sister and that he'd disappeared. She also said she'd be by later to talk to us. Fingers crossed she's hot."

Guilt consumed Aden. Guilt and fear. Ms. Brendal. She claimed to be Thomas's sister. If she had told the truth, she was a fairy. Which meant another enemy of the vampires would be coming to the ranch. Asking questions. Would Aden be forced to kill someone else? A woman this time? He shuddered. *Please, God, no.*

Gravel suddenly crunched up ahead, and Aden saw Dan's truck coming up the long driveway. Nope. He wasn't that lucky. His stomach sank.

Seth tossed the cigarette on the ground and smashed the butt with his shoe. Ryder whipped out a tiny can of body spray from his pocket and hosed everyone down. Shannon coughed and glared, but didn't protest.

"I better get going," Aden said, fighting dread and trudging forward. When he was certain the wind wouldn't carry his voice back to the boys, he muttered, "Elijah, are we coming out of this unscathed?"

Silence.

Aden stiffened, stumbled.

You might, the psychic finally said, *but I don't know about us.*

"Tell me about the voices, Aden."

"I don't hear voices anymore, Dr. Hennessy."

"You're lying to me, Aden, and I don't like liars. Tell me. About the. Voices."

"I don't hear voices anymore, Dr. Hennessy."

The same conversation had been replaying between them for over an hour. Aden was tired and fighting sleep, lying in the doctor's plush recliner, the lights dimmed, and peering up at a plain white ceiling. His lids were heavy, keeping them open a difficult chore. Didn't help that soft music played in the background. Dr. Hennessy sat behind him, papers rattling every so often, but even that had a lulling effect.

Bor-ing, Caleb said with a yawn.

Lame, Julian agreed.

Remain on guard, please, Elijah said, but even he sounded fatigued. *I don't trust this man.*

I'm always on guard, Caleb retorted.

This time, Julian yawned. *You're a liar, and Dr. Hen is pushy. Not a good combo.*

Aden agreed.

"—and as you know, I've read reports from your other doctors."

Great. He'd lost track of the conversation. "So?"

"So, when you were younger, you told several of them that these voices are souls and those souls possess special powers."

"I lied." No way would he trust Dr. Hennessy with the truth. That would only score him more medication, more sessions like this one. "No one has special powers."

"So you admit there are souls, then? They just don't have any otherworldly abilities?"

He ground his teeth. "No. I didn't say that."

"Are you telling me that one of the souls can no longer time-travel?"

Aden stiffened. Eve had been the time-traveler, sometimes sending him back into younger versions of himself. One wrong word, and he would change the future, sometimes returning to a different reality than he'd left.

He didn't think he could time-travel now that Eve had passed on, and anyway, he was too afraid to try. The consequences were too vast, and he was too happy with his life. Well, most of it.

"Aden," the doctor prompted.

"Time-travel is a myth," was all he said.

"As mythical as predicting when other people are going to die?"

"Yes," he croaked. "Where are you going with this, Dr. Hennessy?"

"Oh, I'm sorry. I must have given you the impression that it's all right to question me. It's not. I ask. You answer."

Aden's hands fisted. He'd had a lot of doctors over the years, but this one was by far the worst. As condescending as he was, Aden had to wonder if the man even had a degree. "Better yet, how about if I just don't talk at all?"

"That's all right, too," Dr. Hennessy replied easily, as if that's what he'd wanted all along, surprising the hell out of Aden. "Silence is better than lies."

They would see about that.

One minute ticked by after another, not a word spoken. Soon Aden's eyelids grew even heavier. The ceiling began to blur, becoming one giant white blob. He blinked rapidly, trying to stay alert, but on and on the soft music played in the background. He thought he recognized the melody. "Hush Little Baby." What an odd song to pick for grown patients. But even the voices quieted, listening, falling…

"You're exhausted, Aden."

"Yes," he found himself replying from a sea of black. Black? Yes, he thought. He was floating, the white gone, darkness all around him. His eyelids must have closed for good, then. He tried to open them, but they were glued together.

"You're relaxed."

"Yes." And he was. Lost, still floating. No cares. No secrets or problems. Just…freedom.

Dr. Hennessy asked him another question, but he couldn't make out the words. They were too jumbled. Odd, then, that he responded anyway. What he said, though, he couldn't be sure. Again, odd. And yet, he didn't care. Such peace.

This was heaven, he thought. All that black. So tranquil. So quiet. He wanted to set up shop and stay forever. Perhaps Victoria could even join him. Yes. How kickass would that be? Just the two of them, floating and drifting and relaxing.

Victoria.

He frowned. Here was a care. A care he liked. The thought of her caused the sea to part in a thin line, a little light seeping into his awareness. Where was she? What was she doing? When would he see her again? Tonight, he hoped. They were supposed to meet up, weren't they? Except, what if she stayed away, like she'd done at school?

He was talking again, he realized, but again, the words were unclear to him.

He should leave the black. Victoria couldn't come here. There were no doors, only that tiny line of space. Wait. If there were no doors, how had *he* gotten here? And how was he supposed to leave?

A tiny spark of panic caused the line to widen, and more white flooded that endless sea of black. Another care. This one, he hated, but still he didn't want to shake it. This wasn't right. Something was wrong.

Aden.

The voice called to him, echoing. He should recognize it, he thought, panic rising. Who was here? He couldn't bridge the gap between question and answer.

Aden.

His name had been more insistent that time. Maybe… Elijah?

Aden!

Yes, yes. That was Elijah. What was Elijah doing here? How had Elijah joined him?

ADEN!

"What?" he found himself muttering, and this time he heard himself. His voice rattled inside his skull, and it was like being thumped in the brain, jolting him.

Aden, you have to wake up. I think he hypnotized you.

"What!" His eyelids popped open, practically ripping at the seams. His gaze roved, wild. Dr. Hennessy sat on the end of the recliner, one hand braced beside Aden's knees, the other clutching a voice recorder. He was leaning forward, that recorder outstretched, mere inches from Aden's mouth.

There was something…off about him just then. Underneath his plain, human exterior, Aden saw something soft, almost glittery. Something…pretty. As if he had longer, thicker hair. Pale, like snowflakes. As if he had eyes of sparkling brown rather than dull and lifeless ones, and full, pouty lips.

His stomach rolled. He was *not* attracted to his doctor.

Instinctively, Aden shoved him and the doctor fell off the chair, thudding onto the floor with a gasp. What. The. Hell? "What do you think you were doing?" he demanded.

Dr. Hennessy pushed to his feet with as much dignity as he could muster. He still clutched that recorder, but he quickly stuffed the little black device into his pocket, slid his glasses up his nose and smoothed the lint from his shirt and pants.

"I think that's enough for one session. Mr. Reeves is waiting in the lobby for you."

Bile rose in Aden's throat, burning like acid. *What*

did I say? What did I tell him? He had to get that voice recorder. And wasn't that just perfect? His to-do list lengthened every day.

Dr. Hennessy must have sensed the direction of his thoughts because he strode to his desk and punched a button on his phone.

"Yes?" a female voice asked from the speaker.

"Please let Mr. Reeves know Aden and I are finished. He can now collect the boy."

Well played. Aden's eyes narrowed as he sat up. There was nothing he could do now. Not without causing a scene. He would be back, though. And he *would* get that recorder. No matter what he had to do.

✝WELVE

AT THE RANCH, Aden ate a sandwich. Or five. Afterward, he showered while Mr. Thomas stood in the back of the stall and yelled at him. He had his arms braced beside the nozzle, the hot spray hitting him directly in the face. He tried not to care that his first couples shower was with another guy.

"You smell like my sister," the fairy ghost snarled. "Where have you been?"

So. Ms. Brendal had been telling the truth. "Tell me about her. Your sister." Like, did she attack first and ask questions later? And had she been watching Aden without his knowledge? Other than the ghost prince, he hadn't been around a fairy—that he knew of.

"You will not touch her! Do you hear me? I will kill you first."

"I hear you. I just know that it'll be hard for you to see that threat through since you're dead and all." He shouldn't encourage a conversation, but he really hoped

Thomas would accept what he was and quiet down. "For the record, though, I have no intention of hurting your sister."

There was a heavy pause. Momentary—as always. "I want to leave. Why can't I leave?"

"To depart from this world, you have to do in death whatever you regret not doing in life," he said, turning. That, he knew for fact, since that was how he'd lost sweet, motherly Eve.

Thomas crossed his arms over his chest. "My last wish was to kill you."

"Then I guess we're stuck with each other because you can't get your hands on a weapon." Aden twisted the knob, the water pressure easing, then stopping. He stepped out of the stall and grabbed a towel.

Thomas continued to rant, but Aden easily tuned him out. And not because of any medication.

On the drive home, Dan had told him to continue taking his new pills just to prevent another scare like yesterday's. He'd even walked Aden to his room and watched as he put a little white tab on his tongue and swallowed. Of course, the moment Dan had left, Aden had spit the pill in the trash. He must be getting better at compartmentalizing each distraction, as he'd done with Shannon in the forest today. Or maybe he was simply too distracted to listen.

What had Dr. Hennessy done to him? He'd started to

mention the forced hypnosis to Dan, but had changed his mind when Dan became a supporter of Operation Take Your Pills.

Frowning, Aden patted himself down and wrapped the towel around his waist. He padded through the hall to his bedroom. It was empty. Where was Shannon? He heard muttering from the other rooms, some of it angry, but the doors were shut and he couldn't tell who was fighting with whom. This late in the evening, the boys usually holed up and chilled with their roommates.

With a sigh, Aden dressed in his customary jeans and a T-shirt.

"You're going out again?" Thomas gritted out, claiming his attention. The ghost paced from one side of the bedroom to the other. "Where are you going? You can't leave me here!"

Wear something sexier, Caleb said. *We're gonna see Victoria.*

Leave him alone, Elijah replied. *We have more important things to consider. I mean, really. No one's mentioned Aden's parents in days. When are we going to start looking for them? Finding them will benefit all of us.*

His parents. He'd managed to walk the Forget Them path for days and Elijah's reminder was like being shoved in front of an oncoming bus.

They'd given him up when he was a toddler, and

hadn't checked on him since. For that, he hated them. Still. He had to talk to them. Sooner rather than later. They might know why he was the way he was. They might have a relative just like him.

More than that, however, he would be better able to search for information about Elijah, Caleb and Julian along the way. Like who they used to be, what their final wish had been. Then he could free them. If they still wanted to go.

You eager to pass on or something? Julian asked the psychic.

Aden had dreaded having this chat, too afraid of the answers.

Yes. No. I don't know. I'm just curious about who I was. Maybe, like Eve, I knew Aden's parents. Maybe I did something wonderful with my life. Knowing would be…nice. And if nothing else, the more we can find out about Aden's abilities, the better equipped we'll be to help him deal with everything going on around him these days.

Well, I'm hungry, Caleb said, and Aden suspected it was because the soul was just as afraid as he was. *Do me a solid and see if Mrs. Reeves has extra sandwiches in the kitchen.*

"Give me a minute," Aden replied as he tugged on his boots.

"I asked you a question," Thomas snarled. "Where are you going? Answer me this time!"

"Or what? You'll try to slap me?" he asked dryly.

Hinges creaked, and then Shannon was strolling into the room. He paused, looking Aden over. "Nice." Then he blushed, like he'd done earlier. "I—I didn't m-mean—"

"I know," Aden said on a laugh. "No worries."

Thomas the eavesdropper stilled and quieted.

"I'm g-glad I caught you." Shannon closed the door, shutting them inside, and leaned against the wood, head back, eyes closed. He sighed, the sound weary.

"Something wrong?" Aden asked.

Slowly Shannon's eyelids opened. His green eyes were bright with apprehension. "I—I need to tell you s-something. You need to k-know, and keeping it i-inside..."

"Yeah, I know." Secrets ate at you. Proof: Aden was currently riddled with holes. "You can tell me, whatever it is. I won't judge you. Like I can, you know." He leaned his hip against the side of the desk and crossed his arms over his chest. He glanced at Thomas, who was still listening, and decided to forge ahead anyway. "I'm Crazy Aden, remember?"

"You aren't c-crazy."

"Thanks."

Shannon pushed out a breath. "W-we're roommates, and if y-you find out later, y-you'll be pissed, and t-then you'll want t-to kill me."

Sounds serious. Do you think— Caleb growled. *Do you think he laid a move on our girl Victoria?*

Nah. I bet he murdered his last roommate, Julian said.

"Tell me!" Aden didn't mean to shout, but the thought of Shannon and Victoria together was enough to make him—

"I-I'm g-gay," Shannon said, and the words were uttered with shame and remorse and all kinds of guilt.

Gay. Aden blinked. That was all? Seriously? "Okay."

Those green eyes widened. "O-okay?"

"Yeah."

"But, w-were you not l-listening? I'm queer."

Aden rolled his eyes. "I don't know about that. You're a pain in the ass sometimes, but I wouldn't say you're weird."

"You know w-what I meant," was the snapped reply.

"So, too soon to joke about?"

That earned him a scowl.

"Shannon. Seriously. You're gay, not diseased. It's fine. I'm not worried."

The scowl vanished, replaced by astonishment. "But we're s-sharing a room."

"So? Are you afraid I'll get handsie?"

A smile twitched at the corner of his friend's lips, and

he seemed to shed ten pounds of tension. "You're really all r-right with it?"

"Yes, I'm really all right."

"Thank you."

"Am I the only one who knows?" Aden asked. "Do you want me to keep quiet?"

"R-Ryder knows."

Today in the forest, that blush, Ryder's inability to look at Shannon... Ah. Everything made sense now.

Shannon peered down at his feet, pushed out another breath, then banged his head against the door once, twice. "I t-thought he was, too, but no. He d-doesn't swing that way."

He'd clearly been hopeful, though. "Is your being gay the reason your parents kicked you out?" Aden asked.

A nod. "Part of it. T-they had heard about Dan's ranch and called h-him. I'd started to get into t-trouble, shop-lifting, drinking, t-that sort of thing, and it was e-either come here or hit the s-streets. I came here."

"Good choice."

Another smile began to break its way free. "I think so, too."

A tentative knock sounded at the window, and Thomas hissed in a breath. Shannon straightened and Aden turned. There, beyond the glass, stood a blonde vampire. Victoria's gum-chewing sister.

Frowning, concerned, Aden stalked to the window

and opened it as quickly as he could. Cool evening air blustered inside. "Stephanie?"

She popped a bubble. Moonlight bathed her, illuminating the paleness of her skin. "The one and only."

"Another vampire princess who belongs to Vlad. She. Must. Die." Thomas raced forward with every intention of attacking. Only, he smacked into the same invisible wall Aden had encountered in his world with a thud. When he realized he was blocked, he pounded at the wall with his fists.

Aden forced himself to concentrate on the vampire. "What are you doing here? Is something wrong with Victoria?"

"Physically, no, but I was one of the girls chosen to date you. So yeah, there's something wrong with her mentally."

He did *not* like hearing that. "Take me to her. I need to—"

"Slow down, cowboy. She'll be fine."

Fine. That wasn't good enough. "You're still taking me to her. And FYI, I won't be dating you."

"'Cause you only want Vic. Yeah, yeah, I know." Stephanie rolled her eyes, flattened her hands on the pane and leaned toward him, saying quietly, "I also know she likes you and didn't want strangers laying the moves on you, especially when she can't trust them not to bite and enslave you. So here I am. Chosen, and not fighting it." Now she splayed her arms and turned, giving him a full view of her bright red tank and microscopic miniskirt. "Me, in all my glory. Do you know how lucky you are? Lauren and I were promised to others, but with Vlad's death all bets are off and you get a chance with me. And you might want to rescind your command, oh, mighty king, because if I take you to her now, I'll be taken off the list, and it's better for everyone if I'm on it."

His stomach churned into hundreds of little knots. "All five girls have been chosen, then?"

"Yep. And let me tell you, the council didn't want you dating another of Vlad's daughters, but most of the girls basically had to be forced to agree to see you—sorry, but it's true, you being human and all—even though their fathers want to make that royal connection, and as I was volunteering... By the way, I've met every single girl on the list. So, I change my vote. You aren't a lucky boy."

"I hadn't realized," he replied dryly.

She laughed, and it was a musical sound.

That was the kind of laugh he wanted to elicit from Victoria, at least once a day. Soon, he thought wistfully— and then felt all kinds of guilty. Victoria was perfect, just the way she was. She was smart and dedicated and understood him and his past. Without judging. With acceptance. And he didn't mind working for one of her beautiful smiles. Liked having to do so, even. Was proud and excited when he won one. Except, she deserved to be happy *all the time* and now he was probably making her miserable.

At least, he kind of hoped he was.

More guilt bombarded him. He shouldn't want her to be jealous, but he far preferred jealousy to the indifference she'd shown him at the vampire mansion.

"Aren't you going to invite me in?" Stephanie asked.

He glanced over his shoulder. Shannon still stood against the doorway, expression curious. Thomas was still beating at that invisible wall. "Actually," he said, turning back to her, "I'll join you out there." He was due to meet Riley, Victoria and Mary Ann in the forest, anyway. In…two hours, he realized with a glance at the clock. Not soon enough. Not that he didn't like Stephanie, but he was uncomfortable with this situation. "Shannon," he began, only to be cut off.

"Yeah, I k-know the drill. Go. I'll cover for you."

"Thank you."

As Aden sheathed his blades in their ankle holsters, Stephanie said, "Don't forget your ring."

Vlad's ring. Oh, yeah. He removed the opal from the drawer where he'd stuffed it after returning from the vampire mansion, slid the metal in place and climbed outside. God, it was cold. So cold mist formed in front of his face every time he exhaled.

They walked side by side toward the forest, but just before they reached the line of trees, Stephanie grabbed his arm and stopped him.

"Goblins and wolves are out there." Even as she spoke, a howl rent the air. The howl was quickly followed by a high-pitched screech—a sound no human could have made. He cringed.

"Where should we go?" he asked.

"We're going to be all romantic and crap and sit out here, under the stars. I have to report back, you know, so we have to make this seem real." Grinning, she waved her arm, motioning to his feet. "Behold."

Looking down, he found a black blanket, spread out and velvet soft. So. They really were going to be "romantic and crap." With a sigh, Aden plopped down and stretched out, staring up at the sky, stars twinkling from their perches like diamonds.

Stephanie lay down beside him. "So what do you want to talk about?"

I bet she's soft, Caleb said.

You're gonna get us in trouble, Elijah snapped.

"I want to talk about Victoria."

She snorted. "I'm shocked. Really. Well, what do you want to know?"

"Are you okay with my dating her?"

"Why not? You're cute."

A compliment. Surprising. "Yeah, but your other sister hates me."

"She does indeed. Like a rash."

He smiled; he just couldn't help himself. "Thank you for sparing my feelings."

"Welcome."

"You're...different," he said. He hooked his hands under his head, hoping that would warm them. "Not like the others."

"I know. Isn't it wonderful?" she asked, nudging him with her shoulder. Heat wafted from her, enveloping him.

His smile widened. "Victoria says you used to sneak out."

"Yep. Every chance I got."

"You weren't afraid of your father?"

"Of course I was. We all were. He believed punishment was the only way to train someone, and that man was all about training us to be the undefeatable army he'd always craved as a human. But Lauren was his favorite, his main concern. She is a warrior through and through, after all, so most of his attention was directed at her. Me, I was too...*uninterested,* I guess is the word, but he wanted my mother happy. Females were his weakness, not that he would ever admit that aloud. He admitted to no weaknesses. Anyway, he washed his hands of me, didn't even give me a wolf guard, and left me in my mother's loving care."

She spoke as if her father's desertion didn't bother her, as if the man had done her a favor. "What about Victoria?"

"What about her?"

"He didn't wash his hands of her?"

"We don't share the same mother, and he didn't care to make hers happy. So no, there was no washing." Stephanie rolled to her side, peering over at him, her hands tucked under her cheek. "He pushed her to be his next Lauren. If she laughed, she was punished. If she disagreed with him, she was what? Punished."

No wonder Victoria was so serious. No wonder she rarely relaxed. Aden was suddenly glad the man was dead.

Something about that thought disturbed him, causing the fine hairs on the back of his neck to rise and his brain to ache. Every time he thought about Vlad, he felt this way. Why?

"So what are your plans for us?" Stephanie asked. "For all the vampires?"

"To find you a new king," he answered honestly. "Before that, though, I don't know."

Her eyes widened, her expression pure puzzlement. "You don't want to be king? Really?"

"Really."

"That's just… I mean, wow. Who doesn't want to rule the best vampires on the planet?"

"Me."

She popped a bubble. "That's wise, I guess. I mean, you're just a human. But in the meantime, if you make it to your coronation, I have some suggestions."

"Wait. Remind me when the coronation is taking place."

"Twelve days, my friend. Twelve long, long days."

Long? When time was ticking by so swiftly and so unmercifully he could barely keep track? Still. Once he'd dealt with the witches, he'd have…roughly a week to find his replacement. That was doable. He hoped.

"Meanwhile, you're the man in charge, so your word is still absolute. So will you listen to my suggestions or not?"

"Let's hear them."

"First, no more black robes. You didn't pitch a fit when I dropped mine, haven't said anything about my lack of proper dress now, and I thank you for that. Anyway, we need color. Lots and lots of color. Not just me, but all of us. Only, everyone else is too afraid to risk punishment to act without approval."

"Color. Done." He knew Victoria secretly loved pink.

Stephanie clapped. "Excellent. I'll spread the word when I return. Now. Second suggestion." Another of those high-pitched screeches rang out, this one closer, and Aden sat up. So did Stephanie. "Uh, maybe we should move our blanket closer to the ranch."

A third screech echoed, this one even closer. They hopped to their feet, but not before Aden fisted his daggers. A few feet away, leaves and branches rattled. As he moved in front of Stephanie, a small, deformed man burst through the thicket, heading straight for Aden, as if pulled by an invisible rope.

"Goblin," Stephanie yelped.

Not a man, then. The misshapen creature was the same height as Aden's kneecaps. He had pointy ears, yellow skin and eyes of red fire. Worse, his teeth were like sharpened sabers. Though the goblin wore clothing, the material was slashed to ribbons, revealing a gaping hole where his heart should have rested.

Great. Not just a goblin, but a dead goblin.

"Julian," he muttered. If the soul was close to a dead body, that dead body awoke. Always. And then, of course, that newly awakened corpse attacked Aden, hungry for his flesh. Again, always.

My bad.

Aden had fought corpses a thousand times before and knew removing the head was the only way to stop them. Only, he'd never fought a nonhuman one before. Would decapitation work this time? Guess he'd find out.

When the creature reached him, he arced one of his

blades toward the thing's throat, but just before contact, the goblin ducked and bit into his kneecap.

Aden howled, fire instantly sparking in his leg and spreading. Adrenaline pumped through him, too, quickly dousing the flames and keeping him on his feet. He punched the creature's temple, dislodging its teeth—ripping his own jeans and flesh in the process—and sending the little fiend flying to his side.

The goblin lay there a moment, chewing the bleeding hunk of Aden's skin, ecstasy filling those red eyes—along with hunger for more. Aden swooped in and slashed, using both his blades, crisscrossing his arms like scissors. The goblin rolled out of the way, fast, so fast, escaping the deathblow.

Get him! Julian cheered.

You can do it, Caleb said. *Maybe.*

Steady, Elijah added. *If you can stall him—*

The goblin leapt at him. Aden spun and the creature darted by, hitting the ground before jumping back to his feet. He jolted forward, closing the distance, daggers once again raised. He would succeed this time. Nothing would stop him.

Or maybe something would.

A dark wolf burst from the trees, flying past him and slamming into the goblin, chomping at his midsection. That didn't slow the goblin down, however. The creature scratched and bit, angry, hungry, uncaring about pain. Corpses never cared. Perhaps they simply didn't feel.

The wolf raked sharp claws over the goblin's face. Flesh sizzled, actually burning, and black blood squirted.

"That's not going to stop it," Aden shouted, racing forward.

The wolf tossed him an irritated glance. Dark brown and golden fur was matted to its face, and one of its eyes was nearly swollen shut. A growl of warning sounded.

Move away!

The hard male voice reverberated through his head, unfamiliar...maybe.

"Hold him down." Though Aden suspected the wolf, whoever it was, would attack him for interfering, he raised his blade and struck. Finally. Success. The goblin's head detached from its body and rolled away. That body twitched, then stilled.

Aden was panting as his arms fell heavily to his side.

"Good job, boys," Stephanie said, skipping over to them. "For a minute there, I thought we were all goners."

The wolf turned pale blue eyes on Aden—Nathan, Aden suddenly realized, Riley's brother—before focusing on Stephanie. A moment passed in silence.

She paled, shook her head. "No."

The wolf uttered another growl.

One step, two, she backed away. "But I'm supposed to be here. The councilmen told me to—"

More silence. Another growl.

"Fine," she snapped, and vanished, there one moment, gone the next.

Okay. What had just happened?

Nathan turned his heated gaze to Aden. *I killed the thing, yet it came back to life a few minutes later. How?*

The wolf was speaking inside his head, he realized. He didn't like the extra noise, but he wasn't going to complain. "I did it," he admitted. "I wake the dead, but only when I'm close to them," he added in a rush. "So if there are any more dead goblins in the forest tonight, I'd get rid of them quickly if I were you."

Nathan nodded. *Thank you. For protecting the princess.* The praise was offered grudgingly.

"My pleasure. But, uh, what did you say to her to get her to leave?" He knew the wolf had said *something.* He just didn't know why the vampires kept deferring to the wolves when the vamps were supposedly the ones in charge.

You'll find, Your Majesty, that wolves are the most feared creatures in the land. Even by their allies. Now, please. Leave the area. Just in case. With that, Nathan bounded off.

"He's right." Riley's voice suddenly echoed around him. "Our claws produce the same *je la nune* contained in your ring. That's why vampires are careful not to anger us. That's also why we try not to use our claws on other creatures. *Try* being the operative word. We don't want them getting their hands on the poison."

Aden turned. Sure enough, Riley, Victoria and Mary Ann were striding forward. All three were frowning. Riley with urgency. Mary Ann with fear. And Victoria with…concern? "And yet you serve them," he said.

"Yes." Riley offered no further explanation. "Now, come on." He waved Aden over before he could ask why. "Enough dawdling. We've got work to do—and it's not kidnapping a witch. Lauren already bagged one."

†HIR†EEN

VICTORIA TELEPORTED EVERYONE to where the witch was being held. First Mary Ann, who begged to be left behind rather than be "thrown across the world like a rag doll." Then Riley. Finally, only Aden remained. When she reached out to take his hand, he stepped back, out of range. His shredded knee screamed in protest, but he allowed no hint of his pain to show.

"I want to talk to you first," he said.

Talk? Kiss her first, then *talk!* Caleb beseeched.

Give the boy some breathing room, Elijah countered.

Aden would have thanked him for supporting his cause, but the psychic finished with: *So he can tell her about Dr. Hennessy.*

Hell, no. There was a mood-killer for sure, and they had more important issues at the moment. Dating issues.

"We're not safe here," she said.

Behind him, amid the trees, a wolf howled. Nathan.

Letting him know he and Victoria were, in fact, properly guarded? That there were no dead bodies nearby? He hoped so, but if not, if the howl was to send him running because other corpses would soon rise, he wouldn't have cared. This was too important. He'd fight anyone or thing for the opportunity to finally hash this out with Victoria.

"We'll be fine."

"Well, there isn't time for this," she said then, waving her fingers at him to motion him closer.

I'm with Caleb. Kiss her, Julian piped up.

Stubborn, Aden leaned against a tree trunk and crossed his arms over his chest. The movement, slight though it was, shot another bolt of white-hot agony through his knee. He'd been bitten by a corpse, something that had happened a thousand times before, so he knew this was only the beginning. This corpse had been a goblin, sure, but corpse saliva, no matter its source, was always the same. Poison. And even now, that poison was working through him, burning him.

Tomorrow, he'd wish he were dead. Again.

He almost laughed. Would he ever catch a break?

"Aden." Victoria's voice snapped him from his morbid thoughts.

"Of course there's time for us to talk. The others will be questioning the witch, so we aren't needed for that."

Her eyes narrowed, and she raised her chin. "Fine. We'll talk. Why don't I start?" She crossed her arms, too. Golden moonlight poured over her, illuminating her flawless skin. Her electric blues pierced him, and those bad-girl lips beckoned him. No wonder the boys wanted him to kiss her first and talk later. *Beautiful.*

"Tell me about your date with my sister," she commanded.

Ouch. Should have expected her to start there, he thought. "I wouldn't call it a date. We talked about possible changes to benefit your people. Like pink being the new black. Then we talked about you." Or would have, if the goblin hadn't busted in. "About how much I...love you." There. He'd said it. Said the words. If ever there was a time to tell her, it was now. He didn't want her worried or unsure about his feelings. "You're brave and caring and you see me as an equal, not a hindrance. I just feel better when I'm with you. Better about myself, about everything."

Her mouth dropped open. "You love me?"

"Yes. I do. I love you," he repeated. "You don't have to say it back. I'll understand if you aren't there yet." Yeah, he would understand—but he sure wouldn't like it.

Her expression softened, and she gazed down at her feet, hands twisting together. There was now a rosy flush to her cheeks. Was she embarrassed by his confession, or had she fed recently? If so, who had she taken from?

Jealousy was a fist inside his chest. *You have to get over that,* he told himself. *She's a vampire. That's what she has to do to survive.*

"I…I love you, too, Aden."

Thank God. Every bit of the jealousy drained. She loved him. She really loved him. "Say it again." No one had ever loved him before. No one.

"I love you, too. So much. You're strong and loyal and you understand me better than I think I understand myself. So yes, I love you," she said again.

He would never get tired of those words.

"And because I love you so much," she said softly, "I have to tell you that the other girls will not allow you to simply talk to them. Or rather, their fathers won't. You'll have to romance them. The girls, not their fathers. God, I'm making a mess of this. What I'm trying to say is, there's no way around it. You have to date them properly."

"No. I don't. I can refuse to see them." Simple as that. He loved her, and she loved him.

Nope, he would never get tired of those words.

"You can't. I told you. That will cause problems. Violent problems."

"I don't care. You're more important."

Her lashes rose, and for a moment, there was hope in

her eyes. But then she blanked her features, showing him more of that emptiness. Emptiness he despised. "Actually, I'm not. For all intents and purposes, you're king now. You're the one who's important to my people."

Was that what her father had raised her to believe? That the king was the only one who mattered? Aden wanted to kill the bastard all over again.

Again? As if a second slaying would be possible?

He frowned. "Look, I don't have a lot of time, Victoria, and I don't want to waste it arguing with you. Especially now."

She ran her tongue over her too-sharp teeth. "That's what I said, but then *you* said we had—"

"I meant alive," he interjected. "Not tonight."

The reminder sobered her. She knew about Elijah's prediction; she knew his life would end all too soon. "Oh."

"Your people will need a new king, anyway, and I'll find them one." Like Riley, maybe. The vampires were willing to let Aden, a human, lead them. So why not a werewolf—a werewolf they already deferred to? He nodded, liking the thought. A lot. It was a perfect plan, really. Except…once again the thought of giving up the title…angered him, and that made no sense

He forced his mind to center on the matter at hand. He'd fought for this moment; he couldn't allow himself to become distracted and ruin it. "Like I said, I don't want to spend what time I have left arguing with you. And I don't want to spend it being shut out for reasons I don't understand."

She stood there, silent, watching him, searching for... what? He didn't know. Finally, she sighed. "What do you want to know? I'll talk, I'll explain."

"What are you feeling right now? About me dating those other girls?"

Caleb laughed. *Dude! You sound like a girl, wanting to share your feelings and stuff.*

Dating 101, Julian told the soul. *Sound like a girl and get the girl. Where have you been? I thought you were supposed to be the expert.*

Her arms fell to her sides, and she wiped her palms against her thighs. "Well, I'm...furious."

With him? "You don't sound furious. You don't look furious."

Her chin lifted yet another notch. "I'm bottling my feelings, Stephanie says."

"So unbottle. You'll feel better, I promise." Oh, gag. He must have channeled one of his many doctors.

She shook her head violently, dark hair doing that dancing thing around her shoulders. "That's too dangerous."

"For who?"

"You."

"Try me." Unless... "The monster inside you..."

Now she gulped, backed two steps away. "What about it?"

"Do you think that monster will hurt me if you un-bottle? Is that it?"

"No. I have the wards," she said, but her tone lacked conviction. "Anyway, I take no chances with my beast. None of us do."

"So every vampire has a beast?"

"Yes."

"And over the years, a few vampires have lost control of theirs?" he asked.

"Yes. It's…awful. The damage is…there are no words to describe the horrors that occur."

So. One mystery was solved at least. Despite her pro-test and her assurance, her fear clearly stemmed from what she thought that enigmatic monster would do to him. "Tell me about these beasts. About why you're so afraid—and why I should be, too."

Chin, another notch higher. Any more and she'd be staring at the stars. "Are you sure you want to know?"

Because she assumed they wouldn't be able to be to-gether once he did? Silly girl. There was only one way to prove her wrong. "Yes. I'm sure."

"Very well, then. We are not shifters, like the wolves. We do not change into another form." Her tone was cold and flat. "But the monster *does* come out of us, a separate entity, and the longer that entity is out of our bodies, the more solid its own body becomes. And as its body solidifies, the tether that once leashed it to us withers and dies."

"Wouldn't that help you, though? Getting rid of the beast?"

"Help us?" She laughed without humor, and it was not a pretty sound. "No. As it solidifies, it strengthens, and we become targets of what used to be our darker half. They blame us for trapping them inside our bodies, after all. Actually, no one is safe. And you should know, my beast has been pounding at my head since I met you, louder every time we're together, wanting out."

Good—and horrifying—to know. But he wasn't going to let fear stop him from getting through to Victoria, from proving he could handle anything she dished out. Even if that meant acting like Prince Charming and slaying her dragon. Literally.

"Does this beast talk to you?" he asked.

"No. Usually he's quiet, and he never uses words. Not like you and I do, at least, but he roars sometimes, and when *I'm* hungry, I can feel *his* thirst for blood. We've been very hungry lately."

Aden's mind whirled. How had the vampires obtained these creatures inside them? Most likely, Victoria had been born with hers. She was the product of a vampire union rather than a human transformed by tainted blood like her father and some of his followers had been.

A transformation no one else had been able to make over the years.

Were the beasts why they'd changed—and survived that change—when others over the centuries had not?

"Did I scare you into silence?" Victoria asked coolly.

"Hardly." They were so much more alike than even he had realized. She knew what it was like to battle noise inside her head. She knew what it was like to fear losing control. "We need to get one thing straight, though."

She blinked over at him, surprised. He'd never used such a fierce tone with her.

Was he really going to do this? Was he really going to take this route?

She'd helped him accept himself. He would help her do the same. So yes, he was.

"Am I your king?" he demanded to know. For the moment, anyway.

Caleb whooped with excitement. *Oh, baby, I am loving this.*

Careful or her monster's gonna eat you, Julian warned. *Got the 411 on that, E?*

Sorry, I'm blank.

Victoria's brow furrowed in confusion. "Yes. You know you are."

"And you have to do whatever I tell you to do? Right?"

"Yes." The word was gritted, as if pulled through a meat grinder. Clearly, she knew what he planned to say next.

"So, as your king, I command you to unbottle your feelings. Here. Now. Let them out."

At first, she gave no reaction. Then she said, "You'll regret that order." Then, shockingly, she screamed. Long and loud, so loud he was sure his eardrums were bleeding, but he didn't allow himself to cringe. He didn't want to discourage her.

When she quieted, she was panting. She scanned her surroundings with wild eyes before marching to a large, round boulder and lifting it in her arms as if it weighed no more than a feather. A second later, that boulder was hurtling through the forest and slamming into a tree trunk. That tree cracked in half, the top falling and slamming into the ground.

Aden remained silent, but, uh, maybe this *hadn't* been such a good idea. Someone—probably Dan—would hear the noise and come gunning. No way Aden could explain this.

My God, Julian said. *Such strength…*

I'm thinking, I don't know, run like hell, Caleb said. *Just a suggestion to, I don't know, save our lives.*

Elijah was as silent as Aden.

Scowling, Victoria turned to the tree in front of her and punched. "I can't save you." Punched again. "You're going to die. To leave me. Those girls…they're beautiful and smart, and what if you like them better? You say you love me now, but you haven't spent time with the others yet. They could charm you. They're more…human than I am. Or what if they hurt you? I'll have to kill them. I *will* kill them. You're mine!"

"You're right about one thing. I'm yours. I'm not going to change my mind about that. I don't care how charming they are, how human they act. I love *you*."

Either she didn't hear him or she didn't believe him. The punches never slowed. This tree split just like the other, the top half crumbling to the ground. Then, glowing blue eyes finally focused on Aden.

Aden, listen to me, man. Run. Please. It was the first time Caleb had ever begged. *What if she turns all that anger to your man business? We could lose our favorite body part!*

Victoria's panting intensified, air sawing in and out of her mouth, probably burning her lungs. She stepped toward him, slowly, menacingly. Her hands weren't cut or bleeding from the jagged bark, he noticed. They weren't even bruised.

"Aden," she growled in a voice he didn't recognize. It was layered, as if two people were speaking at once. Raspy. Enraged. *Powerful.* Her beast?

He kept his expression blank, but couldn't stop cold fingers of dread from creeping down his spine. He'd asked for this, had commanded it. He had to take the bad with the good. "Yes?" If she wanted to break him in half, just like the trees, he'd let her. He wouldn't fight back because he wouldn't risk hurting her.

"You should not have demanded this." One menacing step, two, she continued to approach him. Closer... closer still...

His eyes widened. Was that...could it be...? It was; it had to be. She was halfway to him, and there was something rising above her shoulders. Something monstrous. He gulped. There was a glittery outline of wings stretching from Victoria's back, and over her head, he spied a long snout with big nostrils, black scales and eyes he'd see in his nightmares for years to come. Fire swirled in those eyes. Orange-gold flames that crackled with the promise of a painful death.

The demon reached for Aden, claws outstretched. Not in a threatening manner, he realized with shock, but in... supplication? Surely not.

Still. Aden expected to be cut down the moment Victoria reached him. What he didn't expect was for his girlfriend to grab his wrist and jerk him into the heat of her body. Breath pushed from his nose as the world around him faded, as his feet lost their solid anchor, as his mind scrambled for an explanation. What was happening?

A car suddenly materialized around him. He was at

the wheel, Victoria beside him in the passenger seat. She was still panting, and over and over the beast, which was still perched over her shoulders, reached for him, those claws whooshing through air.

What would happen if the creature solidified, as she'd warned?

"Uh, I think your wards have worn off," Aden said, the souls inside him shouting with concern.

Without a word, Victoria removed her shirt, her bra, leaving her bare from the waist up. Aden's jaw dropped. Dear God. Over her heart were two tiny swirling black and red tattoos his eyes could have traced forever.

Caleb fainted.

Elijah and Julian merely gasped.

"No. They're still there." Her voice was still layered. "Now, kiss me," she commanded, climbing over the console and fitting herself in his lap. Tight squeeze, with the wheel at her back, but he loved it. Her knees pressed against his waist, and her hands tangled in his hair, her nails cutting into his scalp.

Her lips smashed into his, and her tongue, which he welcomed wholeheartedly, thrust inside his mouth. Hot, branding. He wound his arms around her, flattening his palms against her shoulders, trailing them down her spine. So much heat… Her skin was as hot as her tongue, and he wanted to be burned.

On and on the kiss continued, until his every breath

was filled with her. Until her taste—cherries, of all things—was all that he knew. Until she was purring, her sweet little moans blending with his groans. The windows on the car had long since fogged.

Elijah and Julian were blessedly quiet, offering no "helpful" advice about how to make this more enjoyable for her, not telling him everything he was doing wrong. They were probably as awed as he was. Just as lost.

"Are you thirsty?" he managed to say when she kissed her way along his jaw, his neck, stopping to lick his hammering pulse. He opened his eyes, and realized the beast was no longer visible.

"No." Another lick of his pulse.

Tendrils of his jealousy returned. "Who'd you drink from?"

"No one. I've been drinking from bags."

The tension drained from him. Sweet, sweet girl. She knew how much he hated her lips—her wonderful, soft, pleasure-giving lips—on anyone else. "Can't taste as good as fresh blood."

"Doesn't." The word was slurred.

"So start drinking from me." *Please.*

"Want to know you're with me because you love me, not because you're addicted to my bite."

Well, he couldn't fault her for that. Being desired for who you were, not what you could do, was a rare and wonderful thing. He knew because he'd experienced the other side of that coin. Throughout his life, he'd been discarded for what he could do, the person he was never taken into account.

"More kissing," she said.

Like he'd argue with that. Their lips met again, and he lost himself again, hands roaming, exploring. Hers did the same, and he thought this was, perhaps, his first true taste of heaven.

All too soon she pulled back, still panting, lips glistening, ending the kiss. "I-I'm calm now. I can feel my beast inside me. We should stop."

Aden's head fell against the seat rest as he stared up at her. Each of his pulse points was hammering wildly. His blood was molten in his veins, blistering everything it touched, and his lungs had long since smoldered to ash.

"You kissed me to calm down?" he asked.

She gave a hesitant nod.

Part of him wanted to be angry. The other part of him was just happy this had happened. "Well, we need to unbottle you more often," he said, trying to lighten the mood.

A laugh escaped her, and she covered her mouth with her hand, as if she couldn't believe she'd found humor in such a horrifying topic.

He didn't care. His chest puffed with pride. He'd done that. He'd made her laugh again, just as he'd hoped. *That's* what he wanted more of, just as much as the kiss.

"So why did you teleport us to this car?" he asked with a wave of his hand. "We don't need it, do we?"

"Riley and I always keep one nearby, just in case, but no, we won't need it. I wanted a little privacy."

"Smart." He reached up and cupped her face. "Don't shut me out again. Okay? I think I proved I can handle your beast."

"I won't." She fisted his T-shirt, expression darkening, and his heart jumped up to meet her touch. "But, Aden, you will have to date those girls to keep the peace, and that will make me angry."

"Maybe you shouldn't tell me that. I *like* your anger."

Another tinkling laugh filled the car. "Be serious."

"I am. I'm not your father. I don't want you to be afraid to express your thoughts and feelings. Besides, I'm not afraid of your beast." In fact, a part of him still thought the beast had actually *liked* him, wanting to stroke him—or be stroked by him. Which was crazy. "And listen. You have my vow. I won't do anything with those vampires. You're the only one I want."

She traced a hot fingertip down the slope of his nose. "How are you so wonderful, Haden Stone?"

He liked the sound of his full name on Victoria's lips.

"You're the wonderful one. Now get dressed and we'll join Riley. He's probably worried about you."

She rolled her eyes as she climbed back into the passenger seat and tugged on her shirt. "His concern is for you nowadays."

The loss of her weight, her heat and the sight of her bare skin left him moaning. Intense concentration was the only thing that kept him talking. "Riley needs a good ass-kicking and if he isn't careful, I'll give it to him."

"Please. You like him. You know you do."

At last Caleb woke up. *What happened? What'd I miss?*

Dude. You missed the Holy Grail of Babe Land. Awe layered Julian's voice. *I never wanted to leave.*

Caleb whimpered.

Aden experienced another tendril of jealousy. "Guys, please. She's mine."

"The souls?" Victoria asked with a smile.

He nodded.

"I've been thinking," she said, tapping her chin with a blunt-tipped fingernail painted silver. Well, not silver, but with the same metal as her opal ring. That way, she could dip a finger into the *je la nune* without injuring herself. "The wards I have keep my monster at bay. What if we tattooed *you* with wards? That might keep the souls quiet."

For a moment, just a moment, he was tempted. Having Victoria all to himself, kissing her like that, without any interference, every time...

The souls immediately began to protest.

"No," he said. "Thanks for the offer, but I like them and don't want to hurt them."

They calmed, but only slightly.

Maybe it's time for a new girlfriend, Elijah huffed.

Victoria began tapping her chin again. "Perhaps, then, we will ward you against the witches. We can't protect you from all their spells—you don't have enough skin for that many tattoos—but we could cover the basics, the most dangerous. Mary Ann, too. No one can be warded against a spell that's already been cast, of course, but after the meeting, when the death magic has worn off, we can ward her against another death spell. Until then, it will be wise to protect her from other curses."

Dan would throw a fit if Aden came home covered in tattoos. And Mary Ann's dad would probably have a heart attack if she inked *anything,* even something as innocent as a rose, into her flesh. "We'll think about it. So why aren't you warded against spells? Why isn't Riley?" He reached out and linked their fingers.

"Some vampires are, but we aren't around the witches enough to concern ourselves, really. For the most part, they avoid us and we avoid them. Wolves, though, can't be warded. Their animal form doesn't hold the ink, so it's a waste. The moment they shift, their wards fade. I suppose we could ward Riley against certain spells for the meeting since he'll be in human form. Knowing him, he'll insist on going with you."

He lifted her hand, kissed her wrist. "I don't understand why *Riley* doesn't just take over the vampire clan. He'd make an excellent king."

And...there it was. The spark of anger that always accompanied talk about crowning a new king. Seriously. What the hell?

"The wolves have more loyalty than any other race. The need to guard is ingrained in them."

"Well, leading is just another form of guarding. We'll talk about that later, though. Let's guard him for once. What do you think?" He was fighting the urge to jerk her back into his lap. If they stayed here, he would kiss her again. Guaranteed. "That witch is probably giving him fits."

Victoria nodded and a moment later, the world around him disappeared.

A DESERTED CABIN, miles from town. From anything. Filled only with wolves, a vampire and weapons. Well, and also a blindfolded witch who was tied to a chair in the center of an otherwise empty bedroom. Not Marie,

Mary Ann had realized upon first arriving. This witch's hair was too short and too dark a blond. She wasn't sure if that relieved her or disturbed her.

Riley had immediately begun his interrogation, and it had gone something like this:

Riley: Where is the meeting between your kind and Aden Stone supposed to take place?

Witch: Go suck yourself.

Riley: Maybe later. Meeting?

Witch: Enjoy death.

Riley: I have once already. Now, decide to talk or lose a body part.

Witch: May I recommend a finger?

Riley: Sure. After I take one of your very necessary hands.

Witch: Look, you mangy mutt. The elders will be here any day now. They had planned on contacting you. After this, well, I'm sure your invitation will be lost in the mail.

At that, frustration had filled the room. Guilt had filled Mary Ann. This had been her idea, but it had done more harm than good.

The same futile exchange was repeated three more times.

"Let me try," Lauren finally said, moving behind the witch and placing her hands on the girl's shoulders. Her fangs were longer than they'd been a moment ago, and there was such hunger in her eyes it actually hurt *Mary Ann*. In that moment, she was willing to hold out her arm and let the vampire go to town. No one should be that hungry.

But then she recalled Victoria's words. Words uttered only yesterday, though an eternity seemed to have passed since then. Witch blood was like a drug to vampires. Once Lauren tasted the witch, there would be no pulling her off. And then Victoria, whenever she arrived—where was she? What was she doing?—would probably join the feasting.

"I'll only nip her," Lauren said, words now slurred. "Only take a little. She'll start talking then. Swear."

"No!" Riley shouted, and Mary Ann thought she saw the witch recoil.

That's when Victoria and Aden at last appeared. Both were flushed, their lips swollen and red, glistening.

Ah. They'd been kissing.

Unlike Mary Ann and Riley, she thought sadly. They'd barely spoken since their argument in the cleaning closet. As a matter of fact, they'd hardly even looked at each other.

He'd paid more attention to Lauren in the half hour they'd been here than he had to Mary Ann, so she was almost afraid he *liked* the ever-growing distance between them. And oh, that burned. Lauren was utterly strong and completely self-assured. Helped that she was weighed

down with weapons and clearly knew how to use them.
She was fierce and brave, reliable, well able to take care
of herself. Unlike Mary Ann.

Had she lost Riley already? Anger and helplessness,
sadness and sorrow mixed together and filled her up.
With the rise in her emotions, a warm, sweet breeze
drifted to her. In and out she breathed, that breeze floating to her lungs, seeping into her veins, soothing every
part of her. Just like that night in town, just like this
morning with Marie, she welcomed the sensation. *So
good.* And the taste...like candy. Sugar-coated, sparkling, fizzing.

Riley told Aden and Victoria what had been happening while forcing Lauren to move away from the
witch.

"Use your voice on her," Aden suggested to Victoria.
"You know, the powerful one." Then, "Shut up, Caleb!
I'm not kidding. Her shirt stays on."

Who was— Ah. One of the souls. Who did Caleb
want to strip?

"Voiced commands don't work on witches," Victoria
replied. She moved into Aden's side, snuggling close, as
if she couldn't bear to be separated from him. "Their
magic prevents it."

Magic. Yes. That's what she tasted, Mary Ann realized. Magic equaled power, and it was a heady sense of
power that surged through her. She closed her eyes and

savored. Felt more of that warmth, more of that sweetness, both consuming her.

She didn't need Riley, she thought. This. This was all she needed. It nourished. It completed. It didn't change its stupid mind.

How she was soaking that magic in, she didn't know and she didn't care. Just as long as she never stopped, she'd be happy.

"Fine, I'll ask, but after that you have to simmer down," Aden said with a sigh. Was he still talking to Victoria? Or to one of the souls? "Did you once know a guy named Caleb?" He focused on the witch.

"No," the bound girl replied, flippant. "Should I have?"

"Did you once know a guy who could possess other bodies? A guy who died a little over sixteen years ago?"

A pause, laden with tension. "Who are you? The boy who summoned us? Don't deny it, I can feel the pull of you. Why do you want to know about the possessor?"

Aden suddenly looked both excited and nervous. "So you did know him?"

"I didn't say that," she snapped. "Now tell me what I want to know!"

"First, let's get a few of your facts straight. The summoning was an accident. I didn't mean—"

Before he could finish his sentence, the witch growled,

and that growl was far more intimidating than any sound the shifters had made. "Is it you who's feeding off my magic right now? Tell me! I demand to know! And I demand you stop this instant, or the moment I'm free I'll curse the skin from your bones. Do you hear me? Stop!"

Everyone in the room stilled. Someone gasped in horror.

"Feeding off your magic?" Lauren said with a frown. "No one would dare. There are no Drainers among us, witch. We would have killed the offender already."

Drainers? Killed?

Feeding—the same word Marie had used. Not *muting,* but *feeding.* Sucking like a vaccum.

Mary Ann chewed at her bottom lip. *Not me. Can't be me.* But…that warmth, that sweetness. That *magic,* filling her up, consuming her. *If it's me, they'll want to kill me? Why?*

Shaking now, she backed up a step and hit a solid wall. She turned, eyes wide, only to realize Riley stood behind her. When had he moved? She'd never seen him leave Lauren's side. He was frowning fiercely, practically vibrating with fury. At her? Because he thought she was a…a Drainer? She could barely even consider the word. Whatever a—whatever *that* was, vampires killed them and witches hated them. So, no, Mary Ann couldn't be one. She just couldn't.

"Victoria," Riley said, his voice tight. His steely gaze never left Mary Ann—a gaze he'd never leveled on her before. A gaze he usually reserved for those who wronged the people he loved. "See if you can reason with the witch. Mary Ann and I are in need of a break." He didn't give Mary Ann a chance to protest. He simply grabbed her wrist and dragged her outside.

FOURTEEN

COLD AIR SCENTED WITH EARTH and pine wrapped around Mary Ann, chasing away the delicious sensation of warmth and power. Lamplight was replaced by moonlight, muted and soft, the only source of illumination. When Riley released her and spun to face her, scowling, Mary Ann drew the lapels of her sweater closer together. His green eyes glittered dangerously.

"What's going on?" she asked.

He was in her face a second later, pressing his nose into hers, his breath trekking over her face. "I was watching you. For a minute there, you looked like you were eating and savoring chocolate." He hurled the statement like an accusation. He didn't add, "You were feeding on her magic, weren't you?" but the words somehow echoed between them anyway.

She gulped, striving for calm. "So?"

"So. You haven't been eating lately. At all."

"How do you know what I have and have not been

doing? You haven't been around." *Don't let your hurt feelings show. Now isn't the time for that.*

His pupils expanded, only to shrink into a thin line. "I can smell food, Mary Ann. The scent of it seeps from human pores. You've had none for several days." He waited for her to issue a denial. She didn't. "At first, I thought you were too riddled with nerves about the death curse, 'cause yeah, I can smell that, too. Then I was mad at you for going into town and forgot to question you about the food. Now, there's no forgetting. Do you want to tell me why the hell you aren't eating?"

"I...I haven't been hungry." Truth. "Like you, I thought it was nerves. I still do. I mean, I can't...I wouldn't..." *Shut up, babbler!* "What's so bad about being a D-Drainer, anyway? It's no worse than being a muter, is it?"

He popped his jaw. "When did you last eat?" he asked, ignoring her question.

She gulped again. "I...maybe the day the witches cursed us. I don't know." The words whispered from her, coated in shame and guilt. *You have nothing to be ashamed of or guilty for,* she told herself. She'd done nothing wrong.

His eyes widened as he straightened to his full height, no longer touching her in any way. "Have you had water?"

"No."

"Humans can't survive very long without water, Mary Ann."

"I plan to have a giant glass of it just as soon as I get home."

"Have you weakened?"

Shivering now from the cold, from an influx of dread, she shook her head. Several strands of hair slapped at her cheeks. "No. That's not a big deal, though," she rushed to add. "I've been living on adrenaline."

"That wouldn't keep the hunger at bay for so long."

"Dieters can go without food for a long time."

"Are you dieting?"

He had a question for everything. "N-no, but that doesn't mean anything."

"You're not hungry, even now?"

"No."

His pupils did that strange expanding/shrinking thing. "You liked being near the witch, yes? You felt warm and safe?"

"Y-yes." *Stop stuttering.* "Is there something wrong with me? I mean, there's nothing wrong with me. I—"

"Yes, there's something wrong with you." He scrubbed a hand down his face, leaving red marks behind. "You were feeding off her magic, which means you really are a Drainer."

The horror in his voice caused her stomach to churn. "I ask again, what's so bad about being a D-Drainer?"

"Everything! By vampire law, hell, by every law in this otherworld, I'm required to kill every Drainer I find. We all are."

Mary Ann backed up a step. Riley, kill her? No, never, she told herself. Not her. They were dating, for God's sake. "You can't just go around killing people. Besides, why would you have to kill a D-Drainer?" And why did she have so much trouble saying the word? "Which I'm not. You can't know that for sure."

His eyes glinted as if a match had been struck inside them. "There was a Drainer in that room, Mary Ann. Witches are always the first to sense them because their survival depends on eliminating them. Victoria and Lauren are out. They might hunger for witch blood, like all vampires, but there's a big difference between drinking from a vein and gorging on energy. Plus, I've lived with them a long time, and would have known. That means the only other option was Aden. Except, he'd recently had a peanut butter and jelly sandwich, so I can cross him off the list, too. Who does that leave, Mary Ann? Go ahead. Tell me."

Distance, suddenly she needed distance from him. All that disgust…all that hate…both radiated from him. She stumbled backward, but didn't try to run even though he'd all but threatened her. With the distance, she could breathe without smelling his dark and spicy scent, without feeling branded by him. He was wrong about her. He had to be wrong.

"What exactly is a Drainer?" There. She'd said the word without stuttering. They'd reason this out together and realize she was no different than ever.

Back and forth he began to pace. "Haven't I already said? Someone who lives off the energy of others."

That didn't sound so terrible.

"I can see your aura and I know what you're thinking, but listen up. Drainers are sustained only by the energy they steal. Without it, they weaken and die. But in the taking, they kill. And if that isn't bad enough, their appetite for magic grows with every feeding."

She was going to *kill* people? No. No, no, no. But…she couldn't stop her next thought. Her mother. Her mother had died at the moment of her birth because Mary Ann had drained her of strength. Oh, God. Even before the witches and Riley had begun tossing accusations at her, Mary Ann had used that very word to describe what she'd done to her own her mother. Drained.

Had she been a Drainer her entire life?

"Soon, magic won't be enough. Soon, you'll take from the vampires and they'll no longer be able to feed." His steps quickened, feet pounding into the ground. "Soon after that, you'll take from the wolves, and they'll lose their ability to shift. After that, you'll take from humans. After that, nature. You'll destroy everything and everyone."

"I would never do that!" she shouted. Then her shoulders sagged. She'd killed her own mother. She was capable of anything. *Stop! Don't think like that. Back then, you ate food. Real food. Riley said Drainers live off energy.* "I just, I can't be a Drainer. There has to be another explanation."

Steps never slowing, he flicked her a menacing glance. "You won't mean to, but you will. Drainers can't help themselves, and they certainly can't stop. Otherwise, like I said, they weaken and die."

He was saying she was—allegedly—a parasite. A murderer. Tapping into living beings as if they were a beer keg, and drinking them dry. The moisture in her mouth vanished, and her heart skipped several beats. "You're wrong. My mother… I ate…"

His expression softened. "You didn't kill your mother. I don't know why she weakened after your birth, but you had nothing to do with it." He didn't sound convinced. "The draining thing, it probably switched on during your first encounter with the otherworld."

"Not true." She shook her head violently, more of those strands slapping at her. "I dated Tucker, and you're the one who told me he was part demon. I made him feel better, not worse." Proof that she couldn't possibly be a Drainer, right?

Riley paused to massage the back of his neck. "And then you met Aden. And then the two of you summoned all of us here. And then you were cursed and received your first taste of magic."

All excellent and irrefutable points. "What happens if I am?" *Don't say that. You can't be, no matter the evidence.* "What happens if I'm a Drainer, I mean?"

"I don't know." He bent and picked up a small, round stone, then tossed it into the trees. A branch cracked; there was a *thump*.

She could only watch him, sick at heart. "Both you and Lauren mentioned that you guys…kill Drainers."

"We do," he said, his tone dead.

As dead as she would soon be?

Light-headed at the thought, she fell backward, her hand flying to her neck. "You would kill me?"

"No!" He whirled on her, hands fisted, nostrils flaring with the force of his breathing. "And I wouldn't let anyone else harm you, either. God, Mary Ann. I can't believe you'd even think that of me."

Okay, okay. He was right. She released the oxygen that had snagged in her lungs. "This is new to me, Riley, and besides that, we haven't been on the best of terms lately, have we?"

His anger diluted, and his expression softened. "No. We haven't."

Hearing him agree was like being slapped—even

though she'd been the one to say it first. "So do you want to…break up? If we were even dating, I mean." Maybe he'd just been fooling around. Oh, God. She wanted to vomit.

"We were dating," he said, hard and unbending now.

Were, he'd said. Her blood chilled as if little ice crystals had formed in her veins. "And now we're not?" Did that needy voice really belong to her?

"We *are* dating, Mary Ann." His head fell back and he stared up at the star-filled sky. "We're just going through a little rough spot."

We are dating. Okay, yes, that was good. Very good. The relief that spread through her was palpable.

Then he added, "I mean, I think we are, at least," and that relief drained.

Drained. Not a good word choice, she thought, laughing without humor. Because if what he'd said before, about Drainers destroying…if that was true, that would mean…. no. No. No! She would *not* venture down that mental path. Like a hypochondriac, she'd only convince herself that her "symptoms" were real.

Riley pounded to the porch steps and plopped down, resting his elbows on his knees. "If you really are a Drainer, you're going to kill everyone I love." He must have been reading her aura, must have realized the direction of her thoughts. "Hell, one day you'll kill me."

Absolute panic filled her at the thought of his death—at the thought of causing it. "I would never hurt you. Ever!"

"You wouldn't mean to, but..." His head fell into his upraised hands. "Damn it! I can't believe this is happening."

"This just can't be right, Riley. I mean, it's happening so fast. I was fine, me, myself, only a few days ago." Now everything was crumbling, leaving only ruins around her.

His laugh was as humorless as hers had been. "That's the way of the world, Mary Ann. Everything changes in a blink."

Not like this. Not for her.

No, not true, she thought next. She'd met Aden and in seconds, her entire world had changed. She'd discovered Tucker had cheated on her with Penny and in seconds, her entire world had changed. She'd learned the truth about her mother and in seconds, her entire world had changed.

She'd met Riley and in seconds, her entire freaking world had changed.

"Is there a way I can stop this? Reverse it?" she croaked out. "If it's true, I mean."

"No." His unyielding tone left no room for doubt or argument.

Still she persisted. "Have you tried?"

"Yes."

"And?"

"And the Drainers died."

"How?"

"Through experiments." He lifted his head and threw a quick glance behind him. He stiffened, sighed. "Now isn't the time to discuss this."

She couldn't end the conversation on such a terrible note. "I don't want to go inside yet." She couldn't pretend everything was okay. Not when tears burned the back of her eyes, not when she was shaking so much she could have been having a seizure. "And really, we can't know for sure what's going on with me." When she got home, she planned to eat more food than her stomach could hold. That would prove her innocence. Right?

"Yeah," he replied, but he didn't sound convinced. "And I don't want to go inside, either. So let's chat about something else. I asked Aden, but now I'll ask you. Why did you pick him to teach you self-defense? Why didn't you pick me?"

That matters? *Now*? she thought. But rather than protest, she grabbed on to the topic switch like a lifeline. This was normal. This proved he still cared.

She could have lied, spared her shredding feelings from further injury, but she didn't. "I picked Aden because I knew I wouldn't pay attention if you were the one doing the teaching. I would have wanted my hands on you, or your hands on me. I would have wanted to kiss you. I wouldn't care about what you were telling me."

Some of the tension left him, and he offered her a half smile. "Okay, then. You made the right choice."

She relaxed a little, too. That smile, so genuine… He hadn't gifted her with one of those in what felt like *forever*. But that smile also upset her—because she recalled something she desperately wanted to ask him. "Answer a question for me."

"All right."

Are you sure you want to do this? You'll probably have to kiss this temporary good mood goodbye. Yeah. She had to; she had to know. "What about you and Lauren?"

Yep. Bye-bye, good mood. He lost all hint of happiness, scowling again. "Why do you ask?"

That was answer enough. "Just say what we both know you're going to say." *Please don't.*

A muscle ticked under his eye. "Lauren and I used to date."

Just as she'd suspected, yet the news was still devastating. How was she—a supposed Drainer—supposed to compete with such a strong, gorgeous vampire? Quite simply, she couldn't. "How long ago did you break up?" *Please say years ago.*

"Let's not do this, Mary Ann."

"Tell me."

He sighed. "We broke up shortly before I arrived here in Crossroads. We were never supposed to date, anyway. Vlad had promised her to someone else."

Stomach churning…"So I'm the rebound girl?"

He snapped his teeth at her, pure wolf. "Mary Ann. You were dating Tucker when I got here. I should be asking you if I'm the rebound guy."

Good point. Okay, she could let the rebound fear go. She walked over to him and eased beside him on the step. "Why did you guys break up?"

His green eyes pinned her in place. "You really want to know?"

Oh, God. *No.* "Yes."

"I didn't like the thought of her in danger, and she was always rushing right into it."

Just like Mary Ann had done by going into town on her own. Only, Mary Ann was human, her skin vulnerable. Just crossing the street could put her in danger. Actually, she'd never felt closer to death than just then, her hopes and dreams burning to ash around her.

"Do you still have feelings for Lauren?" she asked softly.

"No."

Too quick a response? God, she hated this. Hated her doubt. Hated Lauren, even though the vampire had been nothing but nice to her. And by nice, she meant that Lauren hadn't stabbed her.

Do you still have feelings for me? She wanted to ask, but didn't. Couldn't. The answer might be the final nail in her coffin. He'd say yes, but she would hear the "but" in his tone. She knew she would.

"Well, the danger thing is just something you'll have to get over, Riley," she said, as if they were still together and not just a big, fat maybe. "You can't be the one to save the day all the time. You can't do everything on your own. You have to accept help. Sometimes that's the only way to get the job done."

"I know. That doesn't mean I have to like it," he grumbled.

At least he hadn't denied her outright. That was progress, right?

"Right now, I want you to promise me that you won't tell anyone, and I mean *anyone,* not Aden, not Victoria, about the draining thing," he commanded. "Not until I find a way to fix you or reverse what's happening."

Could he, though? He'd already admitted Drainers died when others attempted to fix them. No, not true. He'd admitted that Drainers died during *experiments.*

"Okay?" he insisted.

Admission time. She stood, unable to sit still a moment longer, and shifted from one foot to the other, twisting the hem of her sweater. "I won't tell." She kept her back to him. "But…there's someone who already knows."

There was a rustle of clothes, then hard hands settled

on her shoulders and spun her around. Riley had jack-knifed to his feet, and boy, did he look ready to murder someone. "Who?"

Just tell him. Rip the Band-Aid. "The witch. Marie. The one I saw in town. The one who…appeared at the school this morning and told me she could feel me feeding off her."

Pupils—wide, thin. Wide, thin. Like a pulse. "Why didn't you tell me? Damn it, Mary Ann. I could have hunted her down."

And done what to her? "At the time, I didn't know what she meant."

"She could have killed you!" As quickly as he'd exploded, he relaxed. His head tilted to the side pensively. "Why didn't she kill you?"

"I don't know. She didn't stick around and explain her thought process."

Several heartbeats of time passed in silence. Then, "Someone's developing a smart mouth." Dryly said, without any heat.

"I thought you liked my mouth," she replied, kicking a stone with the toe of her tennis shoe. *Please, still like my mouth.*

He chuckled, and the sound warmed her. "I do."

Thank God. Her knees almost buckled—and might have, if he hadn't wrapped his arms around her waist, holding her up, holding her close.

"You know what I want?" he asked softly.

Her gaze lifted, meeting his. She shivered. "Tell me."

"To go on a date with you. A real date. Just you and me. No war, no being chased, no looking for answers. Just the two of us getting to know each other."

Yes, please. "I would like that," she said on a trembling breath.

"Soon as the witches are taken care of, that's what we'll do." There at the end, he'd sounded depressed, as if he didn't think it was possible. As if one of them would be dead by then.

Perhaps he didn't realize that *he* was killing her just then. Pulling her in one direction, then another, letting her hope before crushing her into nothing. "Nope. After the witches, we'll have to start searching for Aden's parents." A reminder for Riley, for her. Aden was still their friend, and they still had a mission.

"No." Riley shook his head. "Aden won't have time to search for his parents yet. He'll have vampire meetings to attend, laws to pass, punishments to issue. *Then* he can focus on his parents."

"At this rate, he'll have to drop out of school," she said. Her, too.

"Nah. Things'll calm down soon."

"And maybe then we can go on a second date." Fingers crossed. To be honest, nothing had really been worked out between them. Had it? They might be dating, they might not. She might be a Drainer, she might not. Fingers crossed on that one, too.

He chuckled, but it was no more assured than his final words.

The door behind him squeaked, and Riley released her, turning. Victoria and Aden exited the cabin. Both wore grim expressions. Aden looked sick, even. His skin had a greenish tint, and there were bruises under his eyes. And he was limping, dragging one leg behind as if it hurt to bend his knee. Maybe it did. His jeans were ripped and stained with dried blood.

"Are you okay?" Mary Ann asked him.

"Yeah, fine."

"I asked him the same thing, and he gave me the same answer," Victoria said.

Aden smiled, and for a moment, he looked all better. "Because it's true. I'm fine. Just tired."

"You'll be home soon, I swear, my king. So did the witch tell you anything?" Riley asked. He didn't release her, but moved to her side.

"No. So we're going to leave her tied up for the rest of the night," Victoria replied. "Perhaps boredom will make her more interested in talking to us tomorrow."

They were running out of time, though, the week the witches had given Aden to attend their stupid meeting nearing its end. "So what now?"

"Now we spread the word that we've got a witch," Riley said, grim. "If they want her back, they'll call their meeting to order."

"They'll curse us," Victoria said.

"They already have. Therefore, you'll do what I suggested and spread the word."

One by one, Victoria, Aden and Mary Ann nodded.

"As for what's left of tonight, we go home, rest." Riley's gaze met Mary Ann's, just as grim as his voice. "Soon the real battle will begin."

FIFTEEN

Tucker remained in the shadows for a long while, covered by his illusion of trees, darkness and night birds. Thankfully, no one at the cabin had noticed him.

So he'd watched…and listened…

He'd been ordered to follow Aden, which was easy for him, as Tucker could somehow sense wherever the boy went, and he had. Followed, that is. Yet Mary Ann was most often with the boy, and that delighted him, even as it frustrated him.

When it was just the two of them, Aden and Mary Ann, Tucker would lose his ability to cast illusions, forced to hide by regular means. He would wonder what the hell he was doing, following them, watching them and listening to their secrets when he should be protecting them. Oh, yes, there was a small part of him that wanted to protect the two people responsible for saving his dreaded life. And he would hate himself for what he was doing, vow not to do it anymore, and walk away.

But the farther he walked, the more he would hear Vlad's voice, whispering to him across the distance, commanding him to spy on Aden, and so, Tucker would return to Aden's side. If Mary Ann was gone, the desire to please his king would spread again. He would watch, listen and wait. An urge to hurt the boy would bloom, grow.

Thankfully, that hadn't been the case tonight.

Tonight, Mary Ann was with the other boy, Riley. When those two were together, Tucker *could* cast his illusions. For whatever reason. So, knowing Aden was inside, Tucker should have gone inside, too. And he could have, no one would have known—even when Aden was with Mary Ann, Tucker could use his illusions if Riley was there—but Tucker had stayed out here. For Mary Ann, determined to protect her from the rage of the other boy.

As he'd watched them, he'd realized he was glad she had a new boyfriend. She deserved happiness. She deserved love. She was the light to Tucker's darkness, pure where he was tainted. He'd never been right for her. But damn it, why couldn't they remain friends?

And why couldn't Penny be more like her?

Penny. Sometimes—when he was around Mary Ann and calm—he was glad they'd made a baby, even though he most often denied responsibility. Penny would be better off without him. Unlike Mary Ann, she didn't make him feel better about himself, his actions, his future. He would make a terrible father.

Without Mary Ann, he wanted to hurt those around him. Penny, yes, and probably the baby.

The boy. Follow the boy...

As Vlad's command drifted through his head, his teeth gnashed together. How did the vampire always know what Tucker was doing? How did the vampire wield such unbreakable control?

Disappointed, angry, dreading what was to come, Tucker straightened, unable to do otherwise, and headed south, toward the D and M Ranch where Aden lived. That's where the vampire princess, Victoria, had taken him when they'd vanished in a blink. As always, Tucker sensed it, felt a pull tugging him in that direction.

So far, there hadn't been much to report to the king. Aden had gotten sick, Aden had gone to school. Aden had returned to the vampire stronghold—where he'd been treated like royalty.

The last had infuriated Vlad. So much so, Tucker had feared for his own life. For with the former king's fury, invisible hands had wrapped around Tucker's neck, choking him. Finally, though, the vampire had released him and sent him on his way for more spy duty.

What was the vampire's ultimate goal? he wondered. Why was he using Tucker like this? Why wasn't he claiming his throne now? And did Tucker care?

The more distance he placed between himself and Mary Ann, the more the answer solidified in his mind. No. He didn't care. He would do what he was told.

THE GOBLIN POISON SAVAGED Aden, turning his blood to lava, his organs to ash and his skin into one giant welt. He burned, he itched, he vomited thick black goo over and over again. Thank God he'd convinced Victoria to leave him. She'd protested, but he'd done the smiling, "I'm fine" thing and managed to convince her all was well.

Been here, done this, he thought weakly, though he'd never experienced a reaction to this degree. Yeah, this was worse than any other corpse poisoning he'd endured. This one even affected the souls. They were moaning in his head, sometimes screaming, always incoherent.

Except for Elijah. *Death,* the psychic shouted. *Blood. So much blood. She dies. We can't let her die.*

"Who?" The word was like acid in his throat.

He dies, too. So much death.

"Who dies?" he demanded more insistently.

Elijah continued as if he hadn't heard Aden's questions. Maybe he hadn't. Maybe he simply didn't know. *No. NO! They all die. All of them. War. Stop the war. We have to stop the war.*

What war? If that was a prediction…

Through it all, Thomas's ghost remained glued to Aden's side, pacing, yelling, blaming. He wanted to leave, he said. His family would be looking for him, and would find out what had happened. And when that happened, Aden would finally know *true* suffering. Blah, blah, blah.

"A-Aden. You okay, man?"

It was still hard to distinguish real from the sea of noise, but he was still getting better at it, and he knew that someone was now in the room with him. His heavy lashes parted, and through a misty haze he saw Shannon standing at the side of his bed.

"Can I g-get you anything?" Shannon reached out and felt Aden's forehead.

The moment of contact, Aden's entire body jolted with a surge of electricity, and he lost his hold on his own reality. His conscious mind shot from him into his friend, and he was suddenly seeing the world through Shannon's eyes. Shocking, weird. Lying on the bed one second, standing the next. Pain still coursed through him, and he groaned.

His stomach rebelled at the new upright position, forcing him to hunch over and vomit. Again. Thankfully, someone had left a small metal trashcan here. Dan, maybe. Aden thought he remembered the guy checking on him a few times.

"Out," he managed to croak to Caleb. He wanted out of Shannon's body.

The only reply was another moan.

Usually the soul had control. Caleb decided who to possess and when. Sometimes even Aden had control. Caleb might not want to possess someone but if Aden focused hard enough, he could do it. This time, neither of them had control, but they'd still done it.

He tried to step from the body, as he'd done with all the others, but something kept him leashed, tethered there, unable to move. Still. Over and over he tried. Finally, weak, exhausted, hurting worse, he gave up and fell back on the bed. He couldn't hear Shannon's thoughts, so he probably had control of Shannon's mind, too. Which meant his friend would not remember this.

He hoped.

God, what was he going to do?

However long he sprawled there, writhing, he didn't know. Time was immeasurable, endless. Until the *true* fun began.

Aden lost his hold on Shannon's reality, too, and when he next opened his eyes, he found himself in the body of a little boy. Shannon, he realized, as he studied the dark color of his arm. A younger version of Shannon. He hadn't lost Shannon's reality, after all.

Even if he hadn't noticed the physical differences, he

would have known. He sensed the truth, deep inside. He'd just time-traveled—into *Shannon's* past.

That shouldn't be possible, not without Eve and certainly not with someone else's life. Always before Aden had traveled back into his own life. Now he was seeing and feeling what Shannon was seeing and feeling. The physical pain, at least, was gone, and the souls were quiet rather than frenzied.

He sat on a swing, rocking back and forth, tiny sandaled feet pushing at the gravel. His little hands gripped the metal links at his sides. The sun glowed brightly, his only friend.

"Hey, Sh-Sh-Shannon," a kid taunted from a few feet away. Several other kids were clustered around him, laughing. They were outside a school, Aden instinctively knew, and at recess.

There was a slide, a merry-go-round and a jungle gym, but none of the boys seemed to care about those things. They were focused completely on Shannon.

"My mom says you're so weird because your mom is white and your dad is black," the tallest boy said, chucking a rock in his direction.

The stone slammed into Shannon's stomach, stinging. He kept his gaze to the ground. Ignore them, and they'll go away, his mom always said. But he knew they wouldn't. They never did. Unless Ms. Snodgrass noticed and yelled, but she was busy picking the grass out of

Karen Fisher's hair, so he'd have better luck wishing on a star.

Another rock hit Shannon, in the leg this time. He felt the sting, but again, he gave no reaction.

"You have a girl's name, Stutter, you know that?"

More laughter had him cringing inside. Not that he'd ever let them know it.

Aden wanted to jump up, to pound those kids into the dirt, even young as they were. And he could have. He was still in control of the body. But to change the past was to change the future, and not always for the better. Actually, *never* for the better. So he sat there, awash in Shannon's embarrassment and abject sense of loneliness, hoping that's what Shannon had done.

But then the scene shifted, the playground fading and red brick walls closing in around him. Graffiti covered those walls, and in the distance, he heard a police siren wailing.

Smoke wafted in his face, and he coughed. He waved a hand in front of his nose, only then noticing the cigarette resting in his other hand.

"So?" someone said. "What do you think?"

Aden focused. A boy stood just in front of him. Probably fourteen or fifteen, and he was smoking, too. Like Shannon, he was black, though his skin was darker, and his eyes were brown.

He was cute, Shannon thought, though not exactly his

type; still, they'd been secretly dating for three weeks. What made Tyler so appealing was the fact that he was the first boy Shannon knew who admitted, freely, that he liked other boys.

Most people were accepting of him. Some were not, like Tyler's dad, and he often sported bruises. But still Tyler didn't try to hide the fact that he was gay, or that he had a feminine side, was even proud of it, from his lip-glossed mouth to his too-tight pink T-shirt to his red-painted toenails.

Shannon still hadn't told anyone about his own preferences. His dad was clueless, thank God, but his mom… she must have suspected. Flighty as she was, she kept introducing him to girls and then questioning him mercilessly. What did he think of them? Why wouldn't he ask them out?

"Earth to Shannon," Tyler said with a laugh. "Are you listening to me?"

"Uh, sorry. What'd you say?"

Tyler's amusement faded in a blink. "Lookit. Like I've told you a million times already, I said I'm tired of sneaking around. I'm not gonna let you pretend you don't know what I'm talking about this time, either. So either you like me or you don't. Okay? So which is it?"

"I—" Aden quickly shut his mouth. He didn't know how Shannon had replied, only felt the panic surging through the body.

"Say something!"

"I—I—" And then it didn't matter. The scene shifted again, and this time he was standing in the center of an outdoor basketball court. Sweaty boys were all around him, slapping him on the back, telling him what a good job he'd done.

On the ground in front of them was an unconscious boy. Tyler. He recognized Tyler's face, even though it was swollen, bloody and battered. Shannon's hands were throbbing. Aden studied them. The skin on his knuckles was ripped to shreds. By teeth. By *Tyler's* teeth.

He had beaten Tyler? Why?

Guilt and shame bombarded him. Remorse. Sorrow. Self-loathing.

The scene shifted yet again, the emotions falling away like leaves on a tree. Now he was inside a home, sitting on a couch. Pictures abounded. Of him. Of an older black man and a white woman. His parents, he thought.

His cheeks itched, so he reached up with a shaky hand to wipe at them. They were warm and wet. With tears? Someone was in front of him, pacing, screaming. Because Shannon had beaten Tyler?

No, he realized, as Shannon's thoughts and feelings sank into his awareness. Because Shannon had finally told his parents the truth. He was gay. He hated what he'd done to Tyler. He wished he could go back, stop himself from treating his boyfriend that way, as if he were trash. As if he were something shameful.

On and on his father screamed. This was wrong. This was a sin. His mother even joined him, crying hysterically about how embarrassed she was. Why couldn't he be normal?

He and Shannon were so much more alike than Aden had ever realized. He'd been called a freak his entire life, rejected by his parents, tossed throughout the system, unwanted by anyone. Trash. Shameful.

"Shannon?" The male voice called out from a long dark tunnel, and then someone was shaking him. "You're sick, too?"

Tugged back to the present, Aden blinked open his eyes—too bright, burning, tears forming—and found himself inside his bedroom, still on the bed, once again writhing in pain, the souls loud in his head. Dan was staring down at him, frowning with concern.

"You're burning up." His sigh wafted over Aden's face, and even that hurt. "That means whatever Aden has is contagious." Dan looked around. "Where's Aden? Do you need a doctor?"

Several seconds passed while Aden groggily waded through the facts. He was still inside Shannon's body, and Dan wanted to know where "Aden" was. "No," he managed to croak. "Aden's…fine. At school. I'll be fine, too." Then he closed his eyes again and rolled to his side. "Please, go."

"All right, I will, but get some rest. I'll check on you in a bit and bring you some of Meg's chicken noodle soup." Meg. His sweet, beautiful wife. Footsteps sounded, a door creaked open, closed.

So many deaths, Elijah moaned.

Dear God, not that again. The psychic said something else, but another voice soon blended with his, claiming Aden's attention. A female's voice.

"Shannon?" she said. "Where's Aden?"

Victoria, he thought. Once again he forced his eyes to open. The lights had been turned off and the curtains closed, so the room was cast into welcome darkness. He flopped to his back. Like Dan, Victoria stood at the side of the bed, staring down at him.

Thomas was beside her, watching, listening.

When she reached out, Aden scrambled backward. "No touching."

Hurt clouded her expression as her arm fell to his side. "Why? What's wrong?"

"I'm Aden. It's Aden. Trapped." If she touched him, would he possess her body, as well, taking Shannon with him? He hadn't with Dan, and he wanted her hands on him—always—but he wasn't willing to risk it.

First, she appeared confused, then frightened. "I knew it! I never should have left you. I knew you were sick, I just, I wanted you to rest and I was afraid you wouldn't if I stayed, and oh, God, now I'm babbling. I'm so sorry. I'll get Mary Ann. Yes? I'll have to leave you again, but only for a moment."

Mary Ann. Perfect. She muted abilities. "Yes." Maybe, just maybe, her presence would force him out of Shannon's body. If not...

God. He'd be stuck. Forever.

MARY ANN SNUGGLED against the warm, soft—strangely large—heating pad in her bed. She'd never slept this deeply or this peacefully before. Maybe because this was the first real sleep she'd had in what seemed forever, so her body had needed to do something drastic. Or maybe because this just might be her very last sleep.

No. Wait. That kind of thinking didn't make any sense. She would have been scared, up all night tossing and turning, and wondering if she really was a Drainer, if Riley was done with her, if the witches were now coming after her.

Now the tossing and the turning began. What was she going to do? How was she going to— Wait again. No matter where she moved, the heating pad remained pressed into her side. How odd. Even odder, she didn't own a heating blanket. Did she? Her eyelashes fluttered open.

There was a big, black wolf in her bed.

Mary Ann yelped in surprise, heartbeat speeding out of control.

Shh. It's me. It's okay.

The words reverberated inside her head, deep and husky and familiar. "Riley?" His name was more a shout than she'd intended. She rubbed the sleep from her eyes and peered over at him. The lights were off, and the sun hadn't yet risen all the way, so details were hazy.

The wolf was stretched out beside her, dark fur gleaming and green eyes bright.

"Riley," she said, a statement of fact this time.

The one and only.

"What are you doing here?" More importantly, did she look like a mess? She scanned herself. She wore a blue tank, and her covers bunched at her waist, shielding her lower body—boy shorts and bare legs—from his view. She ran her hand through her hair. A few tangles, but nothing too terrible.

You might be a Drainer, and that witch, Marie, suspects it. No way you're sleeping alone again.

He cared, then. He still cared. And he'd said "might be a Drainer," which was an improvement from their last conversation when he'd baldly stated, "You're going to kill me." Her lips curled up at the corners. "So you've been here all night?" Protecting her.

Yep. Came back right after I escorted Aden and Victoria home.

"I'm glad. And thank you."

My pleasure.

Their gazes met, and for a heated moment, he was watching her as he had in the very beginning, before the witches and the feeding, as if she were important, as if she mattered more than anything else in the world. A girl could get used to that.

Grin widening, she fell back onto the mattress and wished she'd woken up sooner. "Now that we're both alert, we should probably talk about last night. We said some things that—"

Suddenly her bedroom door burst open, and her dad flew inside, scowling. "What is going on, Mary Ann?"

"Dad!" Panicked, caught red-handed, she jolted upright, jerking her comforter with her. "What are you doing?"

"You shouted that boy's name. I thought—" His gaze landed on Riley and he stilled, terror darkening his eyes. He was still in his pajamas, a flannel shirt and pants, so he must have rushed straight from bed. "Mary Ann, listen to me, baby. Get up slowly. No sudden movements, okay? I want you to inch your way behind me. Okay? Do it now, honey."

Oh, God. This was *so* not happening. "Dad. The, uh, dog is harmless, I swear." Biggest. Lie. Ever.

To prove his "harmlessness," Riley licked her palm.

Goose bumps broke out over her skin, and then heat flooded her cheeks. She didn't want her dad to think a dog turned her on.

"How do you know that mangy thing is harmless?" Her dad had always hated animals, feared them. "Now, why aren't you moving away from him and toward me? I don't want to scare you, but he could use your face as a chew toy, sweetheart."

Riley stiffened.

"I just do. Know, that is," she said. "He won't hurt me. He's...my pet." *Please don't be mad, Riley,* she thought, even though she knew he couldn't hear her. "He has been for the past few weeks."

Her dad's blue eyes widened, panic and fear giving way to bafflement. "No. No, that isn't possible. I would have known."

"Yes, way. See?" She wrapped an arm around Riley's large frame and buried her face in his soft neck, cuddling him close.

"No," her dad insisted, shaking his head. "You would have told me. I would have known."

Oh, Dad. There's a lot you don't know. She straightened, heart still hammering against her ribs. "I know about your rampant animal phobia, so I kept him hidden. But, see? He's trained. He doesn't cause any trouble. I swear."

He was shaking his head again before the last word

left her mouth. "That thing could have you for breakfast, Mary Ann. I want it out. Now."

"Daddy, please. Please let me keep him," she said, and commanded tears to bead in her eyes. Laying it on too strong? Maybe. But she needed him to say yes. That way, Riley could come and go freely. There'd be no more sneaking around. Really, she should have thought of this before. "He makes me happy. Since...you know. What happened between us." Reminding him of their fight was low, but she was desperate.

Finally, her dad softened. "He might not have all his shots."

He hadn't said yes, but she knew. Victory would be hers. She wanted to laugh, to clap and dance. "I'll take him to the vet myself."

A pause. A sigh. He pinched the bridge of his nose. "You called him Riley."

Uh-oh. "Yes."

"So you named your pet after your boyfriend?"

"Uh, yes."

"Why would you do that?"

Was he reading all kinds of psychological reasons into the situation? "It just seemed...appropriate. They're both protective of me." There. A truth.

A bit more softening. "Does Riley know?"

"Yeah, and he approves. He was flattered."

"That just proves he's weird and you shouldn't hang around him."

"Is that your *professional* opinion?" she asked pointedly.

He was silent for a long while. "I can't believe this. A mangy mutt in the house, all this time. Fine. Keep him. But if he soils the rug, he's out."

She pressed her lips together to keep from grinning. "I understand."

He turned, throwing over his shoulder, "And if he growls at you, even once, he's out. He looks wild."

I am, Riley snapped inside her head.

Do not laugh, she told herself.

Her dad paused at her door. "Where does it stay while you're at school?"

It. Nice. "Outside."

"You could be inviting fleas into our home, Mary Ann."

No. Laughing. "He's clean, Dad. I swear. But if I spot a single little bug, I'll bathe him."

That could prove interesting, Riley said.

"And thank you," she added. "For everything."

"You're welcome." The door shut, leaving her alone with Riley.

Finally allowing her amusement to bubble from her, Mary Ann fell back onto the bed and cuddled her mangy mutt.

SIX†EEN

SOIL THE RUG, Riley growled. As if.

Mary Ann continued to laugh until tears streamed down her cheeks. There'd been so much terror and suspicion, running and waiting, so much time spent dreading what would happen and what was to come that she felt a little weird finding humor just then, but she just couldn't help herself. Actually, she didn't want to help herself.

Riley didn't help. *Fleas. Mangy.* Another growl. *We'll see what he thinks of me when I chew through his kneecap.*

"None of that, now," she said between giggles, "or you'll be thrown out."

He gave another growl, but he did relax against the mattress, against her. *My fur is silky, damn it.*

Finally, she calmed—yet her grin was wide and unhideable. "Very."

He sighed. *Just go back to sleep. You need all the rest you can get.*

She meant to protest. She really did. But as she lay

there, petting him, listening to him practically purr his approval, his warmth and softness drugged her, lulling her back to the darkness as nothing else could have. Her cares melted away, leaving only a sense of bliss.

She'd *missed* this, and knowing he would be here when she woke back up…

When she next opened her eyes, yawning, Riley was still beside her. See! Still beside her. Mary Ann lifted her cell off her nightstand and glanced at the clock. She frowned. She had fifteen minutes before she had to get up and shower for school. She wanted an hour. She and Riley hadn't talked yet.

Oh, well. No help for it. She'd savor these fifteen minutes as if they were her last. In the stark light of the morning, however, all of her worries returned, flooding her mind, last night replaying over and over again.

We are dating, he'd said. *At least I think we are.*

Ouch.

One day you'll kill everyone I love, he'd added. *Hell, one day you'll kill me.*

Double ouch.

No, there would be no savoring. One day, if she was a Drainer as he suspected, she might kill him. Kill this boy who had brought her to life, tugging her from the safe world she'd created for herself, where she had never truly felt, but had only operated on autopilot. No way would she let that happen.

If she had to leave him and everyone she knew and loved, she would. But. Big but. That didn't mean she was unwilling to do everything within her power to prove she *wasn't* a Drainer—or to do whatever was necessary to revert back to her old self if she was.

Hungry? Riley asked hopefully.

His voice slipped inside her mind, as warm as his body. She took stock. Her stomach was empty, but not tight or grumbling. "No," she admitted, though she'd wanted so badly to lie.

Sighing, he jumped from the bed and padded into her bathroom to change into his human form, as well as into the clothes he kept stashed there. This wasn't the first time he'd stayed in her bedroom. Hopefully not the last, either. While he was up, she rushed to her door and turned the lock, then she sat at the edge of the bed to wait for him to emerge.

She didn't have to wait long. The bathroom door creaked open a few minutes later, and Riley stepped out wearing jeans but nothing else and her breath caught at the sight of him. So tan, so lean and muscled, he was every girl's fantasy come to startling life. Seriously, you practically needed an ID to touch that six-pack.

Maybe that was why he exuded such an undeniable bad-boy vibe.

And he's mine, she thought proudly.

Maybe. For now.

Squaring her shoulders, refusing to slink into depression, she pushed to her feet. "I'll just be a minute."

"Okay."

He strode to the bed and she made her way into the bathroom. She quickly brushed her teeth and hair and took care of business. There were dark circles under her eyes, despite her peaceful rest last night. Plus, her cheeks were a little hollowed out.

Not for the first time, she found herself wishing she were beautiful like Victoria. Or Lauren. Mary Ann scowled. Lauren, who had dated Riley and only recently broken up with him. Lauren, who was probably a better kisser, definitely braver, utterly more confident, and wouldn't ultimately kill him and all those he loved.

Mary Ann's self-esteem took another hit.

Disgusted with herself, she stomped back into her room. Once again Riley reclined on the bed, and she settled in beside him, resting her head on his shoulder. He was just as warm as when he'd possessed fur. *He's mine,* she thought again as his heart pounded against her temple. Not Lauren's. Not anyone else's.

Maybe.

She stiffened. Maybe, again. The word was like a cancer inside her brain, eating at her, destroying her. The more time she spent with him, the harder she fell for him. That was a fact. Another fact? The harder she fell for him, the harder it would be to leave him, if that's what she ultimately had to do to save him. And she *would* leave him to save him.

"What's wrong?" Riley had one arm tunneled under her, and that arm wrapped around her, fingertips smoothing over her brow.

"Just thinking," she said.

"About?"

"If I *am* a Drainer. When will we know for sure? *How* will we know for sure?"

He sighed and, of course, he ignored her questions. "Listen, I shouldn't have yelled at you last night. I was freaked out and worried about my family. But you're my family, too, and I'm sorry. I shouldn't have treated you that way."

"You don't have to apologize." That was the truth, but yeah, she did like those words on his lips. "This is serious, dangerous stuff, and if something were threatening my dad—" *or you* "—I would react the same way."

"Still." He pressed a soft kiss on her cheek. "Moment I left you here to escort Victoria and Aden home, the thought of you in danger had me sweating and cursing and practically shoving those two into their rooms so I could return to you. And by the way, I will be sleeping here every night until the witches are no longer a threat to you."

Sweet boy. "Just don't soil the rug," she quipped.

He gave a mock growl. "Funny."

A thought suddenly occurred to her, and she frowned. "You usually hide when you hear my dad coming. Why didn't you this time?"

Riley shrugged, the movement bouncing her head up and down. "I wanted him to see me. I want to be able to come and go as needed without fearing he'll shoot me on sight."

"Smart."

"Genius."

Her lips twitched. "Okay, returning to the subject at hand. I asked some questions a few minutes ago and you ignored me. I'd really like you to answer now. So. First up. When will we know if I'm for sure a Drainer?"

"Actually, let's *not* return to this subject. Let's forget the Drainer thing for now."

"No. I can't." Not when he might be in danger. "Answer, please."

He uttered another sigh, warm breath ruffling fine strands of her hair and brushing them against her brow. "Food will make you sick, because your body no longer needs or wants it. You'll begin to crave close proximity to witches and other creatures, and you'll know them, what they are, what they can do, before you ever even see them."

Stomach churning... None of that helped her case. She'd already begun to sense when creatures were near. She'd known Marie was in town before she'd seen her. And yeah, she would love to experience that rush of power again. Craved it, as he'd said.

"Tell me if any of that happens."

She would do more than tell him. She would show him. She pushed from the bed and strode to her desk.

"What are you doing?"

"Finding out." Maybe she should have waited until she was alone, but he needed to know just as much as she did. Shaking, she pulled a candy bar from the top drawer, where bags of nuts and other candies rested. Her emergency study stash. She peeled back the wrapper, turned to Riley, who was stiff and anxious, and bit into the top.

Usually, she would close her eyes and delight in the sweetness of the chocolate. This time, the food was like ash in her mouth. Her stomach tightened up, ready to revolt, but she did it, she swallowed, and it was like swallowing a lump of coal.

Regret hit her first, then the sickness Riley had promised, strong, consuming, raking every inch of her. Bile rose, burning her throat. Any second now, she would—

Eyes wide, she rushed to the bathroom, hunched over and vomited into the toilet. Over and over again.

When her stomach was finally empty, she brushed her teeth, once, twice, then swished mouthwash for several minutes, until every part of her mouth tingled from the alcohol. All the while, her shaking increased.

No. No, no, no.

"Better?" he asked when she entered the room.

"Fine."

"Could be nerves."

"Yeah." But she knew, deep down, she knew, and so did he. They might not want to face it, might want to deny it with every fiber of their beings, but they couldn't. Not any longer. She was different now. She had changed.

She was a Drainer.

Almost in a trance, she walked back to the bed and reclaimed her spot at his side. She would have to leave him. If she didn't, she would one day hurt him. Was this the last time she would ever be with him like this?

"I'm sure it's nerves. A self-fulfilling prophecy," he said, voice devoid of emotion now. "I told you that you would be sick, therefore you were."

He'd always been the realist, she the dreamer. Now it seemed their roles had reversed.

"Riley," she said softly.

"Nope," he interrupted, as if he suspected where she was headed. "We've covered that topic of conversation. Now we can move on." He pressed another kiss into her cheek. "I want you to know that when I said we were *maybe* dating yesterday, I was still in shock. I didn't mean it, and I want to kick my own ass. We are dating, so don't you dare think about seeing someone else. You're mine, and I don't share."

Sweeter words had never been spoken, and she should have been flying through the clouds, lost to happiness. Except, she found herself saying, "Riley...I just don't know. I mean—"

"Oh, no. Hell, no." He rolled over, pinning her to the bed, his weight smashing into her. He was heavy, but it wasn't unpleasant. She liked it, liked having him there. "Are you trying to break up with me?"

No. "Yes." Oh, God, she couldn't believe she'd just said that. He was her everything, and yet, she was dangerous to him. She wasn't going to risk his life, even to keep him, which she wanted to do more than anything else in the world.

"Things are more complicated, yes, but that doesn't mean we're over."

Tears burned her eyes, springing up, spilling over. "Yeah, it does." *Stop it. Stop talking. Don't do this.* "We're...over." If there were any other way...and maybe there was. She would find it, if so, as planned. Research, experimentation. Whatever.

But until then, no Riley. No feeding her addiction to him. No enjoying him, relying on him, expecting and needing him.

His eyes narrowed. "If that's the case, then you won't mind taking your self-defense lessons from me."

And have his hands all over her? How would she resist him? "That kinda defeats the point of what I'm trying to do." *Protect* you *for once.*

"And what are you trying—"

"Mary Ann," her dad called from downstairs, his voice echoing from the walls and interrupting. "You up?"

"Yeah," she called back.

"Breakfast will be ready in twenty."

"Thanks."

"Welcome."

She squirmed free of Riley and stood, keeping her back to him. "You should probably go. I have to get ready."

He sat up. "I'll leave, but I'll return and walk you to school. Unless you want to skip and head into town to find another witch. The more bargaining power we have, the better off we'll be."

He was asking for her help now, rather than trying to leave her behind to keep her safe. Powerful stuff. He had to know how much that affected her. "Can't. I've got a Chem test, and I can't miss." Not that a perfect grade point average mattered in the afterlife, but part of her wanted to pretend this was a normal week.

"All right, I'll—"

Victoria suddenly appeared in the center of the room, and Mary Ann yelped, hand fluttering over her heart.

The vampire princess was paler than usual, her features tight with concern.

"You have to come with me," she said to Mary Ann. "Aden's trapped inside Shannon's body and can't get out."

Mary Ann had seen Aden possess a body before—Riley's wolf form, actually—and the sight had shocked her to her soul. Now he'd possessed Shannon? "I'll dress and meet you at the ranch."

"No. That will take too long. I'll teleport you."

She stifled a groan. "All right. I have to get past my dad, though, and convince him I'm headed to school." No Chem test, after all. "I'll meet you at the gate to my neighborhood."

"I'm going with," Riley said, standing.

Victoria shook her head, adamant. "You can't. You prevent Mary Ann from using her muting ability. You have to stay behind."

Stubborn, he said, "I'll walk her to the gate, then, and you can leave me there."

After a harried nod, Victoria vanished.

Mary Ann was silent as she tugged a sweater and jeans from her closet; she was silent as she dressed in the bathroom. When she finished, she gathered her books and backpack. Still silent. Riley had already removed his jeans—where had he stored them?—and transformed into a wolf.

Together, they raced down the stairs and into the kitchen. The scent of eggs and bacon wafted through the air. Her mouth didn't water, but her stomach didn't threaten to revolt again, either. An improvement.

"Dad," she said in greeting.

He turned, spied Riley and froze, his expression both disgusted and terrified. There were lines of tension around his eyes, as if he hadn't slept after he'd left her room. "Dear Lord. I didn't realize how big that thing really was."

"Sorry, Dad, but I don't have time for breakfast. I forgot I wanted to get to school early and study for my Chem test."

He frowned. "You've barely even picked at your food lately. Don't think I haven't noticed. At least take a piece of bacon with you. It's brain food."

She didn't want to argue, so she claimed the piece he held out for her. "Thanks."

"Want a ride?"

"Nah." Too casual? "Oxygen to the brain, and all that."

"Good luck, honey."

"Thanks. Love you." With that, she was out the door and running for the gate, Riley keeping pace at her side.

Funny thing. On the way there, she could have sworn she spotted Tucker, running with them, but Riley didn't seem to notice him, and Riley noticed *everything,* so she convinced herself she was seeing things.

Besides, even if Tucker was here, even if he was following her, she didn't have time to stop and question him. Aden needed her. She just prayed she could help him—rather than hurt him further.

SEVENTEEN

TWO VOICES CALLED TO ADEN. Both female. Both alarmed.

"Try something else."

"Like what? I've tried everything! Screaming at him, shaking him, slapping him."

"He's inside that body. Get. Him. Out!"

"What do you want me to do? Reach inside his chest?"

"Yes!"

"You are such a pain! How does Aden stand you? But fine, I'll do it. I'll try."

One second Aden was inside Shannon's body, drifting through his friend's mind and memories, reliving a past as painful and lonely as his own, and the next he was standing beside Mary Ann, his hand resting in hers.

She was panting, sheened with perspiration, gaze glazed with shock and fatigue. "Did you see that?" she gasped out. "Did you? I can't believe I just did that. Tell me you saw that!"

"What happened?" he croaked. God, he ached. Every inch of him ached as if he'd been in a hit-and-run—hit with a baseball bat and run over by a truck.

Victoria moved to his other side, her mouth hanging open with an equal measure of shock. "You're okay. You're going to be okay now."

Was she trying to convince him? Or herself? "What happened?" he asked again.

"She—she reached inside. Jerked you out. You were like a ghost at first, not truly solid, then you were here. I've—I've never seen anything like that."

Any collateral damage? Aden took stock. His knee hurt the most, and he was shaking, but he wasn't puking and wasn't paralyzed. The poison had passed through him. Thank God. He almost collapsed in relief.

Elijah, Caleb and Julian were no longer moaning, babbling and incoherent. They were quiet. There, Aden could tell, but quiet, as if they were exhausted from their ordeal and needed rest.

Despite Mary Ann's nearness, Mr. Thomas was also present. A mere outline of himself, but Aden could still see him. He sat at the desk, arms folded over his middle, expression mulish. He couldn't hide the interest in his eyes, though. He was watching and cataloging every detail.

Odd. Riley wasn't here. Mary Ann should have muted all of Aden's abilities completely. Why hadn't she?

"Uh, A-Aden." Shannon slowly sat up and looked around the bedroom. He scrubbed his face with trembling fingers. "W-what just happened? I was standing in f-front of you. Wasn't I? How'd I g-get on the bed?"

He didn't know that Aden had been inside his mind, then. Thank God for that, too. "You passed out." It was the only thing his fogged brain could come up with so spur of the moment.

"P-passed out? Why?" Shannon looked at the clock and shook his head, rubbed his eyes. "It's n-nine-fifteen. How is it nine-fifteen? I tried to wake you up at six-thirty. I should be at school. C-crap! I'm late. D-Dan's gonna freak. He—"

"He thinks you're sick." Aden remembered Dan's visit, and what he'd said. "And you were. For a little while."

Shannon calmed, focused on the girls and frowned. "What are you guys d-doing here? And when did you get here? God, this is w-weird. I've never passed out before. Never lost t-time like that."

"Shannon," Victoria said, her voice suddenly thick, layered…powerful.

The voice. Aden reached out and grabbed her wrist. When she focused on him, he shook his head. "Don't do it." Shannon had felt defenseless and out of control all his life, and Aden wouldn't add to that—whether his friend realized what was going on or not.

Though she was clearly confused, Victoria nodded.

"Shannon, do you feel up to going to school?" Aden asked.

"Yeah. I—I feel fine. Except for that loss of time."

"You can still make it, if you want."

One dark brow rose. "You going?"

Aden shook his head. "Yeah, but not just yet." At this rate, he wasn't going to get any kind of education anytime soon. "I'm still not feeling one hundred percent."

"O-okay. I dig." His friend's head tilted to the side. "But maybe o-one day, you'll trust me with your s-secrets. See you later," he added before Aden could reply. Motions slow, Shannon stood, bent down and grabbed his backpack, then headed out of the room, out of the bunkhouse, the door beating shut behind him.

So. Shannon suspected something was going on.

Worry about that later. Aden glanced down at himself. He wore boxers and sweat, and that was it. His knee was caked with dried blood, the skin still shredded. His skin was pale with a grayish tint. *Nice.* "Can you guys stay while I shower?"

"Of course," Victoria said.

"Yeah," Mary Ann agreed. She was peering at her hands, turning them in the light. "But will you tell us a little about what happened first? Just a small detail to tide us over before we grill you."

"I...time-traveled through Shannon's past." Aden gathered some clothes—a plain gray T-shirt and jeans.

"That was Eve's ability," Victoria said, "not yours."

"I know. Maybe, I don't know, maybe when she left, her ability somehow stayed with me. Or maybe she gave it to me, even. A final gift in case I ever needed to right a wrong."

"Or maybe you time-traveled so much, your body simply learned how to do it without her," Mary Ann said. "You've heard about muscle memory, right? When a movement is repeated over and over again, a long-term muscle memory is created for that specific task and soon a person can perform that task without any conscious effort."

That made sense—as much as anything in his life did these days. "You, Mary Ann, are a genius."

She grinned. "I know."

He rushed to the bathroom, where he hurriedly washed and dressed. By the time he returned to his room, Riley was there, sitting on the edge of the bed, stiff, obviously uncomfortable. Mary Ann stood as far away from him as possible, leaning against the closet door and looking anywhere but him. Clearly, whatever had plagued them yesterday had yet to be resolved.

Only thing they could be fighting about was that

defense lesson. Was Riley still throwing a tantrum? Baby.

Victoria sat at the desk, composed again. Thomas had moved to the window, no longer an outline but as clear and sparkly as always.

"Oh, good. You're back. I found this." Victoria handed him a sheet of paper. "It's for you, from Dan. Don't worry. He had no idea we were here. I made sure of it."

He peered down and read.

Aden,
You have another session with Dr. Hennessy this evening. Sorry for the late notice. He only called me this morning. I thought you were sick, so I told him no. Then I ran into Shannon, who was better and on his way to class. He reminded me you were better, too, and already there, so I called the doctor back. Glad you're feeling better. I'll expect you to do your chores after school. On another note, I've hired a new tutor, and she's coming to dinner tonight to meet you boys. It'll be after your therapy session, so no worries. Even though she won't be teaching you, I'd like you to be there to help welcome her.
Dan

Great. More Dr. Hennessy. And another tutor? Aden flicked Thomas a glance. Would the next tutor be a fairy, too? Even the harbinger of death that Thomas had promised? He'd find out tonight, he supposed. Aden crumpled the paper and tossed the wad in the trash can.

"So what happened to you?" Mary Ann asked, and he knew what she meant. "*All* the details this time."

"Once upon a time, a goblin took a bite out of my leg…" He told them everything but what he'd learned about Shannon's past. That was Shannon's secret to share. He no longer cared about Thomas getting an earful. Wasn't like the guy could do anything with what he learned.

"I'm sorry I didn't protect you, my king," Riley said, standing and bowing his head. "I take full responsibility for your ordeal."

"I'm not your king." The denial slipped from him automatically. "And the responsibility lies with me."

"Thank you for the exoneration, my king." Such a stiff, formal, *irritating* tone. "I can promise you nothing like this will happen again."

Aden rolled his eyes. "You're such a jerk, Riley."

Victoria wrapped her arms around him and rested her head against his shoulder, her body hot as fire. "You've been injured too much lately. No wonder Elijah thinks you're going to die soon."

"What?" The single word exploded from Riley's mouth.

"Oops," Victoria said with a grimace. "Sorry."

"Looks like I've got another non-fairy-tale to weave." Sighing, Aden explained about Elijah's prediction. That soon Aden would die on a darkened street, a knife in his heart. Though he tried, he couldn't keep the fear from his voice.

"Oh, Aden," Mary Ann said, tears in her eyes. "I already knew, but still. It's—"

"You knew? You knew and you didn't tell me? Thanks for keeping me updated, sweetheart." Riley practically vibrated with sardonic rage.

"First, I only found out the other day. And second, we had other things on our minds," she snapped. "I planned to tell you after this week from hell was over."

The wolf accepted the explanation with a stiff nod. "You won't be hurt on my watch, that I swear."

"Thank you." Later, Aden would tell him that nothing could be done—and yeah, he'd once planned to try something himself, *still* planned to try something himself, really, but he didn't want to get the wolf's hopes up. Later, though. Always later. As Mary Ann had said, they had enough to worry about during this week from hell. "So what's the plan for today?" he said, changing the subject. He walked Victoria to the bed, sat down and pulled her down on his lap. After everything he'd just endured, he wasn't ready to let her go. Thankfully, she cuddled close, unconcerned by their audience.

"We go to school," Riley said, still fighting his

emotions. "My brothers are currently letting every creature in town know we have a witch in our custody. Which means the fireworks should start tonight. Use today to catch up in all your classes. Tomorrow you might be too...sore."

In other words, there was going to be a fight. Great. Worse, there was nothing else they could do right now. Except wait. And hope. And pray.

THROUGHOUT THE DAY, Aden expected a witch to jump out of every shadow and ambush him. Or if not a witch, then something, *anything*. A rabid gnome, maybe, or a vampire with a complaint. Even a fairy making a play for his head.

Instead, he arrived at school in time for lunch, ate, attended his next three classes, and boom, that was it. Class dismissed, time to go home. Nothing happened.

Aden was almost disappointed in the lack of combat. Just two more days until the death curse affected his friends. Two was too close for comfort. A year was too close. He had to do something.

Victoria walked him home and left him at the ranch, as silent and distracted as he was. In his room, he found another note from Dan, telling him not to forget to do his chores or his therapy. Like he could. Aden headed to the barn to muck the stables and feed the horses. He loved the horses and hated that he hadn't spent much time with them this past week. Sometimes, as a special treat for good behavior, Dan let him and the others go for a ride.

The souls loved the horses, too, and cooed at the beautiful animals while Aden worked. And yeah, it felt weird doing normal things. Acting normal, the other boys working alongside him. Redheaded RJ, punked-out Seth. Shannon, Ryder, Terry and Brian. RJ was due to turn eighteen next week, and Terry soon after that. Aden had heard them talking about getting a place of their own. Dan had asked them both to stay, to continue their studies, but the two were determined to get their GEDs and be "free."

What was freedom, really? Once, Aden had thought he knew the answer: to be alone, without the souls, to be able to do anything he wanted, damn the consequences. Now he had friends, a girlfriend, and everything he did affected them. Consequences mattered.

No one could ever truly be free as long as they loved, and life wasn't worth living without love. So freedom? Overrated. He'd much rather have Victoria, Mary Ann and Riley, even the souls.

So how are you going to save them from the witches? The thought was his own, the souls still baby-talking at the horses—and maybe the horses could hear them, because they were calmer than usual, even with all the activity in the barn—and he wished he could blank his mind. He couldn't.

Aden sighed. Once issued, spells took on a life of their own, he knew. So he couldn't stop the magic that had already been unleashed, even by threatening the witch they had locked up.

Hell, maybe they should release her as a gesture of goodwill. Riley would throw a fit, of course, but he would do what Aden told him to do. Aden was vampire king, after all.

Yes. King. The title *was* his and— Aden shook his head, disrupting that line of thought. He wasn't king, didn't want to be king. The end.

When the barn was clean, the other boys trudged inside the bunkhouse to shower, change and prepare for dinner with the new tutor. Seth lagged behind, calling over his shoulder, "Yo, Ad. You coming or what?"

Never ceased to amaze him, how different things now were. Only a few weeks ago, this boy had treated him like a leper. "In a minute," he returned. There was only one shower stall, so there'd be a wait. He'd rather spend the time out here. Besides, he kind of liked the thought of going to therapy covered in horse shit.

Seth paused. He braced his arms against the sides of the barn door, keeping his back to Aden. "Can I ask you a question?"

"Sure," he said, dread leaking into his voice. He

pushed his rake into the ground and leaned against the long, thin handle. "Ask."

"I heard Shannon tell Ryder that you've got girls coming into your room at all hours of the night."

Okay. Not too terrible a topic. "Only two girls, and yes."

Seth swung around, one corner of his lip curved up. "You dating both?"

"Just one, but the other is taken, too." *And Riley will gut you if you go near her.*

"Oh." Seth's shoulders sagged. "Maybe you could invite others and, I don't know, introduce us?"

Aden almost grinned. "Next week, maybe."

"Yeah?"

"Yeah. I know a girl. Stephanie. Very pretty. And she has four friends who I'm sure are pretty, too." No better way to get rid of his unwanted dates than to foist them off on other guys. "I haven't met them yet, but I know you'll love them."

"That'd be great." Seth tossed him a parting grin and loped off.

"Finally. We are alone," a female voice said from behind him.

Aden whipped around as one of the horses whinnied. An unfamiliar girl stood at the end of the barn. She wore a red tank top and a pair of black jeans that molded to her legs. Girls at Crossroads High wore similar attire every day, but on her it looked odd, out of place and uncomfortable.

He studied the rest of her. She had shoulder-length brown hair and dark eyes that slanted up at the corners. Her skin was pale, and she was smiling. That smile wasn't a happy one. Two sharp fangs poked into her bottom lip, revealing the predator she was.

Please tell me this is your next date, Caleb said, finally deigning to speak to Aden.

His next date? Aden tried not to groan.

She appeared older than Victoria by at least ten years, but he supposed that made her young by vampire standards. Vampires aged much, much slower than humans, and the older the vampire, the less their skin could tolerate the bright rays of the sun without blistering. Victoria was "only" eighty-something—that still made him chuckle, since he'd once teased her about being his *grandma* Vicky—and she could still roam freely.

"I see you're looking at my clothes. Stephanie told us colors were now acceptable, and that you actually preferred them. What do you think?" This new vampire twirled, dark gaze remaining on him as long as possible.

"You look beautiful," he said, which was true. She did. She just wasn't his type.

"What's your name?"

"Draven."

An unusual and pretty name. "I'm Aden Stone."

"I know." She moved toward him. Floated, really, so graceful were her movements. As she passed, the horses bucked, but she paid them no heed. "We've met. You do not remember?" A pout curved her bright red lips. "I was there the night you met each of my—your people. You told me you were so happy to make my acquaintance."

Oops. "Uh, now I remember," he lied. Too many faces, too many names. *No one* stood out. And really, he'd said the same thing to everyone.

Tell her she's hot and you could never forget someone like her, Caleb instructed.

We aren't prowling for babes, Julian admonished. *We do have a girlfriend.*

Actually, I have a girlfriend, Aden thought, but they couldn't hear him.

"I'm here because every king requires a queen, and you are in need of one. And I'll be honest. I resisted the thought of being bound to a human at first, but I now think we would be a perfect fit." Her voice dipped huskily, her gaze on the pulse at the base of his neck. "I still feel the pull of you, and I find it…delicious."

He liked when Victoria told him that. Draven? Not so much.

Lucky, Caleb said. *She's hot and she wants you.*

"Actually—"

Draven reached him and traced a white-hot fingertip along his jawline. "You will discover that I'm much better suited for you than Victoria. I," she added, leaning all the way into him and sniffing, "will do anything you ask. *Anything*."

He wasn't dumb. He knew what she was implying, and so did the souls.

I'll take her! Caleb said.

You'll also get us stabbed and killed sooner rather than later, Elijah grumbled. *She's power-hungry. A man-eater.*

Even better.

Dude. Julian *tsk*ed. *Were you a pervert in your other life? Like I already said, we've got Victoria. We don't need this one harshing our mellow. Do you remember those trees Victoria battered? We flirt with this girl, and that'll be our head.*

We? Aden had Victoria, and they needed to start remembering that. "That's sweet of you to offer," he told Draven, then coughed again. *So* uncomfortable. "To do anything, I mean, but, uh, nothing like that will be necessary."

I think I hate you right now, Caleb grumbled.

You should be thanking him, Elijah said with a sigh.

Draven's eyes narrowed, her lashes fusing together. "Well, if you change your mind...the offer has no time limit. Now, what shall we do for our date, hmm?" Hot breath trekked over his face, and he stepped back. "I know humans enjoy having dinner together. We could eat." Her attention returned to his pulse and she laughed. "Or I could."

"I'd prefer not to be the main course, thanks. Or dessert," he added before she could.

She shrugged a delicate shoulder. "Then let's get to know each other better." The words were purred. "That's why I'm here, after all."

She couldn't be more obvious. Elijah's disgust was clear. *She wants to be queen, nothing more. If you marry her, you'll be in pieces by the time she's finished with you.*

"Yeah, I kind of figured that out on my own," he muttered. First, Aden wasn't marrying anyone. Not even Victoria. Not yet. He was only sixteen. Well, almost seventeen. Second…he realized he didn't have a second point.

"Figured what out?" Draven asked, brows furrowed in confusion.

He had that effect on everyone. "Oh, uh. Nothing. Listen." He backed up a few more steps, placing himself out of striking distance. "For our date, we can sit there, in the hay—" he pointed to one of the empty stalls "—and talk about any laws you'd like to see changed." Easy. Innocent.

The grind of her teeth echoed from the wooden walls. "Sitting in hay and talking about laws isn't romantic."

"I never promised romance." God, he wanted this

to end. Did Victoria know Draven was here? If so, was she currently bottling her feelings? Part of him certainly hoped so. Unbottling her was *fun*.

"You studied the stars with Stephanie." Irritation radiated from Draven. "When she met with your councilmen, she extolled the virtues of such a pastime. Now, *I* would like to study the stars."

The candidates really were reporting their "dates" with him. Talk about embarrassing! "Sky's clear right now. If you want to look at the stars, you'll have to come back tonight," he said, knowing full well he wouldn't be available. First, therapy. Then dinner. Then he'd be in town with his friends, hunting. "You aren't allowed to drink from any of the humans here, though, and that's an…order. From your king."

Embracing the role of sovereign? Elijah asked.

No. Yes. Crap. Desperate times and all that. He'd only said what was necessary.

Draven popped her jaw, even as she bowed her head in acknowledgment of his command. "I will not harm your friends, Majesty. You have my word."

"Thank you."

"However, I cannot visit tonight. You may not know this, but guards are posted around our home at all times. We all take turns protecting what's ours. Tonight, from midnight until six, I must patrol the grounds. Unless you relieve me of my duties…" She reached out and drew a fingertip across his collarbone. She was close enough to touch again, yet he'd never seen her move.

He had to arch his back to avoid further contact. "I'm afraid I can't do that. That wouldn't be fair to the others." Impartiality, yeah, that's what he was all about.

Her hand fell heavily to her side. "Very well," she said stiffly. "We will postpone our date, then."

Not if he could help it. "Great. Can't wait." *Except that I can. Forever.*

"Until then." Draven turned and floated from the barn, leaving him alone with a sudden sense of doom.

EIGHTEEN

A few hours earlier...

THE DAY PASSED in a haze for Mary Ann, classes and tests and friends mere blips in her mind. Riley had ignored her, even though they shared the same schedule. That was more than a blip, but not the cause of her upset.

There were only two more days until the witches' death curse took effect. *If* it did. Health-wise, she still felt fine. And yet, she'd never felt so helpless. Or more desperate. "What if" was a constant refrain inside her head. What if she went to sleep in two days and never woke up? What if her heart simply stopped beating? What if a car plowed into her?

If she had to round up every witch in the area and call a meeting to order herself, she would. And she would—hey. Wait. Her eyes widened as her mind whirled. Maybe she *could* do that. What if she used her...aptitude for sensing magic to find the witches, kinda like following her very own yellow brick road, and forced them into the same location?

Finally, a "what if" she liked.

Would calling a meeting to order herself count, though? Or would she simply earn the wrath of some very powerful women?

Worth trying, she thought. And besides, she'd already earned their wrath. So, next question: when to begin? Aden would be busy most of the evening; he had an appointment with his therapist and a dinner at the D and M Ranch. But Riley and Victoria, and even Lauren, could help her. They'd all planned to meet up anyway, but if Mary Ann struck out on her own, she could find the witches, call her friends, and they could bag and tag. Of course, Victoria and Lauren might wonder exactly how Mary Ann was able to sense witches now, and Riley had told her not to tell *anyone* about her new ability. With very good reason.

Crap. Victoria and Lauren were out. Mary Ann would have to rely on Riley. Only Riley. Her stomach clenched. He was clearly angry with her again. After all, she hadn't told him about Aden's possible murder. And she'd broken up with him, had meant it, and she wouldn't change her mind. *Don't cry.* That didn't mean they had to stay away from each other, though. Didn't mean they couldn't be civil. They could work together, amicably, to save their lives. Couldn't they? Yes. Yes, they could. And next time she saw him, she would tell him so. Even yell at him if she had to.

He'd commanded his brothers—the snow-white wolf and the golden wolf who had followed her and Penny that night—to walk her home after school and had taken off. Where he'd gone, she didn't know. She'd asked the brothers, but they had ignored her, merely keeping step beside her.

Now she pounded inside her house, shutting the two out before they could race past the front door. Her dad could barely tolerate Riley. No way she'd introduce him to two more wolves. Wolves she didn't even know, at that. Wolves who clearly hadn't *wanted* her to know them.

"How old are you?" she'd asked both after failing to gain Riley's location.

Nothing.

"Do you have the same parents as Riley?"

Nothing.

"Are you nervous about the death curse placed on him?"

Again, nothing.

Finally she'd given up on that, too. Her relationship with their brother was over—*seriously, don't cry*—so of course they hated her and wanted nothing to do with her.

She sighed. Her dad was still at work, the house silent.

Mary Ann sprinted up the stairs, down the hall and into her bedroom. All the colors splashed throughout blended together and created a bright rainbow haze. Usually she found comfort in that. Today, not so much.

At her desk, she withdrew her cell phone from her backpack and sat down. *Are you really going to do this?*

A moment passed before she nodded. Oh, yes. She was going to do this. There was no other way. Just after she punched the first word in her text, her house phone rang. Frowning, she leaned over to the unit poised at the edge of her desk and glanced at the caller ID. Penny.

Though she felt harried, Mary Ann answered. "Hello."

"Hey, you. You raced out of school today before I could talk to you."

"Sorry. I just—" What? Telling the truth wasn't an option.

"I hardly see you anymore. Unless you're sneaking out, that is. Which brings me to the reason I'm calling." There was so much glee in Penny's tone, Mary Ann had no doubts about what her friend was thinking.

"I can't sneak out again," she lied, and hated herself. Honesty was prized, but she didn't want Penny involved in tonight's hunt. "I need my rest." Now that was the truth. She needed it, but she wouldn't get it.

"Oh. Well, that's too bad because I hear a big group of kids will be making an appearance in town tonight."

Mary Ann groaned. "That's not safe."

"The fun things never are."

"You're going?"

"Nah. Not if you're staying in. The baby…"

"Are you sick?"

"A little. Only, it's not just morning sickness anymore. It's now nighttime sickness, too. And get this. I think I saw Tucker today."

Mary Ann straightened, her ears perking. "Me, too. Yesterday, I mean, but I wasn't sure."

"I know the feeling. He was in the trees when I walked out of school. Not that he bothered to come talk to me, the bastard. And he was gone so fast I couldn't tell if it had really been him to begin with."

What was he doing, lurking about? After surviving a vampire attack, he'd vowed to behave. "Just…be careful. Okay?"

"I will. Love you, Mary Contrary."

"Love you, too, Penn."

As she hung up, Mary Ann spied another of her candy bars from the corner of her eye. Her mouth didn't water, but she found herself ripping past the wrapper, lifting the chocolate sticks and holding them to her nose, sniffing. Not a single hunger pang, no flooding of moisture in her mouth.

She'd been without any food for nearly a week. Well, except for that one bite of Snickers, but it didn't count since she'd immediately barfed. In front of Riley. How mortifying. *His opinion doesn't matter. You can't have him.*

Don't cry.

She swallowed the lump in her throat, set the candy bar aside and reclaimed her cell phone. With trembling fingers, she typed the rest of the text to Riley. He rarely used his phone, but she wasn't going to concern herself with that. It would be his fault if he missed her message.

In two hours, I'm hunting witches. Either come with me or don't. Up to you. Either way, I'm headed out without the others.

Good or bad, she had to try to find them, and she had to go before her dad got home. That way, she could leave him a note—*studying with friends, be back later*—and not have to endure the Spanish Inquisition.

Are you really going to do this?

Yes, she thought again. She was. Though her trembling increased, she pressed "send."

ADEN LAY ON Dr. Hennessy's couch again, the room dimmed, that same tranquil music playing in the background. He waited...craving answers...

"Did you take your medication today?" the doctor asked him.

"Yes," he lied.

"If that's so, why aren't your pupils dilated?"

"I don't know. I haven't had any medical training."

Good one, Caleb said, mentally high-fiving him.

Julian laughed.

Behave, Elijah cautioned. *We have to tread carefully.*

"Do you like the souls, Aden? Is that why you refuse my aid?"

Aid? Ha! For once, Aden opted for honesty with this man. "Actually, Dr. Hennessy, I just don't like you."

"I see." The good doctor didn't seem like he cared.

"What did you do to me, the last time I was here?"

"What I always do. Talk. Listen."

Hardly. "And you plan to talk and listen to me again this evening?"

"Of course. Mr. Reeves is very pleased with your progress. He says you now get along with the other boys at the ranch. He says you're doing your schoolwork and are even impressing your teachers. But he also says you're still talking to yourself, and you and I both know why that is, Aden. Don't we?"

He stiffened, even as the soft lounge beneath him begged him to relax. "You tell me." He would have to act soon. He couldn't risk being sucked under again. No telling what the doctor would do.

"I've encountered your kind before, you know."

"Crazy?"

"No. A...what did you call yourself? A magnet."

And he'd thought himself stiff before. He'd never told Dr. Hennessy he saw himself as a supernatural magnet, but he *had* thought it. He'd told Mary Ann and the others, but none of them would have confided in Dr. Hennessy. Which meant that the doctor had dragged the confession out of him, without his awareness.

What else had he learned?

Not yet. Steady. He wanted to gather as much information as he could before acting.

"No lies to feed me? That's not like you, Aden."

"You mentioned that you've met others."

"Yes."

"Who? When? What could they do?" Did he believe Dr. Hennessy? No.

But lies could be checked out, information verified—or not.

Good. Keep him talking, Elijah said.

"What do you know of your parents?" the doctor asked, rather than answer him.

Not much. He knew they'd once lived next to Mary Ann's mom and dad. That Mary Ann's mother had been pregnant at the same time as Aden's mother. That he and Mary Ann had been born on the same day, in the same hospital. That Mary Ann's mother had died immediately after giving birth and he'd somehow pulled her soul into his head—along with several others, people who had probably died at the hospital, as well.

"Nothing," he finally replied.

Dr. Hennessy sighed. "Perhaps one day you'll trust me."

In unison, the souls snorted.

Yeah. Right. "What of the others? Did they trust you?"

Again, the doctor sidestepped the question. "It's time for you to relax, Aden, and let your troubles fall away."

Subtle. Clearly, there was to be no more talking. Well, then, it was finally time for Aden to act, even though he'd learned very little. He straightened, throwing his legs over the side of the chair.

"Lie back down, Aden."

"In a minute."

Caleb, he said inside his mind, praying the soul could, for once, hear him through the constant flow of chatter. *Get ready.* He closed the distance between himself and the doctor, and as he made contact with the cold skin of the doctor's wrist, Hennessy's eyes—a rainbow of colors now, a pretty mask once more appearing beneath that plain face—widened.

Caleb leapt into action.

Aden moaned in pain as his body morphed from solid mass to insubstantial mist, that mist slipping inside Dr.

Hennessy and taking over mind and body. Never failed to amaze him when this happened.

"Thank you," Aden said, speaking in Dr. Hennessy's nasally voice.

Welcome, Caleb replied with no small amount of pride.

Aden took stock. The doctor's body was cold, empty and hungry...so hungry, but underneath the cold and the emptiness and the hunger was a rush of power, unnatural power, glittering like that strange, clear mask Aden sometimes saw underneath the doctor's face.

Dr. Hennessy wasn't human.

So what was he? *Figure that mystery out later.* Aden glanced at the clock on the wall. Thirty-three minutes until the end of his session. He got to work. He looked through files, but only a few were out in the open and none applied to him. Dr. Hennessy's scribbled notes were quite interesting, though.

More than human, but no powers.

Completely human, but could be useful.

Warmer than most. Reasons?

Linked.

What did that mean? What did any of it mean? The cabinets were locked, and he tried to jimmy them loose so he could read other files. When that failed, he searched for a key.

The desk was neat, tidy, a few unimportant papers. Inside the drawers, there was nothing but paper clips, rubber bands and pens. No photos, no personal notes. No booze. No snacks. And, of course, no key. He moved to the bookcases. To his surprise, he found hidden drawers at the bottom. Inside them? Tattoo equipment, of all things. Everything from needles to body paint to gloves.

Aden made sure to put everything back in its place so that Dr. Hennessy would never know what he'd done. He'd suspect, maybe, but he'd never find proof.

You gotta get into those file cabinets, Julian said. *That voice recorder he stuffed under your nose might be in there.*

"I know. Elijah? Any ideas?"

Sorry. Drawing a blank.

Trying not to drown under a wave of frustration, Aden returned to the desk and fell into the chair. If he couldn't get to the files and the recorder, maybe he could gain the information he wanted by traveling through Dr. Hennessy's past. He still possessed the ability, after all.

Eve, though, had been the one to manipulate time. She'd merely had to visualize a scene, and she had been able to transport Aden there. With Shannon, Aden had had no control. He'd simply whisked from one scene to the next, tugged by an invisible chain. Still. He would try.

"Get ready, guys. I'm gonna try and go back to that last session and see it through his eyes."

Elijah groaned. *I don't like this.*

You can do it, man, Caleb said.

Julian sighed. *God help us.*

Aden closed his eyes, blanked his mind, drew in a deep breath...exhaled...slowly...He thought back, painting the dark canvas of his mind with images from his last visit here. He'd been on the lounge, lying down, staring up at the ceiling. Dr. Hennessy had been behind him.

A spike of dizziness caused his heart to speed up. He continued. Soft music had played, was playing even now. The ceiling had blurred. Darkness had swallowed him whole.

Aden's skin tingled, the dizziness spreading, strengthening, and suddenly he was falling, whisking through a never-ending pit, arms flailing for some kind of anchor. *This was it.* He was doing it, traveling back. In control.

When he stilled, when the dizziness subsided, he slowly cracked open his eyelids. Yet still he saw only... static? There was no office, no desk, no lounge. At the very least, he should have seen himself lying down.

He frowned. He closed his eyes, shook his head, then looked again. Once again, he saw only a void of static, as if the cable had been unhooked from the TV.

What's happening? Julian asked, and he sounded scared.

I see nothing, like when Mary Ann is with you. Caleb's voice trembled.

I have a bad feeling about this, Elijah said gravely. *Something's wrong here.*

"I know." But what? His hands fisted, the answer eluding him. He couldn't picture another scene, because he didn't know any other details about Dr. Hennessy's life. And there were no photos in the room, so he couldn't study them and use them as a guide.

Not knowing what else to do, he willed himself back to the present. As the darkness faded, he began to see the office through Hennessy's eyes. Nothing had changed. He still sat at the desk, that handful of papers around him. Reeling, he could only watch the clock, waiting as time ticked away. When his session reached its limit, he walked Hennessy back to his chair and sat him down. Then Aden pulled himself from the body, returning to solid form, and dropped back onto the lounge. Waiting. Dreading.

There was a moment of suspended silence.

Hennessy would know only that time had elapsed. He wouldn't know what had happened during those missing minutes.

"Time's up," Aden gritted out.

"Well, we were certainly productive today, weren't we?" the doctor said, unemotional as always. His clothes rustled as he stood. Soft footsteps sounded, and then

Hennessy was in front of him, peering down at him, hands fisted at his waist. "Before you leave, I need to issue a word of warning. If you ever again invade my mind and body, I'll cut the souls out of you, one by one. Are we clear?"

Aden and the souls didn't have time to panic. Their entire world fell back into that black, black sea.

nineteen

In the middle of the woods, with trees stretching all around, the quickly dimming sun, a cold wind slithering past every few seconds, Mary Ann stood in the midst of pure testosterone. Riley and his brothers formed a triangle, each at a point before and beside her. They'd arrived right on time, at her two-hour limit, and had escorted her here. Away from civilization.

She'd spent every minute of those two hours trying to research Drainers, magic powers—again—and all kinds of other paranormal stuff. Two hours that now seemed wasted. She'd learned nothing.

Hopefully, that would change now that she was with the wolves. Not that they were informative, or even helpful. Once again, they'd walked beside her, silent.

Now she studied them, searching for a weakness. One word described them all: *gorgeous*. Nathan was all white, from his hair to his skin, with eyes so pale a blue they were almost eerie. But like Riley, he was tall and leanly muscled, with a hard expression that said, *I'll do anything, yeah, even stab you.* Maxwell was tanner…a golden variation of him.

They were warriors, definitely, who looked like they ate glass shards for breakfast and anyone who got in their way for dessert.

"So we're not hunting witches?" she asked. At this point, any other activity seemed extraneous and unnecessary. She'd thought Riley understood that, which was why she'd been so surprised to see his brothers. Had he told them what she was—or rather, what she might be? He still hadn't accepted the truth.

"Hunting?" Finally, something from one of the brothers. Nathan's voice was low and husky, like a shiver over her skin.

"We're teaching you how to defend yourself," Riley said. "Hunting can wait."

"And let me state again that I think this is stupid," Nathan added.

"She's human." Maxwell, the other brother, had a much harder, more determined voice. "She's also fragile as hell. We're…not."

"Just do it," Riley snarled at them.

Mary Ann would have cringed at his tone, but it wasn't directed at her, so she took heart. Besides, he'd never looked sexier. He wore all black, and there were cuts along his forearms, as if he'd recently fought something with claws.

Her knees were actually weak at the thought; she wanted to throw her arms around him and hold on forever, basking in his strength. *You're broken up, remember?*

Don't cry.

Nathan shook his head. "She's yours, Ry, and we know how you are. If we bruise her…"

"I'll behave." Another snarl from Riley. "Just don't scratch or bite her."

She noticed that he didn't disabuse them of their "she's yours" notion. Well, she wouldn't either. Right now she felt a little too much like the cheese in a mousetrap.

"You're right. Learning to fight is important," she began. "But right now there are even more important—"

"No," Riley said, cutting her off without looking at her, "there aren't. Teach her how to defend herself against wolves and vampires. Everything you can in the next two hours, then she and I will be on our way."

Mary Ann gulped as realization set in. Even before saving her from the death spell, he wanted her to know how to defend herself against wolves and vamps. Which meant he thought they would figure out she was a Drainer very soon. Which meant he thought they would try to kill her. Painfully. He wanted her prepared, able to defend herself.

Would they later punish him for that?

A tremor swept through her, and those tears she'd fought against burned her eyes. She'd made the right decision, ending things. She would not hurt him. Ever. Even accidentally. Even after she…died.

Look what he'd done—was doing—to protect her right now. He deserved better than she could give him.

"Fine." Maxwell sighed.

"Sure. Why not?" Nathan shrugged.

Such enthusiasm. Didn't matter, though. She would listen and she would learn. She would never have another chance like this one.

"You're—you're not going to help them?" she asked Riley, blushing at her stutter.

His gaze didn't flick to her, but remained on his brothers as he gave a stiff shake of his head. She remembered what she'd once told him, that if he taught her how to fight, he'd have to put his hands on her, and if he put his hands on her, she would want to kiss him, not learn from him. Did *he* remember? Did he not want her lips on his?

Oh, God. She wanted him to want her, wanted to keep him. *Don't you dare cry.*

How many times would she have to issue the command to herself?

"Do it," he said, backing away from the group. He stopped at a tree, pressing his back into the wide trunk, and folded his arms over his middle. His expression was dark, stormy.

"Do not interfere," Maxwell told him with a finger pointed at his chest.

Nathan snorted. "Like he'll obey you. He always does what he wants. You know that."

She nodded in agreement, and both brothers focused on her. Uh-oh. All that intensity…closing in on her, one in front and one behind. Why had she agreed to this, again?

"You ready, little girl?"

"You gonna sob like a baby if we get a little rough?"

Both were taunting her, and at first, her hackles rose. Then she remembered what Aden had told her. When fighting, emotions could ruin you. They made you dumb, kept you distracted. You had to remain distanced. You had to do whatever was needed to survive.

I feel nothing. Except nervous. Argh! She raised her chin, pretending, at least, to be calm. "I won't cry if you don't."

Surprise flickered in both their eyes, and Maxwell even looked like he was fighting a grin.

"Spirit," he said. "Let's see how quickly we can crush it."

In a snap, they were on her, tossing her to the ground like a doll, their now sharp, long teeth near her neck. She was too shocked—and terrified—to move or even block them. They'd swarmed her so quickly, her gaze had failed to track them.

Slowly, they backed away from her, standing over her and peering down. Something to note: they hadn't chewed her face off.

"We've got our work cut out for us," Nathan grumbled, and offered her a hand to help her up.

Her knees almost gave out when she tried to balance her weight.

"Vamps and wolves are faster than any human you can imagine," Maxwell told her. "Clearly, you're much slower."

"Yeah, uh, I just figured that out. Thanks."

Both chuckled.

"Vamps want your blood, and while they don't have to dive for your neck to get it, that's what they prefer. It's harder for humans to push them away that way. Plus, it weakens the victim faster."

"So basically, we're like cows to them," she said dryly.

"Except, you kill cows. Vamps just drink and discard, their food still kicking when they're done." Nathan shrugged. "For the most part."

For the most part. Such a pleasant add-on. Mary Ann pressed her lips together as she recalled an exception to that "for the most part." She'd watched several vampires torture and kill a boy named Ozzie. They'd splayed him out on a table—Tucker, too—and used him as an appetizer at their party, until the life drained out of him.

Either the wolves read her mind or her pinched expression gave her away. "Yeah, we heard about that," Maxwell said. "Like humans, there are good and bad vampires. Good and bad wolves, too."

"Speaking of, wolves don't feed on humans." Nathan picked up the lesson, expanding it. "If a wolf is attacking you, that wolf just wants you dead. And a wolf's claws can ruin you in seconds, so your main goal when fighting a shifter is to avoid being slashed."

"I never would have figured that out," she said with a roll of her eyes. "So exactly how am I supposed to do that?"

"We'll show you. Just try and keep up."

For every minute of Riley's allotted two hours, the boys worked with her. They tossed her down; they even threw her into trees. She lost her breath, nearly broke her wrist and definitely twisted her ankle, yet still she persisted. Still she made them keep coming at her.

They taught her many things. Mainly, she couldn't

hide from them. Their sense of smell was twenty times greater than a human's. Their hearing was forty times greater. Also, they liked it when she ran. She became a game, a prize, and their heart rate would quicken with the challenge, their need to conquer intensifying.

If wolves approached her while in a pack, she was to remember that they were territorial and very rigidly structured. There was always a leader. Always. That leader controlled the actions of the others. If she could defeat the leader, she could defeat the pack. Unless, of course, the leader told the pack to glom onto her.

Warning signs of an impending glomming: their hair would rise. They would bare their teeth and growl.

Every time Maxwell and Nathan demonstrated that, in human *and* wolf form, her fear ratcheted another notch. They scented that fear, and it upped their hunger level, increasing the odds against her. She would have to learn to control her physical reactions, to show no fear, as Aden had already told her.

How? It was possible to hide an expression. It wasn't possible to stop her heart from racing.

In the meantime, she now knew their noses were sensitive, more so than a human's, so if she could hit them on their noses, she could buy herself several precious seconds to find a weapon. A stick, a rock, anything would help.

If they managed to pounce and push her down while

she did so, she had to try and snap their necks with a firm twist of her wrists before they tore out her throat. Also, it was better to shove her hand into their mouths to keep their teeth busy with her fingers and wrist than to let them bite into her neck. Because if that happened, she was dead, no question. She could live without a hand.

If she was near water, she was to jump in. Wolves had a hard time fighting in water. They could do it, but it wasn't their preference. And if she was lucky, they would give up and move on at that point, eager for readier prey.

By the end, she was sweaty, dirty and yeah, bleeding, not to mention grateful for the darkened sky. The boys hadn't scratched her, per Riley's orders, but the rocks and bark had. A few times, from the corner of her eye, she'd seen Riley stalk toward her, but then he would catch himself and return to his post, watching.

Maxwell and Nathan, at least, were just as sweaty and dirty as she was.

"Good job, human." Maxwell patted her on the shoulder, and she pitched forward. Laughing, Maxwell caught her and helped her straighten. "I expected you to beg for mercy after five minutes."

With that, the two sauntered away, clothes flying behind them as they undressed, leaving her alone with Riley. Howls soon erupted.

"Meet us in town," Riley called. "One hour."

More howls.

Agreement?

"Come on," Riley said to her now. "Time to leave the forest. Goblins are starting to emerge."

Together, they raced to the car he had stashed at the edge of the forest and slipped inside. Soon her heart was pounding in tune to the car's revving engine. From all the exercise, yes, but also from being so close to her now-ex. *Don't cry.*

"Do your brothers know about me?" she asked, even though she knew the answer.

"No, and we won't tell them."

"Won't they realize something's different about me if I lead us straight to a witch? I mean—"

Riley was shaking his head. "Believe me, I'll be taking credit for finding the witch. *If* we find one. So no worries. Right now we're going to the vampire mansion."

"I should go home, shower and change first," she said, very conscious of how she must look. Hobo central.

"Why? You'll just get dirty again."

"At the mansion?"

"In town. That's where we're going after. To hunt, remember. If I don't hunt with you, you'll go alone. Believe me, I haven't forgotten your ultimatum."

She wouldn't apologize for that. Her intentions were too pure.

"Anyway," he said, not quite so grumpy, "you can't go home."

True. Her dad was there, and he'd ask questions she wasn't prepared to answer and think things she didn't want him to think. *What have you been doing? Where have you been? Someone hurt you. Did they force you to do...things?* Then he'd get the police involved. No, thanks.

"So why are we going to the mansion?" she asked.

"I want to take you to Victoria and get some of her blood inside you."

What? "Oh, no. No, no, no. I'm not drinking anyone's blood." She shook her head for emphasis.

"It'll strengthen you, heal your injuries."

In her seat, she swayed back and forth with the bump, bump of the tires. "It'll also force me to see the world through her eyes, and I have enough problems facing it through my own."

"That'll only last a few hours."

"Don't care. I'm not injured badly enough to justify it."

His knuckles tightened on the wheel. Had she not been watching him so closely, she would have missed the telling reaction. "Yeah, but it just might slow down your new ability."

Thanks for the reminder. "Are you sure about that? Because maybe it'll speed the abilities up like the spell did. Not that you're one hundred percent certain I'm a Drainer, remember?" she added in a rush.

He massaged the back of his neck. "Fine." He maneuvered the car off the grass and onto a nearby dirt road, then turned around and headed in the opposite direction. "No blood."

"Thank you."

"Save your thanks. I know you want to break up with me, and that's coloring your reaction to my helpful suggestions, but you have to—"

"Wait. Want? No. Not even close." She wouldn't have him believing he meant nothing to her. He meant *everything.* "I just don't want to hurt you, Riley."

"And I don't want to hurt you." He reached over and clasped her hand, their fingers intertwining. His skin was warm, callused. "So here's the thing. We have two days. Two days before the death curse takes effect, and I don't want to spend those days fighting with you."

Oh, God. She'd never thought of things that way. Two days, yeah, she'd realized—and hated—that, but how she would spend those days? Enjoying them or lost to misery? No. Not even a blip.

"I don't either," she admitted.

He brought her hand to his lips and pressed a kiss into her pulse, hot, soft, his tongue even flicking out for a quick taste. Goose bumps spread. "Good, because I want to be with you while we face this. After that, you can break up with me if that's what you still want. Just don't expect me to like it or walk away without a fight."

Two more days with him, enjoying rather than wallowing over what could have been. She couldn't resist, even though every new minute she spent with him, as if they were a couple, would deepen her sense of connection to him. Even though breaking up with him the first time had nearly killed her, so doing it again would definitely finish her off. She wasn't hurting him physically, wasn't destroying his wolf-side—yet. Two more days with him would be fine.

And that was not an invitation to the Universe to prove her wrong.

"Okay. Yes." With the words, a weight lifted from her shoulders and she suddenly felt ten pounds lighter. "I want to be with you, too."

He pushed out a relieved breath. "All right, then. I can kill my brothers for hurting you now."

She laughed, so happy she could have burst. "No, you can't. You asked them to train me."

"And I told them to be careful with you."

"How am I supposed to learn if they treat me like breakable china?"

"Doesn't mean I have to like it," he grumbled.

Sweet boy.

Grinning, Mary Ann turned her attention outside. With the appearance of the moon, there was a radiant golden glow cast over the forest, dust sparkling in the muted light like glitter, and then, as the trees thinned out and buildings came into view, she saw that the glow and the glitter spread to the brick, creating an eerily beautiful, well, aura. Was that what Riley saw around human bodies? Then she spied the litter dotting the streets, and the glow faded.

Riley parked between a gas station and a laundromat, the shadows cast from both hiding their car. The sidewalks were barren and the stores were empty, as if everyone had gone home early. To prepare for the coming party Penny had told her about?

He opened his door, but rather than step out, he remained in place, peering over at her. "If you sense any witches…"

"I'll tell you immediately. I swear."

With a grateful nod, he emerged and strode to her side before she had time to open her door. He did it for her and extended a hand to help her up and out. Such manners—his mother would be proud—and such endearing sweetness, all wrapped in that bad-boy package.

How had she broken up with him, even for a second? Stupid girl.

Yeah, but you want him to survive.

Oh, yeah.

The air was colder now, with a bit of a bite, but Riley draped an arm around her shoulders, keeping her tucked against him and his delicious heat while they explored. Good thing, too. She sensed no magic, and with every step, she weakened a bit more, her body trembling. What was wrong with her?

"Still cold?" he asked.

"No." Her stomach twisted, utterly empty and ready to erupt into complaints. Was she, dare she hope, hungry? Yes. Yes, she was. She ground to a halt and grinned. "Riley. You're not going to believe this, but I'm starving. I'm actually starving!"

He didn't share her good humor. One of his brows arched as he asked, "For food?"

"Of course." Except, she thought of a slice of her favorite cheese pizza, and the twisting in her stomach became cramping. She thought of beef lo mein, the last real meal she remembered having with her dad, and the cramps gave way to sharp aches. *Don't give up.* She thought of chicken noodle soup, what her mom had fed her each time she'd been sick, and the twisting started up again.

She thought of magic, filling her up, sweeping through her, consuming her, threads of warmth and power weaving inside her, forming a blanket of serenity and strength, and her stomach calmed. Just. Like. That.

Oh…no…

Hope died, burned to ash forevermore. She'd realized the truth before, but just then she knew, bone deep. She *was* a Drainer, and there was no use pretending otherwise or clinging to false hope. She fed off of magic. She destroyed.

"No," she whispered, dejection replacing her joy. "Not for food."

Riley's arm tightened around her. He kissed her temple, an I-still-like-you gesture, and they kicked back into gear. They continued their exploration, silent, and she tried not to worry. As she'd thought, the stores were empty. Even the twenty-four-hour drive-through taco joint that stayed open on Christmas.

"This isolation is weird," she finally said.

"Yeah. Picking up on anything?"

"Not yet." There wasn't a single whiff of magic, and with every second that passed, her hunger for it intensified. She needed...

A few minutes later, Riley's brothers joined them, human and dressed again. Thankfully, Riley didn't threaten or chastise them as he'd claimed. He just drew Mary Ann even closer to him, distracting her from her gnawing hunger.

"Saw several cars on their way here," Nathan said.

"All kids, no adults," Maxwell added.

And sure enough, tires were soon squealing and kids pouring out of several vehicles. Beer bottles were soon clanking together. Someone cranked their radio up as loud as it would go. Laughter sounded, whoops and whistles, and conversations rose.

The party had officially started, it seemed, but every attendee was human, not a supernatural creature among them. Disappointment ate at her as one hour ticked by, then another. There was dancing, a few make-out sessions, unexpected hookups, one fight, lots of drinking, and even a bonfire, right there in the middle of town. The cops didn't show up, and the few adults who did arrive joined the festivities rather than break them up.

Penny was going to find out Mary Ann had come, and there would be hell to pay. Couldn't be helped, though.

Mary Ann watched and waited, no longer quite so distracted from the hunger pains in her belly. She was still weakening, again trembling. Perhaps coming here hadn't been such a good idea. In fact, she'd opened her mouth to ask Riley to take her home when Brittany Buchanan spotted her and raced over. Britt wasn't stumbling, thank God. In Mary Ann's current mood, she didn't think she could deal with a slobbering, slurring, human beer keg.

"Can we talk?" the girl asked, nervously tugging Mary Ann away from Riley before she had time to respond.

He maintained his grip. She tossed him an I'll-be-fine glance, whispered, "If she gets out of line, I'll smack her." He fought a self-deprecating grin, nodded stiffly and finally released her. However, his gaze followed her every movement.

"Is something wrong?"

Britt shook her head, and when they were on the other side of the bonfire, kids dancing around them, her friend leaned close and said, "First, what have you been doing? Rolling in the dirt?" She smiled to lessen the sting of her words. "I don't have to ask who you were rolling with, though, do I? *Anyway*. That's not why I dragged you away. Tell me, who's the hottie and is he available?"

Ah. A crush. "Which one?"

"The one that reminds me of a great big snow-flake."

"That's Nathan, Riley's brother." Away from Riley's warmth, her trembling intensified. "As far as I know, he's single."

Britt's eyes widened. "Really? Introduce me. Please! You promised. Remember? Oh, this is so exciting!" She clapped and jumped up and down. "Do it now, do it now or I'll *die*."

"Come on." Mary Ann led her back to the group of wolf-shifters and made the introductions. Nathan barely paid her any attention. Maxwell, however, shook her hand and smiled at her, a wicked smile that should have melted the girl into butter.

Only, Brittany wanted nothing to do with him. Her attention was primarily focused on Nathan—who couldn't have been ruder. For the most part, he ignored her. When he did finally deign to speak to her, he did so with a cold, clipped tone.

"You're a borderline asshole, you know that?" Maxwell muttered to him.

"Only borderline? I must be off my game," Nathan replied, unrepentant.

Mary Ann wanted to slap him, and would have, if Riley hadn't sensed her intentions and grabbed her wrist.

Finally, Brittany gave up. "I can see our conversation was completely unnecessary, Mary Ann, but thanks for the intro." With that, she wandered back to her circle of friends.

Maxwell punched Nathan in the arm. Nathan flipped him off. The two stomped off in different directions.

Riley drew Mary Ann in front of him and settled her body against his. More warmth. Hunger, fading from her awareness as she savored. Hmm. She wouldn't have too many more moments like this, she suspected, so she had to enjoy them while she could.

"Your brother," she said with a shake of her head.

"The curse," Riley whispered in her ear.

"What?"

"Remember? When one of my brothers is attracted to a girl, she will only see him as ugly. When my brothers are not attracted to a girl, she will see his true self."

Oh. Poor boys. That meant Maxwell had been attracted to Brittany and Nathan had not.

The only way to break the curse was for the boys to die. Like humans, wolves were not always able to be resuscitated. So killing them just to better their love lives? Not gonna happen. The risk—*permanently* dying—wasn't worth the reward.

"Besides, Nathan doesn't date humans. Ever," Riley further explained. "Which is why every female here is eyeing him like he's candy. They want what they instinctively know they can't have."

"A few are eyeing Maxwell that way," she said, oddly defensive of the gold wolf. "And you, too, of course."

"The ones looking at Max aren't his type, and therefore see his true self. And I haven't noticed anyone looking at me but you."

She traced her fingers over his arms and wished they were alone so she could tell him how beautiful he was, inside and out, and then kiss him, taste him, making the most of their time together.

"Should we leave?" Mary Ann asked, doing her best not to sound hopeful. They had a mission, after all. A very important one, at that.

His sigh ruffled her hair. "Yeah. The witches are staying away. They knew we would come."

She wouldn't feel guilty about that. Much. "So why not just fight us?"

"I don't know. Maybe they're planning something. Maybe they're searching for their friend."

She didn't mean to, but she stiffened. What if they succeeded? What would happen if her group lost their only bargaining chip? Nothing good, that was for sure.

"Don't worry," Riley said. "They won't find her. They can't track like wolves can."

Slowly she relaxed. *There's nothing more you can do here. For once, enjoy yourself. Before it's too late.* She twisted in his arms, rose on her tiptoes and pressed a kiss onto his lips. Soft, sweet...but not enough. "Riley..."

He jerked her as close to him as he could get her. His breathing was suddenly labored, sawing in and out of his mouth. "Let's go somewhere private," he said hoarsely.

"Yes," she said, melting into that puddle of butter as Brittany should have. "Let's."

TWENTY

"—SAID YOU WERE GOING TO be out of it because of the medication, but I'm a little worried. Are you okay?"

Dan's voice dragged Aden out of a long, dark tunnel. A bouncy tunnel. He blinked open his eyes. A moment passed before he oriented himself and realized he was in Dan's truck, local shops whizzing past, a party taking place outside them.

"Aden?" Dan prompted.

"What? Sorry."

"You okay?"

"Yeah. Sure." He rubbed his temples, then his eyes. How had he gotten in the truck? Last thing he remembered, he'd walked inside Dr. Hennessy's office, the sun dimming but shining, the air cool. After that he'd… He frowned. He didn't remember. Now, the moon was high and golden.

What had they talked about? How much time had passed?

His frown deepened. He didn't remember that, either.

Medication, Dan had said. Had Dr. Hennessy dosed him without his knowledge? "Hello," Aden whispered under his breath. "You guys there?"

Present.

Accounted for.

Here.

No medication then. If Dr. Hennessy had forced the drugs on him, the souls would be unable to communicate with him. He wanted to ask them if they remembered what had happened, but couldn't. Not with Dan here.

"Are we just now leaving his office?"

"Yeah. You were pretty out of it, so I waited as long as I could before taking off with you, just in case you needed medical attention." There was sympathy in Dan's voice. Clearly, he assumed Aden was regressing. "We've got the dinner with the new tutor, and we're already a little late, so I finally hauled butt out of there."

None of this made any sense. He suddenly recalled sitting in his chair, filled with dread but resolved. Then... nothing.

"If you need to take tomorrow off from school," Dan said, "I'll understand."

"No. I'll be fine." He hoped. He still had witches to hunt. "Did Dr. Hennessy say anything else?"

"Only that he was sorry you had such an adverse reaction to your therapy. Well, that, and you weren't taking your medication properly. That true?"

Aden hated lying to Dan, and had to do so all too often. He wouldn't do it now, he decided. "Yes. It's true."

"Why? Don't you want to get better?"

Surprisingly, there'd been no anger to the question. "I'm not crazy. I don't need to get better."

Dan scowled at him. He was in his thirties, with sandy hair and hazel eyes, and those eyes most often regarded Aden with kindness and understanding. Just then, the anger Aden had expected dominated them. "You still talk to yourself. Of course you're not better. You'll have to do better than that if you want me to help get you off the meds."

Dan would help? Deep down, where every betrayal and rejection he'd ever received festered, unable to heal, Aden simply couldn't believe it was possible. They'd find out the truth soon enough, though. "You want to know why? Fine. The pills make me tired, foggy. When I'm on them, I can't think right, or at all, really. They make me stupid and I have enough to deal with without adding bad decisions and bad names to the mix. And yeah, I'm called names. *Retarded* being at the top of the list."

Several seconds passed in silence, seeming to stretch

into eternity. "Well, okay, then. We'll talk to the doctor about putting you on something else."

Just like that? That was…that was…still unbelievable. He decided to push a little more. "I don't like Dr. Hennessy, Dan. He creeps me out, and I'd rather you didn't talk to him about me. At all."

Dan tossed him a guarded glance. "Creeps you out, how?"

"I don't know. I just don't like the way he looks at me."

The patent stillness of a predator overcame Dan. "Has he ever touched you, Aden? In an improper way?"

"No," he said, and Dan relaxed. Then he added, "Kind of," as he remembered the way Hennessy had perched at the edge of his recliner, holding that recorder. "Oh, I don't know. I just don't feel…safe with him."

"Well, I don't like that. Not at all, and I won't tolerate it. So I'll talk to your caseworker about getting you another doctor, but I'll be honest. This is a small town and we're running out of options. In fact, I remember the list from last time and there was only one other name. Dr. Morris Gray."

Mary Ann's dad. Aden's stomach clenched, even as he realized Dan truly meant to help him. Dr. Gray had been his doctor years ago. They both recalled that, and how Dr. Gray had tossed him out of his office because Aden had admitted to time-traveling—exactly what

Mary Ann's mom used to claim to do. He'd thought Aden had stolen and read his journals about his wife's history, and had erupted.

Dr. Gray still thought so, because he didn't want to admit the truth, that his wife hadn't been crazy, that he'd tried to medicate her for nothing. That she'd died because no one had listened to her, helped her. Therefore, Aden and Dr. Gray did *not* get along.

"No," Aden said with a shake of his head.

"Wouldn't matter anyway. Dr. Gray already turned us down because he had too many other patients."

Yeah. Right. "Maybe we could find someone in the city."

"That's close to a thirty-minute drive one way, and we just don't have time for that, but I promise you I'll be thinking. Something will be done. I don't want you to be uncomfortable. Okay?"

"Okay." That was more than Aden had hoped for, a dream come true. The adult responsible for his care had just proved he...cared. How had such a crappy day taken such a wonderful turn?

When they reached the ranch, Aden hopped out of the truck. "I want to wash up before I eat," he said, and after Dan's okay, he trekked to his room.

The bunkhouse was empty, the boys already at the main house. Aden shut himself in the bathroom, happy with Dan, with the unexpected support, with the fact that he would never have to see Dr. Hennessy again.

At the sink, he twisted the knobs until warm water sprayed and soaked his hands. "Guys?" he whispered to the souls. One by one, they acknowledged him. "Do you remember what happened in that office?"

No, Caleb said. *I'm like a black hole right now, and it's seriously messing with my mojo.*

Who cares about mojo? I barely remember the day at all, Julian said.

It's like my memory has been scrubbed, Elijah said, *and I don't like it.*

So, what had been done to them during all those minutes inside Hennessy's mind? Wait. He'd been inside Hennessy's mind?

Even as the question formed, his own memory seemed to be sprayed with Windex and wiped clean. He frowned at his pale reflection in the mirror, trying to relive the past five minutes. Nothing. The last hour. Still nothing. Droplets of water splashed onto his hands, but he suddenly couldn't remember walking into the bathroom, much less turning on the faucet.

His frown intensified. "What are we doing in here?"

Cleaning up, Caleb said with an unspoken "duh." *We've got a new tutor to meet.*

"Oh, yeah." He shook his head, rattling the sense of uneasiness working through him. "Let's get this over with."

ONCE AGAIN, TUCKER found himself huddled in the underground crypt, dust in his nose, darkness a vise around him and a damp chill stroking him with bony fingers. He was shaking this time. Not because he was weak—he was physically stronger now than he'd been last time— but because he could feel the menace pouring through the air. Thick, like blood. Acrid, like burning rubber.

What was in store for him? Nothing good, that was for sure. And why? He'd done everything he'd been told. He'd followed Aden. He'd kept watch. Yeah, he'd veered off course a few times, following Mary Ann instead, making sure she got to where she wanted to go without any problems, but he'd always gone back to Aden. Always.

"I am not pleased with you, boy."

The smooth voice came from just a few feet away from him, though he couldn't see the speaker, and jolted him far worse than if Vlad had yelled. "I—I'm sorry. I'm trying. Please, don't punish me." He couldn't make himself stand and run, no matter how much he wanted to. God, did he want to. But he also wanted to please this man, this deposed king, the need a part of him, as much as his lungs or his heart, and right now Vlad wanted him to stay put.

"Punish you? Perhaps. You aren't trying hard enough."

"You're not doing anything, either," he muttered before he could stop himself. Then he cringed, expecting a violent retaliation.

"I am healing, you fool. My people cannot see me like this."

"Of course, of course."

"I have questions, and you *will* get me answers. How is the human, Aden, leading my people? Why are they following him? How is he still alive?" Each question was more clipped than the last.

"I don't... I have no—" But he did. From everything Tucker had witnessed, only one answer made sense.

"Tell me!"

Vlad had yelled the words, and Tucker had just realized he'd been wrong. Nothing was worse than hearing this vampire shout his disapproval. The deep, rolling waves of his fury were tongues of fire, licking, feasting. Tucker gulped. Just as part of him wanted to run, part of him wanted to hold his next words inside.

That part of him lost to self-preservation. "The wolves protect him."

"The wolves." Silence followed. Thick, heavy silence. Gut-wrenching, sweat-inducing silence, but finally, blessedly, Vlad spoke again. "Continue observing him. I have much to consider."

Not an order to kill, and yet, Tucker experienced a sickening wave of dread. That final order was coming. Of that, he had no doubt.

DINNER *SUCKED*.

Oh, the food was good—Meg Reeves was an excellent cook—and Aden loved him some pot roast and potatoes. And this room, the "formal" dining room, was wicked cool. Aden never felt more like part of a family than when he was here. Something about the long, square table that Dan had crafted himself, the wallpaper with cherries and wheelbarrows, of all things, and the cabinet brimming with Meg's favorite china. This was what a home should look like.

But the new "tutor"…he shuddered. Or perhaps shivered. The word "hot" didn't do her justice. However, the word "fairy" did. Thomas had been right. His family had come looking for him. The new tutor was none other than Ms. Brendal, his sister.

Aden had immediately realized how precarious the situation was, but he hadn't been able to bail. That would have looked too suspicious. So here he sat. And ate. And pretended to be as normal as the others.

All the boys were around him. Shannon and Ryder, who sat across from each other, refusing to look at each other, were too quiet. Seth was leaned back in his chair, one arm resting on the back slat, his gaze telegraphing *come hither.* RJ, Terry and Brian were openmouthed and dumbstruck. Dan sat at the head of the table and beautiful Meg at the foot. They, too, seemed to be under the fairy's spell, raptly listening to her every word as if she were the savior of the world.

Even the souls were listening to her, waxing poetic about her face and body. Sadly, he wanted to join them.

Ms. Brendal sat across from Aden, and yeah, she *was* beautiful. Probably the most physically perfect being he'd ever seen. She had big, sparkling brown eyes that were somehow familiar to him, but her long, curling blond hair was not. He didn't think. Her skin was so golden and luminous she could have swallowed the sun. And she smelled like jasmine and honeysuckle.

He loved jasmine and honeysuckle, more than anything. He loved Brendal, too.

His hands curled into fists. He had to stop thinking like that, but didn't know how. Even though he knew what she was, he was more drawn to her with every second that passed…had the urge to protect her…hell, even to lay his head on her feet just to be near her. Caress her, kiss her…worship her. And that was dangerous (not to mention embarrassing). For Victoria, as well as himself. This woman, this lovely fairy, was his enemy.

She would want to murder him the moment she learned what had happened to Thomas.

A fact that Thomas delighted in pointing out, over and over again. The ghost stood behind her, desperately trying to gain her attention, screaming at the top of his ghostly lungs, kicking at the table, the chairs, tugging at Ms. Brendal's hair, and when that didn't work, shouting threats at Aden. "My sister will avenge me. This I swear."

Behind that delightful scene was Victoria. She'd come to the ranch a bit ago to wait in Aden's bedroom until this dinner ended, wanting to talk to him, about what he didn't know. But then she'd spied Brendal, and it had been game on—even though—or maybe *because*—fairies hated vampires and preferred to kill them on sight, and Aden had the dubious honor of being king of the vampires. Victoria now paced outside the house, just in front of the window across from Aden. Only he could see her, she blended so well into the night, but that didn't help his sense of doom.

"I hope everyone is ready for dessert," Meg said, standing. She was a petite woman, with delicate features and hair that couldn't decide if it wanted to be brown or blond.

"I'm always ready for one of your desserts," Dan told her with a warm smile. They loved each other, and Aden's chest constricted every time he saw them together.

"I'll just be a moment." Smiling, too, Meg skipped off to the kitchen.

"You keep peering just over my shoulder, Aden." Even Brendal's voice was beautiful, soft, like a song. "Why?" She turned to look, and Victoria swiftly moved out of sight.

Close, too close. He forced his gaze to fall to the tabletop. He was sure everyone was now staring at him, and he hoped like hell he wouldn't blush. He blushed. Fine. Better they stared at him than the window. He hadn't realized he'd been so obvious. "Is looking over your shoulder a crime?"

A pause. Had his bluntness startled her? "I much prefer my students to look me directly in the eyes."

She did, did she? "I'm not your student."

"You could be," she said, leaning forward and reaching for his hand.

He snapped both into his lap just before contact. "I'm happy at Crossroads High."

"And you've been attending for over a month?"

"Yes."

"So you never spent time with Mr. Thomas?"

Thomas knelt beside her, beseeching. "I'm right here. See me. Please, see me." He sounded close to tears, and Aden had to clear his throat to dislodge the lump growing there.

"Aden," Dan said. "Answer Ms. Brendal, please."

Had he just been sitting here in silence? What had she asked? Oh, yeah. "Correct." He prayed he wasn't a neon sign of guilt. "I didn't spend much time with Mr. Thomas." *I only used up half an hour to kill him.*

Necessary, Elijah told him, and he blinked. Usually the souls didn't hear his thoughts. Or had Elijah just guessed? No, he realized a moment later. The topic had given him away.

That, and we're certified bad asses, Caleb said. *I swear, God might have created the world in six days, but we could have done it in five!*

That isn't something to joke about, Julian snapped.

Who's joking?

Aden hated when they argued, but that was far better than the poetry.

Meg returned with a large plate piled high with brownies. She offered Dan and Brendal first choice, then placed the treats in the middle of the table for the boys. Everyone dove in like starving dogs that had just spotted a meaty bone.

"Now that we're relaxed, I'd like to ask some personal questions," Brendal said. She placed her brownie on her plate. "I want to ensure my teachings fulfill your needs.

In that regard, I'd like to know what everyone thought of Mr. Thomas."

"We didn't have time to get to know him," Seth said.

Brendal was undeterred. "Then tell me what you think could have happened to him."

"If he's missing, shouldn't you talk to the police?" Ryder asked.

A moment passed in silence, and yet, in those quiet seconds any resistance the boys harbored melted away. Until the last brownie crumb was consumed, they, and even Dan and Meg, speculated about the man's sudden disappearance. Alien abduction was mentioned. A need for a fresh start. Murder—Aden tried not to squirm— and even a car accident.

"Tell her I'm here, Aden," Thomas said, speaking to him without animosity for the first time since Brendal had entered the room. Their eyes met, clashed. "Please."

He almost caved. That please... *I can't*, he projected.

"You owe me." The anger was returning to Thomas's tone.

Aden shook his head.

Still Thomas persisted. "She might be able to save me."

So you can kill my girlfriend? No. Not now. Maybe after the witches were dealt with, and only if Thomas swore to drop his quest for vengeance against the royal family. Until then, no deal. So he looked away, silently ending the conversation. Thomas began yelling again, snarling, stomping around, and guilt once again welled inside Aden's chest.

"Aden?" Dan said, drawing his attention. "Are you agreeable to Ms. Brendal's suggestion, then?"

"Her suggestion?" He could only imagine what she wanted. His head on a silver platter? His heart in her favorite trinket box? As much as she'd charmed everyone, Aden doubted a single one of them would hesitate to please her.

He searched the boys' faces. They were peering at him with envy. Except for Shannon and Ryder. Earlier they'd gone to such great pains not to look at each other, but now they were locked in some kind of livid staring contest. Both of their eyes were narrowed, both of their lips thinned with displeasure.

His gaze shifted to the window, but Victoria was no longer there.

"Sure," he finally said, sweat beading on his brow. "I'm...agreeable."

"Good." Dan pushed to his feet, his chair sliding behind him. Everyone but Aden followed suit. The boys gave Brendal one last lingering once-over—Seth even wiggled his brows at her—before shuffling from the main house and back to their bunks. Dan walked to

Meg and threw his arm over her shoulders. They waited, watching Aden expectantly.

What was he supposed to do?

"Shall we go, then?" Brendal asked him in that musical voice.

"Uh, sure." Maybe he should have declined her "suggestion."

She moved around the table and toward the front door. Aden remained in place for several seconds, peering out the window. Victoria suddenly reappeared and pressed her hand to the glass. If he wasn't mistaken, someone, a female, stood beside her.

Another date for him? Probably.

Fabulous.

"You'll need a jacket," Dan said, prompting him into motion.

He stood. "I'll be fine." He walked over to Brendal, who held the front door open for him. Knowing she might attack him helped dull his unnatural fascination with her.

Thomas followed him silently into the night, though the ghost disappeared from view the moment Aden stepped from the porch. For some reason, he was only visible—and aware—in the ranch and bunkhouse, not outside in the elements.

Cold, damp air slithered around Aden, biting at his skin. *Should have accepted that jacket.* The moon was partially obscured by clouds, and there were no stars to be seen. The insects were eerily silent.

"We'll begin our tour in the far pasture," she said.

Ah, a tour. *That* he could do. "I'm not sure why you'd want to see a barn, horses and cows this late in the evening, but come on." Unless, of course, she'd simply wanted to get Aden alone. "I'll show you the way." He uttered a quiet prayer that Victoria wouldn't follow.

Ten bucks says the woman is gonna try to nail us. And not the good way! Caleb said.

You don't have ten bucks, Julian reminded him.

Aden will pay.

"If seeing the ranch had been my goal," Brendal said as they started forward, "I would have chosen one of the other boys."

"I guessed as much." The Fae were power-hungry, Victoria had told him. They loved humans—until those humans exhibited signs of their own power. Aden exhibited signs of power. Had she sensed them, or had she figured out who he was and what he'd done?

No. She probably felt the draw of him right now. Without Mary Ann nearby, they all did, all the creatures of this otherworld. Some had called him a beacon in the night, some a chain that tugged without regard. And because he'd possessed Thomas's body, Aden now knew how cold fairies were inside. Deadly cold. Yet, when Thomas had fought Riley, he'd drawn warmth into him. Delicious warmth. Was that why they craved power? Did power equal warmth?

"You guessed, and yet you came with me anyway."

"I'm not a coward." He and Brendal reached the far edge of the pasture, where a wood and wire fence blocked the animals from the surrounding field. Aden had no trouble seeing, despite the darkness, because Brendal now glowed. What the hell? She *must* have swallowed the sun.

"Do you know what I am, Aden?" she asked, her tone now lacking any hint of emotion. She rounded on him, her dress—flowing and white, something girls probably wore to the beach to cover their swimsuits—dancing around her ankles. "You haven't remarked on my radiance."

To lie or not? Why not tell the truth? he thought next. In this, at least. He knew better than most how hard it was to tell truth from lies when the two were intertwined. "I know," he said, and settled atop the top post of the fence, as if he were relaxed, as if this conversation was no big deal. Casual disregard—rather than fear—would throw her off.

Was Victoria nearby? He couldn't see her.

Brendal nodded with satisfaction. "Good. We can skip the formalities. My brother's final report said that you were the reason we were here. That you were the one who summoned us. So here we are. Why? Why did you want us here?"

Careful. A warning from all the souls.

"I didn't, I don't," he said. "It was an accident, summoning you."

She arched the perfect line of a brow. "Yet that accident summoned many others, as well. Our enemies. Enemies to all humankind."

"Yes." He'd argue that vampires weren't an enemy to humankind, though. They fed off humans, yes, but humans fed off animals. What was the difference? And no, he wasn't calling himself an animal. It was simply the circle of life.

"Did you hope to start a war? We have not been together in centuries, and the last time we were, our numbers—*all* our numbers—dwindled significantly."

"I swear to you, I don't want a war to erupt. Especially here. But I can't help what I am and what I can do any more than you can."

Her head tilted to the side, and she peered at him intently. That unwavering stare—and her unemotional tone, he realized—was familiar. Reminiscent of...Dr. Hennessy. His eyes widened as a very repugnant idea sprang up. Was the doctor a fairy, too?

"What exactly can you do?" Brendal asked.

He gave a falsely negligent shrug. "I draw creatures, like you said. Just not with a pen and paper."

"And that is all?"

"Yes."

"Then you must die," she said simply. "Only when you're dead will the pull to you cease."

He didn't hop off the fence, didn't try to run away. One, he didn't know what she could do, ability-wise. And two, he didn't want her to know she'd spooked him, his mind replaying his death by stabbing over and over again.

"You won't kill me," he said with more bravado than sense. Or certainty.

"No, I won't," she replied, surprising him. "Yet. Where is my brother, Aden? And do not lie to me. I have lived for more centuries than you could comprehend. I know when my humans lie."

Her humans?

Uh-oh, Caleb said. *This is dangerous territory.*

Tread carefully, Elijah suggested. *Your next words are highly important.*

Because they might be his last? Yeah, he'd surmised that. For all he knew, Brendal could teleport him into town and stab him, bringing Elijah's vision of Aden's final minutes to life. Or death.

She sure is pretty, though, isn't she? Caleb continued.

I prefer girls with dark hair, Julian said.

Not now, guys, he wanted to shout. He needed to concentrate, to keep his emotions at bay.

"Aden?" Brendal prompted. "My brother would not have left without first contacting his people, without first contacting me. Yet he did. Which means something happened to him. So I ask again. Where is he?"

He wanted to tell her. The truth was there, welling up in his throat, threatening to spill over. All he had to do was open his mouth. She would know, and he would feel better. The guilt would leave him.

His brow scrunched in confusion. Were those his thoughts? On some level, they seemed to be. That guilt… But on another level, they seemed foreign. They were softer, almost like the music of the fairy's voice, like a song in his head.

"Tell me," she said softly. Her eyes, so deep a brown, were hypnotic, swirling, and then, oddly, different colors began flickering. You could get lost in those eyes.

They were very much like Victoria's, only darker.

Victoria.

Aden snapped back from whatever spell the fairy had cast, only to realize he'd hopped off the fence, closed the distance between them and now had his arms resting on Brendal's shoulders, his hands fisted in her hair.

Oh, hell, no. Had he been about to kiss her?

Scowling, he dropped his arms to his sides and stepped back. Brendal frowned. "Listen, I don't know where your brother is. He was here, and then he was gone."

"You lie," she replied, and yet again, there was no emotion in her tone.

Somehow, that made her all the more dangerous.

"Aden," a male voice suddenly called. Dan. "It's time to hit the books. Ms. Brendal, I know you understand how important his studies are. Thank you for coming to speak with us, and we'll see you in the morning."

Obviously, Victoria had voiced him into sending the fairy away.

Brendal stared at Aden for several moments, her expression as blank as her tone, before nodding. "We shall speak again, Aden. That, I promise you."

ADEN PACKED A BAG while Victoria and Stephanie—the vampire who'd been beside her at the window—convinced the boys, as well as Dan and Meg, that he was here, he was sleeping and they'd see him in the morning to wave him off to school.

Actually, he was spending the rest of the night at the vampire mansion.

When the sisters returned to him, he was ready,

standing outside the bunkhouse, bag in hand, the souls chattering happily about this latest turn of events.

"Never thought I'd see the day Victoria broke the rules," Stephanie said with a laugh. "A reason to celebrate. For real."

"What rule?" Aden asked, holding out his free hand.

Victoria twined their fingers. As always, her skin was hot, a brand, and the warmth shot straight through him.

"I'm not supposed to be around you while you date the others, so you'll have to remain inside my bedroom, quiet."

Stephanie laughed again. "Which was why I was so surprised when she brought me here as backup in case the fairy flipped her lid. But better me than Lauren, huh? She would have attacked first and asked questions later." A pause. "I'm not needed anymore, right, so I'll just mosey away. Cool? I'm hungry, and I hear there's a party in town."

"Cool," Victoria replied, the human word sounding weird when spoken in her solemn, formal voice.

"See ya!" Stephanie vanished.

Aden peered down at Victoria. "Won't the vampires living in the mansion smell my blood and feel my pull?" No way did he want to get her into trouble.

"There are other humans there, so your scent will blend with theirs. As for the pull, I don't know. Riley and Mary Ann are there, so perhaps she'll mute it."

Even though Riley negated Mary Ann's muting effect? "Worth a shot," he said. He'd been to the mansion twice, but he'd never been inside Victoria's room. He wanted to see it. Desperately. And if she got into trouble, well, he was the king and he'd just—

Wait. He was the king. That's what he'd just thought. Without reservation or doubt.

But he was still determined to set things right, to pick another ruler. Right?

"Ready?" Victoria asked, releasing his hand to wrap her arms around his waist.

He lost his train of thought. God, she felt good. "Ready."

She licked her lips, gaze falling to the pulse hammering in his neck. "First...a kiss? That's what I came here for. Earlier, I mean. To kiss you."

This might be the best day of my life, Caleb announced.

"My pleasure." Aden tuned Caleb out and pressed his lips to Victoria's; her head tilted, and she immediately opened up, his tongue sliding into her mouth. Tasting. Exploring. The heat, the electricity, they made him feel

like he'd stuck his finger inside a light-socket, every cell
he possessed sparking to life.

"More," she whispered.

They strained against each other. She was so soft. All
the while she made little purrs in the back of her throat,
urging him on. His blood quickened in his veins, burning him up, rendering his organs to ash and remaking
him into a new being.

A being that could fly, he mused, his feet losing their
solid anchor. Victoria's hands were in his hair, though,
her nails scraping his scalp—which he loved, needed
more of—so he didn't care.

"I want to bite you," she said, and she sounded intoxicated, her words slurred.

"Yes." He didn't hesitate. He loved when she bit him.
Could even be considered a blood-slave, he was sure,
but again, he didn't care. He loved this girl. Would be
anything she needed him to be.

"I shouldn't."

"Please do."

She trailed little kisses along his cheek, his jaw, then
his neck, her tongue flicking against his skin. *Yes.* This
is what he'd dreamed of, before he'd even met her. Just
being with her, giving and taking like this. Kissing on
and on, forever.

"Sure?"

"Do it. Please."

Her teeth sank into his vein, sharp and insistent. There was no pain. Her mouth, tongue, teeth, *something* produced a drug, a chemical, and it numbed his skin before slithering through his body, caressing him from the inside out. *Yes, yes.*

His eyes opened to half-mast, and he realized he was no longer outside. Four walls surrounded him. They were painted white. *Everything* in the room was white. There was a large, canopied bed with white fur draped over the top. A vase of white roses that scented the air rested on a vanity. There was no dresser, but there was a computer and game system, though neither looked as if they'd ever been used. Too much dust.

"So good," she whispered. "So..." She jerked away from him, panting. "Dangerous."

A bead of blood trickled down his neck, he felt the heated glide of it, but he didn't wipe it away. "I like it," he reminded her, and he, too, sounded intoxicated.

She cleaned her mouth with the back of her hand. "I like it far too much. Next time, you have to tell me no."

"I never want to tell you no." As he spoke, lethargy swept through him. Blood loss, combined with all those sleepless nights, all the tension, the worry, the battles, that drugging kiss, suddenly caught up with him and his knees buckled.

Victoria rushed to him, arm wrapping around him and holding him up. She helped him walk to the bed. He fell on the mattress, his eyes already closing.

"Sleep," she said. "I'll take care of you."

He believed her, and so he obeyed. He slept.

+WEN+Y-ONE

I'M IN BED WITH RILEY. And he's not in wolf form, Mary Ann thought. Giddily. He was human, and they were back together. For the moment. And in less than two days, they could die. Right now, things were innocent. They were dressed, they weren't kissing. They were simply snuggled together, her head resting on his chest, his heart beating against her ear, his hand caressing her back. They were talking. Or had been.

They were silent now. His bedroom was next door to Victoria's and they'd heard the vampire return. With Aden. There'd been a short, muffled conversation, then a telling silence. A silence that had drifted into this room, bringing tension with it.

Sexual tension. Awareness.

Mary Ann tried to distract herself from thoughts about what was happening next door—and what could happen in here. She studied Riley's inner sanctum, a place of absolute relaxation and comfort. Game stations, a computer, pillowed chairs, a mat for lounging. Only thing that kept her from thinking this place belonged to a bored human billionaire intent on distracting himself was the wall of weapons. Knives of every shape and size covered every inch. Cleary, he took his duties of protector seriously.

"How long have you been Victoria's guard?" she asked.

"Since her birth."

"That's a long time."

"Not in this world."

True. "What'd you do before that?"

"Trained, mostly. When a wolf is assigned a charge, he dies with that charge. Therefore, a wolf is only ever given one charge. She was mine."

"So you're connected?"

His breath ruffled several strands of her hair. "Nothing like that. If she dies, then that means I failed in my duties. That means I deserve to die, too."

They would murder him? "No!"

"Yes." His fingers moved to her arm, stroking up and down. "No one would trust me again, and I would be shamed. Believe me, death is preferable to that."

His caress *almost* managed to distract her. "But you're stronger than the vampires. You can kill them with that liquid stuff in your claws. I heard you tell Aden."

"That doesn't make honor any less important."

She fisted his shirt, wrinkling the material, afraid to let go. "Have you ever thought about leaving the vampires?"

"No. We aren't slaves. We aren't even servants. But Vlad brought us into this world, and his people were once our guardians. How can we not return the favor?"

Loyal to a fault. Exactly as Victoria had said. "But it's the vampires you protect, and Aden isn't a vampire, yet still you follow him. Would you do so if the vampires turned against him?"

Several beats of quiet followed her question. Then, "I have watched people live and die for centuries, and I've seen the chaos that springs from lack of leadership and rules. Vlad created our rules himself. If anyone was stronger than he was, they were to take his place. Dmitri did that. Then Aden proved himself stronger than Dmitri. That means Aden, no matter his origins, is fit to lead vampires and wolves alike. I will defend him as I have always defended Victoria."

With his dying breath, she thought. Had he given that same loyalty to his past girlfriends? And why did she suddenly want to beat those exes into a bloody pulp? Violence wasn't usually her first choice. Or her second. Or her third.

"How many girls have you dated?" she asked.

He handled the switch in topics with ease. "Lots."

"Countless?"

He sighed, weary, as if she'd just asked him how fat her butt looked in her jeans.

"You do know I've lived a long time, right?"

"Yes." But she still had to know how many girls had won his heart. Otherwise, she might always wonder, might always feel like she was standing on a stage, a beauty pageant in full swing, his exes all around her, pointing and laughing. Silly, but true. Especially since she and Riley wouldn't last past the witches' curse. "Just ballpark it for me."

The gentle stroking stopped. "I thought we weren't going to fight."

"We aren't."

"If I answer you, we'll fight."

He couldn't even ballpark it, then. Ouch. "Have you ever been in love?"

"No."

What about with me? she wanted to ask, but didn't. "How long do your relationships usually last?"

"Some longer than others," he answered cautiously.

Which meant some hadn't even been relationships? Just quick, easy conquests? "Did you break up with them or did they break up with you?"

He groaned. "You're killing me here, you know that?"

She was killing *herself*. But maybe, just maybe, she was doing this, insisting on answers, so that leaving him—when the time came—would be easier. She'd be able to tell herself she'd been one in a group of thousands, meaningless, temporary. That would hurt her, destroy her, but eventually, she would heal. Right? She wouldn't try to track him down and start something all over again. He would stay safe.

"Please answer." His T-shirt ripped where she still fisted it. One by one, she forced her fingers to release the material.

He uttered another sigh. "Mostly...I did the breaking up."

"I see. Why?"

"Different reasons."

Like...he'd gotten tired of them? Bored? "I know you dated Lauren, and you told me before, when we first met, that you'd once dated a witch and she was the one who cursed you and your brothers, but that you died soon after and when you were revived, you were freed from that curse. You told me why things ended with Lauren, and I can guess why they ended with the witch."

"Wait. I didn't die soon after the curse. More like a few years. I was stabbed in the side and bled out. Victoria gave me some of her blood, and that helped bring me back. But anyway, I'd gotten a taste of the non-dating life in those years since no one wanted to date me. So I guess you could say I went a little crazy afterward, when girls started noticing me again."

"Are you trying to tell me you became a slut, Riley?"

He choked out a laugh. "Maybe. Does that disappoint you?"

"No." He was who he was, but she *was* worried. His answers weren't convincing her of anything. She wasn't distancing herself. "You've slept with a lot of girls, then?"

Every muscle in his body stiffened. Underneath her cheek, his heart sped out of control. "With some."

"With Lauren?"

His hand left her completely and scrubbed down his face. "I won't talk about that. Just like I would never talk with other people about what you and I do."

So that was a yes. She was jealous, of course, and suddenly so self-conscious she wanted to scream. Lauren was gorgeous, perfect, strong. What was Mary Ann? Imperfect in every way, dangerous to his health, his well-being. "I'm your first human? To date, I mean."

"Yes."

Was she a novelty, then?

"I know what you're thinking," he said, and rolled on top of her. His weight pinned her down, and she…liked it. "Your aura is a very sad, very depressing color. You think you mean less to me than all the others. That *you* are somehow less."

His opinion shouldn't matter. If they survived the

curse—*you will*. She wouldn't believe otherwise—she was going to break up with him, she reminded herself. "Let's just say I'm not exactly sure what you see in me."

"We've covered this before. I see your beauty..." He kissed the shell of her ear, softly, sweetly.

She shivered. "Beauty fades."

"I see your intelligence." Another kiss, this one on her chin.

Another shiver. "I could lose my mind." And was probably close to doing so even now.

"I see your bravery." Another kiss, once, twice, this one just under her bottom lip.

Shiver...shiver... "Lots of girls are brave."

"I see a pair of hazel eyes that view the world with an enviable mix of innocence and optimism. Those same eyes, when turned on me, go soft and hot at the same time, the innocence blending with wickedness, and that does something to me." He kissed her lips then, tongue sliding out for the briefest taste. "What do you see in me?"

His words...they were drugging, delicious, suddenly as necessary as breathing. No matter what the future held.

Their gazes locked, and he braced his hands beside her temples, caging her in, waiting.

Oxygen somehow trickled into her lungs, and she

said, "I see the hottest boy alive," and leaned up to kiss his jaw.

He shook his head. "Someone wise once told me that looks fade."

So the tables had been turned, had they? She almost grinned. "I see the sharpest wit I've ever encountered." She kissed his chin.

"Humor is subjective."

"I see strength." She kissed just below his lip.

"One snap of my spine, and I'm useless."

"I see...a boy who would stand between me and my enemies a thousand times, dying a thousand times if it meant keeping me from the smallest of scratches." Truth. "I see a boy who knows what I need before even I know, and then delights in giving it to me." Again, truth.

She pressed a soft kiss into his lips.

He hadn't lingered with his kisses, but she did with hers. She pressed again, then again, until he opened his mouth, and she opened hers, until their tongues were twining, exploring. He was heavy against her, but he didn't crush her. Having him there actually felt good. Her hands had room to move, along his back, kneading, squeezing.

His, too. They roamed, and soon both their shirts were off and they were skin to heated skin. *Nothing* had ever felt that good. His taste was in her mouth, somehow in her blood, warming her up another degree. His hands were just as hot, soft and hard all at the same time.

Soon they were moaning, she was swallowing his breath, and he was swallowing hers. She was clutching at him, no longer content to knead and squeeze. If he'd been human, she would have feared she was hurting him, but he seemed to like everything she did, each new, inexperienced touch she gave, because he constantly growled his approval.

For a moment, his fingers played at the waist of her jeans. Her skin tickled there, and she found herself arching up, seeking more, but he stiffened, growled—and this time it wasn't in approval, but in…pain?

"We have to stop," he rasped.

He'd stopped them last time, too. This time, she wanted to scream. "Why?"

"This is your first time."

"I know."

"But I don't want you to be with me because you're afraid of dying."

"I'm not." She was, but that wasn't the only reason she was with him, doing this.

His eyes were grave, haunted. "Mary Ann, only this morning you were done with me."

"To save you. I don't want to hurt you."

His forehead pressed against hers. Both of them were sweating, shaking. "Oh, yes, you're killing me tonight, and one day I'm going to get a medal for this. You have no idea how hard this is for me." He snorted, as if he'd made a joke. "Listen, your first time should be about love. Only love."

"Was yours?"

"No, and that's how I know how important it is."

He rolled off her, but didn't sever all contact. He pulled her into his side, and once again she rested her head just above his heart. The organ pounded wildly, and that soothed her. He wanted her, and stopping had been difficult for him. But he'd done it. No other boy would have stopped. She knew that, and it was another reason she was falling so deeply in love with him.

Despite how upset her body currently was with him.

"I want you to be sure," he said huskily. "Of me, of us. I don't want you to ever look back and regret. I don't want you to wish things had been different. I want the things we do to each other to be about nothing but us."

But what if she never reached that point? She sighed, kissed his chest. Either way, he wanted the best for her, the sweet darling boy. "Thank you."

"I'd like to say it's my pleasure, but...I feel like I'm dying."

She laughed. "Your fault, not mine."

"No. It's absolutely your fault. Now let's get some sleep." He hugged her tight for a minute. "Okay?"

"Okay."

"Good. 'Cause we've got a big day tomorrow."

She didn't want to think about tomorrow, the day before the spell kicked in. Sleep, though, proved impossible. Her body was achy, and she couldn't stay still. She needed something, but she didn't know what. And then, minutes later, perhaps hours, her stomach began to hurt, twisting and cramping, so terribly empty. Like what had happened in town, only magnified a thousand times.

Hungry...hungry.

"What's wrong, baby?" Riley asked, concerned. She didn't think he'd fallen asleep, either, because he'd never truly relaxed, but had adjusted his long frame to her every time she'd moved, trying to make her more comfortable.

"I...I don't know," she said. A lie. She tried to raise her head, to look at him, but she didn't have the strength. A tremor was slipping and sliding the length of her spine and vibrating into her limbs. "I can't move anymore. And I hurt." Oh, God. Panic set in. "Riley, I can't move! I'm paralyzed."

"Don't worry. I can fix this." Riley popped from the bed, dressed, then helped Mary Ann do the same. She didn't have the strength to do *anything*. He even had to tug her hair out from under her shirt.

"Am I dying? Already?" *So...hungry...* She'd thought she would have more time. *Hungry...* A moan escaped her. "Riley!"

"Calm down, just calm down. I'll take care of you," he said, easing her to the side of the bed and propping her up. "I'll make it better." He strode to the door that connected his bedroom to Victoria's and knocked.

What was he doing? Did she care? No. Another moan escaped her. *HUNGRY...*

There was no answer. He knocked again. Finally, the door swung open and a frowning Victoria glared up at him. "You're the hundredth person at my door. I know. You sense Aden. So did they. But to prevent upheaval, I didn't lie to them, so I hope you're prepared. Tomorrow, though, and not tonight," she rambled. "Tonight he's trying to sleep—I commanded him to sleep actually. We'll deal with the consequences in the morning because I won't have him disturbed."

"Are you finished?"

She hissed at him. "I'm not sending him away, Riley."

"I didn't ask you to. In fact, I'm glad you're finally standing up for what you want. Now, enough about you, brat. I need you to take us to the cabin."

The cabin, where the witch was being kept. Understanding dawned. Riley was going to feed her. Mary

Ann wanted to protest, but she also wanted to feel better. She'd never been this weak, never been this helpless.

"All of us?" Victoria looked back at her bed, and Aden sleeping there. "Why?"

"Just Mary Ann and me, and because I said so. Leave us in the cabin and then come get us in an hour. Okay? Actually, during that hour, go to Mary Ann's house and convince her dad she's there tonight and in the morning so he doesn't worry."

"Why do you want to go to the cabin?" she asked again, gaze sliding to Mary Ann.

Starved, dying, scared, agonized...

"I need your blind trust," Riley told the vampire. "As I've often given you."

Victoria nodded without hesitation. "All right. Yes, of course. Who first?"

"Me, but be careful with Mary Ann. She's...ill."

A second later, the two disappeared. Mary Ann could only sit there, her mind starting to hurt, too. Then Victoria was there, gripping her hand, the bed was falling away, and she was floating, spinning, stopping, then starting all over again. Finally, solid ground appeared. She wanted to vomit, but had nothing in her stomach and ended up dry heaving, intensifying the pain in her body.

"What's wrong with her?" Victoria asked.

"Like I said, she's ill."

"And you think the witch will cast a healing spell? I assure you—"

"Thanks for your help. Now go back to Aden," Riley said, scooping Mary Ann in his arms. "Please." She was floating again, only this time she had an anchor. Strong, magnificent Riley. "Out. I'm serious, Vic."

Victoria growled, but disappeared.

"What's going on?" a familiar voice asked. The witch.

Suddenly warmth and power swept through Mary Ann, easing her hunger, her pain. She sighed in ecstasy, drinking in every molecule she could. Yes. Yes. This was what she'd needed, what she couldn't live without. Strength returned to her limbs, her body becoming hers again.

"Drainer," the witch cried. "No. No! Get back! Get away!"

"Well," Riley said dryly, "if either of us were in any doubt, that doubt is now alleviated."

TWENTY-TWO

ADEN AWOKE MORE CLEARHEADED than he'd been in what seemed forever, but also a little peeved. He was in the vampire stronghold; he remembered being whisked here, kissing Victoria, feeding her, loving her, but now he was alone in her massive bed and there was no sign that she'd ever been here. No Victoria meant no more kissing or feeding.

At least he wasn't twitchy and in withdrawal, *needing* her to bite him again. Therefore he hadn't become a blood-slave last night.

He sat up and looked around. The room was as white as he remembered, and he could guess why she'd chosen such a blank canvas. Her father remained true to the I'm-an-evil-badass stereotype: black, black and more black. Colors, which Victoria loved, hadn't really been allowed, so she'd done the next best thing. The opposite of what her father had wanted.

A small rebellion, but so wonderfully telling. Deep

down, she hadn't wanted to be like her father. Here, in the privacy of her bedroom, she'd allowed herself to be herself.

This place gives me the creeps, Caleb said.

"Why?" He glanced down at himself. He was still wearing his jeans and T-shirt, but his boot, socks and blades had been removed. By Victoria? Had she run her hands all over him? He wished he'd been awake for that.

'Cause there's no naked girls.

Aden laughed. Typical Caleb.

Well, I like it, Julian said. *Add your clothes in the closet, and this would feel more like home than the ranch.*

"And why do you say that?" he asked, gaze straying to the closet in question. The entry was dark, too dark to see what rested inside. Probably black robe after black robe.

It's almost like we're smack in the middle of an unwritten book. Like there's nothing here but blank pages.

Which means we can write the story however we want. And anyway, you don't see this room as it will one day be, Elijah said. *There are colors, so many beautiful colors.*

That put a smile on Aden's face. "Will I be here?"

Elijah didn't reply.

Aden took that for a no, and said goodbye to his blossoming good mood. How could he have forgotten, even for a second, that he was going to die? *I don't want to die,* he thought.

Once, he'd simply accepted his pending demise as fact. Then he'd been stabbed in the heart to save Thomas from the pain. Now he was starting to think crazy thoughts— for the first time, despite what the world thought of him. Thoughts of changing his future, even though he knew that would only make his death worse.

Was there something worse than being stabbed?

Yeah, and watching his friends die topped the list. A sobering reminder. He had work to do. "Have you figured out where the witch meeting is being held, Elijah?"

No.

"Caleb, you seem to like them when no one else does. Do you know where the meeting will be?" Aden was beginning to feel guilty he hadn't done more.

Wish I did, buddy, but I've got nothing.

One day left, tomorrow, yet he'd made no progress. Six days had passed, and he'd learned nothing. Yeah, he'd been busy fighting goblin poison, meeting the vampires and dying. Twice. But when it came to the safety of his friends, there really was no excuse for his lack of results.

The door creaked open, and then Victoria was standing in the open entry, wearing a pink tank top and a blue miniskirt. Her dark hair hung to her waist, glittery green ribbons woven into the strands. She'd never looked so human. Or so hot.

"I cooked you breakfast," she said, grinning as she approached him. She kicked the door shut behind her, her hands occupied with a tray of food. "I'd never cooked before, but one of the blood-slaves helped me. I hope you like the results." She sounded unsure, nervous.

His chest did that constricting thing. "Thank you. I'm sure I'll love it." And even if he didn't, she'd never know.

Still grinning, she closed the rest of the distance and sat at the edge of the bed, balancing the tray in his lap. "I hate to rush you, but you're expected below. I wasn't able to keep your location secret—everyone sensed you, and since you're here, the councilmen would like you to preside over their morning meeting."

The scent of pancakes, sausage and syrup wafted to his nose, and his mouth watered. "We don't have time for a council meeting." Not that he planned to go to school. Was this even a weekday? He couldn't remember. Still. They *had* to get some answers out of their witch. They'd run out of time.

"It will only last an hour, and it'll be better if you attend. They decided not to punish me for breaking the rules and seeing you, since they were desperate to speak with you. If you don't, you'll be hounded or even followed. If you do, we can leave without incident afterward."

A worthy reward. "What will be expected of me?" He took a bite of the pancakes and lost his train of thought. They were oversalted and raw in the middle, but he didn't allow himself to cringe. He chewed and he swallowed.

"Well?" she asked hesitantly.

"Delicious," he said, and smiled.

Her own smile bloomed. "I'm glad. So what do you think of my outfit?" She stood and twirled. "I borrowed everything from Stephanie."

"You look amazing." And she did.

Her grin widened as she reclaimed her seat beside him, her hip pressed against his. All that heat and softness... "Are you nervous?" he asked, his voice huskier than he'd intended. "About the meeting?"

She didn't have to ask which meeting he meant. They weren't discussing the council any longer. She nodded. "A little while ago, Riley told me that he went into town last night, and there were no witches. None. If they left Crossroads, that means they left us here to die."

Aden pursed his lips and thought back to when the witches had surrounded him, Victoria, Riley and Mary Ann in the forest.

"We will call a meeting in one week's time," one of them had said, "when our elders arrive. You will attend that meeting, human. If you fail to do so, the people in this circle will die. Doubt me not."

"Only I have to attend," he said after swallowing a bite of the runny eggs. "But they were waiting until their elders arrived. The witch we captured told us that the elders were due to arrive any day. Maybe they're finally here." His eyes widened. "Maybe…maybe we don't have to look for them. Maybe they'll find me."

"That is my hope, though I will destroy them if they even scratch you. But we cannot rest our hopes on that. If we are wrong…"

Everyone he loved would die. His hopes sank. What could he do, then? How could he gain the information he sought? As he cleaned his plate, making sure to moan and grunt a few times as if he were consuming heaven itself, the souls tossed ideas around.

Mostly, they contemplated possessing the body of the captured witch, walking her into town and shouting until one of her friends appeared. Not bad, but that might just get Aden thrown into jail for disturbing the public or something like that.

The possessing thing, though… That might actually work.

"Here's what we're going to do," he said, resolute. "When I finish with your people, I need you to take me to our witch. I'll possess her, and try and travel back through her life, to last week and the following days, to see if she ever spoke to anyone about us."

Victoria's electric blues widened. "That's brilliant!"

"Thank you." He only prayed he didn't encounter static like he had with the nonhuman doctor.

Wait. What? Static? When had he been inside Dr. Hennessy's head?

"Before you face off with the witch, you need to be warded," Victoria said, pulling him from his thoughts. "And perhaps I'll add extra wards to my body, too. I think I told you that my beast has been snarling for release more than usual lately. Ever since our kiss in that car..." She shivered, then shuddered. "I can barely stand the roars in my head—and the fear that comes with them. What if he gets out? Solidifies? What if he attacks you, like he seems to want?"

"I don't think he will," Aden said. "Attack, I mean." He couldn't know for sure until he actually faced the beast. He just remembered the way the thing had reached for him, as if to caress rather than rip apart. He could be wrong. He certainly had been before. "Let's worry about that later, okay?"

"You're right. Come. I'll take you to the meeting, and while you're in session, I'll gather the supplies we will need for the wards."

ADEN AND THE COUNCILMEN sat in a room of black. Black walls, black metal table, black chairs, domed black

ceiling with a chandelier dripping with black crystals.
The only decoration to be found was those strange symbols. The wards. They covered every flat surface in the
chamber.

All eyes were focused on him, and some of those eyes
were glued to the pulse hammering away in his neck.
Some of the vamps even licked their lips. He was almost
afraid they'd demand a snack, and his blood would be
the only food available.

Un-com-fort-able, Caleb sang.

Maybe, I don't know, do something, Julian said.

Elijah sighed. *I want to leave. I don't like this.*

Aden cleared his throat.

Several of the men shook their heads and found their
wits.

"We have much to cover today, so let's get started.
First order of business," one of them said. Aden was
having a hard time telling them part, and for the life of
him, he couldn't recall their names. "Many challenges
have been issued."

"Challenges?" Aden asked.

With the question, an entire conversation took place
around him, as if he weren't even there.

"Several of our elite wish to challenge you for control
of the crown."

"I'm only surprised they didn't cut the boy's throat
while he slept."

"They feel there's no need for subterfuge, that he's too weak to handle them. They'll learn otherwise, of course."

"Anyone strong enough to kill the man who killed Vlad deserves our respect. But I think their refusal to launch a sneak attack is based more on their desire to have the entire congregation witness the new king's defeat. Such confidence is foolish, I think, and they deserve what they get."

"And don't forget the wolves. The elite wanted to act honorably so they wouldn't anger the wolves."

Nice, but Aden couldn't worry about any of that now. "Hello, everyone. Have you noticed my presence? I'm here, and I'd appreciate it if you spoke to me rather than about me." When they nodded, shamed, he added, "Thank you. Now, I'm happy to address your concerns."

"We are on your side, Majesty."

"And I'm grateful. Please tell my detractors that I accept their challenge. Later. We'll set dates for…two weeks from now?" Hopefully by then, the witches would be taken care of and he'd have already picked out his replacement, so the challengers could fight themselves.

The thought brought a tide of anger. A replacement? Hell, no.

He shoved the silly emotion—and the thought—aside.

What are you doing? Elijah demanded.

Caleb gasped. *You're actually going to fight them?*

"Excellent. We did not doubt, not for a single moment, that you would take your duties seriously." All of the councilmen nodded, and one of them banged a gavel—a black gavel, of course—over the tabletop. "Next order."

"The use of colors," someone said with obvious displeasure. "There have been complaints."

"Why did you authorize the incorporation of such... human colors? Not that I wish to question your judgment, but we have traditions, you see."

The councilmen's eyes flew to him. They looked so serious, so grave. "*I'm* human," he reminded them.

A murmur of "as if we could forget" arose.

"Perhaps, if we limited the use of color to personal bedchambers..."

"And clothing," Aden said, a picture of Victoria in her pink tank top rising in his mind.

There was a sigh, a few nods.

"Agreed," the one with the gavel said, and then added, "done," and then he tapped that gavel over the tabletop. "Next order. The dating."

Another murmur arose, only this time, Aden couldn't make out the words. Victoria hadn't exaggerated. As quickly as this meeting was moving, it wouldn't last more than an hour.

Then he heard the words "Your chosen," and stiffened.

"You haven't given the girls a sufficient chance, Majesty, yet you shared a bedroom with Princess Victoria last night."

"I don't need to give the others a chance." Aden gripped the edge of the table. "I know what I want. Know who I want. I've made that clear from the beginning."

"Why can't you simply wed them all?" someone suggested. "Vlad had many wives."

The man makes a good point, Ad, Caleb said. *You should consider—*

I want to slap you, Julian muttered.

Boys, Elijah interjected. *Let Aden answer the guy.*

The answer was simple. Because one, Aden didn't want the other girls and two, Victoria would go crazy. While some Neanderthal part of him still liked the thought of her jealousy, he wouldn't put her through that. "I'm not Vlad," he ended up saying. "I desire only one."

You're ruining everything! Caleb sulked.

"Besides, Victoria and I aren't getting married." Yet. "We're too young."

Another murmur. This time, he had no trouble discerning what was being said.

Difficult. Stubborn. And yet, even while calling him names, they somehow remained respectful.

He could do no less in return. "Besides, I can't have vampires coming to the ranch where I live. My friends will discover the truth, and I don't think you want that. You've gone to great lengths to keep what you are hidden."

"We can kill your friends, then." Simple. Easy.

"No!" he shouted, forgetting all about respect. "There will be no killing, and that isn't negotiable."

More sighs. "Why don't we propose a bargain, yes? You will see the females we have chosen for you, at least once, but you will do so only while here at the mansion?"

"This may not be an issue, anyway, with the upcoming challenges," he pointed out, trying to buy some time.

"True."

"Still, Majesty. We need to offer the people hope for a future alliance."

He scrubbed a hand down his face. God, he wanted to fight them on this, but the sooner he got out of this meeting, the sooner he could scour the witch's brain. "Deal," he said. "I'll date the girls here. Once each."

"Done." The gavel descended. *Boom.* "Next order."

They spoke of a feud over a blood-slave, and Aden had to decide who won the rights to said blood-slave. They spoke of some vampires wishing to travel back to Romania, and Aden had to decide if that was acceptable. They spoke of an upcoming peace talk with another faction of vampires. Vampires led by someone they called Bloody Mary. Aden recognized the name from his history books, but wasn't sure that was who they meant. Could be her, but he didn't want to ask and reveal his ignorance.

He was supposed to travel to England for this meeting. Apparently, Bloody Mary and her crew could feel the pull of him, too, though they hadn't traveled to Oklahoma to find the source, for whatever reason. They *were* curious about him, however, enough to reach out to Vlad's council for information.

"Could be an ambush," one of the councilmen said.

"Or another attempt to control our people."

So. On top of being enemies with nearly every other race, the vampires were also at war with each other. Sweet.

"We'll protect him. Or rather, the wolves will. They are behind him one hundred percent." There was a bit of displeasure in this councilman's tone.

"*We're* having trouble keeping our teeth off him. There's no way Bloody Mary will be able to do so. She's a savage!"

"Guys," he said, interrupting their debate. "I have school. I can't leave until summer, anyway, so we'll discuss a trip to England then."

"You could drop out of school. We have tutors, after all," one said.

"Nope. Sorry." Not even they could talk him into abandoning Crossroads High. And how was he supposed to pack up and go to another country when even sneaking here was a problem? And really, he'd had several recent encounters with so-called tutors. Look how well those had turned out. "Summer or never." And if he decided to go, he was taking Victoria and Riley with him.

Or maybe not Riley. Many Ann would be upset about losing her boyfriend, even for a short period of time, and Aden hated the thought of upsetting her.

More murmurs resounded, but one by one, the councilmen nodded.

Next order. Many of their blood-slaves were missing. No one knew where they were. Vamps were angry and hungry and demanding new slaves. To obtain them, they needed Aden's permission.

"For right now, they can feed, but they cannot kill. They can feed, but they cannot enslave." Because of Victoria, he knew that if they drank from a human only once—or twice—that human could walk away without becoming addicted to the vampire bite, as he had. More than that was iffy.

Though the councilmen were disappointed, they called the next order of business. Aden's supernatural pull, or "hum." As they spoke about how strongly they were drawn to him, more and more of their gazes swung to Aden's neck and stayed. He had to stop the hum-ming nonsense, they said, over and over again, as if they were locked on the words and couldn't move past them. Maybe they were entranced.

"I can't stop," he replied, shifting nervously.

The souls grew restless in his mind, as nervous as he was. Especially Elijah. The psychic began muttering about "blood" and "death," and those mutterings were somehow familiar. As if Aden had heard them before. Where? When?

"The pull is stronger the longer we're with him, isn't it?" someone asked.

"Yes. Or maybe it's because we're so hungry."

"What do you think he'll taste like?"

"Nirvana."

Finally, there was silence. Absolute, utter silence. Was the meeting over? Aden looked around. All eyes were on him again, piercing, narrowed. Then the silence was broken as lips were licked and breath emerged from flar-ing nostrils. A few of the councilmen had their nails embedded in the tabletop, as if trying to hold themselves back.

They wanted to devour him, but they were fighting the urge.

What should he do? Stand and run? Or just stay here, like this, until they got themselves under control. If they could. Should he shout for Victoria? No, he didn't want her in the line of fire, just in case. Besides, he had to learn how to deal with these people if he was going to lead them.

Not that thought again. He wasn't going to lead them.

Slowly, Aden pushed to his feet. The councilmen rose with him, their gazes never leaving him. *Do not show fear.* "I have a lot to do," he said. "I'll leave you now."

No reply.

He stepped around his chair, never turning his back to the vampires. One step, two, he moved away from them. Slow, easy, as if he hadn't a care. But they were predators, and he was their prey, and with his retreat, they lost control.

With a cry, the closest man launched himself at Aden—and that was all the permission the others needed to follow suit. They flew at him, teeth bared.

TWENTY-THREE

OUT OF HABIT, Aden had his daggers drawn before the first vampire reached him. Of course, bringing a dagger to a vampire fight was like taking a feather to a boxing match. Useless. He slashed, made contact with his opponent's chest, but the metal bent. Yep, useless.

Both of his wrists were batted away. The daggers flew from his grip, skidding to the ground. Teeth sank into his shoulder, stinging. One of the vampires had teleported behind him, and a second set of teeth sank into the base of his neck. Adrenaline pumped through him, giving him strength, and he managed to wrench the vampires off him and toss them aside. But when one was removed from him, two more would appear. Soon they were all over him, trying to push him down, their teeth sharper than anything he could have imagined. Unlike when Victoria had bitten him, there was no pleasure. Only pain. Burning, agonizing pain.

He should have expected this, prepared for it, but too

many other worries had consumed him, and honestly, he'd grown lax. He'd been here before, and no one had attacked him. And damn it, he was king! They shouldn't treat him this way.

The vampires were heavy, their hands roving. They were like sharks who had scented his blood, and were biting, heads shaking, trying to rip pieces of him into their mouths. Finally, they managed to buckle his knees. When he hit the cold, hard ground, he lost the air in his lungs and a wave of dizziness swept through him.

Fight! Elijah growled.

"Am!" Aden kicked, sent someone flying. "But what else can I do?"

You have the ring. Use it!

The ring. Hello. Aden jerked his hand from between the jaws of a councilman, the ring glinting in the light. With the pad of his thumb, he slid the opal out of the way, then flung his arm out, liquid flinging in every direction.

Flesh sizzled. Vampires howled, releasing him to clutch at their now burning faces. Aden scrambled to his feet, panting, sweating, determined to hit the doors as fast as his feet would carry him.

Only, he saw their beasts, the ones they'd been warded against, rising from them—from *all* of them—mere outlines, yet visible enough for him to discern outstretching wings, eyes blazing red, snouts dripping with…something. Poison? Acid? He stood frozen.

Those beasts spotted him, and like Victoria's had done, they reached for him, as if they were desperate to feel him. He should have been scared. Well, *more* scared. But those fiery eyes…they somehow calmed him. Maybe because they weren't projecting menace. They were almost like puppies—granted, beastly demonlike puppies—who just wanted him to scoop them up, take them home and pet behind their ears. Weird. Most likely wrong.

Snap out of it! Julian growled.

Seriously, dude. Caleb knocked on his skull. *Now isn't the time to just stand there.*

Run! Elijah commanded.

Too late. His hesitation cost him, big-time. Though the vampires were bleeding, gaping wounds having melted their flesh, they were forgetting their pain, finding him with their eyes, and straightening. Stepping toward him. Teeth chomping, mouths probably watering for more of his blood. He held out his ring to threaten them, but there was no more liquid inside. He'd used every last drop.

Worse, his arm was shaking, puncture wounds all over it, and his action merely wafted the scent of his blood in their direction. They closed their eyes, savoring—until savoring was no longer enough. Until they wanted more.

Aden's heart pounded in his chest, and the vampires hissed, excitement reaching a new level. Again someone flew at him. Again the others quickly followed. More teeth sank into him. More stinging, more burning.

Aden fought with every ounce of strength he possessed. He kicked. He hit. He even bit, but nothing broke that tough vampire skin. Nothing proved strong enough to push them away.

Dirty, get down and fight dirty. There was Caleb again.

And yeah, Caleb was right. Aden hooked his fingers into one of the vampire's open wounds and tugged. There was another howl, and that vamp wrenched himself away. Over the howl, Aden thought he heard… roaring? There it was again, and again.

Yes, roars. So many roars, they were reverberating off the walls. And then the vampires were being snatched off Aden, not one at a time but all at once. There were snarls and growls, teeth chomping, screams, all blending together in a soundtrack of horror.

What the hell was happening?

He sat up, intending to scramble out of the way. When he saw what was happening, he froze. The beasts had solidified. Victoria had said they needed time to do so, yet somehow, someway, they'd solidified in a blink. Their scales were iridescent, their teeth like ivory sabers. They smelled of sulfur—rotten eggs—and the tips of their wings were like daggers.

Even they couldn't penetrate the vampires' skin, but they could hold vampires between their huge jaws and shake. Probably breaking bones, rattling skulls. Each vampire was screaming in pain.

The tall double doors burst open, and several more vampires raced inside. When they saw what was going on, however, they stilled, gaping in terror.

"Beasts!"

"What do we do?"

"This has never happened before!"

"Stop," Aden shouted. "Please."

All of the beasts stilled and looked at him. Bodies were dropped with a thump. Those vampires didn't rise, but curled into themselves, crying. One of the beasts roared, and the new vampires backed away, pressing themselves against the wall. Aden remained in place.

Even when one of the beasts approached him.

Victoria flew into the room, then, shouting his name. He didn't turn away from the creature in front of him, but held out his arms to stop Victoria, least she try to pass him and fight to protect him. Of course, she ignored him, and her body slammed against his.

All of the beasts roared this time.

Victoria's hands clutched at him, trying to pull him into her side so that she could teleport him. "They'll kill you. We have to leave."

"No," he said, "no. Move away from me, Victoria."

"No!" More tugging.

More roaring.

"Please, Aden." Utter fear layered her voice.

"Move away from me. Now! They're not going to hurt me." He hoped. "They're protecting me." Again, he hoped. No matter what, he didn't want her in the crosshairs.

A moment passed in suspended silence before her hands fell away and the heat of her left him. Without another word, Aden forced his heavy, puncture-infested legs to move him forward. The beast closest to him issued another roar, wings flapping. The others moved, some flanking his sides, some behind him, becoming a wall of fury and menace.

What are you doing? Julian demanded.

Run, Caleb begged.

I—I see nothing, Elijah stated. *I don't know what you should do anymore. And I don't like it. I don't like this.*

Still Aden forged ahead. "I was right," he said gently. "You were protecting me, weren't you?"

No reply.

Could they understand him?

"Why would you do such a thing?"

The one in front tucked those deadly wings away and crouched down, placing his face inches from Aden's. Moist breaths sawed in and out of huge black nostrils.

That dripping mouth, with those protruding teeth, nudged Aden's arm.

For a moment, fear petrified him. Then he realized there were no new injuries on him, no new stings. *Then* realization set in. "You want me to pet you, don't you, boy?"

Again, no reply, but Aden reached out. Even though he was almost positive he was right, his hand shook. He flattened his palm behind the beast's ear and rubbed. Rather than a snapping of teeth, a wound, a torrent of pain and the loss of a limb, he received a purr of approval from the beast.

The others clomped closer to him, claws scraping against the floor as they settled at Aden's feet, seeking his touch.

"I don't understand this," he whispered.

Me, either. Julian, dumbfounded.

But, dude. We rock! Guess who? Caleb, a strutting peacock.

I never saw this coming. Elijah, awed.

Why did the creatures like him? Why had they protected him from the very people they lived inside? It made no sense.

All he could think was that they must *like* the pull of him, the strange vibration he emitted, drawing the vampire, witches, fairies and goblins to Crossroads. Those creatures hated the pull, though. That's why the witches had called their meeting. To decide what to do with him. That's why Thomas and then Brendal had come to the ranch: to save themselves and "their" humans from his evil.

"Aden?" Victoria's voice was soft, gentle as she attempted to return to his side.

Several of the beasts hissed and snapped at her.

"No," Aden told them, stopping his petting. "She's a friend." He didn't know what he expected the admonishment to do, but what he got was pitiful mewling. His arm was even nudged, a demand for more pets.

He gave them, even as he said, "Victoria, approach us slowly." He couldn't allow these beasts to threaten or hurt her in any way. Ever.

He could hear the soft fall of her footsteps. Again the creatures hissed and snapped. Their bodies stiffened, scales rising, almost like armor being engaged, preparing for attack.

"Stop," Aden told her *and* the beasts.

The footsteps ceased. The beasts calmed.

"Another step."

She obeyed, and more of those hisses erupted.

"Stop."

Again, she obeyed. Again, the beasts calmed. He sighed. They would have to try again another time. These monsters just weren't ready to accept anyone else, not that he could tell, and he wouldn't be able to hold them back if they lunged for her.

"How do I get them back inside their vampires?" he asked, still petting.

"They're solid now," she told him, voice trembling. "They don't have to go back."

Ever? "Can they, though?"

"Yes, but I've only seen a return once. Usually the vampire hosts are dead by the time the beasts reach this point."

"Are the councilmen…"

"No. They're alive," she said. "In pain, bones broken, but alive. They'll heal."

Aden peered into the eyes of the monster in front of him. "I need you to return to where you came from," he said. He couldn't have them running about, scaring people. Eating people.

That earned him a derisive snort.

They understood, he thought, taking heart. "I need you to return," he repeated more firmly.

This time, he got a shake of the beast's head.

"Please. I'm grateful for your help, but those men, they're also helping me. I can't visit this home without them. So if you don't return to them, I have to leave, and I can never come back. If you do return, however, I can talk to them about their wards, about letting you come out and visit with me."

He was taking a gamble. Did these creatures care about him? He didn't know for sure. Did they want to spend more time with him? He didn't know that for sure, either, but it was the only bargaining chip he had.

They stared at him for a long while, eyes narrowing, nostrils flaring, clearly angry, but at least they didn't attack him. Finally, huffing and puffing, they rose, one after the other. Gradually their color faded and the scent of sulfur thinned. By that time, they were once again nothing more than outlines, like ghosts.

Astonishing. Those outlines floated to the writhing vampires and disappeared inside them as if sucked up by a Hoover. Aden watched everything through wide eyes. *Amazing.*

A commotion behind him had him turning. Victoria was rushing to him; when she reached him, she threw herself into his arms, the impact nearly flattening his lungs. As he struggled to breathe, he hugged her tight. The other vampires who had entered the chamber were chalk-white, muttering and peering at him with a strange mix of awe, horror and disbelief.

"How did you do that?" someone finally asked him.

I'm wondering the same thing myself, Elijah said.

"I've never seen anything like that…" another said.

"The beasts were tamed. Actually tamed!"

Beast Tamer. That should be our new nickname, Caleb said with a whoop.

A big, burly vampire with red hair stepped forward, head bowed. He even dropped to one knee. "I do not know if you were told of my challenge, Majesty, but I humbly withdraw it."

A second vampire echoed his words and gestures, followed by a third, a fourth.

"Good. That's good," Aden replied, because he didn't know what else to say. "Victoria and I are going to take off for a little bit. Okay?"

"Yes, yes."

"Of course."

"Please, enjoy yourself, Majesty."

"Do whatever you'd like. This is your home."

Though he was shaking, Aden twined his fingers with Victoria's and allowed her to lead him out of the chamber and up the stairs toward her bedroom. There were now pink and green ribbons tied along the banister, he noted. Clearly people were taking his color mandate seriously. But with the council's insistence that changes be limited to bedrooms and clothing, he wondered how long the ribbons would last.

Riley and Mary Ann were waiting for them upstairs. They sat on the edge of Victoria's bed, silent, not looking at each other.

When he shut the door behind him, closing everyone

inside, Victoria whirled on him, her eyes as wide as his probably were. "That was *incredible*. How did you do that?"

"Do what?" Riley asked, frowning.

Victoria told him, and the wolf paled, pushed to his feet and shook his head. "I should have been there. I'm sorry that I wasn't, sorry you were attacked. I—"

"It's no big deal," Aden told him, trying not to waver on his feet. "I had things under control." For the most part.

"Are you all right?" Mary Ann asked. "You look like you've been in a boxing ring. While playing with knives."

For the first time, Victoria raked her gaze over him. She frowned. "She's right. Your clothes are torn and your skin is eaten up with bites and you...you smell divine." Her voice lowered, husky with desire. "Shall I give you some of my blood to heal you?"

"No, thank you." He didn't want to see the world through her eyes. Not that he minded. He actually liked it—when he wasn't seeing through Dmitri's eyes, too— but for the next couple of days, he needed to be in control of himself. "Were you able to get the tattooing equipment?"

She nodded, forcibly jerking her attention from him. Then she motioned to the vanity. There were tubes, vials and needles scattered along its surface.

"If you don't mind," she said, prim now, "Riley is going to do the tattooing. It's going to hurt, and well, I don't want to hurt you."

They shared a smile as Aden sank into the chair in front of the vanity. "I don't mind." He wouldn't want to hurt her, either.

"Does it speak poorly of my character that I'm looking forward to this?" Riley strode to him and pulled a second chair in front of him. He busied himself with the equipment, asking, "How many wards do you want?"

"How many do I need?"

"As many as you can handle. Were the situation reversed, I'd cover myself in them. But these are permanent, you know? With vampires, they fade as their skin heals from the *je la nune* we have to prep the needles with to leave marks on them at all. Not so with humans. And no, I won't be using any of the *je la nune* on you."

"Is the ink magical or something?" Aden asked.

"No. The designs themselves are spells. Well, antispells. You'll see swirling lines, but the lines are actually a series of words."

Cool.

"Anyway, choose carefully, because you'll be stuck."

He pondered his options. "We don't have a lot of time, so I'll give you two hours. How's that? Give me as many as you can in that time frame."

"Six. I can give you six."

"That seems like a lot for such a short amount of time."

"I've been doing this for, like, a century. I'm very good. So. What do you want to be protected against? Mind control? Ugliness? Pain? Death? Anything you can think of, they can cast a spell for. Impotence. Love. Hate. Rage. Oh, and we'll have to give you a ward to protect your wards, so that they can't be tampered with, well, unless they…never mind, that's not important right now, but anyway, I guess that means we only have time for five others."

"Wait. Go back to that *never mind*," Aden said.

Riley sighed. "Wards can be closed with more ink, which negates their power."

Aden arched a brow. Why would someone want to *negate* one? "Is there a ward that will keep me alive forever?"

"Yes and no. That's a weird one, and one we don't really have time to discuss. What I can do is give you a ward that will protect you from a death spell." Riley's self-recriminating tone lingered long after the words were spoken.

"Can you protect Mary Ann and Victoria with such a ward?" Victoria had already told him the answer to that, but it couldn't hurt to get a second opinion.

"No. I could tattoo the ward on them, but the moment I finished, that ward would crackle and burn away, rendering it useless since they've already been bespelled."

Too bad. "Okay, then, I'll give you an hour to work on me, which means I get three wards. Then I want you to ward Mary Ann against some stuff."

"Tattoos? I don't know about that," Mary Ann said, nervously shaking her head. "My dad would kill me."

No one pointed out the obvious. You had to be alive to be killed.

Riley nodded again, for Aden's benefit. She needed to be warded, therefore she would be warded. End of story. It would be one less worry for all of them. She'd realize that and cave, Aden was sure of it.

Riley held up a silver gunlike device. "So. Besides the ward to protect your wards, what two would you like, Majesty?"

"One against a death spell, like you said." No question. And he was tempted to ward himself against hate. What if they bespelled him, and he thought he hated these friends of his? What if they cast a rage spell, and he injured his friends in a fit of violence? But in the end, he said, "Protect my mind."

"Good. We'll start with that one. So far, the witches have wanted you alive. If they were to capture you, they'd probably try to scrub your head for information. This way, they won't be able to do anything like that. Now, take off your shirt."

With a quick look to Victoria—she was watching him—Aden obeyed. Riley raised the device to his chest and got to work.

There was a constant sting, but nothing Aden couldn't handle. In fact, he could have taken a nap. And did. He closed his eyes, mind drifting, until he heard Riley curse under his breath.

Aden blinked his eyes open, suddenly noting the burning in his chest and the scent of sizzling flesh that saturated the air. He looked down. There was a tattoo on his chest, but lightning snapped over its surface, wiping away the color, causing steam to rise.

"You've already been cursed," Riley said gravely. "Why the hell didn't you tell me?"

What? "I haven't. Believe me, I would remember something like that."

"Well, the only other thing that would cause this kind of reaction is if you have a ward that *prevents* me from warding you."

"I think I'd remember that, too." But there was a niggling sense in the back of his mind, a sea of darkness, of static. "Maybe I'm having memory problems, though. I mean, I was thinking that I'd encountered static in Dr. Hennessy's mind yesterday, yet I can't recall even trying to enter his head."

"Memory problems, huh?" Riley frowned, set the

equipment aside and stood. "Take off your clothes. All of them."

He choked on his own breath. "Excuse me?" A shirt was one thing. *Everything* was another.

"You heard me. Strip. I'm going to check you for wards."

We are not *giving everyone a peep show,* Julian sputtered.

Nothing wrong with showing a little skin, Caleb said.

"I think I would have noticed—"

Riley's severe head shake cut him off. "Not always."

Still he persisted. "The girls—"

"Will turn their backs. Stop stalling. You don't have anything I haven't seen before, you big baby."

Aden glanced over at the girls, and sure enough, they'd turned their backs. So, with a sigh and flushed skin, Aden stripped. Riley looked him over. Frowned again. Growled low in his throat.

"Damn," he said as Aden hastily dressed. "No wards."

"Did you check *everywhere?*" Victoria asked.

Meaning his family jewels? Aden's cheeks flamed.

"Yeah, I checked there. There are a few more places I need to look, though." Riley checked behind his ears, in his hairline, under his arms. Still nothing.

With a push to his shoulders, Aden flopped back into the seat. Riley sat and lifted one of his feet, then the other. Bingo, Aden thought, because Riley was shaking his head and studying both as if they held the secrets of the universe.

"How?" Aden demanded. "I would have known afterward, even if I wasn't aware during." Wouldn't he? "Walking would have hurt."

"No. You were warded twice, and one of them prevents foot pain. After you woke up, you never would have felt a thing."

Dear God. There really *was* a ward for everything. "You mentioned foot pain. What's the other ward for?"

"Preventing you from being warded *against* mind manipulation. Which means whoever warded you wanted your mind malleable. Wanted to control you. Probably *has* controlled you. And if you're having memory issues related to your doctor, chances are good that he's the one who did the warding."

Shock swept through him. Shock and fury. How would Hennessy have known to ward him? What's more… "Why would he do such a thing? What would he have wanted me to do?"

"We'll pay him a visit tomorrow and find out."

If they were still alive, he didn't add, but they were all thinking it.

"As for now, I'm going to negate the mind manipulation ward by smearing the words. Then I'll give you another antimanipulation ward. *Then* I'll give you a ward protecting your wards. That way, he can't negate ours like we're doing to his. Warning, though. Not many people want the ward protecting ward because it makes any wards you get now, as well as any you get later, permanent. And if another ward is ever added without your consent... Anyway, with you, with our circumstances, it's worth the risk."

"Thank you." Aden was still numb with that shock, still on fire from the fury. The dual sensations created havoc inside his head, the souls now equally numb and upset, demanding answers. "Will there still be time for the death-prevention ward?"

"We'll make time. Anyway, I'll leave the anti-foot-pain ward alone. You're gonna need it." With that, Riley got back to work.

TWENTY-FOUR

TUCKER HAD NEWS TO SHARE. News he knew Vlad would hate, but share he would. He had to. His blood vibrated with a need he couldn't fight.

Why are you doing this? Stop, his mind screamed.

Truly, he couldn't. The need was too strong. He flew across the manicured vampire lawn, bypassing bonsai trees, skirting around black rose bushes. In the center of the property was a wide ring of cement poured in swirls to create an intricate design. Almost like a crop circle he'd once seen on the news. A strange electrical pulse rose from it, and birds and insects stayed as far away as possible. *Like I want to do.*

As he had done a thousand times before, he stood in the center of the ring, unnoticed by the few vampires working around him, pulling weeds and digging in the dirt. They saw only the golden sunshine around him because that's the image he projected at them.

Perhaps they smelled him, though, because every single one of them straightened and sniffed the air.

Hurry. Tucker planted his feet inside two grooves of cement. When his heels hit the back of those grooves, the swirls around him began to move. Whirling, interlocking, separating, twisting. He continued to project sunlight, glaring bright...brighter...until the vampires looked away.

The center he stood upon began to descend, slowly, slowly, lowering him into the earth, into the darkness. No one would see the opening he left behind; he made sure of it. For a moment, as the sunlight illuminated the yawning pit below, he saw what awaited him.

Dead bodies littered the hard ground. In fact, when the metal finished lowering, one of those bodies was crunched, bones snapping. The smell...metallic, as if blood had sprayed. Rotten, as if the bodies were already decomposing.

He wanted to vomit. Was this the fate that awaited him?

Probably. That didn't stop him from stepping inside. Without his weight, the platform rose, higher and higher, finally closing the circle above. Darkness swathed him. Such darkness. He reminded himself that when he was ready to return, he had only to flatten his palms in the grooves on the wall, and the ring would open again. Until then...

"Who are these people?" he whispered.

Vlad, always awake, never sleeping, heard him. "They were unimportant slaves who outlived their usefulness, and you will dispose of them." His voice was stronger, far less raspy than it had been during their other meetings. "The sight of them offends me."

"Of course." Tucker didn't even think about refusing.

"And you will bring me more."

"Yes." How was he supposed to do that? *You'll find a way. You want to please this man. You have to please this man.*

"Now why are you here? I didn't summon you yet."

Don't do this. There was his other side, fighting, wanting to live a better, sweeter life, thinking things could be different, pretending he hadn't used his power of illusion to terrify an innocent family last night, letting them think they were covered in spiders and grinning while they screamed.

That had always been his favorite trick.

"Well?"

"I—I have news." He told Vlad what he'd seen when he'd used his illusions to sneak inside the mansion. Vampires attacking Aden. Horrible monsters rising from those vampires, protecting Aden. Aden, petting those monsters, cooing to them. Asking them to return to their hosts, watching them obey.

"How did he not die before the beasts showed themselves?" Vlad asked, and as usual, his mild tone was somehow mind-numbingly frightening.

Tucker gulped. "He sprayed some kind of liquid on their faces."

There was a rustle of clothing. "Liquid? From a ring?"

No longer pretending at calm, Vlad had sounded furious. "Y-yes."

"And how did he win the loyalty of the beasts?"

"I don't know. No one knew."

Before the last word left Tucker's mouth, Vlad was screaming. He must have been stomping around, ripping up stones and tossing them into the walls, because Tucker heard the grind of rock against rock, felt the rumble of the earth as everything around him shook and cracked.

He clutched at his ears, but it was too late. Warm blood leaked, that high-pitched scream having busted his eardrums. Sharp pain exploded through his head before lancing through the rest of him.

For once, the desire to flee outweighed his desire to please and he stumbled to the wall, feeling for the grooves. But a strong hand clamped on his shoulder, stopping him in his tracks.

THIS MIGHT JUST BE her last day on earth, Mary Ann thought, then chided herself for such a morbid outlook.

Now that she'd fed from the witch, she felt better, stronger than ever before. No way she'd simply drop dead. She hoped. But she felt guilty, too, as she remembered how the witch had cursed and screamed at her, then wilted, silent.

How could I have done that to her?

And how could she return to the cabin? But she was returning, as soon as Riley finished tattooing her. Aden planned to possess the girl's body and try to time-travel into her past. Maybe…maybe Mary Ann would remain outside during the attempt. That way, she wouldn't take anything else from the poor girl.

Yes. Yes, that's exactly what she'd do, she decided. Victoria would simply assume Mary Ann was a coward, afraid to face so powerful a creature even though she had been warded.

The wards. Ugh. Mary Ann frowned. Unlike Aden, she hadn't wanted her tattoos on her chest. She hadn't wanted to see them every day, to know they were permanent, a part of her forever.

So, she'd removed her shirt—blushing like crazy and thankful she'd worn a pretty bra, even if Riley had seen it the night before—and given Riley her back. And dear God, getting them *hurt*. Like having fire poured straight into her bloodstream.

"All done," Riley finally said. He sounded pleased.

She pushed to her feet, grabbed her shirt and strode to

the full-length mirror in the corner. Twisting, she saw two beautifully elaborate tattoos. One would protect her from mind manipulation, just as Aden had chosen, and one would protect her from mortal wounds. At least physical ones.

That second one wouldn't help if, say, her heart suddenly stopped because of the death spell, but Riley had insisted on that one, so that one she had picked. And it hadn't sizzled and disappeared, so obviously physical harm—like a stabbing—wasn't the way the death spell would kill her.

Apparently, for wards of that magnitude, the tattoo had to be *bigger,* so the second ward stretched from one shoulder blade to the other. God, her dad was going to *die.* After he murdered her, of course.

She pulled the tee over her head, wincing against the sharp sting as the material rubbed her sensitive skin.

"Ready?" Victoria held out one delicate hand.

She nodded and twined their fingers. A second later, the vampire had her teleported to the outside of the cabin. Victoria disappeared without a word, returned a few seconds later with Aden, disappeared again, then returned a few seconds later with Riley. She was getting better at the teleporting thing.

"Let's do this," Aden said, his urgency catching like a virus. Everyone but Mary Ann pounded up the stairs.

"I'm staying out here," she announced.

They stopped, looked at her.

Mary Ann studied Aden, and she couldn't help but wonder if this would be one of the last times she saw him. *You have to stop thinking like that.* He was such a beautiful boy. He was a natural blond, but he dyed his hair black. His eyes were multicolored, blue, green, gray and brown, each representing a soul, as well as Aden himself, and when those colors blended, his eyes looked completely black.

He was as tall as Riley and just as muscled. Where Riley was ruggedly appealing, dangerous, Aden was model handsome. His lashes were long and cast spiky shadows over his cheeks. His lips were perfectly pink and soft-looking.

"Everything okay?" he asked her, frowning with concern.

She loved him like a brother, and when she left this group, she was going to miss him terribly. "I just think it's better if I stay out here," she said as Riley said, "Mary Ann's not feeling well."

They shared a smile, though neither of them was amused. Last night, after he'd realized beyond any doubt that she was a Drainer, he had fallen silent. He had held her while she absorbed the witch's power, strengthening, and then, after Victoria returned them to his room, he had gotten back into bed with her. Still without saying a word. She hadn't spoken, either, though.

She doubted either of them had slept. They'd simply lain in each other's arms, knowing their time together would one day end.

With a sigh, she returned her attention to Aden. She stepped up, reached out and clasped his hand. His skin was warm, callused. "Good luck," she said, "and be careful."

He squeezed her fingers. "Always."

"You were feeling fine a moment ago," Victoria said with a frown of her own. "Are you…afraid? You shouldn't be. You're protected now."

"Only against certain things."

"Oh." Victoria shook her head, long dark hair waving around her arms. She was a beautiful girl, the perfect match to perfect Aden. Pale, flawless skin, lips of the deepest scarlet. Eyes of sapphire blue. No wonder Aden had fallen for her so quickly and so hard. "I see," she said.

But she didn't. Her expression had *coward* written all over it, just as Mary Ann had known it would. That was okay, though. This was better than Victoria knowing the truth—and trying to kill her.

So many death threats, she thought. And that she wasn't running, screaming for help, proved just how far she'd come.

Victoria and Aden turned and strode into the cabin.

Riley remained with her for a few seconds, watching as the pair disappeared.

"I'll be fine," she assured him.

"I know."

It was the first time he'd spoken directly to her today, and she relished the sound of his voice.

"Are you nervous?" he asked. "About tomorrow?"

She opted not to lie to him. "Yes. It just doesn't feel real, though. You know? I'm fine. I feel fine. How can I die?"

"I know," he said again. "I regret that we weren't... together last night."

Just then, so did she. She regretted so many things. She should have spent more time with her dad. Should have forgiven him sooner for how he'd lied about her mother. He wouldn't recover if he lost Mary Ann, too. He would be alone, no one there to look out for him.

She couldn't leave him like that. He might blame himself, tormented by thoughts that he could have done something to save her.

"I was trying to do the right thing," Riley said, bringing her back to the present. "For you."

"I know," she was the one to say this time. "We've had a wild few weeks, haven't we?"

"We certainly have."

"And I'm sorry, I really am. You wouldn't be in this situation if it weren't for me." If she hadn't met Aden, she wouldn't have met Riley, and if she hadn't met Riley, she wouldn't have spent every spare moment of her time with him, binding them closer and closer together, changing the course of his life.

"Hey. Don't talk like that. The one thing I don't regret is meeting you," he said gruffly. "Never that."

To be honest, she didn't either. He was one of the best things to have ever happened to her. No matter how this thing ended, she couldn't regret meeting him.

From inside the cabin, the witch cursed. At least she'd recovered from Mary Ann's draining enough to do so.

Riley sighed wearily. "I better get in there."

"Okay. I'll be here."

He leaned down and pressed a swift kiss to her lips, then strode up the rest of the steps and into the cabin, leaving her alone. Suddenly feeling just as weary as he'd sounded, she settled on the bottom step, elbows resting on her knees, chin resting on her upraised palms.

The sun was bright, throwing orange-gold spots in her line of vision, and the air warmer than it had been in weeks. She—her thoughts skidded to a halt as, in the distance, limbs rubbed together and brittle leaves crunched. She straightened, gaze homing in. Soon, a familiar face and form came into view. A boy. A football player. Tucker, her ex. He lifted a hand in a brief wave.

Mary Ann was on her feet before she realized she'd moved, mouth opening and closing, heart pounding.

She raced to him, praying he wouldn't bolt. The closer she came to him, the more clearly she saw him. He was so pallid she could see the blue tracery of veins beneath his skin. When they'd dated, he'd been beautifully tanned. Now his face was gaunt, as if he'd lost weight. His sandy hair was matted to his head, and his clothes were wrinkled and stained, ill-fitting. Torn, as if he'd recently been in a fight.

The moment she was within touching distance, she saw the scars. Small, round, side by side. Punctures. From vampires. They'd healed quickly—too quickly—no longer scabs, as they should have been, since very little time had passed since he'd been served up as an hors d'oeuvre at the Vampire Ball, but already scars. On his neck, his arms, even his face. No, wait. There was a fresh pair of punctures on his neck, beads of blood still leaking.

Not so long ago, she'd hated this boy for cheating on her. Then she'd seen him strapped to a table, near death. Her hate had drained, pity and fear taking their place. Just then, that pity and fear intensified.

"Tucker," she said. "How did you find us? And what are you doing here? You should be in a hospital right now."

"No. No, I have to warn you." He grabbed her by the wrist and jerked her deep into the forest, so deep the trees hid them from cabin onlookers. He whirled on her, mouth opening to speak. He stilled, closed his eyes, pressed his lips together. A smile lifted the corners of his mouth. "Peace. I had forgotten how wonderful I would feel, being this close to you again."

She gripped his shoulders and shook him. "What's going on, Tucker? What do you have to warn me about?"

"Just...give me a minute." His eyes remained closed. "Please. I didn't think I'd ever get you alone again, but here you are. Here I am. And it's better than I could have imagined."

He radiated such bliss, she couldn't deny him. So she stood there, silent, shaking with the force of her curiosity and dread. One minute passed, two. Three, four. An eternity.

Finally, blessedly, his eyes opened. He frowned. "I shouldn't be here," he said. "He'll probably punish me." He laughed without humor. "Probably? He'll destroy me, no question."

"Who, Tucker? Talk to me!"

He licked his cracked lips. "I've come this far. I might as well just tell you, right? It's..." A beam of sunlight hit his face, illuminating the dark circles under his eyes, making him look like the living dead. "It's...Vlad." His voice dipped into a tortured whisper.

"Vlad?" Her brow crinkled in confusion. "Vlad's dead."

He shook his head. "Not anymore. He's very much alive. He called me while I was in the hospital."

"Like, on the phone?"

"No. Inside my head. He called me, and I went to him. I couldn't stop myself. He's underground, in a crypt behind the vampire mansion."

"Tucker, I—"

"No. Listen. He wanted me to watch Aden, to report what he was doing. And I—I did. Have. Will. He's angry right now, Mary Ann. Very, very angry, and all of that anger is directed at Aden for daring to take his throne." Tucker's gaze darkened. "I don't know what Vlad will do to him, and I don't know what he'll command me to do, but you should know that I'll do it, whatever it is. I won't be able to help myself."

"This is—this is—"

"True."

The implications of this were vast. Too vast. Too frightening. And, she thought, almost more than her already fragile state of mind could bear. "You have to tell the others what's going on. They'll—"

"No. No." He jerked from her hold, backing away. "I won't go near them. Not while they can see me, at least."

"Tucker, please. They won't hurt you." She wouldn't let them. "You have to tell them everything Vlad has said to you. Everything he's asked you to do and everything you've told him."

"No." He gave another shake of his head. "You don't understand. When I'm with you, I feel good. Normal. Happy. I can control myself. But when I'm with the others, I...can't. I do bad things."

"I'll be with you. I won't leave your side. I swear!"

"Doesn't matter. Not when you're with them."

"Tucker. Please."

"I'm sorry, Mary Ann. So sorry. Consider yourself warned." He turned on his heel and ran off as fast as his feet would carry him.

TWENTY-FIVE

ADEN STOOD IN FRONT OF THE witch. She was sitting in the same chair as before, only she'd scooted herself across the room as she'd screamed about a drainer. She wore a blindfold, but this one was a different color than the one she'd worn before. Had she managed to destroy the other one? Why else would someone switch them?

Her ties were different, too. Had she tried to escape? Almost succeeded?

She was paler than before, her skin almost…yellow. Her cheeks were more hollowed. There was a brittle quality to her hair now, as though the strands had lost their shine and had dried into hay. Before she'd hummed with power. Now…not so much. She could have been a human.

The wolves had been caring for her, feeding her, that kind of thing. But she had to be uncomfortable. Miserable, actually. And he felt bad about that. He really did. He didn't like that she was suffering, bored, stiff, uncertain, scared, but more than that, he didn't like that his friends could die because of her and her kind.

"I'm not here to hurt you," he told her gently. "I'm not going to drain you of anything."

Her panting breaths echoed between them. "You're the Summoner." Even her voice was different. Weaker. Raspier.

"Yes." If only he could tame witches with the same ease he tamed flesh-hungry beasts, none of this would have been necessary. "What are you so afraid of being drained of?"

Don't engage her, Elijah instructed. *Just do your job.*

"Your blood?" he found himself adding.

Good going. Dryly uttered.

"As if you don't know someone among you can and has—"

Riley entered the small room and propped himself against the closed door, snarling, "Quiet, witch. We gave you a chance to share. You refused. Now, you can deal with whatever's done to you."

Caleb, highly agitated since seeing the witch in such a weakened condition, prowled through Aden's head, huffing, puffing, and now growling at the wolf. *She can talk if she wants to talk! Aden, man, you can't leave her like that. You have to save her.*

What's with you? Julian asked. *Save her?*

Look at her. She's sick. She needs help. I know I helped come up with our current plan, but that was before I saw her like this.

"We'll save her," Aden muttered. "After." *So let's get this done.* He glanced up. Victoria stood across from him, behind the witch. "Ready?" he mouthed.

She nodded, expression tight with nerves.

"Save who?" the witch demanded. "Me? Well, that's not going to save *you*. Not after everything you've done."

Aden! You wouldn't tolerate this kind of thing if your vampire girlfriend was the one tied up, Caleb said, unwilling to give up. *Let the witch go. Now. Please.*

Why do you care so much about this witch? Elijah asked. *And really, even the others. From the time they approached us and cast their death spell, you've been as drawn to them as they are to Aden.*

I don't know, was the agonized reply. *I just know I don't want her hurting.*

Aden suspected the witches were part of Caleb's past. Plus, this witch had stiffened when he'd mentioned a guy who could possess other bodies. "Maybe we can find out," he said. After all, he kinda needed Caleb's cooperation for this. And he *had* promised to discover who the souls had been when they'd lived. He'd promised to help them with their final wish, to send them on, even if he would miss them terribly, even if he now wanted to keep them. "When we're inside, we'll search for information about you."

"Inside?" the witch asked, struggling against her bonds. "What are you planning? What the hell are you planning? If you hurt me, my sisters will hunt you down and curse you with pain, such terrible pain. They'll curse your family, too! Do you hear me?" Her chair rattled, bouncing up and down with her motions.

"I already told you, I'm not going to hurt you," he said. But really, she'd already threatened to punish him no matter what happened, so her newest threat missed its mark.

I don't know about this, Caleb said. *What if we change her past? What if that change destroys her?*

"We'll be careful, but we have to do this. Tick-tock on the deadline, you know? There's no other way."

A pause, then, *Fine. Do it. But don't injure her in any way.*

Aden took offense to that. "As if I would." Not purposely. "You know me better than that."

"Know you better than what?" the witch snapped.

Time to act. Reaching out, he removed her blindfold. She blinked against the bright light of the room, eyes watering, nose wrinkling, lips pursing. Aden cupped her chin and forced her attention on his face.

"Relax." The moment their gazes met, Caleb took

over, Aden's body dissolving and slipping into the witch's. He expected pain, had braced himself against it, but there wasn't even a flicker of discomfort. Maybe, after everything that had happened to him, his pain threshold had increased. Or maybe Caleb was getting better at this. Maybe Caleb had done everything in his power to keep Aden from feeling pain because, if Aden had felt it, the witch also would have felt it the moment they linked to her, whether she was aware of the link or not.

Now seeing through her eyes, Aden took stock. His wrists and ankles were bruised and cut from tugging at the rope. His muscles were stiff. "Free me," he told Riley. The oddity of speaking with someone else's voice always startled him.

A frowning Riley strode to him, claws sharpening, and slashed at the ties. Aden pulled his hands into his lap and massaged his wrists. When his feet were freed, he stood. His legs were so weak they almost collapsed, but he managed to walk around the room, increasing blood flow.

She wouldn't know he'd done this for her, but she would feel better.

"Thank you." As he walked, he let his mind wander through hers, the world around him fading away. Unlike with Dr. Hennessy, he didn't see static. He saw—wait. There was that thought again. Static. He *must* have entered Dr. Hennessy's mind. Otherwise, he wouldn't keep thinking about what had happened there. How long had he stayed? Why couldn't he recall?

Don't think about that now.

Aden returned his attention to the witch. But unlike when he'd been in Shannon's mind, he didn't see scenes from her life. He saw...boxes? There were thousands of them, scattered across a sea of white, each boasting a thick silver lock.

He frowned as he clamped one of the locks between his fingers, and an electric shock tore through him, burning. "What would cause such a reaction?"

Wards, Caleb said, and he'd never sounded more confident. *She has wards of her own. Her memories are in the boxes, and the boxes are warded against invaders.*

"How do you know?" Aden asked.

Don't know. Just do.

Well, Aden needed inside them. Each ward could do only one thing, so what—or which—wards did she have and how, exactly, did they protect her mind? There was only one way to find out.

He searched the room until he found Riley, who was once again leaning against the door. "I need you to leave," he said.

The wolf shook his head. "That would be—"

"The right thing to do," he interrupted. "She's warded, so I can't reach her memories. Therefore we have to see what wards she has, and I don't think she'd want a guy looking."

Oh, no, Caleb said. *You're not stripping her down.*

Usually, Caleb was the one begging for a peep show. "We'll work around her clothes, okay?"

"If I'm gone," Riley said, "I won't be able to protect you."

"Don't care. Go." He pointed to the exit.

"Fine. But if she somehow realizes what you're doing and rips at *your* mind, I can't be blamed." The shifter threw open the door, stomped out and kicked it shut behind him.

"If that happened, you wouldn't be able to help me anyway," Aden called. "Victoria, you look the body over."

"Yes." She glided to him, as graceful as a ballet dancer.

Aden closed his eyes. One piece at a time, she moved the witch's clothing out of the way, searching. At first, her motions were quick and efficient. Then she slowed... slowed...lingered.

"I've never studied a witch this intently," she said, voice heavy. "Usually I avoid them. I don't know why. Your scent..."

"Bad?"

"No." She'd finished her search, but her grip tightened on his arms, holding him in place. "Good. *Soooo* good."

He recognized that tone. It was the same one the councilmen had used just before flying at him and chomping at his veins.

Red alert, Elijah suddenly announced.

"I know." Aden opened his eyes and tugged from her. He rushed to the far end of the empty room. When she attempted to follow, he shook his head. "Stay there."

Her eyes were glazed, her fangs longer than ever before. "Just one taste," she pleaded. "I'll make it feel good. You'll like it."

"Riley," he called.

The wolf entered the room a second later. Clearly, he hadn't gone far. "Decide you needed me, after all?"

"We have a slight…problem." Victoria had crouched, ready to leap.

"What—" Riley noticed and grabbed her by the waist, holding her in place. "Oh, no, you don't." She struggled against him. "There are bags of blood in the other room. She'll feed and she'll be fine. We'll be back," he said, and hefted her out the door.

Several minutes passed. Aden waited, wishing he could be the one to feed her, the one who calmed her. But he wasn't ready to leave the witch's body, and Victoria couldn't be allowed to drink from the witch. He remembered what she'd said about the allure of the witches, how addicting their blood was, and he didn't like the thought of her strung out like a drug user.

When the pair finally returned, a subdued Victoria walked by Riley's side. He shut the door and stayed there, but she kept moving, careful to give Aden a wide berth. She perched against the far wall, her cheeks rosy with color.

"Sorry about that," she muttered.

"Don't worry about it," Aden said, just glad to see her clearheaded again. "Can you tell me what wards she possesses?"

Victoria nodded. "Her wards are tiny. Actually, I've never seen wards so small. I would think them ineffective, yet when you run your finger over them, you can feel their intense power."

"How many does she have?"

"Nine. Two are purely cosmetic, preventing anyone from cursing her with ugliness. One is for the protection of her wards, so that no one can tattoo over them and ruin or change them."

Smart witch. Though Riley had told him not many people chose to have that particular ward.

"One is to protect her from mortal injury, one to protect her from mental injury, which is probably what's hindering your progress. One to anchor her to this world, I guess so that she cannot be taken into another dimension by a fairy. One against goblin poison, one to protect her against a lying male's seduction and one to prevent her from speaking secrets. Which means she couldn't have told us what we wanted to know, even if she'd wanted to."

Riley fisted a handful of his hair, released the strands, then fisted them again. "We should have thought to look for wards before."

True. "In our defense, we've had a lot to think about."

"And we normally avoid witches," Victoria said. "We've never willingly spent time with one. Why would we have known what to do?"

Good point. "Okay, so. She can't speak secrets, and her mind is protected from injury. I don't mean to harm her, but she can't know that. Even if she doesn't know I'm here, inside her, her mind probably recognizes me as foreign and therefore views me as a threat."

"Can you hide yourself from her?" Riley asked.

"I don't know, but it's worth a shot." Maybe if she were conscious, unaware of his presence, her mind would relax. Maybe those boxes would open up on their own. "Here, tie me back up."

I don't like this, Caleb said.

Aden didn't either, but there was no other way.

He plopped into the chair, stretching his arms behind his back and pressing his wrists together. In less than a minute, Riley had him bound back up. Yep. Uncomfortable. Poor girl.

You swear you'll set her free after this? Caleb asked on a trembling breath.

"Yes." After this, they'd have no more need of her.

"Yes what?" Riley asked, then shook his head. "Never mind. You weren't talking to me."

The wolf was learning. "Put the blindfold on me. And yes, this time I'm talking to you."

Riley did as instructed, and suddenly darkness surrounded him.

"I'm going to try and fade to the back of her mind. Hopefully, she won't know I'm there. Try to keep her talking, distracted. And if she won't talk to you, you talk to her. Try to say things that prod her memories of the death curse." She couldn't speak her secrets, but he would soon find out whether or not she could think them while someone listened.

"I need you to be quiet now," he said, "and no, I'm not talking to you or Victoria." He didn't want the witch to hear the souls. "Please."

Fine, Elijah said on a sigh.

Sure, Julian said.

All right, Caleb grumbled, *but only because I want her released.*

Aden breathed in, held…held, then slowly released every bit of air. As he did, he threw himself into a shadowed corner of the witch's mind. He could have eased to the back, but then she would have become gradually aware of her surroundings, might have had time to notice something was amiss. This way, it was like ripping a Band-Aid. He was there, front and center, and then he wasn't.

"Well?" the witch demanded as if their conversation had never ended. "Know you better than what?"

Good. She didn't recall Aden removing her blindfold, looking into her eyes and disappearing.

"Enough," Riley said. "Tell us your name."

Contrary wolf, she thought, and Aden almost whooped. He could hear her, and she didn't seem aware of him. "I thought you didn't want me to talk."

Riley kept up a steady chatter, but Aden tuned him out, concentrating on the witch. *Blah, blah, blah,* she was thinking now. *Where'd the Summoner go? I can't feel the pull of him anymore. If he left… Argh! I've got to get out of here and take him with me. The girls are going to be so pissed. I can't believe I got caught. Stupid vampires. I'm going to be teased about this forever. I may not be able to die by physical means, but I'll probably die of embarrassment.*

Nothing useful there.

He turned his attention to the vast sea in front of him. The boxes had disappeared, the memories that had been inside them now floating freely. There were so many, each like a tiny TV screen. He didn't know which to focus on. If he picked the wrong one, he was afraid he'd waste hours, lost, and learn nothing. That was better than waiting, doing nothing, he supposed.

He scanned the images before him until he caught a glimpse of the blond witch who had spoken to him in the forest a week ago, the one Caleb had reacted to so strongly. The one who had spoken the curse that could kill his friends.

When he saw her, Aden automatically reached out. The moment his fingers touched the screen, dizziness flooded his mind, catching him in a surprising whirlpool, spinning him out of control, tossing him like a ragdoll. And just when he thought he could take it no more, he stilled. Or rather, his body did.

He closed his eyes, shook his head.

"Hey, are you okay?" a female voice asked him. A familiar voice.

In the back of his mind, Caleb whimpered.

"Quiet." Slowly he cracked open his eyes. The blond witch stood in front of him in all her pale glory. Her hair hung to her waist, curling slightly. Her skin was flawless, her eyes a dark, navy blue and her lips like a frosted plum. She looked to be about twenty years old.

She wore the same red robe she'd worn that day in the forest. For that matter, so did Aden. They stood outside a chapel-like building comprised of white brick, with a pointed roof that seemed to stretch to the sky. Rose bushes covered the front, hugging the sides of steps that lead to a wraparound porch. The air was hot and humid, fragrant with the scents of summer.

"Well?"

Aden waited a moment, trying to decide how best to answer. He didn't want to change the past, and thereby alter the future, but he couldn't remain silent as he'd done while inside Shannon's head. Shannon was ashamed of his stutter and often ignored those around him; Aden had a feeling this smart-mouthed witch never had.

"What were we discussing?" he asked in that female voice.

The blonde rolled her eyes. "Look. I know you're scared about punishment. You told the human about your powers, and now we have to move before the witch hunt begins. But…"

She continued speaking, but Aden tuned her out. This wasn't the right memory. He closed his eyes and imagined himself back inside the witch's head. He didn't know if it would work and he—there was another whirlpool, more tossing about, but suddenly he was there, back in that shadowed corner, little TVs floating in front of him.

Thank God.

He must be getting good at this.

This guy going to shut up? she was thinking.

Riley continued babbling about right and wrong, life and death, how all he wanted to do was protect his friends and to do that, he had to get Aden to that meeting, yet he couldn't do that if he didn't know where the meeting was. His voice was hoarse and Aden wondered how much time had passed.

Again, Aden tuned him out. He watched those TV screens until he again spied the blonde. Once again, he reached out.

TWENTY-SIX

THE SCENE ADEN NEXT FOUND himself in was vastly different than the first. Night had fallen, and he stood in a circle, surrounded by witches draped in red robes. There was a drizzle of rain, soaking him. The moon was high, the air so cold mist bloomed in front of his nose every time he breathed. Yet he wasn't cold. A fire crackled in the center of the circle, wafting heat at him.

His skin tingled, the fine hairs on the back of his neck standing on end. He looked around.

The blonde was across from him. She said something in a language he didn't understand, and the women at his sides reached for his hands. That startled him, but he didn't allow himself to jerk away.

Everyone but him began muttering something under their breath. He listened. Now they were all speaking in that strange language. This must be a spell-casting, he thought, but for what?

Caleb repeated the words. *I think...I think they're asking for protection from dark forces.*

If Aden had ever doubted that Caleb had an affinity with the witches, those doubts faded.

"Someone is impeding our power," the blonde suddenly snapped. Her gaze scanned the circle, then backtracked to Aden, locking down. "Jennifer," she said. "Why aren't you chanting?"

Finally, the witch's name. Jennifer. So very...human.

Rather than reply, Aden pulled back from the memory and settled inside Jennifer's mind with only the slightest unease, once again watching those TVs. They moved back and forth.

Had his blunder changed anything in the future?

He looked around. Riley was currently draining a glass of water and Victoria was talking about her desire to save the humans. Thank God. Nothing had changed, really. There was no window inside the room, so Aden couldn't peer outside and determine what time it was. He'd try one or two more times, and then leave the witch, informed or not.

Choose carefully, Elijah said. Did he sense something? Dread had layered his voice, and he wouldn't have spoken, fearful of alerting Jennifer, without reason.

Aden wanted to ask for Caleb's help, but didn't. He wouldn't risk it. So many screens passed him, some of

Jennifer as a little girl, some of Jennifer with a boy, obviously in love, some of Jennifer crying.

Then he saw the unexpected. Dr. Hennessy. Aden stopped breathing. He reached out before he'd realized what he was doing, inserting himself into a new scene. Dizzy only for a moment, he blinked and was clearheaded. This time, he found himself in the very woods he walked through every day. Only, the blonde witch and Dr. Hennessy were keeping pace beside him.

Again, it was night and the moon was high, the air frigid. In the distance, he could hear the howl of several wolves.

The blonde witch tensed.

"Do not worry about the wolves," Dr. Hennessy said. "They can't see or sense us."

And why was that? A spell? What kind of power did the doctor possess?

"So what are you doing here?" the blonde demanded of the doctor.

So beautiful, Caleb said. *And mine, I think. We have to talk to her, Aden. Please.*

Hush! Aden hissed, but he wasn't sure if the soul heard him or not. *Do you* want *to alert Jennifer?*

Now is not the time for chatter, Caleb, Elijah reminded the soul, perhaps sensing Aden's thoughts. The psychic was more attuned to him than the other two.

There's never a good time.

"The same thing you are, I'm sure," Dr. Hennessy replied, yet his voice was different, softer, more feminine. "You, too, felt that explosion of power, Marie, then the tug of whatever's here."

Marie. Another name. This conversation must have happened when they'd first arrived in Oklahoma, when they hadn't yet known Aden was the source of the "tug."

"Yes," Marie said. "We did. Are you saying you didn't cause that tug to lure us into a trap?"

"Of course that's what I'm saying. We're allies. Unless *you* meant to lure *us* into a trap. This feels like black magic to me."

"As you know, we do not deal in the black arts."

"Then we're still allies."

The tension eased. "Great, but admitting we're still on friendly terms is not the reason you called this meeting, I'm sure. And will you please drop the mask? You're hideous like that, and I can't stand to look at you a second longer."

Dr. Hennessy frowned. "Subterfuge is necessary."

"With the humans, yes, but not with us."

"Oh, very well." White light seeped from the doctor's pores, brightening...brightening...before exploding in a shower of sparks. When those sparks faded, Aden could only gape. Ms. Brendal now stood in Dr. Hennessy's place.

They were one and the same?

Did I just see what I think I just saw? Caleb asked.

I never suspected, Elijah breathed.

I'm...I'm... Julian couldn't finish his thought.

Why had Brendal come to the ranch as herself, then, after pretending to be Dr. Hennessy? Because Dan had told "Dr. Hennessy" that Aden would be finding a new doctor? No, because the dinner invitation had come before the firing. This was...this was...too weird. He—she—was a fairy.

"Better," Marie said. "And thank you."

Again, Brendal shrugged, but her gaze snagged on Aden and she quirked a brow. "I'm beautiful, yes, but there's no reason to stare at me."

"Uh, sorry." Aden cast his gaze to his feet. He wore sandals under his robe and his toenails were painted neon green. What the— Oh, yeah. He was in Jennifer's body.

Marie nudged his shoulder, and he glanced up. She was frowning at him, a what's-with-you glare in her eyes.

"So what do you plan to do about the tug?" Brendal asked, returning them to the only topic that mattered.

"Tell us your plans first," Marie said.

Brendal gave another of those casual shrugs. "Very

well. We must first discover the source of the allure. Is it human? Something man-made? Something just found beneath the earth?" She closed her eyes for a moment, inhaled deeply. Her step never faltered. "We are close to it, whatever it is. I can feel it more strongly than ever."

Aden tried not to cringe.

"Me, too," Marie said.

"Me, too," Aden echoed, just to blend in. "What do you plan to do with it when you find it?"

"Dispose of it, of course," the fairy said.

"Maybe we should keep it instead," Marie suggested.

Brendal blinked in confusion. "Why would we want to?"

At Aden's left, branches and leaves rattled together. Then several goblins sprinted out, their short legs moving faster than Aden would have thought possible. They were grinning evilly, grins that said this was all a game, blood dripping from the corners of their mouths. Two wolves burst after them, leaping through the air and slamming into their backs, sending them hurtling to the ground face-first.

A second later, high-pitched screams, growls, snarls and pleas erupted, then silence reigned. As Brendal had promised, neither the goblins nor the wolves noticed the trio.

Aden watched, horrified. He didn't recognize the

wolves, and he knew what they were doing was for the best, for the protection of the people, but…all that violence.

Brendal and Marie continued walking, unconcerned. When they realized Aden had fallen behind, watching the action, they turned. Frowning again, Marie motioned him over with a wave of her hand. He hurried to catch up, and they kicked back into gear as a group.

"This is a rare opportunity," Marie went on as if they'd never been interrupted. "Let's assume the tug comes from a human rather than an inanimate object, which I believe it does because we're being pulled in different directions all the time, usually at the same time each day. The power required to do something like that must be tremendous. And therein lies the opportunity. Because not only were we summoned, but the vampires and their furry friends were, too.

"If we capture this human, we can harness its strange power for ourselves and lead *our enemies* into a trap. I mean, think about it. If we slaughter the vampires and the wolves, we'll no longer have to worry about being used as a blood bank or medicine chest, and you'll have protected your precious humans from the giant ticks we so abhor."

Ticks. Aden's hands fisted at his sides. Victoria was not a tick.

"Neither of our people is known for sharing, Marie.

This you know," Brendal said. "How would we share this human? If we are indeed looking for a human."

"We'll work out a custody plan. Anything is better than destroying someone—thing—so powerful."

So. She didn't want to destroy him. That was good to know, and finally something he could use.

"Unless that something powerful can be used against *us*," the fairy said.

Marie sighed. "True."

"Well, we'll continue to search for it and reconvene when we've found it. Meanwhile, we must keep each other informed of our progress. Agreed?" Brendal asked.

"Agreed."

Silence. Expectant silence, at that.

Brendal flicked Aden a glance. "Your apprentice is quiet. Have you no thoughts, girl?"

Once again, Aden found himself pulling back. He couldn't think of an answer to give the fairy, and didn't want to alter the future too much, so he imagined himself back inside Jennifer's head. This time, when he settled into his shadowed corner, he realized the TV screens were no longer floating about and the boxes had returned.

Why? Had he given himself away? Or *had* he altered the future?

With a sigh, Aden stepped from the shadows.

Who's there? Jennifer immediately demanded.

Without replying, Aden reached an arm out of her body, then the other, then a leg, then the other, until he was standing in front of her, sweating, panting. His knees gave out and he dropped, putting himself at eye-level with her. Or more accurately, blindfold-level. Body-possessing always weakened him, but the act had never done so this quickly. He must have stayed there too long.

"What did you do to me?" Jennifer shouted. "You're the reason for my blackouts, aren't you? Because it just happened again. Answer me!"

Blackouts. That's how she saw the times he'd gone back. He'd changed the future, then. Made her weary and wonder what had been done to her.

She's alive and she's healthy, Caleb said with relief. *Good job, Team Aden.*

"Thank God," Victoria breathed, suddenly behind him, arms wrapping around him, body heat seeping into him, strengthening him. "We didn't think you would ever emerge."

"How much time passed?"

"About six hours."

His eyes widened. That long? The day was wasting away, a mere blink of time left. "Help me up," he said, urgent.

She stood and dragged him with her, stronger than

a girl who looked so delicate should be. With her arm around his waist, they left the room and the still-shouting witch. Down the hall and into another room they stumbled. There was a couch and a chair, both empty.

"Where's Riley?" Aden asked as he plopped on the couch.

"He and Mary Ann went to get something to eat." Victoria settled beside him. "Did you learn anything?"

"Nothing that helps us with the meeting."

Her shoulders drooped with disappointment. "Then what did you learn?"

"I learned I have worse luck than I thought. Not only did Dr. Hennessy hypnotize and ward me, but it turns out *he* is really a *she,* and *she* is really a fairy. Nice, huh? She and the witches are working together, planning to use me to draw the vampires and wolves into a trap so both races can be slaughtered."

"Okay, that's a lot to absorb."

"I know, and I'm sorry to throw it at you like this. But why haven't they just snatched me up? Both the fairies and the witches now know I'm the one pulling at them, and they've had the opportunity."

"Because you were protected by the vampires and the weres, maybe?"

"Maybe."

"So...what are we going to do about that meeting?"

I have an amazing idea, Caleb said. *The best you'll ever hear, if I do say so myself.*

Elijah groaned. *I know what you're going to say. Don't listen to him, Aden.*

Now I'm nervous, Julian piped up.

Caleb outlined his plan. Afterward, Aden was the one to groan. Of course Caleb thought his plan was a gold-star idea, because he liked those witches, but he wasn't using his brain, merely his hormones. Still, Aden could think of nothing else to free his friends from their curse.

"I'm going to give myself up," he said flatly, and Caleb patted himself on the back.

Told you it was the best.

Victoria gasped, shook her head, strands of black hair hitting her cheeks. "No. That's dangerous and foolish and—"

"The only way. I'm the only one who has to make the meeting. If we pretend to set Jennifer free, she can—"

"Jennifer?" Victoria interjected with a twinge of anger. "Who's Jennifer?"

"Our delightful hostage." He motioned to the doorway with a tilt of his chin. "Anyway, if we let her go, she'll likely want to capture *me* and take me to her friends. I'll be with them. They'll ask me questions. That counts as a meeting, right?"

Victoria chewed on her bottom lip. "They could decide to destroy you, despite your origins."

That was a chance he was willing to take. For her. For the others. He reached out and cupped her jaw. As always, she was hot, so hot, and utterly soft. "We've run out of time."

And the idea is made of awesome, but whatever.

She leaned into the touch. "Well, I'm not willing to risk your life. I'll let her capture me, too, and that way—"

He shook his head before she could finish. "Witches and vampires are a bad mix, as you know. I'm sorry to say this, but they're more likely to take me if you're not there. And we need to do this before Riley returns." As protective as the wolf was of his king, he, too, would insist on going with Aden. If he "allowed" Aden to go at all, that is.

But most of all, Aden recalled the conversation that had just taken place. The witches and the fairies wanted to destroy the vamps *and* the weres. He wasn't going to let Victoria and Riley become their first victims.

"You're king," Victoria said, fisting his shirt, "so I can't stop you if you insist on doing this, but you have to—"

"I'm not your king," he said. "I'm your boyfriend."

Her gaze pleaded with him to understand. "And I want my boyfriend to stay alive."

He softened, inside and out. "I'm going to die soon. We both know that." He pried her fingers from his shirt and slid her palms underneath, above the scabs on the right side of his ribs. He'd possessed scars in the vision Elijah had shown him. Soon, these scabs would become scars. Soon after that, he would die.

No fear, though. He wouldn't let her see his fear at the thought of being stabbed in the heart again. Only his willingness to do what was necessary to protect his friends.

"There's a difference between knowing you might soon die and courting danger," she cried.

"Listen. These are scabs, not scars. Not yet. I've still got a little time. Which means the witches won't kill me." A lie. They could keep him for weeks, months, enough time to turn the scabs to scars, and then kill him. But he didn't want Victoria to worry the entire time he was gone.

A sigh left her as she absorbed his words, and he knew the exact second she accepted his claim; hope brightened her irises, making them glow like twin sunrises over the ocean. "If you do this, you need more wards," she said, scooting closer. "That is nonnegotiable."

"If by nonnegotiable, you mean we should negotiate, then yes. I agree. There isn't time for more wards, sweetheart."

She scowled. "So I'm just supposed to let you leave with the witch and hope everything turns out okay?"

Yes, but he didn't say it aloud. "Will you make sure no one misses me at the ranch?"

Her scowl deepened, but she nodded.

"Thank you. And just in case you've forgotten, I love you." He kissed her then, tasting her, deep and thorough, as if this was the last time they'd ever be able to do this.

Maybe it was.

Her hands tangled in his hair, and she angled his head for even deeper contact. At some point, he thought he tasted blood—perhaps he'd accidentally swiped his tongue on her fangs—but even that didn't slow him. In fact, they stayed like that, locked together, kissing, the souls quiet, until the front door creaked open and footsteps pounded.

They sprang apart, and Aden noticed Riley's brothers standing a few feet away, grinning.

"Okay, well," Aden said, and popped to his feet. He wavered, still weak, but didn't fall.

Victoria stood beside him and smoothed her pink shirt. "Hello, boys."

"I never thought I'd see the day Victoria got her tonsils cleaned, did you?" Maxwell asked Nathan.

Nathan barked out a laugh. "That wasn't a cleaning. That was a full-on surgery."

Aden's cheeks heated. "Enough." He turned to Victoria, pulling her close for a final hug. "Distract them," he whispered in her ear, "and I'll take off with Jennifer."

She kissed the side of his face before drawing away, her hand remaining on his arm as long as possible. When she was positioned in front of the wolves, who were still grinning like loons, she looked at Maxwell. "Take my hand."

"What? You want to perform another surgery? Sure, I'm game." He clasped her outstretched fingers.

They disappeared a second later. Nathan spun, frowning. Then Victoria reappeared, alone, and grabbed his arm before he could stop her. They, too, disappeared, this time leaving Aden alone.

Now! Caleb commanded. *You have to act now.*

Aden, Elijah began. *Think about this.*

"Thinking time's over. I'm doing it, and that's that." Chin high, he stalked back down the hall to the witch's door, drew in a breath and turned the knob.

TWENTY-SEVEN

MARY ANN CHEWED ON her bottom lip as she peered up at Riley. A fuming, steam-coming-out-of-his-nostrils Riley. She was once again in his bedroom at the vampire mansion, perched at the edge of his very soft bed, the door closed, footsteps echoing beyond it. She doubted anyone would barge in—even if she screamed, which she wouldn't, he wouldn't hurt her, but company would have been nice just then. Riley paced in front of her, an intimidating sight.

"Let me get this straight," he said, each word measured. "Tucker was in the woods. Outside the cabin. You saw him. He waved you over. And you. Actually. Went." The last was uttered with disbelief.

"Correct."

"You talked to him."

"Yes."

"You were within striking distance of him."

"He wouldn't hurt me. Not that way," she added

before Riley could remind her of the mental anguish Tucker had caused and the tears she had shed.

"You don't know what he's capable of, Mary Ann. He's a demon."

"Part demon." And the father of her best friend's baby. If he decided to help Penny and be a part of the baby's life, then he was going to be a part of Mary Ann's life, as well, because she planned to be there for her friend. Riley needed to learn that now. "And he's calm around me. You know that."

"Then," Riley continued as if she hadn't spoken, "you waited a few hours to tell me what had happened."

"Yes, again." She'd given Tucker time to get away. Riley was a wolf, an expert tracker, and easily could have found him. They would have fought. There wasn't time for a fight. So, once she was sure enough time had elapsed, she'd made an excuse to Victoria about being hungry and dragged Riley out of the cabin to fill him in. He should have thanked her for telling him anything at all. Instead, he'd brought her here to yell at her.

Riley scrubbed a hand down his face. "Why do I bother protecting you, if you're just going to throw yourself into dangerous situations?"

"Because you like me." Until this mess with the witches was over. Then they had some major issues to work out. Or not. She still planned to leave him. A knot formed in her throat.

He stopped, sighed, the anger seeping from him. "You're right. I do like you. Even though at times likes these, I'm not sure I like that I like you. So tell me again what Tucker said about Vlad."

That, she could do. "He mentioned the former vampire king is alive and well and living in an underground crypt behind this house. That said former vampire king ordered him to watch us and report his findings. And that said former vampire king is mad as hell that someone else is commanding his people."

"Yes, Vlad would be, but he couldn't have survived total body *je la nune* poisoning. No one could have."

"How do you know?"

"I've seen others die that way."

Was that...guilt darkening his green eyes? Had he killed others that way? The fact that she wasn't disturbed by the possibility proved just how immersed she was becoming in this otherworld. "Maybe he healed. You once told me Vlad was the strongest among you, and that his people hoped he would somehow recover. I mean, seriously. That's why Aden hasn't been crowned officially."

"First, if Vlad was alive, he would have come to us." Riley's head tilted to the side. "Unless he was too weak, but then...no. No. He wouldn't have sent a kid to spy. Second, Vlad was also staked. Maybe he could have healed from one injury, but not both. Not in such a weakened condition." A heartbeat later, he added, "God, I can't believe I'm talking about this with a human. Vlad killed for less."

"Well, there's a new guy in charge and I have a very good feeling he'd tell you to tell me what I want to know. So, backtracking. I thought vampire skin couldn't be penetrated. *How* was Vlad staked?"

Riley frowned, hesitated, but eventually said, "Did you hear me tell Aden that when we tattoo wards on the vampires, we have to prep the needle with a little *je la nune* first? That's what allows the ink to penetrate. It's the same principle with a staking. You cover a blade in *je la nune* and stab the heart. The poison melts the skin and infects the organ."

"Maybe he heals faster and from more severe injuries than anyone else."

Head tilting to the side, Riley stood there for a long while, silent, pensive, grim. Finally, he sighed and held out his hand. "There's one way to verify this."

She shook her head, already knowing what he planned. "Feel free to go alone."

"No way. Let's go check the crypt."

Her eyes widened. "A very much alive, very hungry, very angry dethroned vampire king might be down there. That's dangerous, and I'm not supposed to place myself in danger. Remember?"

"You're my very capable backup. Now, come on."

He waved his fingers. "Afterward, we'll go back to the cabin, find out whether Aden has left the witch's body and whether he learned anything."

And if he hadn't? she wanted to ask, but didn't. Time was ticking away, no solution in sight. She was trying not to let nerves overwhelm her, wasn't letting herself think about how significant tomorrow was. What better way to distract herself than to pay a visit to old Vlad? A man who'd once enjoyed removing human heads and displaying them on pikes.

Shaking now, she took Riley's hand and he pulled her upright. Why did he want her to go with him, anyway? The real reason, and not the "capable" crap he'd spouted. Riley was a protector first, and a flatterer second. Because he still didn't believe Vlad was alive? Because he wanted to prove to her that Tucker had lied to her?

Instead of leading her out the room, he dropped her hand. What, she was supposed to walk behind him now, like a good little inferior human? She was *not* disappointed—except that she was *very* disappointed. Only, he didn't leave. He strode to his closet and dug out a coat, then wrapped that coat around her, pulling her hair from underneath. Okay, she really wasn't disappointed anymore.

He reclaimed her hand. "Just…stay behind me and do what I tell you, when I tell you. Got it?"

"Got it. But I'm really not a dimwit when it comes to my safety."

"Let's not get into a debate right now."

Funny. They strode into the hall. Going from Riley's normal bedroom to the all-black hallway was a bit of a shock, but she soon grew used to the drab surroundings. The black walls, the black windows, the violent tapestries, the swirling circles—wards—etched on *everything*.

"Do you think Tucker plans on ambushing us?" Even as she asked, she deduced the answer. If he thought that was a possibility, he wouldn't take her. Unless he wanted her to see Tucker's "evil" firsthand. She barely stopped herself from rolling her eyes. "Never mind. Don't answer. Just listen. I. Want. To. Survive. I won't do anything to place myself in unnecessary danger."

"Good. Because your survival is my goal, too."

See? A protector.

Two vampires, both female and pretty, suddenly snaked a corner. Both slowed their steps, giving Riley a long, lingering look, practically eating him up. That always happened at school, too, with the human girls. He was just too hot for his own good.

He waved to them with his free hand. Apparently, they interpreted that wave as an invitation to chat because they homed in like heat-seeking missiles, barely flicking Mary Ann a glance.

"Riley," the brunette said, tone heavy with familiarity.

The redhead just smiled, her lashes dipping flirtatiously.

I'm not jealous or angry. Really. Mary Ann's time with him was almost over, anyway. So why did she suddenly long for a giant bucket of vampire poison and a knife?

"We're kind of in a hurry, girls, so…" Riley tried to slide around them, tugging Mary Ann with him, but the brunette jumped in his path.

"Not so fast, wolf. I have business to discuss with you."

"Draven," he said on a sigh. "Not now. Please."

Draven. A pretty yet dissolute name. It fit its owner. She was as delicate as an angel, yet there was something… depraved in her eyes. Something cold and calculating.

"I'll only take a second," the vampire continued, "and you're the one wasting time right now."

He nodded stiffly, and his grip tightened on Mary Ann. "Very well. What do you wish to discuss?"

She lifted her chin, all attitude and self-confidence. "As you know, I was one of the females chosen to tempt the new king."

Riley nodded again, wary this time.

"As you probably do *not* know, I issued a challenge."

"You wish to be king yourself?" Riley laughed,

suddenly relaxing. "Good luck with that. Now, if you'll—"

"Actually, no. I don't wish to be king." She smiled, yet there was no humor in it. Only satisfaction. "I went before the council and challenged Victoria. For rights to Haden Stone."

"What?" The single word was a roar and a gasp blended together.

Why was Riley so furious and shocked? Aden was king, and he'd never allow another girl to have "rights" to him.

Draven raised her chin another notch. "Challenges can be issued to anyone at any time about anything. You know this well. If a challenge is not accepted, the challenger automatically receives the prize."

"The princess is mine to protect," Riley growled, "which means your challenge is directed at me. And I accept. You and I shall—"

"Oh, no." Laughing now, Draven shook his head. "That is not how our law works, and you know that, too. If *Victoria* accepts, she must fight me. And you, her guardian, are not allowed to interfere."

A muscle ticked below his eye. They'd entered dangerous territory, though Draven didn't seem to care. "Aden will change the law," Riley stated.

"He may do so, yes. *After* my challenge has been met. Otherwise, everyone will know of my challenge, and of Victoria's refusal to meet it. Everyone will know that Aden belongs to me, and Victoria will then be condemned by our people."

Condemned. What did that mean in vampire terms? She wanted to ask but held her tongue. She didn't exactly know the protocol for asking a vampire bitch to explain something. And if Mary Ann had thought Riley furious before, she'd had no idea how deeply he was capable of feeling the emotion. Rage rolled off him in great waves, palpable, stinging, even heating the air around them.

"I will tell her," he said through gritted teeth. "She will accept. The match will be set for sometime next week."

For the first time, Draven frowned. "I wish to get this done today."

"No. You will wait until next week. If those terms are unacceptable, you will have to forfeit. The king can choose the time of the match, and will insist on watching. This I know, as well. He won't be available until next week."

"Very well. Accepted." Draven inclined her head, her smug satisfaction as strong as Riley's fury. She tossed a quick sneer at Mary Ann. "Until then."

The vampire pair floated away, talking and laughing now, as if the bombshell they'd just dropped on Riley was insignificant, without consequence.

"Is Victoria a decent fighter?" Mary Ann asked quietly as Riley jerked her back into motion.

"Yes. I trained her myself."

"Is Draven?"

"Yes. Regrettably, I trained her, too."

"Who's better?"

His jaw clenched.

Mary Ann would take that to mean Draven was the better fighter. Her stomach clenched. "What will happen if Draven wins? To Aden? To Victoria?"

"They won't fight to the death, but until one of them admits defeat. The winner will own Aden."

"Own. How? He's king!"

"Yes, but he is also human, and there's the loophole Draven is using. We've never had a human king before, and our laws regarding humans were designed with blood-slaves in mind. And blood-slaves may be passed around like baseball cards. Aden will have to change the law, but Draven was right. He cannot do so until this challenge has been met. Otherwise, Victoria would look weak."

"And be condemned. But what does that mean, really?"

"It means that everyone will see her as easy pickings and challenge her for every single thing she owns. For the rest of her eternal life, until she has nothing left. No guardian, no clothes. No room, no furniture. No food. Until she's forced to strike out on her own to survive."

What a harsh reality these vampires and werewolves lived in. "And what happens if Draven loses? Seems unfair that if she wins, Victoria will lose everything she owns on top of losing Aden. Yet if Draven loses…"

"She will become Victoria's property. Which is why this kind of challenge isn't issued often. No one wants to chance such an outcome."

Draven was utterly confident of her success, then. Great. Another worry. Would they never stop piling up?

"Come on, pick up the pace. We have a task to complete." Down the winding stairs they finally pounded.

Several other vampires passed them along the way, grouped in twos and threes. Each group was discussing Aden and his taming of the beasts. They were clearly awed, shocked and a little frightened. Thankfully, though, no one else stopped Riley for a chat.

Outside, the air was colder than it had been that morning, and a dreary mist dampened her hair. She was immediately grateful for Riley's coat. There were no vampires out here, no wolves either. Too cold and wet for them? Riley didn't seem to mind the weather. He wasn't wearing a coat, just a thin T-shirt, but he wasn't shivering. Or were they too busy? If so, what were they doing? For that matter, what did they usually do during these daylight hours?

She might never know.

You weren't going to think like that, remember? Nothing else seemed relevant, though.

Mary Ann sighed. If she only had a day to live, she didn't want to spend it doing this, she realized. Visiting a crypt. Searching for a possibly dead, possibly alive vampire king. Hunting witches. She wanted to be back in bed with Riley. She wanted to go home to her dad and hug him tight. Victoria had convinced him they'd interacted recently, but they hadn't, and she missed him.

If Aden had made no progress with the witch, that's what she was going to do. In that order.

"You're not going to die tomorrow," Riley said.

"How did you—never mind." He'd read her aura again.

He stopped in the center of a large winding circle, placing his feet in...concrete grooves? He pulled her flush against him, his body heat seeping into her, and wrapped his arms around her, his chin resting atop her head.

When the ground began moving, she yelped, floundering.

"I've got you," he said, gentling her. "We'll descend and start spinning in just a few seconds. Just hold on to me."

"Spinning?" She gulped, imagining the carnival rides she'd enjoyed as a child. But then, she'd been strapped into a seat.

"Slowly. Promise."

She relaxed. And sure enough, they began to slowly spin and inch downward, into a wide chasm that formed even as the concrete or metal or whatever it was re-arranged itself at their feet. The lower they went, the more the scent of dust and—her nose wrinkled—old pennies saturated the air.

"That smell… I would have bet… I can't believe… human death," Riley finally finished, grave. "And very recent." He very gently, but very quickly moved Mary Ann behind him, but not before she saw the claws sliding from his nail-beds. He was preparing for attack. "It's too late to get you topside, so when we reach the bottom, I'm going to push you against a wall. Do not move from that spot. Okay? You won't be able to see, so you won't know where to step."

"But you will?" she asked on a trembling breath.

"Yes."

The foundation jolted as they hit bottom, jarring her, and all that darkness Riley had promised enveloped her instantly. His strong hands gripped her waist and shoved her backward, until something hard and cold met her back. Then the comfort of his hands vanished, and she was left alone. With the darkness.

She heard the drip of water, the shuffle of feet, a frustrated curse from Riley. Several curses, actually, and her tremors intensified. Would Vlad, if he truly was alive, really attack a favored wolf? Would Tucker really ambush him? Tucker would never hurt Mary Ann, she was certain of that, but he'd always been a fighter, and that courtesy might not extend to her current boyfriend.

A scrape of stone against stone, followed by another curse from Riley, tugged her from her thoughts.

"He's gone," he croaked. "Vlad's gone. Unless his body was snatched, which no one here would have done, he's out there. And like Tucker told you, he's probably planning to ruin Aden."

TWENTY-EIGHT

ADEN GAVE HIMSELF A PEP talk as he tugged the witch, Jennifer, through the misty forest. *This will work. Your friends will be saved. You'll get through this just fine.*

She was still blindfolded, her arms still tied behind her back, and demanding to know what he was doing with her. So far, he'd ignored her, but finally they were far enough away from the cabin that no one, even a wolf with supersonic hearing, would pick up on the conversation.

"What am I doing?" he responded, still chugging forward. "I'm letting you go."

"I don't believe you!" She stumbled over a twig, his grip the only thing holding her up. "Otherwise you'd cut the rope. I mean, really. Your Drainer used up most of my powers, so I'm pretty helpless now. You don't have to worry about my casting a spell or anything like that."

"You've said that before, about the Drainer, but as I told you, I don't know what that is."

She laughed without humor. "Whatever. Just untie me. Please. We'll go our separate ways and pretend this never happened."

As if. She'd never forget. Neither would he, for that matter.

Now or never, Caleb said, determined.

He's right. This is the spot. Elijah sounded solemn. *Something will happen here, I can feel it.*

With a sigh, Aden stopped. Jennifer didn't realize and bumped into him, stumbling backward. Once again, his grip prevented her from falling. For a moment, he just stood there, watching her, feeling her desperation. If he did this, there was no going back. *You don't want to go back.* She would be on the loose, would want revenge against those who had wronged her.

But he might also be taken right into the lion's den…

Steeling himself against the threat of magic, he removed her blindfold, quickly moved behind her and cut the ties with one of his daggers. Instantly, she whirled on him. Again, he steeled himself, expecting a spell, or, at the very least, a punch. Something. She merely backed away from him, blinking, frowning.

What would he do if she ran from him? *Without* taking him with her?

"Why did you do that?" she asked. "Did you think a nice deed would cause me to spill my guts and tell you about the meeting? Well, guess what? There won't be a meeting. Not now. Not after everything that was done to me. Your friends are as good as dead, human."

She tossed the words at him as if they were weapons.

Don't listen to her, Elijah said.

He blinked in surprise. "You think they'll be okay?"

"Didn't I just tell you they wouldn't?" she demanded.

I don't want to lie to you, Ad, so don't ask me that question. All you need to know is that she's going to take you with her. That, I can promise you.

Like Aden could really leave that alone. "I have to ask. Will they be okay?"

"Why do you keep asking me that?" Jennifer snapped.

Ignore Elijah and beg the witch's forgiveness, Caleb pleaded. *If you're nice to her, she'll make sure there's a meeting. I know it.*

Don't listen to him, Ad, Julian said. *He's too involved. Not objective.*

Shut up! Caleb shouted, and it was the angriest Aden had ever heard him. *I know what I'm talking about.*

The conflicting advice, suggestions and demands razed his nerves to the breaking point. "Just tell me what you know, Elijah!"

"Who's Elijah?"

A sigh. *Do you remember when we were in that vampire meeting, and I told you about blood and death? When I said those things, I wasn't talking about the attack you endured at the hands of the councilmen. I was talking about this, with the witches. And your friends...I saw them on the ground. All three of them. Mary Ann, Victoria and Riley, each splattered in red.*

"No," Aden said, shaking his head in denial. "No."

"No, what? What's going on?"

I didn't tell you then because, like Caleb, you have no objectivity in this. You would have tried to alter things, and that would have made the situation worse for you.

"I don't care about me! Only them."

Jennifer said something else, but he couldn't make out the words, was too focused on Elijah.

I know. But I care about you. I've always cared about you.

Yes. Yes, Caleb suddenly said, and there was joy in his tone. *Finally.*

You want *them to die?* Julian screeched.

No. Look.

Aden pulled himself from the hated, confusing conversation—he was shaking, breathing heavily, his heart beating savagely—only to realize he was now standing in a circle of witches. Shocked, he spun. They wore their ceremonial robes, their hands joined, the circle closing him in. Jennifer, he noticed, was grinning.

Elijah moaned.

"Well, Summoner, we meet again. Did you think we wouldn't find you?" the blonde he recognized from last time said. The one from Jennifer's memories. Marie. "We've merely been waiting for you to move your hostage from the cabin. There were too many wards there, preventing us from even stepping foot on the property."

"Hello, witch. *How* did you find us?" he asked as calmly as he was able.

"Magic, naturally," Marie said smugly. "Several times in the past few months, our friend acted strangely, completely unlike herself. And afterward, when I questioned her, she had no idea what I was talking about. She'd had these little blackouts, you see, and we began to fear she'd have them when we weren't around to protect her. So we placed a tracking spell on her and disguised it as a ward."

One of the "cosmetic" wards, he would guess. And added because he'd possessed her body. He'd done it to find the witches, so, mission accomplished. "Smart," was all he said.

"Aren't we, though? And now that I've assuaged your curiosity, answer a question for me."

He gave a single nod. Now wasn't the time to play hardball.

Caleb practically purred. *Her voice…it's so sweet.*

"To whom were you speaking to a moment ago?"

For once, there was no reason to lie about the souls. "To the three souls in my head."

Her brow puckered in confusion. "People live inside your head?"

Here was his opportunity. "Ask me anything and I'll answer." That would make this a meeting. Right? That would mean his friends—

The witch laughed. "I can guess what you're thinking. You think *this* is our meeting. I'm afraid not, Summoner. A meeting must be officially called to order. And as Jennifer told you, we won't be having our meeting. Not now. Your actions have revealed exactly whose side you're on."

"You will call a meeting to order!" he barked, stepping forward—until his feet glued themselves to the ground, preventing him from moving. What the—the answer slid into place. *Stupid magic,* he thought darkly.

Jennifer's eyes slit as she inserted herself into the conversation. "We should have killed your friends rather than curse them, but we thought to use them to control you. Now I see the flaw in our logic. One of your people is a Drainer, and Drainers must be eliminated as quickly as possible. One of your people is a wolf, and wolves protect our greatest enemies. One of your people is a vampire, and vampires are our greatest enemies. All three deserve to die."

"How many times do I have to say it? I don't know any Drainer. I don't even know what a Drainer is, unless you mean a vampire drinking until every drop is gone, but that didn't happen, so again. No Drainer." He wanted to kick his own ass for not asking Victoria for details. "And the wolf and the vampire mean you no harm, then or now. Tell them, Jennifer. You weren't forced to feed anyone."

"Enough," Marie snapped. "So they didn't drink from her. *This* time. We are still drugs to them, and addicts can never be trusted. Now. Silence, human. Sisters, let us move him to a more…private location."

A second later, their chants filled the air. He tried to reason with them; they ignored him. And then it didn't matter. His world began to spin, dancing to a beat he didn't recognize. Spinning, spinning, colors whirling together, darkening, that dark consuming him, blinding him, tossing him around as if he were stuck in a washing machine. The souls were shouting, and those continued shouts were deafening.

Then, suddenly, he stilled. The souls quieted.

Pinpricks of white grew among the black, and colors soon followed. His feet were still rooted in place, but he was now in new surroundings. He was inside a… cave? The walls around him were comprised of dirt, orange-colored stones and clay. Somewhere nearby was a waterfall. He could hear the urgent rush and crash of water, the air cold and damp.

The witches, still circling him, dropped their arms to their sides and perched atop boulders. All but one, that is. Marie approached him, a perfumed cloud accompanying her. Caleb purred his approval.

Without a word, Marie claimed his hands and raised them above his head. Aden wanted to grab his daggers. He didn't. He needed their cooperation, not their fury. "What are you doing?" he asked.

"Taking precautions."

As she spoke, something cool and soft wrapped around his wrists. Frowning, he looked up. Ivy had sprouted from the cave's ceiling, descended and bound him. His molars gnashed together as he tried to jerk free. The vine held steady.

"We draw our powers from Mother Earth," she explained. "You're lucky you're warded, otherwise we'd do a lot worse to you." She laughed when his expression tightened. "Oh, yes. I know without looking what you're protected against. We all do. We can feel the power of the wards." She backed away and sat on a boulder like the others.

"So what do you plan to do with me?"

"Your actions will determine that."

"Come on. Help me out here. What actions? What do you want from me?" Aden's gaze roved over them, stopping only when one of them—the only one left standing, the only one wearing a *black* robe—walked from a shadowed corner and pushed away her hood. Another blonde, though this one wasn't a witch.

Her face was beauty personified. Her skin glowed as if it had been dipped in a honey pot, and her eyes gleamed like liquid ebony. With only a look, she lured, entranced, made him ache to do whatever she wanted. Not that he'd succumb.

"Hello, Aden," Ms. Brendal said smoothly.

He hadn't noticed her in the circle before. Which meant she had been waiting here. Waiting to pounce. "Dr. Hennessy," he said, his jaw so clenched the words barely escaped. "I'd like to say I'm surprised, but I'd rather not lie. I know how you hate it."

Her pupils flared briefly. "So you knew I was not who I pretended to be. How?"

"Why don't you invade my head again and find out?"

She traced her tongue over her straight, white teeth. "I looked through your mind, yes, but all I encountered was a sea of noise. Voices and more voices, one stacked upon the other, talking about the silliest things. Things I cared nothing about. But I could find no evidence of my brother, Mr. Thomas. Where is he, Aden? I know that you know."

Now's your chance, Elijah said. *Bargain.*

Wait. What? Bargain with what? Caleb demanded.

Aden knew. "Convince the witches to call a meeting to order," he said, "and I'll tell you."

Brendal eyed each of the witches. Each of them shook her head no.

"Aden," she said, her voice no longer smooth. "You will not fare well if I'm angered."

He shrugged as best he could with his arms in the air. "Why? You'll morph into a giant green monster?"

Breath hissed between her lips. "I figured you would prove stubborn. However, you have underestimated me. I'm leaving, but don't shed too many tears, for I will return. With your friends."

A clear threat. He wanted to shout at her. He wanted to fight his bonds. He did neither. Displays of emotion in any battle meant defeat. Isn't that what he'd taught Mary Ann? And in this battle, the most important of his life, he needed any edge he could get. If he threw a fit now, he would lose what little bargaining power he had.

"Have you anything else to say to me?" Brendal asked.

"Yeah. Good luck with your search."

"Very well." She stepped backward, her narrowed gaze locked on him, and disappeared from view, there one moment, gone the next.

She'd entered that other plane, he supposed. To capture—perhaps torture—his friends. *They can take care of themselves,* he assured himself.

Let me take over, Caleb pleaded. *Let me talk to the witches for you.*

Oh, no. Aden could allow the souls to assume control of his body. They couldn't do it without his permission, and he'd once given permission to Eve. That's how she'd spent the last day of her "life" with her daughter. But Caleb was too concerned with the witches. He might place their welfare about Victoria's, above Mary Ann's and Riley's, and *that* Aden couldn't allow.

"Call the meeting to order," he said, ignoring the soul, "and I'll answer anything you want. Don't, and I'll answer nothing."

Aden, please, Caleb persisted.

"I'm sorry." And he was. He hated for Caleb to want something this much and not get it. He hated for Caleb to beg.

Focus, Aden, Julian said.

Yes. He blinked, blanking his mind. The witches had removed their hoods, and each was watching him curiously.

"You have souls trapped inside your head," Marie said.

"Yes, I have souls inside my head." He'd already admitted as much. Denying it now would serve no purpose.

"And once, you asked me if I'd ever known a man who could possess other bodies. Someone who died sixteen years ago. Is he, this body-possessor, one of the souls?"

Aden! Tell her! She might have known me. She could tell me about my past.

Guilt washed through him. He ignored it. He had to stay on course. "Call this meeting to order, and I'll tell you."

She grinned without humor. "I don't wish to know that badly."

Wh-what? Caleb sputtered with his affront.

"I'm willing to bet we can extract the souls and give them bodies of their own." Marie tapped a fingertip to her chin. "That way, he can answer all our questions himself."

Aden tried to hide his alarm. "And where would you get these bodies?"

"People die all the time. If you reanimate a fresh corpse with a new soul…"

"How? It was the body that died, not the soul. The soul simply moved on." That he knew. "Reanimating a body isn't the same as healing a body." Right? "Which means a new soul won't be able to make a lifeless corpse work."

"Magic can do many things," was all she said.

Yes, Caleb rushed out. *Yes. Let her try.*

No, Elijah and Julian said in unison.

It wouldn't be that easy, Elijah added. *It never is. There will be a catch, I promise you.*

Caleb growled his frustration.

"If you can sense my wards," Aden said, "you know my mind cannot be manipulated. Therefore, the souls' minds cannot be manipulated." Could they?

One of her brows arched, making her the picture of superiority. "I don't need *your* cooperation. Just his."

She was bluffing. She had to be bluffing.

Uncomfortable, he shifted his weight from one foot to the other. Blood had already rushed out of his arms, and now his hands were cold, his shoulders tingling. "If you can do such a thing, why haven't you? Why are you just sitting there?"

The brow fell back into place, creating a smooth line. "We have more important things to do at the moment."

Yep. She'd been bluffing.

"Your résumé is growing," she said suddenly, as if they were seated across from each other at a job interview.

He'd play along. "What do you mean?"

"First vampire king, now beast slayer."

How had she heard about that? "I didn't slay them."

"Tamer, then. Beast tamer." The very nickname Caleb had suggested. "How did you do that?"

So she could defeat them herself? "Call this meeting to order and I'll tell you." His answer would be, "I don't know," because that was the truth, but she didn't need to know that yet.

"You want to save your friends?" Jennifer piped in. "Fine. Renounce your claim to the vampire throne, and give us a blood vow that you'll remain with us, serving and aiding us."

Do it, Caleb said.

No, Elijah and Julian repeated in unison.

"Sorry." Serving and aiding them would require hurting the vampires; he knew it with every fiber of his being. Otherwise, he would have said yes without hesitation.

"Then you don't care about the others, the cursed, as much as we thought," Marie said.

"Not true," he gritted out. "I care about them more than you realized. If I gave you what you wanted, would you give *me* a blood oath not to ever hurt the vampires or the wolves?"

"No. Of course not. None of us would."

The other witches laughed at him for daring to suggest such a thing, Jennifer the loudest among them.

"If you won't aid us, Aden, that means you will work against us, aiding *them*. If that's the case, you will never walk out of this cave."

So they would kill him, too, was what she was saying. Before she could make the threat outright, he switched gears. If he could soften her, just a little, he could gain the upper hand. Maybe.

"The soul, the one who could possess other bodies," Aden began. "What was he to you? To any of you?"

Caleb went eerily silent, waiting.

Marie shrugged, but a vulnerable gleam lit her eyes. "He was…everything and nothing," she said, then gave an angry shake of her head. "And now," she added, standing, "we will leave you. We have reached a stalemate, and you need time to think. And perhaps you should consider the fact that I could have and should have killed your friend Mary Ann days ago, but I didn't. I let her go. For you. I have regretted the action ever since, and my sense of mercy has been depleted. The more you resist us, the less I want you happy."

Wait. What? "You never wanted me happy. Now call the meeting to order," he demanded, panic blooming.

The others pushed to their feet.

"As you left me bound," Jennifer said, "we leave you bound. Maybe the isolation will loosen your tongue."

"I demand that you stay! I demand you call the meeting to order!"

One by one, they strode from the cave, silent. Jennifer watched him until the last possible second. Marie stopped at the dark, yawning mouth and looked back at him over her shoulder. "When the clock strikes midnight, your friends die. I am sorry, I truly am, but there are always casualties during war. You know what you have to do to save them." With that, she, too, left him.

Over and over he screamed for her to call the meeting to order; over and over he pleaded, even though he was alone, his voice echoing off the cavern walls, mocking him. He screamed until he was hoarse, jerking at the ivy until blood ran.

The vine never gave, and the witches never returned.

TWENTY-NINE

ANOTHER SUMMONS.

Tucker tried to resist. Tried with every bit of strength he possessed. But Vlad's voice called to him—*Come to me*—and his feet moved forward before he realized he'd taken a single step.

He jumped from the roof of his mom and stepdad's house, the impact jolting his entire body. He'd been watching his six-year-old brother play in the drizzling cold, nose wet, coat soaked, hands shivering as he talked to an invisible friend.

Twice Tucker had almost revealed himself. Both times, he'd convinced himself Ethan was better off without him and remained hidden. Now, as he strode away, he felt a hollow ache where his heart should have been. He would never go back, he decided. Ethan was all that was good, all that was right, with a bright future ahead. Tucker had never caused him anything but pain.

It was past time for a clean break.

The ache intensified. *This is for the best.*

Tucker blanked his mind as he ran out of the neighborhood and into town, where it seemed everyone he knew—or rather, once knew—was stuck in party mode. Some kids were driving around, throwing beer bottles at the buildings. Others were on the streets, dancing to a beat no one else could hear. Among them floated a beautiful woman, a woman with long blond hair and skin so fair it practically glowed.

She would look a kid in the eye, speak, and that kid would shake his head. She would speak again, then the kid's shoulders would slump, head ducking, before he bent down and cleaned up the mess. The blonde would then move on to someone else.

Night had long since fallen. The myths about vampires and sunlight weren't exactly true, he knew, since Victoria could stand outside all day without consequences. Vlad, though...would he burn to ash? A guy could hope.

Come to me...

Closer now, Tucker thought. With dread. With happiness. Vlad was no longer in his crypt. He was here, in town. Hidden.

Tucker rounded the corner of the local laundromat but saw only a cardboard box. He frowned. Still. He knew, as he always seemed to know, exactly where Vlad was. He bent down and peered inside. Yes, there was Vlad, a dead human flung over his lap, blood dripping down his chin.

Most of the king's body was still charred, still black with deadened skin, but patches of pale, smooth flesh were visible.

"Next time you make me wait, you will be the one I feed from," the king said calmly. "Do you understand?"

A tremor of fear moved through him, and his gaze returned to the dead man, whose neck was torn apart as if a wild animal had feasted. A painful way to die. Vlad had fed from him during that last visit, yes, but only briefly, and only as a warning. If *that* had been misery incarnate… He shuddered and each of his already scarred puncture wounds throbbed. "Yes. I understand."

"Now. What more have you learned?"

"The witches have taken Aden." Tucker had watched them suddenly appear around Aden. He could have helped. Maybe. Had wanted to help. Kind of. But he hadn't allowed his concealing illusion to fade, his need to please Vlad still too strong to be denied. Even then.

Vlad laughed, a cackling sound that caused his body to hunch over in a spasm of coughing. When he calmed, his lips pulled back, sharp teeth red and gleaming. "Go to them, but do not let them know you are there."

To the witches? "How will I find them? They vanished."

"You can feel the pull of Aden, can you not? We all can."

Reluctantly Tucker nodded. Truer words had never been spoken. First time he'd met Aden, he'd feared he was, well, attracted to the boy. As in turning *gay*. Even though he had always preferred girls. He'd wanted to be near the bastard, though Aden hadn't calmed him like Mary Ann did. Aden stirred him up, though, and sometimes even made him want to be *worse*.

"Good. Now, for your most important task. You will kill Aden. You will stab him in the heart, as if he was a witch's sacrifice."

"I—I can't."

"You can. Listen closely, and I will tell you how…"

MARY ANN WAS SCARED. Very, very scared. Apparently, Aden had kidnapped the kidnapped witch, and no one knew where they were. Yet. Victoria had told Riley what had happened, what Aden planned, and then teleported away before Riley could scream at her. Or tell her that her father was still alive. Where had the princess gone? To help Aden?

And God, how was she going to react to the news about her father? Mary Ann had never met the guy, and she was still reeling. After discovering the truth, she and Riley had searched the grounds but had found no sign of him.

Riley was distraught. Mary Ann had never seen him so upset. His new king—*was* Aden still his king now that Vlad was walking around?—and his princess had been—were—in danger, and he hadn't protected them. At least he and his brothers could feel Aden tugging at them. Well, as long as Mary Ann was out of the way. When Mary Ann *was* with them, and Riley at her side, they could still feel the tug, but it was somewhat muted. So they were now on the hunt for Aden. Without her.

Mary Ann had thought to use the time searching for Victoria, but no. That idea had been quickly discarded. Where would she begin looking? She couldn't go to the vampire mansion on her own and simply driving around town, which was all she could have done, wouldn't have been productive.

So here she was. At home. Riley had driven her and dropped her off after giving her the quickest, most distracted of kisses. She'd spent the past hour with her dad, hugging him as she'd wanted and telling him how much she loved him. He'd laughed and joked with her, and it had seemed as if they'd gone back in time, before she'd found out about her mother. Victoria's Voice Voodoo had worked its magic, because he never once interrogated her about where she'd been.

But her nervousness was growing with every minute that ticked by. Was Aden okay? Were Riley and Victoria okay? Was this her last night alive?

"You're distracted again," her dad said with an ever-patient grin.

They were sitting at the kitchen table, playing cards. War, of all things. She glanced down at her pile, picked a card and flipped it over. An eight of hearts. Her dad's card was a three of diamonds, so she gathered that round into her deck.

"Want to tell me what's on your mind?"

"I'm fine," she lied. She hated the necessity, but wouldn't cave. He didn't believe in the paranormal, even when the evidence of it was right under his nose, and she wasn't in the mood to fight. Or receive a therapy session.

"Problems with Riley?" he persisted.

Riley, her sweet Riley. The boy she would date for one more day, then never speak to again. At that, her heart actually lurched inside her chest. "Dad, what do you do when you know you're no good for the person you love?"

He looked at her for a moment, then sighed and pushed his cards aside. He propped his elbows on the table and stared over at her intently. "I hadn't realized you and Riley had reached the *I love you* stage yet."

Her cheeks heated. "We haven't said it to each other, no."

He relaxed a little. "So why isn't he good for you, sweetie?" Gently asked.

She squirmed uncomfortably in her seat. She couldn't tell him that it was the other way around. That *she* wasn't good for *Riley*. He wouldn't believe her. "What would you tell a patient who asked you the same question?"

His lips twitched at the corners. "I see what you're doing. Deflecting. I've taught you well. So, are you asking what I'd say to a patient if she refused to share all the details with me?"

She nodded.

Another sigh. "I'd tell her to ask herself a very important question. Will the person cause her harm, emotionally or physically?"

He still had it backward, but the answer was *yes*. She, too, pushed her cards away. She'd been right, then, to break things off with Riley. She'd been wrong to let things start back up again. But she couldn't regret her actions. She'd had that one glorious night with him, and she could die without regrets. For the most part.

Die. She swallowed the lump in her throat.

"If the answer is yes, I always tell my patients to leave the relationship." He reached over and took her hand. "Always. Now. Do I need to get my shotgun? What'd that boy do?"

She laughed. "You hate guns, and therefore don't own one. Besides, Riley hasn't hurt me or anything like that. He never would, either. He's very protective." *And I need to be protective of him.*

"Then what's the problem? You can tell me. This is a safe space."

Another laugh, though this one was forced. "That may be true with your patients, but that's never been the case with me." Which she understood. She was his daughter. Everything was personal. "So anyway," she said, quickly changing the subject. "I've been wondering. If you knew you only had one more day to live, what would you want to do?"

"Planning on killing me?"

She rolled her eyes. "Be serious."

"You've never been this morbid before, but I guess I can play along." He released her and tapped a fingertip against his chin. "I'd pay the premium for a higher life insurance policy, make sure you were going to be properly cared for, and then spend the rest of my time here, with you."

Tears filled her eyes, burning. "Thank you."

"And I'd want to tell you the truth about something, since I've learned my lesson about keeping secrets."

Her mind locked onto that one word—secrets—and she froze. Even her heart skipped a beat as panic whipped through her. "Wh-what?"

"I, well, I met someone," he said, a blush staining his cheeks.

Her eyes widened. "Really? Who? When? Where? Tell me everything!"

He laughed. "So many questions at once. Yes, really. I met her yesterday, at the grocery. And I, well…I asked her out on a date."

"Dad!"

"I haven't been on a date in ages, but I couldn't help myself. She was just so intelligent and, well, pretty."

Mary Ann was…glad. He deserved to be happy. Especially if she…if she…no, she wouldn't think like that. He just deserved to be happy. "You're leaving details out. What'd you guys talk about? What's she like? Where are you going to take—"

The doorbell rang, and they both jumped.

Her dad grinned sheepishly. "We'll resume this conversation in a bit. I'll get the door." He uncoiled from the chair and strode off while Mary Ann cleaned up the cards, marveling at the turn of events. Her dad. On a date. Oh, he'd been on one or two over the years, but nothing serious, and not once had he lit up like that. His interest had always been detached.

A few seconds later, she heard a female voice and laughter. Her dad's laughter, and it was such a sweet sound. What was going on in there?

"Mary Ann," he called. "Come on in here, honey."

She padded into the living room, hands stuffed into her jean pockets. Soon she was standing in her mother's rainbow living room, staring over at her dad, who was grinning like a loon and saying something to a young, gorgeous blonde wearing a white silk blouse and a flow-ing white skirt. Her skin was flawless, almost too much so. Her features were perfect and heart-achingly lovely. Could this be the mysterious grocery store babe?

Mary Ann cleared her throat.

Her dad glanced over at her, radiating so much excite-ment she actually had to look away. "Mary Ann, this is the woman I was telling you about."

The blonde nodded in greeting, though her gaze didn't leave Mary Ann's dad. She was petting his cheek, as if he was a favored puppy. "Mary Ann. I've heard so much about you."

From their one conversation at the grocery? *Don't be petty.* This was a good thing. "Nice to meet you," she said.

Finally the newcomer turned and faced her, and Mary Ann gasped in horror. Those eyes…glowing, wide and brown, revealing the sheen of glitter in her too-perfect skin. This was no human.

This was a fairy.

"Leave my father alone," she barked. "He's done nothing—"

"Mary Ann," he said, clearly shocked and disappointed by her behavior. "That isn't how you—"

"Be a dear and go to your room," the fairy told him. "Stay there, no matter what you hear."

"Of course," he said, and walked off without another word, heading up the stairs and never looking back.

Mary Ann's heart threatened to beat its way out of her chest. She wanted to run, but she remained in place. She would protect her dad, no matter what she had to do. But the simple fact was, she'd never dealt with a fairy before. She knew only what Riley and Victoria had told her.

They couldn't control people with their voices, like vampires could, but humans were so entranced by them, they usually obeyed their word without question. They craved power and didn't like anyone who was stronger. They were cold, icicles on the inside, yet desperate for warmth.

Despite all of that, or maybe because of it, they considered themselves protectors of mankind. Mary Ann was part of mankind. Maybe. With her ability...

She opened her mouth—to say what, she didn't know.

"Do not scream for your boyfriend," the fairy said with a frown. "At the moment, the wolves are busy fighting a swarm of goblins. I made sure of it. And you'll only distract them. Do you want their blood on your hands?"

She gulped. "I wasn't going to scream." She wasn't a coward. Anymore. "What are you doing here? Who are you? What do you want?"

A grin met her words, and yet, the expression lacked any hint of amusement. "I am called Brendal, and as to why I'm here, I would think that was obvious. I want you to follow me."

"Why?"

"Answers will come later."

"Hardly. Did you lead my dad on to get to me?"

"Of course. We do what we must."

Spoken without a hint of remorse. Bitch. Anger sparked.

"Now. Come," Brendal said, and motioned her over.

Mary Ann raised her chin. She felt no compulsion to do as the fairy wished. Because she muted the fairy's powers? Maybe, but she wasn't fully muting them, since her dad had climbed those stairs on command. *Remember what Victoria told you. Your ability doesn't work on someone's natural gifts.* "I think I'll stay here, thanks."

Dark eyes narrowed. "You desire answers, fine. I want you to follow me because I have a use for you. You repel, while your friend Aden attracts. You dull, while he magnifies. You, too, are a weapon, though most probably you do not realize it."

"You'll have to do better than that."

"He pulls them in, and you finish them off."

As if. "Just who am I supposed to finish off, hmm?"

"The enemy, of course."

According to the fairies, vampires and werewolves were the enemy. "Is that why you're here? You think I'll help you?"

"Not me, no." Brendal strolled to the left, increasing the distance between them, her hand brushing along prized knickknacks. "You wish to help your friend Aden, do you not?"

Mary Ann's stomach twisted painfully. "What do you mean?"

"The witches have him, and they aren't happy with him. And yes, I know about the required meeting and how you're most likely going to die tomorrow. Aden loves you, though, and refuses to give the witches what they want until they call their meeting to order so he can save your life. He refuses to give me what I want, as well."

Don't give her a reaction. Don't you dare give her a reaction. "And you want?"

"To know what happened to my brother. I'm willing to do anything to find out. *Anything.* Even…betray my allies."

Was she saying what Mary Ann thought she was saying? That she would betray the witches in exchange for information about her brother? That she would help Mary Ann rescue Aden?

"That's why you're coming with me, Mary Ann."

She shook her head. She couldn't afford to trust this being. "No. I told you. I'm staying here."

Brendal arched a golden brow, ever the picture of calm acceptance. "If I told your father to kill himself, he would. Happily. Your ability to dull my influence might stop him, yes. I know that's what you are thinking, but I can call others of my kind. They can drag you away. Then…"

For a split second, Mary Ann imagined flying at the fairy, a catapult of fury, nails bared, teeth ripping. No one threatened her dad. No one. Only Brendal's promise to summon others stopped her. One on one was manageable. More than that, iffy. "How, exactly, do you expect me to help you?"

Frustration bloomed, the first true emotion to touch the beautiful female's face. "I told you. You will come with me. You will weaken the witches while I obtain the boy."

"And that's all?"

"Yes."

Did she know Mary Ann could drain the witches of their power or did she simply mean for her to mute their abilities? "And what will you do with Aden?"

"As soon as he tells me what I want to know, I will release him."

Or try to kill him. Because Mary Ann knew the answer this fairy craved, and knew she wouldn't like what she learned. Her brother was dead and Aden was the reason. "You'll free him? No matter what?"

She nodded. "No matter what."

"How can I trust you?"

"Do you have any other choice?"

God, she wished Riley was here to tell her whether or not fairies kept their promises. "And what about the witches meeting?"

Triumph replaced the fairy's frustration. "I cannot force them to call a meeting to order."

At least she'd been honest. About that. "All right. I'll help you." After that…

†HIR†Y

THE KISS ON THE COUCH, when he'd tasted blood. It hadn't been his own, Aden realized now. It had been Victoria's. She'd given him several drops—accidentally? purposely?—but that had been enough. Now he was inside her head, hearing her thoughts, seeing the world through her eyes. Feeling her pain.

And oh, was she in pain. There was a burn in her chest, directly over her heartbeat, as if the skin had been singed away. She barely seemed to notice, though.

She stood in front of Riley, gaze cutting through the darkness. They were in the woods, wolves and goblins fighting all around them. Snarls rent the air, as did shouted commands and groans of agony.

"—found him," she was saying. "He's in a cave, an entire state away."

Riley swiped at the blood dripping from his hairline. "I know. We can feel him, too. We just can't leave this forest until this swarm of goblins is taken care of. Otherwise, they'll hunt humans."

"Well, I need a few of your men to follow me to the cave—after they return to the mansion and gather as many vampire warriors as possible."

Riley shook his head. "You'll get the wolves and the vampires, but you aren't to enter the cave alone."

Stubborn. As always. "I can move faster than you can." To prove it, she grabbed a goblin racing past by the neck, swooped down and bit, hard, sucking him dry in seconds. The body fell, and she tried not to cringe as she swallowed that last drop of blood. Goblins' blood always tasted like bile. "You'll just slow me down, and Aden could be…hurt."

"You'll be distracted by the witches, Victoria." Riley's gaze was pointed. "You know you will. You'll do more harm than good."

No. She wouldn't. Aden was priority one. "As you just saw, I ate. I'm not hungry, and this conversation is wasting precious time. I'm only here to tell you not to let your wolves or the vampires inside the cave while I'm in there. They'll ruin everything. Okay? They are only to fight the witches outside."

Now he frowned, suspicion dancing in his eyes. "Why? What will they ruin? What are you planning?"

What's necessary. She didn't say the words aloud.

"And anyway, I need you to listen to me. Your father—"

Is dead. She already knew. "Goodbye, Riley," she said, and rose on her tiptoes to kiss his cheek. Then, before the shape-shifter could grab her, she teleported. The ground abandoned her feet, wind rustled her hair and she spun... spun...darkness closing in, sounds fading away. When she reached her new destination, the darkness gave way to beams of light. Panting breaths disrupted the quiet.

Suddenly, Aden was looking at himself.

"Aden." Her voice stroked his ears. "Aden. Wake up."

A sharp sting lanced his cheek, then another, as he watched Victoria slap him. Slowly he blinked open his eyes. The cave seemed coated with Vaseline. He blinked again, once, twice, his own image fading and Victoria's taking its place.

She was here. With him. "Leave," he croaked. If they found her... "Now."

"Shhh." She tugged at the ivy around his wrists, but when she cut one vine, another quickly grew in its place. "Was the meeting called to order?"

"No." The admission shamed him. "What time is it?"

"Almost midnight. The true countdown has begun." Still she tugged and clawed. "They kept us busy or I would have been here sooner."

"Leave me here, and try to get the witches to return to me. That's the only way."

"No. I won't. If I don't do this now, I may not...I may..."

Be dead, he finished for her.

"And you'll be stuck," she whispered, still chopping at the vines. "I can't allow that."

He couldn't fail. He couldn't. Wouldn't. "Do you know where the witches are?"

What are you planning? Caleb asked, speaking up for the first time in what seemed an eternity.

Aden ignored him. When it came to the witches, the soul had no objectivity.

With a screech of frustration, Victoria grabbed the vine, pulled herself up and slashed the root with her teeth. Aden's arms fell heavily to his sides as she spat the leaves onto the ground.

"The witches?" he prompted, trying to rub feeling back into his shoulders.

You're not thinking about hurting them, are you? Caleb demanded.

And if he is? Irritation pulsed from Julian. *What if it's them or us?*

Guys, you need to— Elijah began, only to be interrupted.

"Couldn't get enough of me, princess, and decided to find me?" Jennifer asked. "I'm touched, really."

"Yes, thank you for joining us," Marie said. "Now I won't have to go to the trouble of sending you an engraved invitation to the night's festivities."

The witches had returned.

At the sound of Jennifer's voice, Victoria had spun around, arms splayed to act as Aden's shield. He shoved her behind him. They wanted him alive. Victoria, not so much. When she tried to return to her position in front of him, he reached back and squeezed her wrist.

"Do you think we failed to realize the exact moment you had stepped onto our land, tick?" Marie said. One by one, the witches marched to their boulders, claiming their spots around him. They still wore red robes. "Now we can watch you die and revel in the knowledge that we have one less bloodsucking enemy to contend with."

"No," Aden barked. Despite the cold, sweat beaded over his skin. "Call the meeting to order. Now."

Marie nodded as if she had every intention of obeying. "I will. As soon as you give me your vow of loyalty."

"And trade one death sentence for another? No."

She gave another of those acquiescent nods. "Then you have brought this on yourself, Haden Stone. I had hoped it would not come to this, but... You will not help us, and so you must die with your friends. Sisters?"

Arms outstretched, fingers interlocked, completing their circle.

Behind him, Victoria stiffened. "On my signal, drop," she whispered. "I'll take care of the witches."

No! Caleb shouted.

It's the only way, Elijah said. *Like Julian told you, it's the witches or us.*

Then it's us! They are to be left alone.

Aden blocked them out. In less than a single second, he had figured out Victoria's plan, and he wanted to vomit. The pain in her chest…she'd closed her ward. She was going to free her beast, let him kill these witches to protect Aden—but by doing so, she'd also kill every chance of a meeting being called to order.

Victoria planned to die, but she intended to take those who threatened Aden and her people with her.

He had to stop her. Had to save her. What good was his life without her in it?

"Stop," a soft voice called before he could decide on a plan of his own.

Brendal strode into the cave, a visibly frightened Mary Ann trailing close behind her. No. No! Aden cursed under his breath. Not her, too. Not here. Not with Victoria's beast so close to bursting free.

Victoria groaned, the repercussions hitting her, as well.

"Don't do it," he whispered. "Please."

"Oh, good. All we lack is the wolf," Marie said. Her tone was optimistic, but her features were almost…grim. Definitely haunted. "I'm sure he's on his way. Where that one goes, he goes."

"I didn't see any hint of the wolves outside," Brendal said.

"They'll come, so remain on alert. For now, take the girl outside." Marie waved to the mouth of the cave with a suddenly trembling hand. She looked at it, frowned. "Take her now."

"I feel like…I'm being…" another witch began, rubbing at her chest as if she were pained.

"My powers are…"

"Drainer," the witches said in unison, and there was enough horror in their voices to make Aden cringe. Only Marie and Jennifer appeared unsurprised.

"Remove her and hold her until the spell takes effect," Marie snapped. The howl of a wolf echoed through the cave, and she stiffened. "As predicted, the wolves have arrived."

Brendal shook her head. "I don't think I will. Take her out, that is."

"What are you talking about?"

"Mary Ann," Victoria suddenly shouted. "Run!"

No, no, no! The signal. Aden dropped to the ground as Caleb shouted a tortured denial. Victoria's beast flew overhead with a roar.

Mary Ann yelped, but ran as commanded, slowing only when Brendal grabbed the back of her T-shirt. She whipped around and shoved her flattened palm into the fairy's nose. There was a moan, a spray of blood. She was released and darted away.

After that, Aden lost sight of her. The witches ran for the exit, but the beast beat them to it, flashing sharp, dripping teeth, roaring. He chomped at them, and they scrambled backward. He didn't let them get very far before he batted them with his tail and his wings. So much strength…they propelled into the cave walls, dust pluming around them.

Most of the witches must have been warded against physical injury because no cuts appeared, even when those razor-sharp teeth bit into flesh. But they did scream, as if they could feel the damage that should have been done to their bodies. A few were *not* warded; they bled. And bled.

Aden jumped to his feet. A shaking Victoria clutched at him, trying to hold herself back, muttering, "So good. Just a taste. A little taste."

First things first. "Don't kill them," Aden told the beast. "Please." He needed them.

Please, Caleb echoed.

Those large, dark eyes flicked in his direction. They radiated hunger, it seemed, and anger. Anger at the treatment Aden had endured. Just then, Aden could practically hear the beast's thoughts. The witches were a threat to him, and all threats must be eliminated.

"Please," he repeated, and received an almost imperceptible nod. "Thank you."

And now, for his vampire. Aden backed Victoria against the wall and pushed her into a corner. The beast had spent nearly a century inside her, but she had no control over it, and might be considered another threat. Aden was taking no chances.

He faced her, saw that her eyes were alight, glazed and focused behind him. She licked her lips over and over, as if she already tasted the sweetness she craved. Should he try and feed her his own blood or would that just make her craving worse? "Victoria." He shook her, adding, "I need you to stay here. Do you understand?"

She didn't respond, was still staring behind him, at the blood.

He kissed her then, hard and fast, but enough to finally gain her attention. She blinked up at him. "Aden?"

"Stay here," he commanded. "Okay?"

He moved forward, dodging one frantic witch after another. Someone grabbed his arm and jerked, and he tripped to the side. He freed himself and crouched, remained searching...scanning...there. Marie.

Panic clouded her features as she guided her sisters out of harm's way. She was closing in on him...almost there…he leapt at her, knocking her down, rolling and pinning her to the jagged floor.

Careful, Caleb pleaded.

She struggled, but Aden held tight. "Call the meeting to order."

"No!" Panic receding, she gripped his chin and forced his eyes to lock with hers. "Hear me well, Haden Stone. You love me. You want to obey me." Power pulsed from her, growing, spreading, wrapping around him. "Yes, you love me so much."

Yes, Caleb said. *Yes.*

A spell, Aden realized. She was weaving a spell, the desire to love and adore her suddenly *there.* Impossible. He was warded against mind-manipulation. Wasn't he? Or was he feeling *Caleb's* love for her? *Caleb's* need to obey her? Or was love an emotion of the heart, rather than the mind, and she could make him feel whatever she wanted?

Someone tried to physically turn his head for him. Victoria, he thought. He recognized the heat of her hands. Still, he resisted. Caleb was muttering about the rightness of Marie's claim, how everything was going to be okay if they just did whatever she wished.

"Aden!"

The voice, so familiar, beloved, reminding him that there was something he needed to do. Something about his friends. His friends! Yes. He needed to save them.

He gave Caleb a mental shove, and the need to please Marie faded. He glared down at her. "Call the meeting. Now! Call it, and the beast will stop."

"Hear me well." Her eyes swirled, luring Caleb back to the surface, catching him, snaring them both, beseeching Aden to obey, to forget his purpose a second time. "You love me. You want to—" She shrieked as the beast chomped her by the arm and tossed her through the air.

She landed with a hard *thwack* and slumped, fighting for breath. Aden's gaze remained glued to her. Love... obey...

"Aden," Victoria said, shaking him. "Aden! Listen to me. Hear *me*. You have to fight this."

Marie gained her bearings and stood on shaky legs. She raised her arms, eyes narrowed and still pinned on him. "You love me. You will obey me."

Love, obey, Caleb said.

"She's hurting him," Victoria cried to the beast, and a second later, Marie was screaming, tossed into another wall, but again she stood, ready to finish her spell.

MARY ANN STUMBLED OUTSIDE, into the moonlight. There'd been a...a dragon in the cave. An honest to God dragon. She shouldn't have run, she thought, but the urge to flee had been instinctive. She'd panicked. She'd obeyed Victoria without hesitation.

Perhaps, though, she wasn't any safer out here. Another war was being waged.

Where minutes before there had been calm in this rocky canyon, now vampires and a few wolves battled more fairies than Mary Ann could count. And those fairies were vicious. They might not have had access to *je la nune* poison, but they fought with swords, hacking at fur and flesh, aiming for the vampires' eyes, ears and mouths, blood spraying.

Riley was here. She knew he was. He would have followed Victoria. So where was he? If he was hurt, she would—

Behind her, there was a screech of fury, and then a heavy weight was pushing her down. She flipped midair and realized Brendal had trailed her out, then she hit the ground and lost her breath, her train of thought.

"You cannot leave," the fairy snarled at her, grabbing her by the shirt and hefting her to her feet. "You must convince Aden to tell me about my brother."

Midnight would arrive very soon, and the winner—and loser—of this battle would be decided. One way or another. If Mary Ann died, this woman would never learn the truth about her brother. Had the situation been reversed, had Mary Ann's dad been the one missing, she would have been just as determined and desperate for answers as Brendal.

"Your brother…your brother is dead," Mary Ann told

her gently, still fighting for air. She tried not to cringe when someone screamed behind her.

Shock. Disbelief. Rage. All three passed over the fairy's expression. Brendal shook her head, pale hair slapping her ashen cheeks. "No."

"Yes. He is. I'm sorry."

Eyes narrowed. "Then where is his body?"

"I don't know."

"Who does?"

"Please," Mary Ann said. "Just tell your people to leave the wolves alone."

"Who knows?" As she spoke, she shook Mary Ann so hard her brain rattled against her skull. "The boy? The wolf? The vampire?"

Again, Mary Ann ignored the question. She'd given the fairy an answer, but she wouldn't condemn her friends.

"Would you tell me to save your own life?" Brendal reached behind her, and when her hand reappeared, she was gripping a blade. She held its gleaming tip to Mary Ann's throat, slicing her skin, burning. Not enough to kill, just enough to hurt.

Fight. You know how. But as Mary Ann moved to smash the woman's nose into her brain, the blade sank a little deeper. She froze, panting, a cold sweat breaking over her. She was stronger than she'd ever been, yes, and had some training now, but this, this she had no idea how to combat.

There was a howl, a blur of black in the corner of her eye, and then Brendal was soaring to the side, away from her. Riley, in full wolf form, landed on top of the fairy, doing his best to subdue her. Mary Ann's relief didn't last long. He wasn't having much luck, his motions slowing, becoming sluggish.

Was he being drained? Was the fairy somehow weakening him?

I'm the Drainer, Mary Ann thought darkly. If anyone was going to be weakened, it was the fairy. Determined, she lumbered to her feet and stumbled her way to the still-straining bodies. Riley must have sensed her, because he snarled over his shoulder. When he realized it was Mary Ann approaching, he returned his attention to Brendal.

"Hold her as best you can."

As Riley dropped all of his weight on his opponent, pinning her, Mary Ann crouched and placed her hand on the woman's neck, where her pulse hammered. She hadn't had to touch the witch to feed from her, but then she'd been starving and the draining had been involuntary. This time, she suspected she'd have to use force.

She closed her eyes, tried to blank her mind. An unwanted thought arose. If she did this, everyone would know what she was. Her secret would be out. She would be marked for death. Well, more than she already was. Not just by the fairies, but by the wolves and vampires.

Another thought formed. If she didn't do this, Riley could be injured. And besides, she might not survive the night, anyway. So, really, what did she have to lose?

Finally, her mind blanked. *I'm hungry,* she told herself. *So hungry.*

She waited. The warmth remained at bay, out of reach.

I'm starving. I need the fairy's energy.

Again, nothing.

Time to regroup. So far, the ability had worked only on the witches. Riley had said that Mary Ann would begin with the witches, but then her need would expand to fairies, then to all other types of creatures. Perhaps it was still too soon to feed from anyone else.

No. No. She could do this. She had to do this. Mary Ann concentrated, focusing completely on the fairy. Brendal's skin was soft, her pulse strong, so strong, like a drum. A song. Mary Ann listened to that song, allowed it to play inside her mind, absorb in her blood.

Brendal jerked against her hold.

Mary Ann absorbed the motion, too. The warmth she'd craved soon followed, sinking inside her, and oh, it was nice, too. Like being inside a cabin, snow all around, yet a fire leaping to life in front of her, soothing her.

The song slowed, however, and she frowned. She wasn't done listening, and now, the melody wasn't quite as pretty. It was lacking somehow. And then, even the warmth faded. She wanted more warmth. *Needed* more warmth.

Enough. You have to pull away, Mary Ann, or you'll kill her. I know you don't want to kill her.

Riley's voice shouted through her head, jolting her, and she ripped her hand away from the fairy. She blinked open her eyes. Brendal lay motionless, barely breathing, but thankfully alive.

She'd done it. She'd actually done it. She had drained the fairy.

Can you drain the others? Riley asked, urgent. *Just enough to weaken them?*

Trembling, she scanned the still-raging battle. Most of the wolves were as sluggish as Riley had been, the fairies seemingly stronger than ever. She was ashamed of the little spark of glee that flickered in her chest. Not because she wanted to help, but because she want to hear more of those songs, feel more of that warmth. "I'll try."

THIRTY-ONE

VICTORIA STEPPED IN FRONT of Aden and kissed him, just as he had done to her. She was there, in his arms, exactly where he liked her, and with the touch of her hot, soft lips, his senses snapped back into place, Caleb's pleading drowned out, the witch's hold on him broken. Before he could thank her, however, she jumped away from him—flying toward Marie.

"What are you—"

The two clashed together and rolled to the ground in a tangle of limbs.

Victoria's skin couldn't be cut, so Aden didn't worry about her. Yet. He approached the beast, who had positioned himself back in the doorway, keeping everyone inside, and raised his hands, as if he meant to pet. The beast—he needed a name. Chomper, maybe—huffed and puffed through his nostrils, clearly agitated by all the violence.

"Can you place the witches along the wall for me?" Aden asked.

There was a moment of suspended silence, where no one moved or breathed, everyone waiting to see what would happen. Finally the beast dipped his head and began gathering the witches with his mouth, sometimes several at a time, and tossing them along the wall. The ones still conscious tried to dart away, but he snarled in their faces, and they settled against the wall willingly.

Finally, only Marie was left. Her fight with Victoria hadn't slowed. Or gentled. Nails slashed, teeth bit, fists punched and legs kicked.

When the beast moved for her, Aden said, "Not her. Not until I remove the vampire. Okay?"

Chomper snorted as he nodded.

"Good boy," Aden said. "There'll be lots of pets for you when this is over."

Chomper's tongue rolled out, red and wet, and his tail actually wagged.

Aden turned to the still-fighting girls. They were rolling on the ground, their punches more concentrated—nose, throats, stomachs—and their kicks more vicious. There was no hair-pulling or slapping. This was knock-down-drag-out, and to the death. Without a single drop of blood spilled, since neither was bleeding.

What was the best way to break up a witch and a vampire?

Caleb babbled, and Aden tried not to allow himself to become distracted. "Victoria. Separate. Please."

A moment passed before she reacted. Then she flung herself away and pinned herself to the wall, arms splayed, nails digging into rock, as if they were the only thing holding her in place.

Marie spun, facing Aden. "Not much time left," she taunted.

He raised his chin, refusing to back down. "There's not much time for either of us, then, because I'm taking you to the grave with me."

"You'll try."

"I'll succeed."

"Really? What about her?" Grinning, Marie held out her hand and wiggled her fingers, revealing a ring very much like the one Victoria always wore.

Aden realized what was about to happen, and his stomach twisted.

Victoria threw herself to the right, away from the witch, even as Aden leapt forward, intending to block, forcing the liquid to splash him instead. But he was too late, and Marie moved too quickly. Every poisonous drop hit Victoria's profile. Her face, her neck, her arm and side. Immediately she dropped, screaming her pain, clothes and flesh sizzling.

Aden changed his direction and slammed into Marie; they rolled until he was on top, straddling her and holding her down. He was so angry, he almost hit her. Almost. But he'd never hit a girl before, and didn't want to start now. Instead, he hopped to his feet and moved out of the way.

"Get her," he pushed through gritted teeth.

Chomper grabbed the witch and once again threw her against the wall. A gust of air left her on a pained moan.

"Hold her down."

The beast went back for her, pinning her to the ground as Aden had, using his teeth instead of legs.

She struggled against the hold. "Let me go!"

Aden raced to Victoria. He gathered her trembling body in his arms and held his wrist over her mouth. She immediately bit down, sucking his blood. "Call the meeting to order," he told the witch.

"Why don't you come over here and request that to my face," Marie sputtered.

So she could ensnare him again? Ha!

Do what she says, Caleb beseeched. *We have to do what she says.*

Caleb! Dude. It's not gonna happen. Leave the boy alone. She's bad news. Julian.

No. She isn't!

Julian cursed at him.

He's ensnared, Elijah explained, *just like Aden was. Only*

Caleb hasn't snapped out of it yet. You won't be able to talk any sense into him until he does.

Victoria's trembling eased and her teeth loosened on Aden's wrist. With his free hand, he smoothed the hair from her face. *His* trembling increased, making him a little lightheaded.

"I think I'll stay here," Aden said. Victoria's eyes were closed, and she was breathing heavily. She radiated tension, but she wasn't screaming. "Now call the meeting to order, Marie, or I let the beast have you. And if you're warded against death, you'll get to live in his stomach, probably melting from the bile and acid there. Always in pain, never allowing death to relieve you."

"I don't care! Do you hear me? I don't care. I could call the meeting to order, you're right about that. I don't need the elders. But your friends need to die, and so they will. At midnight. They're dangerous. They're evil. They *will* die."

She wasn't going to relent, and if she was telling the truth, they would die in just a few minutes. He was just going to have to force her to do what he wanted. And there was only one way to do that.

He settled Victoria gently on the ground and stood, then closed the distance between him and Chomper. "Whatever happens, keep holding her," he said, patting the beast's side.

A slight nod.

What are you doing? Caleb demanded. *Don't hurt her. Please don't hurt her. We love her.*

"There's only one way for this to end happily for everyone, Caleb." He hoped.

Possess her?

"Yes." He would force her to call the meeting to order. He only prayed it counted. "And while we're in there, you can search her memories for bits of your past. Sound good?" If he had to bargain with the soul, he would bargain.

You won't force her to do anything to harm herself?

"I didn't punch her when I had the chance, did I?"

All right, then. Yes.

"What are you doing?" Marie's struggles increased. "Stop. Don't come any closer!"

"I thought you wanted me to approach you." Aden crouched down, grabbed her wrist and closed his eyes so that he wouldn't accidentally be ensnared. He shouted as he turned to mist and tried to push his way inside her, but there was some type of block around her, keeping him out.

A ward.

Damn this! He solidified again. "Looks like we will have to hurt her," he said on a sigh, "but it's only to save her, Caleb," he added before the soul could protest.

No!

Undaunted, desperate, he searched every one of the witches. He confiscated every ring he found—only four—and returned to Marie. "Tell me which ward to burn away or I'll destroy all of them." A vow. "And it will hurt, Marie. You know it will."

Aden…

She saw the rings in his hand and stilled, panic filling her eyes. Panic and fear. He would do it; she had to realize that. He didn't want to, but he would do it.

"No," she said. "I—I won't. I can't! Try to understand."

There was a ward tattooed on her wrist. "I don't have time to understand." He latched on to her arm and poured several drops of *je la nune* on the ink. She screamed, her body bowing as the pain slammed through her. The scent of burning flesh rose.

He tried again to possess her, but met the same block. *Steady.* "One more chance, Marie, then I'm not stopping until they're all gone."

"If I…call the meeting…will you vow to release us? Alive."

"Yes," he and Caleb said at the same time. Though Aden didn't dare to hope. Yet. "If you will vow not to cast any spells on your way out."

"I do," she gritted out.

Thank God. Thank God, thank God, thank God. This might work. This might happen. "Then call the meeting, and I vow upon my life—and death—that you and your coven will have free passage from this cave."

"No one can follow us."

"I vow that no one will follow you."

She pushed out a breath as her head fell to the ground. She stared up at the ceiling, tears leaking from her eyes. If she meant to waste time, to wait until it was too late…

"Do it now! Or I start pouring." He took hold of her other arm, revealing the ward tattooed there.

She squeezed her eyes shut. "This meeting is…called to….order."

He waited several seconds, but nothing happened. He wasn't sure what he'd expected, but this certainly wasn't it. "That's it? That's all you have to do? All you have to say?"

"Yes."

"My friends are saved?"

"Yes, damn you!"

His knees gave out. Thank God. His friends were safe. They were finally safe, free of their curse. He stayed just as he was for an eternity, shaking, basking, relieved, shocked, numb then excited, numb then sick—how close they'd come to losing—then, finally, blessedly, accepting.

Another battle, another victory. Only, this one was so much sweeter. They. Were. Safe.

"You can release her now," he told Chomper, and

the beast instantly obeyed. "Will you please guard the vampire while I take care of the witches?"

Another nod, and the beast was clomping off to hover over Victoria, teeth bared at all the witches in warning.

"Carry the ones who can't walk on their own and follow me," Aden told the women who'd almost destroyed all he'd come to love. Without waiting for a reply, he stood and stumbled his way to the cavern's opening. Footsteps soon echoed behind him, some dragging, most heavy. He snaked left and right through a long hallway, but finally reached the outside.

What he saw shocked him anew, and he stilled, the witches slamming into his back. Fairies littered the ground. Wolves and vampires stood around them, all staring over at Riley, in wolf form, who was in front of Mary Ann and growling. He was...protecting her? From his own people?

Meanwhile, Mary Ann was pale and clutching her stomach, as if in pain. "Aden," she said on a moan.

All eyes swung to him, and then the vampires were kneeling. The witches gasped and took a collective step backward.

He'd find out what was going on in a minute. "Allow the witches to pass. Don't look at them. Don't touch them. Don't follow them. Just allow them to pass." He waited until both the vampires and the wolves had nodded before stepping aside.

Though hesitant, the witches filed out, their unconscious sisters propped between them. The vampires parted, creating a pathway, and Aden released a breath he hadn't known he'd been holding. No one reached out, no one attempted to stop the robed women.

Now for his friends. "Riley, take Mary Ann home." She was clearly sick and in need of rest.

"But, my king," a vampire covered in blood said as he rose. "She's a Drainer. She must be killed."

Someone was going to have to explain the drainer thing, and soon. As for now, he said, "I don't care what she is. No one touches her, and no one follows her, either. Riley, take her home like I told you. Now!"

The guard moved behind Mary Ann and nudged her forward. Again, the vampires and wolves heeded his command—though all of them were stiff and clearly eager to act. More so than they'd been with the witches.

Such blind obedience. In a sudden moment of clarity, he realized these were his people. And he…he was their king. Yes. *Yes.* The admission felt right, so unbelievably right. He'd earned the title with this victory. More than that, he had somehow tamed their beasts. He *was* king, and he wasn't going to fight it anymore.

"The rest of you…stay here. Don't move." He turned and strode back to the cave. Chomper and Victoria were exactly where he'd left them, only Victoria was now sitting up.

"Better?" He squatted beside her and cupped her jaw. He gently moved her head left and right, gaze intent on her skin. The burns were already fading.

"Better." Those blue, blue eyes regarded him with concern. "Are you?"

"I'm just fine."

"I'm so glad." She threw her arms around him, placing little kisses all over his face.

Chomper snorted to remind Aden of his presence. Grinning, Aden reached up and petted his new protector behind the ears. So much could have gone wrong tonight, he thought. He could have lost everyone he loved, but with this creature's help, things had turned out okay.

Better than okay.

After he convinced a reluctant Chomper to go back inside Victoria—where he could better protect them both, Aden explained—he and Victoria walked back outside, hand and hand. This time, he wasn't surprised to discover his orders had been obeyed. The vampires and wolves hadn't moved.

Aden looked over at Victoria, and she looked over at him. They shared a grin, happy to be alive and with each other. "I'm king," he said.

"Yes," she agreed. "You are."

He faced the waiting crowd. "Return home. Rest. I'm proud of each of you." Next week, after *he* had rested, he'd hold a meeting of his own. Things were going to be different now.

As they began to teleport, disappearing from view, Victoria said, "Now I'll take *you* home."

A moment later, he was standing in his bedroom, Shannon snoring softly from the top bunk. Aden peered up at his friend. He would stay here a while longer, he thought, before moving into the vampire mansion with Victoria, where he would rule as was expected. There were a few things he had to do first. For the boys. For Dan. He wanted to make sure they were forever taken care of, forever safe.

He didn't see Thomas, and wondered where he was.

"You go home and get some rest, too. Because tomorrow," he said, placing a soft kiss on Victoria's lips. "We're going on a date."

She grinned slowly. "Is that an order from my king?"

"That's a plea from the guy who loves you."

"Then I accept."

"YOU HAVE TO LEAVE, Mary Ann," Riley said, stuffing her clothes in a bag, several pieces at a time. Even as she pulled those clothes out. "And I'm going with you."

"I'm not leaving my dad. And no, you're not."

"It's the only way. If you're here with him, he'll be killed to get to you. Everyone knows what you are now. Aden can command the vamps and weres to leave you alone, but he has no power over the witches or the fairies. And they'll be *very* eager to destroy you. Especially after tonight. So just so you know, there's no way I'm staying behind. I want to protect you."

He was right about the danger. She knew he was right. That didn't make this any easier. "I can't just leave."

"Write him a note," Riley continued as if there was no question of her course of action. "Tell him goodbye. That's the only way to save him."

Save him. Nothing else could have propelled her into action. Tears filled her eyes, but she stopped stopping Riley from packing and walked to her desk. She wrote her dad a letter, telling him she loved him, but needed to get away for a little while and she'd call him when she could.

He was going to be distraught and blame himself. God, she hated herself just then.

"All packed," Riley said, resolute.

"My dad...he's still in his room. The fairy told him to stay there, no matter what he heard. I think he's been there all night." She'd been home less than half an hour, but she'd checked on him twice. Both times, he hadn't heard her, hadn't noticed her, had merely remained perched at the edge of his bed, his eyes glazed.

"I'll contact Victoria and she'll release him from the fairy's compulsion. Any other objections?"

"Yes. No one knows Vlad is still alive. What's going to happen to Aden when everyone finds out? You need to stay here and protect him. Or have you lost your loyalty to him?"

His lashes fused together, but she could still see the way his pupils expanded and retracted. "No, I haven't lost my loyalty to Aden. No one else will, either. Believe me, he has more than proven himself, taming the beasts, and our people would now rather deal with Vlad's wrath than Aden's. He'll be fine. Now, let's go."

Gulping, she stood and faced him. Telling her dad goodbye wasn't the only tough thing she had to do. "No," she whispered, then added more firmly, "No. I told you. I'm going alone."

"Not just no, but hell, no." He slung the bag over his shoulder. "Let's go. Together."

"I'm going alone or I'm staying here." She wasn't going to allow Riley to give up everything for her, not when such an act would get him killed. If not by her, then by the people he left behind. Protecting her after the battle with the fairies was explainable. She'd saved the day, defeated their adversary. He'd felt obligated. And yet still the others had growled and hissed at him as if *he* were the enemy. They would have killed him right then if Aden hadn't stepped out and ordered them to back down.

They'd forgive him, though, welcome him back into the fold. Surely. Unless Riley chose her over his brethren a second time. Then they'd hunt him down—as they were going to hunt her.

"I'm not kidding, Riley. If I stay and he's hurt, I'll blame you. You have to let me go alone."

"And just where will you go?" he snapped.

She didn't know, but she wouldn't have told him if she had. "It's best if I keep that to myself."

He popped his jaw.

"For both of us," she added, and had to fight a fresh spring of tears. *This is for the best. Don't forget.*

"Fine," he said, his knuckles white as they clutched the bag's handles. "Do it. Go."

"I will." The words choked from her as she pried his fingers loose and anchored the heavy nylon in place. "I guess this is goodbye, then." She turned away before the tears started falling and strode out of her bedroom. Then stopped in the hall. She couldn't leave like this. Couldn't end things like this.

Quickly she backtracked, pausing in front of a scowling Riley, grabbing him by the back of the neck and jerking his mouth to hers. The kiss was swift, hard and teased her with the wildness of his taste, the unwavering strength of his body. Seconds passed, and she wished for eternity. This was it. The end. Their last kiss. She committed the moment, the boy, to her memory.

She'd need it.

With a groan, she released him and spun. She ran out of her house and into the bright sunlight.

She threw her bag in the car Riley had stolen last night, recalling how he'd sped along the roads, whisking her from somewhere in Texas to Oklahoma in record time. Then she drove, just drove. She never stopped crying.

ADEN SAID NOTHING about his plans to Dan or the boys while they ate breakfast and discussed Ms. Brendal and how she'd seemed to disappear exactly as Mr. Thomas had. And how Dan wanted to give up on tutors entirely and try and enroll the other boys at Crossroads High with Aden and Shannon.

They were, of course, excited.

He said nothing as he gathered his books and backpack, the souls chattering inside his head—Caleb making plans to find the witches again, Julian amusing himself by pointing out the flaws in each of Caleb's ideas, and Elijah trying to figure out why he saw more turmoil in the future than ever. Aden ignored them, still flying high. Even Shannon and the other boys remarked on how happy he seemed, how light his mood was.

He didn't know what he'd tell them yet, or even how

he'd tell them. But he wasn't going to worry about that now. After everything that had happened, he was simply going to enjoy the day. And the evening, of course, when he took Victoria on their first official date. He grinned. He frowned. Would evening never arrive?

The school day passed with agonizing slowness, the classes sheer torture. Despite the fact that he was free. Free of the witches' curse and its consequences. Victoria was absent, but then, so were Mary Ann and Riley. Aden wasn't worried. They needed a break. Hell, he needed a break, but he kinda owed Dan.

After school, he rushed through his chores. Or tried to. Finally, though, he finished shucking and bailing and showered. He changed into his best clothes, jeans and a black T-shirt, just as the moon made its appearance in the sky. He wanted to buy Victoria flowers, but didn't have any money and didn't want to destroy Meg's roses.

He would just have to give her his heart. Again.

Because he didn't have a car, and wasn't allowed to date while living at the ranch—girls equaled trouble, Dan said, because they kept boys from working hard and studying—Victoria had to pick *him* up and convince everyone to think he was right there with them.

And God, did she look beautiful. Some of her wounds were still in the process of healing, and there were scabs on her arm, but she wore a tight blue sweater and a barely there miniskirt in a lighter shade. The colors transformed her from Vampire Chick to Little Slice of Heaven. Her hair hung down her back in silky black waves, and all he wanted to do was find a dark corner and run his fingers through them.

They climbed through his window and strolled away from the ranch hand in hand.

"Do you like?" she asked. She even pulled from his hold to twirl in front of him. "I borrowed it from Stephanie, naturally. And speaking of my family, the girls have decided you're, and I quote, not so bad. You tamed their beasts, outwitted the witches and sent the fairies to their knees."

"I *love*," he corrected. In the distance, an owl hooted. "And tell your sisters I think they're not so bad themselves."

They shared a smile. They were doing that a lot lately, he thought, proud. Bit by bit, she was losing her serious, somber edge.

"So…what should we do?" she asked. "I can't believe we don't have a death curse hanging over us or goblins to fight."

"I know what you mean." Tonight, they were just two people, hanging out and having fun. "Want to go into town? I mean, a town other than this one, where no one knows who we are. We can see a movie, maybe." What did girls like to do? He'd never been on a date before.

"I would love to!" She reclaimed his hand, and a

moment later, the world tilted, wind kicked up and his surroundings faded. He blinked, that was it, and his feet settled, buildings suddenly stretching at his sides.

He laughed. "You're getting good at that."

"I know, *right*."

How human she sounded. How sweet. He looked around. They were in a darkened alley, a busy street sidewalk a few feet away and an even busier road a few feet from there. "Where are we?"

"Tulsa. Not too far from home, but not too close either."

"Perfect."

Aden, Elijah said. *Go home. You have to go home.*

"I'll be fine."

"Of course you will, but instead of going to the movies, what do you think of going to a dance club?" Victoria asked, unaware he'd been talking to the souls. He didn't correct her.

"I think that's...doable." He didn't know how good a dancer he was, never having danced before, but for her, he would try. And he would get to hold her close, so that was even better.

Aden, please.

One night, Aden thought. That's all he wanted. "Tomorrow," he said.

"The souls?" Victoria asked, getting it this time.

"Yes."

"They'll be our next project." Victoria's skin was hot against his as they strolled down the street, joining the crowd. "I can't believe we're doing this. I mean, I love you, you know that, but this feels so…frivolous."

"Frivolous is what we desperately need right now." *Do you hear that, Elijah? I need this.*

"So true. So guess what?" Too excited to wait, she answered before he could reply, releasing his hand to jump in front of him. "I know a human joke."

"Oh, yeah?" He hooked several strands of hair behind her ear. "What is it?" From the corner of his eye, he saw a strange movement and frowned. Had that trash can just moved several inches on its own? Surely not. Surely he was simply paranoid now, looking for danger in every shadow.

"There was once a boy who—" Victoria frowned, too, and followed the line of his vision. "What is it?"

Aden. Aden, leave now.

A second later, Tucker seemed to appear out of nowhere, suddenly right in front of Aden, tears streaming down his face. "What the—"

The crowd and cars disappeared—Victoria, too— leaving Aden on a deserted street. A deserted street he'd seen in countless visions. One he'd dreaded finding. One he'd hoped to avoid.

Aden backed up, gearing to fight. Tucker followed.

"I'm sorry, so very, very sorry," Tucker said. "He

told me you would be here. Why did you have to be here?"

Before the last word left his mouth, before Aden could go on the offensive, a sharp pain he recognized, hated, dreaded, expected, lanced through him, slicing through bone, through muscle, through…organ. Every beat of his heart sliced the wound deeper, wider.

The very heartbeat that kept him alive was killing him.

Tucker fled, footsteps pounding.

The pain exploded, as sharp as the blade. Aden looked down, saw the hilt dripping crimson. A gasp of blood gurgled from him, and he heard Victoria scream his name. Where was she? He still couldn't see her. He was alone. Was going to die all alone.

Not even a day. He hadn't even had a day of rest. Even God had had a day of rest. Strange thoughts, he mused. "Worth…it," he said, hoping Victoria would hear him, wherever she was. She was worth anything, everything. He wouldn't trade a moment of his time with her.

The deserted street shimmered, faded, the busy street coming back into view.

Oh, Aden, Elijah said.

Caleb and Julian shouted denials.

Not alone, then. He had the souls. Made sense. They'd started life together, and now they would end it together. Oh, God. End. End. This was the end. With the word echoing in his head, he realized he wasn't ready. But the pain soon dragged him down…he was falling…a shroud of black was sweeping him under a burning tide…

He knew nothing more.

SOMEONE MUST HAVE USED electric shocks on his brain, because suddenly Aden's entire body spasmed, and he felt the pain, so much pain. Too much pain. The shroud of black quickly wrapped back around him, thank God, thank God, thank God, but the electric shock pulled him back out. The process was repeated over and over again.

"—save him," Victoria was pleading to someone. "You have to save him."

"He's been injured too badly," an unfamiliar voice said, "and you've given him all the blood you can stand to lose. Any more, and you'll both die."

"He's not going to die," she screeched. "We can't let him die. He's our king!"

I'm here, he tried to tell her, but he couldn't force his mouth to move. The souls were still with him, he thought, because he could hear them crying, but they couldn't form a single word, either.

Was this it? The end?

The end. Familiar words.

"Try and turn him," Victoria said on a rush. "Drain

him completely and fill him back up with what remains of my blood."

A sigh, weary and sad. "We've tried that before, princess, with others. This you know. Not since Vlad's time has a turning ever ended successfully."

"I don't care."

"Sometimes the donor died, as well."

"I know that, too! Just do it! There's no other way, and I have to try. I have to try," she repeated on a sob.

No, Aden wanted to shout. *Don't risk your life, Victoria.* Anything but that.

Another sigh left the stranger. "Very well. He's all yours. But know this. When your people discover his weakened condition—and they will, we can't keep this a secret for long—there will be a struggle for the crown. No matter how worthy a king Aden has proved himself to be, there will always be those who hunger for power. Contenders will want to strike him while they can."

"They'll have to find him first. And when he returns, *and he will,* I'm sure anyone who dared issue a challenge will be punished. Severely."

A knock sounded, several hard thumps. Footsteps. A gasp.

"Riley?" Victoria said.

"What happened to him? What the hell happened?"

"Stay back! Don't touch him. I'm turning him. Just stay here and keep everyone calm. I'm taking him away."

"Turning him? Away? Victoria, you can't do that."

"I can and I will. Stay back!"

A pause. "Okay, okay. I'll stay back. But there's something I have to tell you. Several somethings, actually. And I can't stay here for long. Mary Ann ran away, and I followed her to make sure she made it someplace safely, and I only came back to talk to you. I have to return to her before she decides to head somewhere else and I lose her trail. So listen up. You've been challenged by Draven for rights to Aden. Your father is alive and—"

"A challenge? No! Not yet! Is Mary Ann okay? And… and what you do mean my father is alive? Riley, he can't be alive. He can't be alive. He'll hurt Aden, he'll… *No!* I won't let him!"

Silence, then. Floating. Darkness. Then, Aden felt as if his neck was being ripped open, and this time, he did make his mouth move. He screamed.

He thrashed, he fought, he stilled. Nothing, he had nothing left.

The shroud, that blessed shroud. It covered him, protected him. Slipping away…

…cold, so cold…

Stupid shroud…he tugged it back in place.

…hot, so hot…

He pushed it away… Better, but not for long. Slipping again…

—COLD, SO COLD—

He tugged.

—HOT, SO HOT—

He pushed, as hard as he could. He kicked. No shroud. No more shroud.

…pain, so much pain…

—PAIN, SO MUCH PAIN—

Time was an endless ocean of change. He drifted on the waves, was pulled under, struggled, was jerked back up, drifted some more…cold, so cold…and wondered… hot, so hot…if he'd ever find his way home. Home, where was home? The answer eluded him. Too much chatter, incoherent, bothersome. The pain had returned. But not the shroud. Thank you, God, not the shroud.

The ocean vanished in a sudden blink. He saw a cave, he hated caves now, saw himself, how sick and pale he looked, writhing, sweat pouring from him, washing away the blood that coated him, and he saw Victoria, how sick and pale she looked, lying beside him, thrashing, moaning, and he heard her thoughts, all her thoughts from all her life, so loud he couldn't deal with them, couldn't listen to them, there were too many memories inside his head, her memories, his own, her pain, his own, more than could possibly fit, and if something didn't give soon, he would break, break into a thousand pieces and never fit back together.

He wanted the shroud back.

Then there was silence. Calm. They came, but they

didn't last. In the distance, he heard a roar. No, not in the distance. Louder…louder…closer…so close. *Inside* him. The roar was inside him, filling him up, nearly ripping from his pores. At least the chatter stopped. Hot…he was hotter than before. Burning, blistering, smoldering to ash. Reforming, weaving back together, harder, heavier, still hotter.

"Aden."

Where was the cold? He wanted the cold to return.

"Aden, please." The voice blended with the roar. "Open your eyes."

His mouth was as dry as cotton, his gums and tongue swollen, his lips bruised. His muscles and bones felt like they'd gotten up close and personal with a baseball bat.

"Aden!"

His lids popped open of their own volition. He was panting, still sweating. A wan Victoria loomed over him, her dark hair falling like a curtain around his face. There were circles under her eyes, eyes that were glazed with pain, and she was clutching at her ears, cringing.

Was this a dream? Or had he died and gone to heaven? No, he couldn't have gone to heaven. He still heard that godawful roar, still felt as if he were on fire, battered and bruised.

"Aden," she moaned.

He jolted upright. Dizziness hit, then subsided.

Pain hit, and remained. "What's wrong?" The words
were slurred, pushed through teeth he didn't recognize. Through...fangs? He flicked his incisors with his
tongue—no, no fangs. He wasn't sure what that meant.
Wasn't sure what was wrong with him or what had
happened.

Oh, he knew Victoria had given him some of her
blood. Knew she'd tried to turn him from human to
vampire in order to save his life. He hadn't forgotten
the conversation he'd heard. But he didn't know any
more than that. How was he alive if the change hadn't
succeeded?

He wanted to ask.

"The souls," she said before he could. "I have the
souls. Inside me. Talking. Why won't they stop? And
you...you, I think you have my beast." As if she'd managed to maintain her strength only long enough to issue
her confession, she collapsed, falling into his arms.

Unable to process what he'd heard, Aden gathered her
close, held her tight. His brain hadn't sparked back to life
yet, his thoughts fragmenting quickly, fatigue beating
through him. He eased to his back, taking Victoria with
him.

They were alive. That thought was clear. Whatever
had happened to them, they were alive. The rest could be
figured out later. And whatever changes they'd experienced, whatever they would next need to do, they would

triumph; he had no doubt. They'd defeated the witches and the death curse. They could get through this, too. They had each other, and that was all that mattered.

"Don't let go," Victoria said against his chest.

He was surprised she had roused, surprised but glad. "I won't. I'll never you let go."

Yes, they had each other, would always have each other. They could handle what came next.

He hoped.

★ ★ ★ ★ ★

Glossary of Characters and Terms

Blood-slaves   *humans addicted to a vampire's bite*

Bloody Mary   *queen of a vampire faction that's rival to Vlad's*

Brian   *resident of the D and M*

Brianna Buchannan   *friend of Mary Ann's, sister of Brianna*

Brittany Buchannan   *friend of Mary Ann's, sister of Brittany*

Caleb   *a soul trapped inside Aden's head. Can possess other bodies*

D and M Ranch   *a halfway house for wayward teens*

Dan Reeves   *owner of the D and M Ranch*

Dmitri   *deceased betrothed of Victoria*

Dr. Hennessy   *Aden's new therapist*

Dr. Morris Gray   *Mary Ann's father*

Drainer   *a human who feeds from and ultimately destroys those with supernatural abilities*

Draven   *vampire female, chosen to date Aden*

Elijah   *soul trapped inside Aden's head. Can predict the future*

Eve   *a soul formerly trapped inside Aden's head. A time-traveler*

Fairies   *protectors of mankind, enemies to vampires*

Goblins   *small, flesh-hungry creatures*

Haden Stone   *known as Aden. A human who attracts the supernatural and has three humans souls trapped in his head*

je la nune   *a poisonous liquid that can be fatal to vampires*

Jennifer   *a witch*

Julian   *soul trapped inside Aden's head. Can raise the dead*

Lauren   *vampire princess, Victoria's older sister*

Marie   *a witch*

Mary Ann Gray   *human. Repels the supernatural*

Maxwell   *werewolf shape-shifter, Riley's cursed brother*

Meg Reeves   *Dan's wife*

Ms. Brendal   *fairy princess, sister to Mr. Thomas*

Mr. Hayward   *Crossroads High Anatomy teacher*

Mr. Klien   *Crossroads High Chemistry teacher*

Mr. Thomas   *fairy prince, ghost*

Nathan   *werewolf shape-shifter, Riley's cursed brother*

Ozzie   *deceased former resident of the D and M*

Penny Parks   *Mary Ann's best friend*

Riley   *werewolf shape-shifter, guardian of Victoria*

RJ   *resident of the D and M*

Ryder   *resident of the D and M*

Seth   *resident of the D and M*

Shane Weston   *human teenager, friend of Tucker*

Shannon Ross   *Aden's roommate*

Stephanie   *vampire princess, Victoria's older sister*

Terry   *resident of the D and M*

Tucker Harbor   *Mary Ann's ex-boyfriend, part-demon illusionist*

Vampires   *those who live off human blood, and have a beast trapped inside them*

Victoria   *vampire princess*

Vlad the Impaler   *former king of Romanian vampire faction*

Witches   *spell-weavers, magic producers*

*More pulse-pounding danger
and thrilling romance are in store
for Aden and his friends!*

Don't miss an all-new
INTERTWINED *novel*

TWISTED

*Coming from
Gena Showalter
and Harlequin TEEN
in September 2011!*